Footprints in the Sand

Sarah Challis

First published in 2006 by HEADLINE REVIEW

An imprint of HEADLINE PUBLISHING GROUP

First published in paperback in 2007 by
HEADLINE REVIEW

8

Cataloguing in Publication Data is available from the British Library

A format (ISBN 10) 0 7553 3150 8
A format (ISBN 13) 978 0 7553 3150 5
B format (ISBN 10) 0 7553 2169 3
B format (ISBN 13) 978 0 7553 2169 8

Typeset in Bembo by Palimpsest Book Production Limited,
Grangemouth, Stirlingshire

Printed and bound in Great Britain by
Mackays of Chatham plc, Chatham, Kent

Headline's policy is to use papers that are natural, renewable and recyclable products and made from wood grown in sustainable forests. The logging and manufacturing processes are expected to conform to the environmental regulations of the country of origin.

HEADLINE PUBLISHING GROUP
A division of Hachette Livre UK Ltd
338 Euston Road
London NW1 3BH

www.reviewbooks.co.uk
www.hodderheadline.com

For Diana, dear friend and trusty fellow traveller, whose inspiration, courage and humour made this story possible.

With love and thanks to my Tuareg friends who have looked after me in the Sahara, and in whose company I have never felt so safe, or so honoured.

Emily

When I arrived at the church, late and sad, for Great-Aunt Mary's funeral I had been in tears for nearly a week. My face looked as congested and blotchy as that of my cousin Clemmie's father, Uncle Peter, and it must take at least half a bottle of whisky a day to maintain his corned-beef complexion. Our village church is tiny and it was already filled with neighbours and Kingsley relations from far and wide. As I made my way up the aisle I sensed a slight shifting and sighing amongst the congregation as my tragic appearance was noticed and a murmur of sympathy travelled up and down the pews as I took my seat next to my parents at the front.

My father turned to me briefly and squeezed my elbow. He looked tall and distinguished in his funeral overcoat, inherited from his father and now going a faint green on the shoulders. He could have been mistaken for any kind of professional man. Only his weatherbeaten face, the frayed cuffs of his shirt and his large, raw-looking hands gave him away as a dairy farmer. My mother leaned across him to pat my arm. Her expression was bright and social, which seemed jarringly inappropriate in the stony, dank gloom of the ancient church. She and my father sat a little way apart from each other, not even the sleeves of their coats touching, and I noticed that she had placed her handbag on the pew between them.

I had been hurrying not to be late and it was so cold that my quickened breath floated in a faint white mist, like an airy snail's trail, while behind me people turned up their collars and rubbed their frozen hands together. Then there came a mournful wheezing noise and up in the chancel a ghostly little white gargoyle face bobbed into view in the mirror above the organ. It seemed incredible that Miss Timmis was still vigorously alive while stout Great-Aunt Mary, her friend and companion, was dead. I watched her neat little feet in polished lace-up shoes dashing about the pedals like a pair of darting brown mice, and her arthritic, knobbly hands energetically pulling out the organ stops, and the music swelled into a dirge that seemed to have no beginning and no end but gurned tunelessly like a groaning, dying beast.

In the pew behind me I heard my cousins whispering and jostling. They were all there, all seven of them, squashed in together so that their shoulders were forced up round their ears. They always did everything en masse so the idea that they might take two pews and spread out a little would not have occurred to them. As an only child it made me feel lonelier and sadder than ever that there was only my mother, father and me to occupy our own chilly stretch of polished wooden seat.

I turned to give them a sombre smile and my eyes passed over the boys, Stephen, Will, Jake, Hugh, Felix and Pete, the youngest, and rested on Clemmie, their sister and my dearest friend. Her face was pinched with cold under a coal-scuttle black hat and her pale blonde hair spread out on her shoulders like a mantle. She was sitting bang in the middle of her brothers, three on each side, looking like a medieval princess surrounded by her knights. Instead of returning my smile, she gave me a beady, assessing look, one golden eyebrow raised.

There was a muffled disturbance at the back of the church and Great-Aunt Mary's coffin came slowly round the corner, tipped forward at a slight angle and carried by six straining bearers. I recognised one of them as Neil, my father's relief milker, and even he, a sturdy lad with broad shoulders and square purple hands, was staggering. It was just as well that Great-Aunt Mary had left instructions for a wicker coffin or I don't think she would have made it up the aisle.

She had forbidden any flowers and so here she was, in an unadorned basket-woven box, and it was shocking to think of her lying there, cold and dead, only an arm's length away from where I stood. I imagined her wrapped in tissue paper, her hands crossed on her great monobosom, and then, for no reason at all, I thought of Ted and I began to cry again.

Ted. Small, stocky, brown-haired, handsome enough to make my heart stop whenever I saw him; vain, mean and unfaithful. I had loved him since our schooldays and we had lived together, tempestuously, for four years since university. Over the last miserable six months I had known in my heart that there was something wrong, but wanted to believe him when he said that it was my fault, that I was insane, jealous, possessive and suspicious. Then the hard evidence fell into my lap via his mobile phone and a pornographic text message to him from a close girlfriend of mine. A friend who had given me advice about Ted in the past. A girl with whom I had giggled and gossiped and confided awful and shaming truths. So it was a double treachery that tore my heart apart. How could they have done this to me? Lied and lied and covered their tracks and told me that I was mad? When I confronted him, Ted looked first shocked, then cornered and then angry. He said he loved me but when I pressed him he admitted that he had been sleeping with Tatty on and off for two years. Two years! After that I threw him out, had a sleepless night and telephoned him the next day to beg him to come back. I had no shame. I also telephoned her, the über-bitch, but she switched off her mobile when she heard my voice.

Ted did come back but things could never be the same again, and after a few days of tears and rows (my tears, his provoked rows) he took a bundle of clothes under one arm, his toothbrush out of the bathroom, kick-started his motorbike and wheeled away.

I was bereft without him. Our flat was full of his things, his clothes, his CDs, his books. He was everywhere but he was gone. After a few days I borrowed a van and packed up my own stuff and moved out. A kind colleague at the primary school where I teach lent me her spare bedroom in which to weep and pass my sleepless nights and it was from there that I had travelled down to Dorset this morning for Great-Aunt Mary's funeral.

A funeral was right for the mood I was in. I wanted everything to be cold and grey and miserable, and I wished that it was me in the wicker coffin and Ted weeping in the front pew. It would have served him right if I had died of a broken heart.

So it was not for Great-Aunt Mary that I wept. She was my father's eldest aunt, and not even a proper blood relation. She had been married to Great-Uncle Timothy, Dad's father's younger brother, who had been dead so long that there was a thick crust of moss on his grave in the frozen churchyard outside. Ours is a large and untidy family, and in this part of Dorset there are a lot of us Kingsleys scattered about, most of whom now crowded the church. Some of them, a batch of second cousins once or twice removed, I hardly know. Great-Aunt Mary had been closer than that. For the last quarter of a century she had lived almost next door to where I grew up and where my parents still live – a farm in a small village tucked beneath a bare Dorset hill. Quite what Great-Uncle Timothy did for a living I'm not sure – something to do with the wine trade in London – and then he and Great-Aunt Mary, childless and in late middle age, retired to a small house in the village. According to Dad, Uncle Tim opened the front door on his first morning in Over Crompton, looked up at the lowering hill, said, 'Nothing but bloody sheep!' and promptly dropped down dead, leaving his widow complaining that it was she who was buried as a result. In the country, she meant.

Why she stayed and did not run back to London is lost in history. She continued to complain and to see herself as an exotic outsider, and a memory of my childhood is of dark green Harrods vans lost in the lanes round the village with a delivery of some unheard-of luxury for Great-Aunt Mary on board. 'Small reminders of civilisation' was how she referred to the boxes of Elvas plums, the lapsang souchon tea, the tins of foie gras and crystallised ginger in Chinese jars. If Clemmie and I met a lost delivery van when we were out riding our ponies, we made a game of giving the driver the wrong directions so he ended up in a muddy farmyard or on wandering lanes which petered out at a silage clamp or a lonely corrugated barn on the top of a faraway hill.

What probably kept her was a certain fondness for

other members of her late husband's family and the fact that she was an only child and had none of her own. Uncle Peter, her godson, persuaded her to join a racing syndicate which ran a promising horse he had bred at home on the farm and she went point-to-pointing every spring. Then, after our darling Gran died, she struck up an unlikely friendship with my grandfather, George, until his death two years ago. She invited him to lunch two or three times a week and they watched the afternoon's racing on the television and grumbled about the government and old age and everything else in cheerful alliance.

Great-Aunt Mary's cooking was almost the most important thing about her. She was a wonderful, wonderful cook in a slapdash, noisy, clattering, careless way. Children did not much interest her and she made it clear that she found us boring company, but spasmodically she enjoyed feeding us – educating our palates, she called it. Once when she caught Clemmie and me gorging on white-bread sandwiches filled with pink and white marshmallows – our idea of heaven at that time – she threw up her hands in horror and took us home to sit at her kitchen table while she cooked us beignets; tiny airy golden balls, puffed crisp in deep fat and dusted with icing sugar. After that we were summoned once or twice every holiday to be fed. Her roast chicken, fragrant with garlic and herbs, was so unlike the stringy, wet, flavourless bird my mother slapped on the table that it was hard to believe they were ever related. Her chocolate cake was rich and dense with a slick of glossy dark icing studded with tiny crystallised violets. Her roast beef was crisp and brown on the outside and soft and pink within – a revelation to me, accustomed to the overcooked fibrous slabs served up at home, on which one chewed and chewed to no effect.

Regrettably for us children, as Great-Aunt Mary got older and stouter there was less and less room for her to move round her cottage kitchen and she became disinclined to cook, and then Miss Timmis appeared on the scene as a companion and the cooking went out of the window completely. Harrods vans had long since ceased to call and Great-Aunt Mary took to shuffling about, one hand leaning on a walking stick, the other holding a cigarette, the butt stained red by her violent lipstick kiss, and to eating shop cakes and ready-prepared meals, dished up by her nervous little friend.

Despite her spreading bulk her face was still strong and handsome in a fleshy, operatic style and her fine black eyes, overhung by jet-black arched brows, sparked with animation, but she was old and slow and bad tempered and I have to confess that recently I had no longer made the effort to call on her when I was home from London for a weekend. To be fair, she never indicated that she would welcome a visit and neither had I expected that she would die without a moment's warning.

Now she was gone and I already missed her because she was a character and part of my childhood and I hated things to change. My own life seemed so insecure and wavering that I took comfort in the belief that down in Dorset things went on the same for ever, and of course they didn't. To my profound dismay my parents' marriage had recently developed cracks.

Even as a child I had been aware that my father was what Gran called 'a ladies' man'. Clemmie and I used to think he was just being silly and embarrassing when we saw him with an arm round a woman at a party, or paying ridiculous compliments to some simpering girl hardly older than we were. As I got older, I discovered that his various local dalliances were well known and that my mother seemed to put up with it because although his affairs were intense and short-lived and made him whistle about the farm for a few weeks, they inevitably ran out of steam. He always came home with his tail between his legs, declaring his love for her and begging forgiveness. He reminded me of my childhood collie, Patch, who was also given to straying, staying out all night and appearing sheepish and hungry at the back door the next morning. Although his absences drove me wild with anxiety it didn't make me love him any the less, and I supposed my mother felt the same about Dad.

But now she had struck back and had had an affair of her own – a 'fling', she called it – with the Artificial Insemination man, a regular caller to the farm. At fifty-four! My father had the nerve to take it badly, and although they seemed to have patched things up to a certain extent, he was now threatening to sell the farm, which had been in the family for ever, and go off to live in Spain. He said that he was sick of cows and wanted to learn to play golf.

It was for all these reasons that I sobbed in tiny, freezing St Michael's, Over Crompton, but most of all I sobbed for myself because Ted had broken my heart.

After the service had come to an end and Great-Aunt Mary had been shouldered out of the church, we filed slowly from our pews and I fell in with Clemmie, who clasped my elbow. Even through the thick wool of my coat I could feel her sharp little nails digging into me.

'Bugger Ted!' she whispered fiercely. 'You're better off without him. He was never the right man for you!'

'He was an arrogant arsehole,' said Stephen from the other side.

'A wanker,' said Will from behind my shoulder. I sniffed and wiped my eyes with a wodge of wet tissue.

'Would you like us to beat him up for you? Go to London and do him over?' asked Pete and Felix eagerly.

'It's tempting,' I said, 'but he's not worth the effort.' I didn't really believe this, of course. I would have done anything in the world to have him back and I lived in a state of nervous, gut-churning anticipation that at any moment he would call or text me and everything would be all right again.

'That's my girl!' said Clemmie, her little diamond ear studs glinting in the wintry grey light that seeped through the clear glass windows of the church.

Outside, we milled about in the lane while Neil reversed the farm pick-up truck in the back of which Great-Aunt Mary was to travel to the crematorium, driven by my father and accompanied by Uncle Peter. I saw that someone had thought to brush out the back of the truck of the usual litter of straw and sheep nuts and had laid a tartan rug over the metal floor on which Great-Aunt Mary now rested, like a giant picnic, in her wicker coffin. This unorthodox ultimate journey had been arranged because she disliked unnecessary expense and had a deep suspicion of funeral directors, whom she considered thieves.

'Why couldn't she have gone to the kennels?' asked Clemmie, stamping her frozen feet in her black high-heeled boots. 'And been fed to the hounds like other fallen stock? She'd have kept them going for weeks.'

'I hope there is someone to help unload at the other end,' said Jake, turning up the collar of his long tweed coat, the elbows of which were holey and frayed. 'Do crematoriums have fork-lifts?'

This irreverent attitude to death was not a reflection of a callous disregard for poor Great-Aunt Mary, but rather a family trait born of a loathing of sentimentality and an inability to talk openly of anything that remotely touched our hearts. My dear granny had shocked the ladies' hairdresser in Market Newton where she went once a week to have her hair washed and set, by looking crossly at her watch as she waited to be collected by Grandpa and saying loudly, 'Where *is* the daft old man? Dead, I expect!' He countered this when he eventually hove into view by opening the door and addressing the salon at large in his booming Dorset countryman's voice. 'I've come to collect the corpse!' It was their way of dealing with old age and ill health. Granny was half blind and suffering from Parkinson's disease and Grandpa was devastated by the prospect of life without her.

Neil slammed up the back of the truck and Dad and Uncle Peter climbed into the cab and with a parting tootle on the horn set off down the village street. As we stood watching them go, kind-hearted Clemmie hooked her arm through that of little Miss Timmis, whose nose was very pink, through grief or cold I couldn't tell, and we trooped off towards the village hall where there was to be tea for the mourners. Since my mother had gone off the rails she refused to do anything helpful at home or we would have gone back to the farm and gathered round a cheery fire in the drawing room. As it was, it had been left to Dad and Uncle Peter to organise caterers to master the tea urn and set out the thick white crockery in the dusty hall. The mourners' feet clattered on the frozen lane and the sound echoed back from the pale winter hills on which nothing moved. The village seemed eerily empty and silent. Smoke from one or two cottage chimneys travelled white and straight into the pearly sky and some rooks batted about on the top branches of the bare elms behind the Old Vicarage; otherwise there was no sign of life, only a strong smell of livestock, warm and pungent, in the air.

The caterers' white van was pulled up outside the village hall, and inside, Mr Tooth the caretaker was lurking in the entrance, wearing his anorak and cycle clips and woollen hat, a worried expression on his face. He wanted to buttonhole someone about the water heater in the kitchen. He didn't want her left on or her'd blow a fuse, he said. It had happened before, after the playgroup jumble sale. I assured him we'd switch the boiler off when we had washed up the tea things, and invited him to stay, but he said, no disrespect but he had to get on, he'd got his fowl to feed, and he wobbled away into the grey afternoon on his bicycle, on the back of which were lashed three tall and knobbly stalks of Brussels sprouts.

Inside the hall the long trestle tables were laid with white cloths and plates of sandwiches and cakes and at the far end there were glasses and bottles of whisky and sherry. The mourners seemed to cheer up when they were out of the cold and within sight of something to eat and drink, and in a matter of minutes the cousins had formed a loud, laughing group in the middle of the room. They made so much noise that everyone else had to drop their muted funereal tones in order to make themselves heard.

There was nothing the Kingsleys liked better than a funeral, except perhaps the entertainment of a good row, or someone else's farm sale. Kingsleys who had hardly known Great-Aunt Mary, who could have passed her in the street without recognising her, had come from far and wide in order to run a critical eye over their relations, tease and provoke one another, stoke up on gossip and rekindle old feuds and alliances. Great-Aunt Mary could not have died at a better moment in terms of providing an opportunity to witness my parents' marital fall-out first hand.

I felt quite sorry for my mother, who was being determinedly bright and smiling. Her fuchsia lipstick had worn off except where it had crept into the lines about her mouth. She wore too much make-up these days, too much jewellery, and her clothes were too short and too tight. She thought it made her look youthful, whereas the effect was more sad and desperate.

It looked as if, at any moment, she would be suggesting that we went out clubbing together. Now she passed round the plates of sausage rolls with a tinkly laugh here and a touch on an arm there, knowing all the time that great waves of family disapprobation were breaking all around her.

It was all very well for my father to stray and fall charmingly in and out of love with most of the pretty women in the neighbourhood; that was what was expected of a man of his type. It was quite another thing for a woman to flout the rules, especially my mother, who was marked down as being an outsider from the start. Poor Mum, the daughter of a Reading chemist, who met Dad at university where he was reading agriculture and she was studying political science. What had they ever had in common? She was never going to be a country girl. She arrived in Over Crompton as a socialist who disliked animals in general. Even worse, she was anti-hunting. Nothing was more condemning in the eyes of the Kingsleys, who were made up of Jorrocks-faced men who farmed up and down the county and hunted three days a week on stout cobs, and iron-arsed women who rode in point-to-points.

She was pretty though. I had studied the wedding

photographs and there she was, a laughing girl with sooty eyes and dead-straight curtains of shiny black hair, wearing a pink mini-dress and a large flowery hat. I suppose she had tried to like the farm at first but by the time I was born she had given up the effort, and as soon as I went to school she got a job running the housing association in the nearest town and angrily championing lost and unpopular causes. 'Busybodying,' Grandpa called it. 'Should be at home cooking John a proper hot dinner,' sniffed Gran, and theirs was the mildest criticism.

Apart from our family, the other mourners were mostly ancient, the slightly less old and incapacitated ferrying the extremely old and doddery in cars which were parked erratically outside the church and would later prevent the milk tanker from getting through the village to our farm. Funerals were one of the few outings left to them in their old age. You could always expect a good gate when one or another of them fell off the perch. I noticed that hardly any mention was made of Great-Aunt Mary. They were more interested in what was in the sandwiches and in getting their whisky glasses topped up. Beady-eyed, hung about with handbags and sticks and walking frames and adjusting their hearing aids in and out of whiskery ears, they were as alert and lively as anyone else in the room.

'Which one are you?' they boomed at me and my cousins, and when we shouted back our names they generally went on to tell a tale about our fathers when they were boys, followed by wheezy laughter.

'You can see that this is the generation that won the war,' said Clemmie to me, as she made a sortie towards the drinks end of the table on the arm of an ancient retired colonel who was clearing the way by using his stick like a metal detector in front of him.

I spotted little Miss Timmis twittering to the vicar and went to speak to her. My approach gave him the opportunity to duck away with a caring expression on his face and a little trill of his fingers in my direction.

'Miss Timmis,' I said, taking her arm. 'How are you? I mean, *really*?'

'Oh, my dear!' she said, blinking up at me through her smeary glasses, her little pouchy, powdery cheeks trembling. 'It was such a shock! So sudden! But you know, just the other day Mary said she thought it was time she died. She believed that God had forgotten about her.'

This was an arresting idea. I thought of the avenging

God of the Jews, the forgiving God of the New Testament and Great-Aunt Mary's version; absent-minded and disorganised. I imagined Him slapping the side of His head and saying, 'Mary Kingsley! Completely slipped my mind! She'll be expecting me!'

'She'd asked for a poached egg for breakfast and I took it in to her on a tray, cooked just as she liked it, and she said she wanted the salt. It was so silly of me, I always forgot the salt, but when I went back with it only a few minutes later, she was sitting motionless in her chair and there was something about her which gave me a fright. "Mary?" I said, giving her arm a little shake, and then I realised that she had gone. Just like that, with the poached egg still warm on the toast.'

'What a waste,' I said, before I could stop myself.

'Oh, no, Emily, because naughty Pugsy jumped up and ate it when I was waiting for your father. He licked the plate quite clean.' Pugsy, a pop-eyed, wheezing fawn barrel on antique bow legs, is one of Great-Aunt Mary's two rather repulsive dogs. 'Your father came at once and was so kind. He realised what a shock it was to me! I've been with Mary for eight years, you see, and known her since she was a girl in London before the war. Oh, my dear, I shall miss her.

She was such a *character*. Such a strong person, even towards the end, when she found life difficult.'

'What will you do now, Miss T? Will you want to stay in the cottage on your own?'

Miss Timmis's little furry face brightened. 'Oh no, dear. I'm going into a home. Mary had it all arranged for me, if she went first. I have had a room booked for some time. As soon as your father has the opportunity to help me sort out the cottage of Mary's things, I shall move.'

'But will you like that?' I asked anxiously, thinking of a dreary place smelling of pee and cabbage, inhabited by dotty old women shuffling about in nylon nighties.

'Oh yes, my dear!' sighed Miss Timmis. 'I have visited The Willows several times and know I shall be happy.' She lowered her voice. 'They have a very nice type of person living there. Old Lady Forbes is a resident, you know! I shall enjoy the company.' I looked at her eager little face and saw that genteel snobbery could be a comfort to the end.

'What will happen to the dogs?' I asked, thinking of naughty Pugsy, who rogered anything that moved, and his sister Millie, stout and snuffly with only one oily blue eye.

'Your father says they can go to the farm. He said that your mother, you know . . .'

I did, only too well. Poor Mum, I thought. Why couldn't Dad give them to one of his girlfriends to look after?

'Now, how about you, Emily?' went on Miss Timmis in a brighter tone, twinkling up at me. 'Are you engaged yet? To be married to that nice boy? The one with the motor bicycle?'

'No, I'm not!' I said, trying hard not to look as if I cared. 'In fact, I have broken up with him. Just recently. I'm a single girl again.'

'Oh well,' said Miss Timmis. 'You are so young. There is plenty of time to settle down and I am sure there is a *queue* of young men at your door!'

Oh Miss Timmis, wrong on both counts. Not so bloody young. I shall be a dreary twenty-six next year. And no queue either.

My mother whisked past at that moment with a tray of sausage rolls and caught my arm with her free hand. 'Sorry to interrupt, Miss Timmis,' she said. 'I need just a word with Emily.'

'Of course! Of course! I don't want to . . .' Miss Timmis twittered and patted at the scone crumbs caught at the corner of her mouth, but my mother took no notice.

'What's the matter?' she said, drawing me to one side. 'You look awful. Are you ill?'

'No. I've just had a bit of a bad time,' I began. 'Mum, I've broken up with Ted,' but she wasn't listening.

'Has Dad said anything to you?'

'What do you mean? *Said* anything. Of course he has.'

She sighed impatiently. 'About *us*, I mean. About him and me and so on?'

'Mum! What is there to say? Everybody seems to know anyway.'

'I just want to know what he's *saying*. Especially to you. I want you to hear my side of the story.'

I winced. 'Mum! Please! It's up to you and him to sort it out. I don't want to take sides. I don't feel it's anything to do with me.'

'I've done nothing that I'm ashamed of,' she said fiercely, jamming a whole sausage roll into the mouth of a passing child. 'Nothing! When I think what I've put up with over the years . . .'

'Mum!' I said desperately. 'I don't want to know!' I dreaded hearing that she had only stayed with my father because of me, but even left unsaid, the implication hung heavily between us.

'But you should know,' she said, 'because if you had *any* idea . . .'

'Please, Mum!' I said, but was unwise enough to add, 'If you're so unhappy, why don't you leave him?'

She stopped and stared at me. 'Leave him?' she demanded. 'How do you imagine I could do that? We have been married for more than thirty years. Do you think I could just chuck all that away? I am fifty-four years old, Emily. I can't start all over again. I don't want a lonely old age, thank you very much.'

'Well . . .' I said helplessly. 'What do you want? What about the Artificial Insemination man?'

'Don't speak of him!' she spat. 'He's gone. Took bloody fright and asked to move areas. He's serving Yorkshire now.'

Her anger and hostility made my eyes water. She bared her teeth in a ferocious smile as she surveyed the roomful of gathered Kingsleys. 'Look at them!' she snarled. 'Like vultures round a corpse!'

I glanced about us. Her analogy wasn't wholly accurate, because Kingsley men were mostly squat and square, red-faced Dorset countrymen, although the women did tend to be sparse and lean and beady-eyed.

'Did you love him then, Mum?' I asked awkwardly. 'The AI man?'

'Of course I didn't. Don't be ridiculous, Emily.' She

turned her fierce gaze on me. 'But he provided a diversion. Took my mind off your father and the bloody farm. And,' her voice softened and took on a wistful tone, 'it was so good to be *noticed*. Appreciated, for once.'

'Dad appreciates you in his own way. He'd be lost without you.' I really meant it. My father relied on my mother for everything but romance.

'Hmm!' she said. 'I'm sick to death of being told that. Of always being here ready to forgive him and take him back. I tell you, Emily, if I do stay, things are going to change.'

I stared at her angry face. She looked too old to be experiencing this sort of stuff, so like what I was going through, but nearly thirty years down the line.

'Do you still love Dad?' I asked.

My mother paused. She ran a hand through her hair, recently coloured an unflattering auburn, and her mouth sagged at the corners with emotion.

'Of course I bloody do, Emily. Why else would I still be here?' She looked around angrily. 'Anyway, it would be what this lot would like. To see me off. But I won't do it. Not to please them, anyway.' She took a glass of whisky off a passing tray and downed it in one. I didn't remember her drinking whisky before.

'What did you say about Ted?' she asked. 'Did you say you had split up?'

'Yes,' I said and felt my lip tremble and my eyes fill with tears.

She put her arm round me. 'Don't let them see you!' she hissed. She looked over my shoulder and I heard her murmur, 'So fond of Aunt Mary.'

I scrubbed at my face. 'I don't mind who knows! Clemmie and the boys know already.'

'Maybe they do, but the others don't need to. All their ugly daughters are smugly engaged or married with their photographs in *Pigkeepers Monthly*, I expect, with rings through their noses. I don't want them to see you unhappy.'

'Oh, Mum!' I didn't care. I was long past bothering about my pride.

'What went wrong?' she asked, softening for a moment. Her eyes narrowed suspiciously.

'I found out that he had been sleeping with Tatty.' Even now the words hurt me.

'Bastard!' she spat. How angry she was about everything. 'God! Men are all the same! How long had that been going on for?'

I found that I didn't want to talk to her about it. I shrugged. 'I don't know. It doesn't matter anyway.

I've moved out of the flat. I've been staying with a teacher from school.'

'Forget him!' she said. 'I always thought he was untrustworthy. Sexy and good-looking and all that, but thoroughly untrustworthy.'

'Please, Mum!' I did not need reminding of what I had lost. 'Poor Great-Aunt Mary!' I said, to change the subject. 'I can't believe that she has gone.'

My mother looked thoughtful. 'She snuffed it at the right moment, in a way. Your father and I hadn't spoken for two weeks but you can't deal with a death in the family in grunts. Now at least we are talking again. I shall miss the old bat. She was always good for a laugh, and of course, she loathed all this lot.' My mother gestured with her hand at the surrounding Kingsleys. 'Look at them! They are getting worked up about the will now. There have been endless telephone calls trying to find out how much she left and to whom!' My mother snorted with laughter. 'They are in for a shock!'

'Why?'

'She didn't leave much. She has provided for Miss Timmis to go to a very expensive home and that's about as far as it goes. Oh yes, apart from something weird about you and Clemmie.'

'What do you mean? Weird?'

'I can't remember exactly. Nothing to get excited about. You're not an heiress or anything. It was something to do with her ashes. Old Godders will tell you.'

Mr Godfrey was the family solicitor. I had seen him in church, small, round and jolly, twinkling and bobbing, even at a funeral, jammed into his fawn overcoat like a plump little sausage in its skin. I wrinkled my nose. I did not like the sound of Great-Aunt Mary's ashes becoming my responsibility. I had heard tales of the scattering of ashes at sea or on Exmoor or at the open ditch at Wincanton racecourse. I imagined Clemmie and me detailed to do the same with Great-Aunt Mary in Harrods food hall. God forbid.

'Right!' said my mother grimly. 'Back into battle!' and with a horrid smile fixed on her face she continued on her way with her plate of sausage rolls.

She was brave, I thought. I had to give her that. Braver than I was, groping in my bag to check my mobile phone to see if I had a text message or had missed a call. I still couldn't make myself believe that Ted had gone, and most of the time I felt that I would give anything to get him back. I admired my mother's anger, but given her current mood I didn't rate the chances of Pugsy and Millie if my father was unwise enough to expect her to take them on.

I looked about me and nodded and smiled to neighbours and relations but it was Clemmie for whom I searched. I spotted her in the corner with her rheumy-eyed old colonel and worked my way across to relieve her. The colonel's lower lip trembled, wet and pink, and he had Clemmie pressed up against the table and was leaning over her as if she was a plate of mouth-watering cakes.

'Excuse me, Colonel!' I said, edging in. 'I don't want to interrupt but I need to talk to Clemmie rather urgently.'

The colonel made a harrumphing noise in his throat. 'My dear Emily. Enchanted, my dear.' His horny old hand moved over my bottom as if it was the price to be paid for releasing Clemmie, who ducked out from the corner.

'Thanks, darlin'!' she said, and gave the colonel a fat wink. She took my arm. 'Poor old Aunt Mary. I can't really believe it, can you? I feel so mean that it is weeks and weeks since I last saw her. It was the summer, wasn't it? At Dad's birthday party. She was scoffing strawberries and cream and wearing an enormous straw hat and a vast dress that looked as if it had been made out of the sitting-room curtains, do you remember? Larger than life she was then, and now she's gone.'

'Have you heard about her will?' I asked.

'No? What about it?' Clemmie's beautiful oval face looked at me from under the brim of her black hat. She pursed her lovely wide mouth, carefully glossed with a pale lipstick.

'There's something about us in it. You and me, Clem. My mother says so.'

'What about us? Has she left us everything? We always were her favourites.'

'No, nothing like that. It's something about her ashes.'

'Yuck. No thanks,' said Clemmie. 'You can have all of her in a pot on your mantelpiece. I don't want my share.'

'No. I don't think it's like that. Mr Godfrey knows. He's over there. Let's ask him.'

Mr Godfrey was having a hard time keeping the Kingsleys at bay. He was surrounded by them, all wanting to know details of the will, and batting them away with little flurries of good humour. 'No, no,' he was saying to Frank Kingsley, a cousin of Dad's who farmed the other side of the hill. 'I can't say anything else at the moment, but I can assure you that there is nothing of interest to your branch of the family. She made a few small bequests, but her estate was not large.'

I touched his arm. 'Mr Godfrey! It's us, Clemmie and Emily!'

'Ah, girls!' he twinkled. 'I wanted to see you. I think we need to arrange a meeting.'

Cousin Frank bristled and glared. I could see he thought that something was going on, that wool was being pulled over his bushy badger eyebrows.

'When do you have to be back in London?' Mr Godfrey asked us.

Clemmie shrugged. The modern art gallery in which she had sat behind a desk filing her nails and bored witless had closed a month ago. Now she was waitressing and doing bar work in the run-up to Christmas. 'Doesn't matter too much to me,' she said. 'But why do we have to meet at all?'

Mr Godfrey drew us to one side. 'In her will, your Great-Aunt Mary made a rather unusual request regarding the disposal of her ashes,' he said in a confidential tone. 'She has left a sum of money to cover the expense incurred and she has nominated you, her two great-nieces, as executors. She never spoke to you about this?'

Clemmie and I looked at one another blankly. 'No,' I said. 'Not to me she didn't. Clemmie?'

'No!' said Clemmie emphatically. 'Never.'

'I can't take time off,' I said. I was working as a supply teacher at an east London primary school where every man counted. It had been hard enough to arrange for my class to be covered while I attended the funeral. 'Couldn't we get this over with now? It can't be that complicated.'

Mr Godfrey hesitated. 'I do have the relevant papers in the car,' he said. 'Perhaps we could adjourn there for a short meeting? It shouldn't take long.'

We followed Mr Godfrey outside and buttoning up our coats walked back down the village street to where his smart solicitor's car was parked near the church. He took the keys out of his pocket and the car doors winked and unlocked themselves obediently.

'Hop in,' he said, fishing his briefcase off the seat. Clemmie climbed into the back, her coat falling open to reveal her slender legs in black fishnet tights. I slid into the passenger seat and we both sat and waited while Mr Godfrey flicked through papers which he rested against the steering wheel. 'Ah!' he said. 'Here we are,' and he began to read: 'I appoint my two great-nieces, Emily and Clementine Kingsley, to be executors of this part of my will. I request that my ashes be transported to Mali, formerly French Sudan, in western Africa. My final resting place is to be,' he hesitated over the pronunciation, 'Timadjlalen in the Sahara Desert, and the last part of my nieces' journey will have to be completed by camel. Sufficient funds from my estate have been set aside to cover the travel expenses and any loss of income that my nieces may incur. I realise that they may be a little surprised and dismayed at this request and perhaps unwilling to comply with my wishes. However, they must trust me when I say that this journey will be the most important of their lives. The man they must seek to facilitate their travel is well known in the Kidal area. His name is Salika ag Baye.'

Clemmie and I sat in stunned silence for a moment, while Mr Godfrey cleared his throat and shuffled his papers.

'Well!' said Clemmie eventually, from the back seat. 'Why on earth does she want to be scattered there? I've never even heard of Mali.'

'I must admit I was equally surprised,' said Mr Godfrey. 'I had no idea that your great-aunt had any connection with Africa. I had a quick look on the internet. Mali is rather a large and empty west African country, the northern part all desert. I could find no trace at all of the particular place mentioned.'

'I have never heard of anything so mad!' I said crossly. 'It's ridiculous. How can we be expected to comply with such a stupid whim? She must have lost her marbles.'

'I don't think so,' said Mr Godfrey, shaking his head and searching through a document-holder. 'The will was a model – beautifully drawn up. She had thought of everything. Here!' He produced what he was looking for and waved an envelope at us. 'She even bought your air tickets. Open-ended and valid for a year.'

He held out the envelope, at which I glared, unwilling to take it from his hand. I didn't want anything to do with it. Clemmie reached across my shoulder and snatched it and ripped it open.

'Air France. Two tickets. Paris to Bamako,' she said. 'Wow!'

Her excited tone irritated me. 'For God's sake, Clem. Don't start thinking I'm up for this. It's all very well for you—'

'Oh shut up, Emily!' she interrupted. 'Don't be so pathetic. This is an adventure. It's exactly what we both need. I'm sick to death of my boring life and it will get you away from London and help you forget horrible Ted.'

'If it is of any interest,' said Mr Godfrey, patting my

hand and smiling at me cheerfully, 'I discovered that there *is* one place in Mali that you've probably heard of.' He paused and his eyes twinkled. 'Timbuktu,' he announced with a flourish.

'Oh!' cried Clemmie. 'I've *always* wanted to go there.'

Clemmie

FROM THE VERY beginning I knew that Emily and I had to do what Great-Aunt Mary requested. Mr Godfrey's news was a total surprise, of course, but as we sat in his car and he told us about Mali, I had the strangest feeling that I had been anticipating something like this; that at some point my life would take an unexpected turn. It was as if I had been waiting for the call, although I would never have expected that it would come via Great-Aunt Mary.

I was never very academic at school, and when Emily and I left and she went off to university, already knowing that she wanted to be a teacher, I drifted into any old job, earning enough to keep myself but not really knowing what I wanted to do. I felt that I was marking time, filling in the hours and days and weeks until my real life began, though I didn't know which direction it would come from. I'd tried astrology and tarot cards and palm readings and I had sat alone and thoughtful in empty churches hoping for a sign from above, but so far, nothing. I was well aware, and have had it pointed out to me often enough, that you can create your own destiny and make things happen, but I knew instinctively that this was not what this feeling was about. I did not need an interesting hobby or to take up a new sport, or to meet more people or go speed-dating or find a new job – it was not like that at all. My life was full enough in that sense, it didn't lack *activity*, but I felt as if there was an empty space at my centre which was waiting to be filled.

Emily and my other girlfriends all thought that what I needed was a man, that I needed to fall in love and get married and have a stack of children, and of course they might be right, but I knew that just finding and attaching myself to a suitable guy, like a limpet to a rock, was not the answer to this frightening feeling of emptiness. At that time I was always meeting men. I worked all over that Christmas as a waitress and I remember being asked out nearly every night by boozed-up and happy men. Although it was flattering and some of them might have turned out to be worth knowing, when I looked into their flushed faces and hot, excited eyes and heard the encouraging yelps of their testosterone-driven mates, I picked up their credit cards from the table, pocketed their tips, smiled sweetly and declined. Instinct told me that going out with any one of them would not be the answer I was looking for to fill the void I felt inside. On the contrary, it would make it worse.

Great-Aunt Mary's will changed all that. It gave me a purpose. I liked being charged with something important to do and I enjoyed the mystery of her request and the fact that it needed a bit of unravelling. I remembered the last time I had talked to her, back in the summer, at my dad's birthday party lunch. I had sat beside her under a tree in the garden and she had asked me about my life in her usual direct style, her brow furrowed, her scarlet mouth drawing on a cigarette. I shrugged and said not much, work was okay, my friends were okay, no, there wasn't anybody special. My standard response. She was quieter than usual, more thoughtful, and what she said stuck in my mind.

'The trouble with you, Clemmie, is that you were born in the wrong age.'

Emily wandered over at that moment and overheard what Great-Aunt Mary had said. She sat down on the grass beside me, keeping one eye on Ted, who had drunk too much and was fooling about with the boys, scrapping on the grass and trying to push one another into the stream which runs at the bottom of the garden.

'What do you mean?' I asked.

'You need a man who was born to bear arms and love women.'

'What about me?' said Emily, who is a typical only child and always likes the conversation to turn to her, and Great-Aunt Mary laughed and said, 'You, Emily? You are a child of your time. As I was. There's no doubt of that!' and Emily had looked a bit crestfallen because she took it to mean that I was special in some way and she was not.

It was going to be hard work to persuade Emily. At the funeral she looked so forlorn and wrapped up in her own misery that she was not willing or able to be enthusiastic about anything else. She was at the stage of a disintegrating love affair when a girl wants to hole up in a corner, lick her wounds and talk about nothing but her ex-beloved, as if by saying his name twenty times in the same number of minutes she can somehow keep him alive in her heart.

Poor old Em. She and Ted had always been a mismatched couple and everyone knew it but her. I could understand what she saw in him in a way, because he was good looking and could be fun, but he had always been far more in love with himself than he ever was with her. Bossy, good, kind Emily treated him like an indulged spoilt child and in return he abused her love for him. He was the one unsensible thing in her whole life, and I sometimes wondered whether she was the sort of girl who needed to be needed, even if it meant that she suffered as a result with a waster like Ted. He sponged off her shamelessly and lay in bed while she went off to work, but instead of repaying her generosity he undermined her confidence, telling her that she was fat or boring or a nag. Sleeping with one of her best friends was the final treachery. The best thing for Emily now was to get Ted out of her life, and going to Mali looked to me to be a useful start.

To be truthful, I am not the one to give advice on the snaring and handling of men. I am pretty useless at it myself but for different reasons from Emily. I start out with good intentions. I desperately want to fall in love and think each time that maybe this is the one, but it never is. I just can't seem to love a man as much as, for instance, I used to love my old pony Blazer, who, truthfully, I would have died for. It still makes my eyes fill with tears when I think about him. I take my feelings for him as a sort of benchmark, and no man has ever come close. So you see, I think there is something wrong with me, that I've got a piece of vital girl equipment missing. It's as if I can never find the right falling-in-love top gear and all my relationships labour along in third.

Apart from thinking that it would do Emily good to get away, I really wanted and needed her to go to Africa with me. She has been my companion and friend since we were born, a few months apart, in the same hospital in Dorchester, and we have shared all our best adventures ever since. Clemandem, my brothers used to call us, because we were always together, whiling away the long school holidays, mucking about with nothing much to do except dream up stories with ourselves as the heroines, cutting our arms with penknives and mixing our blood because we were that close. Blood sisters. Now the real grown-up adventure was about to begin and I couldn't contemplate setting off without Emily as my partner.

When I got back to London after the funeral, I felt fired up by the whole idea of our trip with Great-Aunt Mary and set out to learn more about Mali. I stopped off at the public library on my way to work my shift at the pub and ran off some maps and printed some stuff off the internet, then telephoned Emily to ask her to come round after school. Her voice sounded flat but at least she agreed.

'After all, I've got nothing else to do,' she said gloomily. At least you're not washing Ted's socks, I thought. Having nothing to do seemed a preferable alternative.

Then I telephoned Miss Timmis. There hadn't been an opportunity after the funeral to speak to her about Great-Aunt Mary's peculiar request and I wanted to find out how much she knew about it. Nobody else in the family had a clue. They were all as stumped as we were.

'Africa!' my mother had exclaimed when I told my family what Mr Godfrey had said. We had just got back from the village hall and she was leaning on the Aga in the kitchen, en route for the hen house, her apron draped over the front of her best coat, a bowl of scraps for the chickens in her hand. 'Why ever Africa? I never heard her even mention Africa in passing. Not once.' Absent-mindedly she offered the bowl to the rest of us, as if she was at a party, passing round the canapés.

'It's Beryl Timmis you must speak to,' said my dad, fishing out a piece of old toast and putting it in his mouth. He had had too much to drink at the funeral and stood swaying gently backwards and forwards like a sapling in a wind. 'She and Aunt Mary grew up together. She's the one who will know why.'

'Mali's a wonderful country,' said Will. 'The music is the best.' He works for a music label as a sound recordist and knows all about weird world stuff. 'God, I'd love to come with you. If Emily won't do it, take me, Clem.'

'Or me,' chorused my other brothers.

'No way!' I said. 'This is girls' stuff. This is for Emily and me. It's what Great-Aunt Mary wanted. It has to be us.'

Miss Timmis answered the telephone on almost the first ring. 'Oh, Clemmie!' she said in her little wispy voice. 'How nice to hear from you, my dear!' It made me feel guilty that I had rung for a particular reason and not just to find out how she was. We chatted about various things before I said, 'Miss Timmis, Great-Aunt Mary made a rather peculiar request. She wants Emily and me to take her ashes out to Mali, a country in Africa, and scatter them in a particular place there. A very faraway place as far as we can tell. Dad says that you are the only one who might know why . . .'

There was a pause at the other end. I could hear Miss Timmis's breath in a faint high whistle.

'Miss Timmis?' I said. 'Are you still there?'

'Africa?' she said softly, wondering. 'Well I never . . .'

I waited for a long moment. 'Miss Timmis?'

'No,' she said finally. There was a firmer tone in her voice. 'No, my dear. She never talked to me of Africa.' There was another pause, during which I had the feeling that she was about to speak again. 'France, though,' she said eventually. 'That I would have understood. You know, of course, that Mary's father was French?'

'No, I didn't. I never knew that. She never talked about it.'

'Oh, yes. He was a charming man. An army officer. She spent time in France when she was a girl. After she left school she went to live with her father for a while.'

'It's amazing how little the rest of the family seem to know about her. No one had a clue about France or Africa. We had never even heard of the country she wants us to take her to. It's a mystery, Miss Timmis. A complete mystery.'

'Yes, it's very strange,' she said slowly. 'I never heard her speak of Africa.'

When Emily arrived later that evening she looked very pale and tired, which was not surprising since she was battling her way towards the end of the long autumn term at her East End primary school. She was wearing unnecessarily depressing-making clothes, baggy and shapeless and in various shades of sludge, and her lovely dark hair was flat and greasy and scraped back off her face. She slumped down on my sofa and said that she had been round to the old flat after school. She said that she'd had a feeling that Ted would be there, waiting for her to come back but too proud to telephone. Instead she found that he had returned at some point to collect more of his belongings and had left a cheque for her on the kitchen counter. Just a cheque to cover his share of the rent, which was something, I suppose, but no note. Not a word. She said that the sight of his writing had made her feel so ill that she had retched into the sink.

I made her some tea, which she bent her head over, holding the mug in two hands close to her chest, like you imagine a down-and-out might drink, glad of a little warmth and comfort.

'Look, Em,' I said, getting out the maps of Mali and spreading them on the floor at her feet. 'It's a huge country. As far as I can tell the top half is desert. The bottom of the Sahara, in fact. There's a whopping river which divides the country that does a sort of unusual type of U-bend. What's it called?' I put on my glasses and traced the line with my finger. 'The Niger. The countries on either side are Algeria in the north, Burkino Faso, Mauritania, Ivory Coast and Niger.'

'It's all bloody civil wars and massacres and droughts,' said Emily. 'Those are the only reasons anyone has ever heard of those countries. It's not like Kenya or Botswana or Tanzania, where people go on holiday. I've never known anyone go to any of those west African countries unless they are forced to.'

'Don't be so negative!' I said. Outside my dirty window it had started to snow in huge wet grey flakes which melted and slid down the glass. 'There's another map here,' I went on. 'Of the transport system. Mali seems to have a main road from Dakar to the capital, Bamako, but there's nothing else marked. The rest is just a big blank.'

'Hmm,' said Emily. 'That would account for the camels.' She snorted impatiently. 'Honestly, Clemmie, it's all such bollocks. We should ignore the whole thing and go and scatter Great-Aunt Mary on the hill at home. What does it matter where she is? She is dead, after all.'

'She'd haunt us for the rest of our lives. She hated the hill. You know she did. She never really liked the country.'

'Well, anywhere, then,' said Emily. She had laid herself down on the sofa with her big biker boots stuck out over the arm and was staring gloomily at the ceiling. 'Anywhere that doesn't involve a bloody great hike to some godforsaken place in Africa. Do we know *why* it has to be there?'

'A mystery,' I said. 'None of the family seems to have a clue. The only person who might be able to throw some light, who knew Great-Aunt Mary before any of us, is Miss Timmis, but she says she doesn't know either. She was a bit peculiar about it, actually.'

'What do you mean, peculiar?' said Emily, turning her head with a spark of interest in her voice.

'I telephoned her today to ask about Africa and she said she didn't know. She sounded odd about it though. She went very quiet for a long time. Then she said that Great-Aunt Mary's father was French. Did you know that?'

'French?' said Emily, frowning. 'Are you sure? She never seemed at all foreign, did she?'

'Well, there was the cooking,' I reminded her. 'That

was very French when you think of it. Had she been completely English, she would have grown up as part of the Spam and rice pudding generation, wouldn't she?'

'Yes, I suppose that does make sense. What was her maiden name?'

'I don't know,' I said. 'I never thought to ask. She seemed too old to have a *maiden* name, I mean.'

'Mali was French, you know,' said Emily. 'It was a colony up until at least the sixties.'

'How do you know that?' I asked, surprised. 'I thought you didn't know anything about it.'

'It's not exactly classified information,' she said witheringly.

'Find out some more,' I prompted. 'Look it up on the internet at your school. I tried the library on my way to work this morning, but when I typed in Kidal, the name of the place that Great-Aunt Mary mentioned, it asked me if I meant Kendal, as in mint cake. I didn't have time to look any further.'

'I suppose I could,' said Emily carelessly, 'if I had any intention of going there, which I haven't.'

'Well I'm going, and I'm not going without you, so you'll have to come. Do you want some supper? Mum sent me back with loads of eggs. We could have an omelette.'

'Yeah, okay, thanks.' Emily lifted her great boots off the sofa and swung them down to the floor. 'I've got some decisions to make, Clemmie,' she said in a weighty tone of voice. 'There's only three weeks to the end of term and then my contract comes to an end. I can get it renewed, I'm sure, there's such a shortage of teachers willing to work in deprived inner London, but do I want to? I'm only working there because of Ted, because it suited him. Then there's the flat. I can't afford the rent on my own and I don't want to live there without him anyway, so I must give notice and clear the place out. I'll have to find somewhere else to live. I can't stay where I am. Janet's been really kind to put me up and she obviously needs the rent, but her flat's too small for both of us and her two kids. I'm in her daughter's tiny bedroom while she's been moved in with her brother. No wonder she gives me death stares all the time.'

I let her ramble on while I beat eggs in a bowl. I had a terrible sense of her life having come to a full stop. She was feeling the awful loneliness of being an unwanted person crowding Janet's family, knowing they would rather have her space than her company.

'I keep thinking of *her* with him,' she said, coming to stand in the way in my tiny kitchen so I had to stretch round her to drop the whisk in the sink. 'In bed together, showering together, fooling about, watching television. All the things we used to do. He used to come up behind me and kiss me on the back of my neck when I was cooking.'

She went on and on like this all through supper, and then to cheer her up I made her come to the pub on the corner for a drink. Unfortunately, the bar was full of happy couples. I saw her noticing a hand touching a shoulder, an arm round a waist, a man bending to kiss his girlfriend's mouth. Even the girls cackling with laughter next to us at a corner table, a stack of glasses and an overflowing ashtray in front of them, were out on a hen night.

We said goodbye on the cold street where the snow had melted into an inch of brown slush. A bitter wind stung our faces and a homeless man with a bedraggled grey beard rifled through a bin outside a kebab shop.

'I'm not even getting thin,' said Emily glumly, looking for her gloves in her pocket and pulling out a crumpled chocolate wrapper. 'I seem to have the sort of misery that needs feeding.'

The next few days I was busy, working long lunchtime and evening shifts and waking up in the morning with a headache and a taste of cigarette smoke in my mouth.

The only thing I had time to do was to ring a friend's sister who worked in a travel agency and find out that there was only a handful of companies who arranged trips to Mali. She gave me their names and told me to get in touch because they might be able to help with the journey once we had arrived at Bamako.

Then Will dropped round with a CD of Malian music which he had promised me and Emily telephoned to tell me that she had decided to stay on at her school.

'They need me, Clemmie,' she said in a defiant voice, as if I had suggested something to the contrary. 'I can't cop out now, halfway through the year. Those poor kids have had four different teachers since they started Primary Three. I've told them I'll stay.'

'That sounds more like you,' I said, and it did. Emily was the last person to give up on something and she was passionate about her teaching. That morning I had had a cheque through the post for the money owed me by the gallery I had been working for. 'Tell you what, let's go out tonight,' I said. 'I'll treat you because I'm in funds, and in return you bring over all you can find about Mali.'

'Okay, that's really kind of you, Clemmie,' she said in a resigned voice, and then added, 'but it doesn't mean I'm going with you. Let's get that quite clear. No way. I shall need the Christmas holidays to find a new flat.'

'Just come over,' I said, 'and bring the stuff.'

When she arrived that evening, she looked better. She had washed her hair for one thing and it was loose and shiny on her shoulders, and she wasn't wearing tracksuit bottoms and an enormous jumper. She had on a short denim skirt and a tight top which showed off her magnificent bosoms and I took her improved appearance as the first early sign of recovery. However, she was as negative as ever about Mali.

'To kick off, you might like to see this list of endemic diseases,' she said, 'and read about all the shots you will need before they even let you into the country.' She passed over a stack of printed sheets which I flicked through quickly.

'All this looks boring,' I told her. 'I don't want to know percentages of irrigated land and GDP. This is just dull facts.'

'It's what you get,' she said tartly, 'when you look up countries on the internet, and it isn't boring at all if you intend to go there.' She was using her annoying teacher voice. 'You *should* know that life expectancy is forty-five years, that the people are desperately poor and that it is impossible to travel into the desert except between October and March. There are no hard roads in the north, where you want to go, just sand tracks that get washed away in the rainy season, and it's too hot to travel in the dry season.'

'But there is a tourist industry,' I protested. 'Lots of French companies take tours there. It can't all be as difficult as you make it sound.'

'They stay in the south,' said Emily. She was such a know-all. 'I looked at some of their itineraries. They go on the river Niger in a boat thing called a pinasse, and they visit a weird tribe of people called Dogons, but they don't go up north into the desert where Great-Aunt Mary wants you to take her. There's nothing to go there for. It's just empty desert. Mali is like two different countries, one below the Niger and one above.'

'Have you seen any photographs?' I asked her, refusing to be put off. 'Have you seen the Tuareg people from the north? The desert people? Em, they are sensational! They are very tall and graceful and they wear these wonderful coloured robes and big turbans which they wrap round their heads so that only their eyes can be seen. They have a terribly fierce and blood-thirsty reputation. They are like a wonderful warrior class, like noble knights in the Middle Ages.'

'They're always fighting, if that's what you mean,' said Emily irritably. 'And they used to be slave-owners. They fought the French and then after independence they fought the government in the south. The war only ended in 1996.'

'I know all that!' I said. 'I read all about it here.' I picked up Will's CD and passed it to her. 'This is music from the wildest festival in the world, which takes place in the desert outside Timbuktu. The Tuareg started it after they gave up fighting the government, like you said. It began as an annual get-together of desert people who had been through so much, droughts and then the civil war, and instead of fighting they met to make music, and now people come from all over Mali and the world. It's all here in the notes. But look, Emily. Look at the pictures!' I pushed the little leaflet into her hand and watched as she flicked it open. She skipped the shots of the open-air stage and the shaggy-looking performers and concentrated on the grainy black-and-white photographs of the Tuareg.

Mysterious veiled riders on towering camels were shot against luminous skies. The camels reared their heads haughtily, dressed up in sumptuous cloths and with tasselled reins and decorated saddles. The men were swathed in voluminous robes that fell in graceful folds while their slender naked feet rested on the necks of their camels. The most striking thing was the fact that their faces were veiled, with only dark glittering eyes visible through the slits of their head cloths. Even Emily had to be impressed.

'Yeah,' she said. 'I see what you mean, but I expect all this dressing up is a tourist stunt. Just for the festival visitors. It would be like foreigners coming to England and expecting all our men to look like Morris dancers.'

This was such a silly idea that we both laughed.

'But wait until you hear the music!' I went across to my CD player and inserted the disc, then sat down next to Emily on the sofa. A hollow knocking sound filled my little room, and then from afar, as if from the dark sky outside the window, a hypnotic chant began. A hand and drum rhythm joined in, marking the time of the long slow gait of a camel, and then faster, as if the camel was trotting and then galloping, and human voices called and echoed back and forth with strange ululations and cries and a stringed instrument rinsed and rang in the background. It was the most unearthly sound I have ever heard and it made my skin feel as thin as tissue and the soles of my feet tingle.

I was on the bus coming back from work the following afternoon when my mobile phone rang.

'Hallo? Hallo?' I had to shout above the noise. There was a twittering sound from the other end, and then I made out the high, soft voice and the rushed sentences of Miss Timmis.

'Oh my dear! I am so glad to speak to you. There is something I must tell you. Oh my goodness, you seem to have gone. Are you there? Clementine? Can you hear me? Oh dear me, she seems to have gone.'

'No! I'm still here, Miss Timmis!' I shouted. 'But I'm on the bus.'

'The what?'

'The BUS! Let me telephone you when I get back to the flat.'

'Where ever are you, dear? I thought you said a bus.'

'I'll ring you back in fifteen minutes!' There was no point in going on like this.

I ran all the way home from the bus stop, my bag banging against my legs. Although it was only early afternoon the light was already draining from the steel-coloured sky. The shops were garish with Christmas decorations and I ran through blasts of festive Santa music as I dodged and wove amongst the shoppers. I have a tiny flat at the top of an Edwardian villa. When I first moved there I felt as if I was being kept in a box with the lid on, it is so cramped and dark.

This afternoon some careless person had left the front door ajar and the inside hall with its scuffed paint and floor littered with flyers for a pizza joint looked grim and unwelcoming. Notices and unfriendly admonishments from the landlord were pinned to a scarred cork board under the stairs next to a dead plant in a pot which had been there since I moved in a year ago. A bicycle frame, chained to the banisters, with both wheels removed, was the other permanent fixture.

I clattered up the stairs, unlocked my door and sat straight down on the sofa to call Miss Timmis. She took ages to answer and when she did she sounded nervous and flustered.

'Well, you see, Clementine, there is something else. I was going through some of your great-aunt's things and I found a letter. I have a letter here, you see. Yes, a letter. Perhaps I should have given it to Mr Godfrey. Or to your father, but the thing is that it is quite clearly intended for you. Yes, your names are on the envelope.'

'A letter?' I said. 'From Great-Aunt Mary?'

'Oh yes, my dear. She left it, you see. Amongst her things.'

'But that's wonderful, Miss Timmis!' I said. 'I expect it will explain everything. It will tell us why we have to take her to Mali. It will probably tell us how to find this unpronounceable place.'

'Well, yes, my dear. Of course it might. There's something else too . . .' She hesitated.

'Something else?' I prompted.

'Yes. It has been on my mind that I haven't been entirely truthful. There is something else that I should have told you.' I waited while her voice tinkled away into silence.

'Are you going to tell me now, Miss Timmis?' I asked, trying to be patient.

'Tell you?' she echoed. 'Well, no, my dear. I don't think I can explain on the telephone. I think you had better come and see me. You and Emily.'

Emily

'SO, MY DEARS,' said Miss Timmis on Saturday morning. 'I am glad that you could both come. There is something else which perhaps I should have told you. It is not exactly that I forgot, more that it all happened so long ago that I haven't thought about it for years and I did not believe that Mary had either. Not until you told me about her will.'

It seemed strange to be sitting on the windowsill in Great-Aunt Mary's sitting room, now stripped almost bare of her things. There was one small basket-weave chair on which Miss Timmis perched and a folding card table where our cups of milky coffee and a plate of digestive biscuits rested. The carpet was marked with bright rectangles where the furniture had once stood and was stained and faded in between. The grate was black and empty apart from a charred log and small balls of discarded paper. In one corner a stack of paperbacks leaned against the wall, and a desk drawer had been turned out on the carpet leaving a scattering of paperclips and old Biros and long-forgotten postage stamps.

'The furniture was all your great-uncle's, you see,' explained Miss Timmis. 'It's all gone up to the farm or to your father, Clemmie. I don't believe that Mary had much of her own. A dressing table of her mother's and a little gate-legged dining table, that's all.'

Across the hall in the kitchen I could see the cupboard doors standing open and the table stacked with a depressing selection of old, unwanted china and cooking utensils. I had already poked about, hoping that I might unearth a recipe book that would allow Great-Aunt Mary's culinary secrets to pass to our generation, but there was nothing. She must have cooked straight out of her head. Everything I touched was smudged and dirty and sticky with the years. I imagined that it would all go into the skip, already half full outside. Her large striped apron still hung on a hook behind the kitchen door, the front stained and discoloured where she had wiped her hands, and scattered with a grapeshot of burned holes from the carelessly dropped ash of her cigarettes.

This is what a life amounts to, I thought. Piles of useless junk that nobody wants or has any use for. It seemed dreadfully sad that the old cottage which I remembered as inhabited so completely by the formidable energy and spirit of Great-Aunt Mary should now stand empty and silent, grubby and threadbare. She had gone, that was for sure. There was no sense of her lingering behind to haunt us. A lick of paint, a new carpet, and all traces of her would vanish for ever.

'You see,' said Miss Timmis, smoothing down her neat tartan skirt with her arthritic, knobbly little hands, 'I *can* tell you a little more than I intimated.' She paused. 'Oh Emily, you have let your coffee get cold! Let me warm it for you.'

'No, no thank you, Miss T. But let me warm *yours*!'

'Oh, well thank you, my dear. I would prefer it, if it is not too much trouble. Clementine, another biscuit?'

Miss Timmis was like a little cat that won't settle until she has gone round and round preparing her bed entirely to her satisfaction, and we would have to be patient.

I came back with the heated coffee and we began again, but this time Miss Timmis saw a magpie on the bird table and Clemmie was instructed to jump up and bang on the window to scare it away. Meanwhile her bright little eyes danced behind her glasses and I saw she was alert as a robin.

'Where was I? Oh yes. You see, I realise now how little your family knew Mary. Really knew her, I mean. I wouldn't say that she was secretive, but selective, perhaps, in what she allowed anyone to know. It is different for me because we grew up together. Our mothers were themselves childhood friends. They both grew up in Shropshire and at one time shared a governess. My mother told me that Mary's mother, Constance, was rather a lonely child. Her father was a diplomat and often posted abroad and her mother accompanied him, leaving Constance alone in a large, empty house, looked after by servants. Later on she was considered old enough to go with them, and it was while her father was posted to Dieppe that she met her future husband, a young French army officer.'

Clemmie and I exchanged glances.

'What was his name?' I asked.

Miss Timmis looked surprised. 'Mary's maiden name? Don't you know? She was Marie Barthelot. A name which was rather made fun of in England, but it was a distinguished family that Mary's father came from, a noble family. Somewhere in the past an ancestor had been a Prefect of the Seine.' She paused.

'Go on,' Clemmie and I said together.

'Mary's parents' marriage was not what you would call a happy one. I don't know the full story, one didn't talk about such things in those days, but Mary was brought up mostly in England at her grandparents' house in London. She and I went to the same London day school. She was sent away to France in the holidays and she spoke perfect French, but her grandparents on her father's side were very stiff and formal and I don't think she enjoyed it much, although she was extremely fond of her father. Then at about sixteen she was sent to be finished in Paris and I rather lost touch with her. She told her mother she wished to live with her father and I believe that she accompanied him abroad, where he was something in colonial administration in French West Africa. I can remember her English grandparents and her mother being most concerned. They considered that Africa was dangerous and altogether unsuitable for a young woman. However, being Mary, once she had made up her mind there was nothing anybody could do to stop her and she remained abroad for the next few years, returning to London only when war broke out.'

'That explains it!' said Clemmie. 'There's the connection we did not know about. It must have been Mali that she went to.'

'Of course it wasn't called Mali then,' I pointed out. 'It was French Sudan, I think. All the names were changed after independence. And it doesn't exactly explain why she wants us to ship her back there.'

'There is something else,' said Miss Timmis, leaning forward confidentially. 'What I wanted to tell you is that something happened to Mary while she was away.' She stopped and sat back.

'Something happened?' echoed Clemmie. 'What sort of thing?'

'Well,' said Miss Timmis. 'There was a great fuss in England when it looked as if war was inevitable, and Mary's mother became terribly concerned about getting her home. I can only remember the *anxiety*, not the details. All sorts of strings were pulled and eventually she managed to get back. Of course I was excited about seeing her again and hearing all about her time abroad, but I was disappointed.' She took a little sip of coffee.

'Why?' I asked. 'Why were you disappointed?'

'Because,' said Miss Timmis, putting down her cup, 'something had happened to her. She came back a different person. Of course one would expect her to have changed in terms of growing up. We were hardly more than children when she went away and she returned a young woman. But there was something else, something more than that. To begin with she was very unwell – some unpleasant tropical fever – and she remained isolated for some time, seeing no one. When she was a little better and I was allowed to visit her she was pleased to see me but she refused to talk about where she had been or what her life had been like since I last saw her. Not a word. Her mother advised me that it was better not to refer to it, that Mary had experienced things which a young girl should not have to go through. She suggested that her father had been remiss in looking after her. I don't know, perhaps she was referring to something to do with *men*, and that the journey home had been very unpleasant, travelling alone and with ordinary courtesy and good manners forgotten in the upheaval of approaching war. Her mother covered it up, perhaps to make things easier for her daughter, and told people that Mary had been living with her father's family in France, which of course I knew not to be true. It was as if between them they had closed a door in her life and nothing would make them open it again.

'Sadly, Mary's father did not survive the war. It was rumoured that he joined the Vichy French and there was some disgrace attached to that. Later her mother remarried, happily this time, and it was as if the whole French side of Mary's family no longer existed.'

'Whatever could have happened to her?' said Clemmie, frowning. 'Why all the mystery?'

Miss Timmis sighed. 'When I saw her for the first time I was quite shocked. Of course she had been ill, but she went away rather a plump schoolgirl and came back very thin, and her hair was long, which was not at all fashionable at that time. We were all having bobs and permanent waves. Nobody of our age had hair that they could sit on, but she wouldn't have it cut. She started to wear it in that rather severe bun which she had for the rest of her life. But it wasn't just her appearance.'

Miss Timmis paused again and looked out of the window. Out of the corner of my eye I saw that the magpie was back on the bird table, but she did not seem to notice. Her eyes had a distant expression and I realised that she was not seeing the garden outside the cottage window. She was looking into the past.

'Go on!' urged Clemmie.

'It was as if she had experienced great sadness, or been through something which had affected her very deeply. She was withdrawn and melancholy, most unlike either her old self or how you will remember her. It was as if her spirit had deserted her. Then, thank heavens, she slowly started to improve. She put on a little weight, and as soon as she was fit enough she joined the Wrens and began war service. In a way it was the war which saved her because it was so exciting. They were thrilling times, you see, if you were young. Terrible, but thrilling. Our lives changed completely. Especially carefully brought-up and overprotected young women. Once Mary had something worthwhile to do, she snapped out of her depression or whatever it was. She started to smoke and drink and was popular because she was rather bold and daring and enjoyed male company. By the end of the war she was engaged to your Great-Uncle Timothy, and the rest you know!'

'But what do you think had happened to her in Mali?' persisted Clemmie. 'Do you think she witnessed atrocities or something?'

'I really don't know,' said Miss Timmis, with a little shudder. 'She never talked about it to her dying day, and as far as I know had no contact with anyone from that time of her life. As I said, it was as if a door had been firmly shut. I sometimes wonder if what she had suffered, in modern terms, was a nervous breakdown.'

'It's hard to believe,' I said. 'She was such a robust sort of character.'

'If it was something bad that happened to her while

she was in Africa,' said Clemmie thoughtfully, 'why on earth would she want her ashes to be taken back there?'

We stared at each other blankly. Miss Timmis seemed as stumped as we were.

'Oh, but the letter!' she said suddenly. 'We've forgotten the letter!'

'Perhaps it will give us the answer,' said Clemmie.

Miss Timmis drew her handbag on to her lap and took out a long brown envelope. I could see that our names were written on it in Great-Aunt Mary's large, firm handwriting.

'Now we'll find out what this is all about!' said Clemmie, taking the envelope and ripping it open. She unfolded a sheet of paper with a jagged edge as if it had been torn out of a notebook. She began to read and then looked up, puzzled.

'Well?' I said.

'I don't understand,' she said slowly. 'It's just a bit of a poem or something. I don't know what it means.'

'Read it out!'

Clemmie cleared her throat and began.

'I saw Eternity the other night,
Like a great ring of pure and endless light,
All calm as it was bright;

And round beneath it, Time in hours, days, years,
Driv'n by the spheres
Like a vast shadow mov'd; in which the world
And all her train were hurl'd.'

'Is that it?'

'Yes.'

We looked at one another and I slowly shook my head. I was right. Great-Aunt Mary was barking.

On Sunday evening, as we sat on the train crawling back to London, Clemmie took the envelope out of her pocket and read the lines again.

'What does it *mean*?' she said. 'You're a teacher and everything, Em. You should know. It seems like only a bit of something longer. Where does it come from, for a start?'

I shrugged. 'I've no idea, but I can find out. It's beautiful though, isn't it? I love the way Eternity is seen "the other night".'

'What do you mean?'

'Well, Eternity is something so huge and mysterious that it's almost impossible to imagine, and yet the writer says he saw it "the other night", which sounds so ordinary and by the way.'

'It sounds dreamy to me,' said Clemmie. 'I sometimes dream that I'm flying above the earth and looking down on it and I can see all the deserts and mountains and seas, and even though I am so high up I can see tigers in India and crocodiles in the rivers and people going to work on bicycles in China and all the little sheep and cows in the fields in England and a traffic jam all the way round the M25.'

It was somehow typical of Clemmie to have a detailed vision like this in which people and animals were going about their daily business. I thought that the poem was much more frightening. Eternity might have been calm and bright but the poor old world was being hurtled about down below, under the stern shadow of a ticking clock.

'The question,' said Clemmie thoughtfully, 'is only partly what the poem might mean. It's also a question of why Great-Aunt Mary bothered to write it out and leave it for us. It seems such a weird thing to do when what we need is a proper explanation and some instructions. Although I don't understand what she meant by the poem, and I've probably got it wrong from a lit. crit. point of view – at school I was the dim one who always got the wrong end of the stick, you remember – it seems as if she knew we both need something. I don't know what, I don't know how to say it, Emily – but maybe to see Eternity. You know, something grand and mysterious and immense, way beyond anything we've ever seen before. Way beyond Dorset and dirty old London, way beyond grubbing a living and waiting for love. Is this journey more about us than it is about her? What happened to her out there in the Sahara that so changed her? Why did she choose you and me to take her ashes to Mali and not the boys, who'd love an adventure like that?'

'It's as if she has sent us off on a treasure hunt,' I said. 'As if she is playing games with us.'

'What do you think she meant by it?'

I shrugged my shoulders. 'I don't know. It's just stupid as far as I can see. Even if she wasn't exactly senile, the past often gets distorted in old people's minds. They don't remember things right.'

Clemmie wasn't listening. 'Tomorrow,' she said, 'I'm going to find out how we can get up to the north of Mali. I've got the names of some travel agencies which go there.'

I closed my eyes and pretended to go to sleep. I wasn't going to listen. Instead I would think about Ted. I wanted to try to remember the good times we had had together, to remember that he had once loved me and to try to find a way to ease the pain in my heart.

The following afternoon my mobile phone rang as I was waiting for a bus to take me back to Janet's. I had been standing at the bus stop for fifteen minutes and I was cold and tired after school, where the kids, winding up to Christmas, were noisy and excitable and it was impossible to get them down to any work. It had been another bitter grey November day with drizzle in the wind and the light had already gone. I went to work in the dark and came home in the dark and I felt as if I was trudging down an endless gloomy tunnel.

It was Clemmie. 'Hi!' she said, her voice bright and eager. 'Where are you?'

'At a bus stop,' I said. I knew what it would be about and I didn't want to hear.

'I've got lots to tell you and I've got Will here. Can you come round?'

I took some time to think about it, so as not to seem too keen. 'Okay,' I said eventually. Clemmie's enthusiasm made me feel stubbornly resistant to being cheered up. I knew I was being a misery, but I couldn't help it.

I crossed the road and caught a bus going in the opposite direction and then walked the rest of the way to her flat. 'Come in!' she shouted when I banged on the door, and when I opened it, she and Will were side by side on their knees on the floor with papers and brochures spread about them. They both looked up and grinned a welcome. Clemmie's pale hair swung forward in a high ponytail and she was wearing a pair of tight faded jeans with a short black lacy skirt over the top, and a pair of flip-flops. She looked both carelessly dressed and stylish, which is a particular knack that she has.

I was pleased to see Will, who is my favourite male cousin. As the eldest of our tribe he had a benevolent influence on our growing-up. He was always kind and fair and gentle, and blessed with the same angelic golden looks as his sister. He was the best sort of man, in my view, and I often complained to him that no boyfriend could ever match up and that in the end he would have to marry me as an act of kindness, whatever the Prayer Book might have to say about marrying one's cousin, and even though we would probably have a load of wonky children. Meanwhile, he was more than happily settled with a lovely shiny black Jamaican girl called Divinity who made a lot of money creating bespoke handbags shaped like liquorice allsorts.

'This is just so exciting, Emily!' he said, indicating the stuff on the floor as he got up to kiss me. 'God, I envy you. I've always wanted to go to Mali. It has the most wonderful music in Africa in my view and you might even be there in time for the festival in Timbuktu.'

'I won't be,' I said, 'because I never said I was going.' I went and sat on the sofa, hunched in my coat, my hands tucked in the sleeves. I was behaving exactly like an eight-year-old child in my class called Krissie Bignall when she was in a sulk. Will came and sat beside me and withdrew one of my hands.

'Oh, Emily,' he said gently, holding it between his. 'Come on. Like Clemmie says, going away is the best thing for you, and this is such a cool thing to do. Really. Believe me, you won't regret it. Come on, cheer up!'

I gave him a wan smile. No one could touch me like Will, and if he wanted me to be more cheerful, then that was what I had to be. 'What do you make of the verse Great-Aunt Mary left for us?' I asked. 'Did Clemmie show you?'

'Yes, she did. It's beautiful, isn't it? I looked it up

and it's from a long poem by Henry Vaughan written in the 1600s. I love all the cosmic imagery, but I never would have thought that Great-Aunt Mary was much of a one for poetry, especially something metaphysical.' Will had studied English at university and knew about such things. 'It seems out of character because she was such a dry old stick in a way. It's as if she wanted you to share some really intense experience, isn't it?'

I shrugged. 'I suppose so. A proper explanation for this wild-goose chase would have been of more practical use.'

Clemmie looked up from the floor. 'I telephoned the travel agencies today. Some of them were no good because although they go to Mali they do similar tours to those French companies – they don't have any demand to travel into the north of the country where we have to go. Some of the others just do posh animal safaris to East Africa, you know, with hot showers in the bush and guaranteed lions. But would you believe it, the very last one I tried, called Trotts Travel, has got a group of four people going out to Mali just after Christmas. They sound much more adventurous and are going further north to look for migrating elephants, and we could travel with them as far as they are going, about halfway up the country, and then make our own way after that!'

I slouched down lower on the sofa and pulled my hood over my face.

'I spoke to the owner of the company, whose name is Jimbo Trott, if you can believe it. I told him the whole story and he was really helpful and enthusiastic. He said he thought it was splendid that we were going to strike off on our own and he would do all he could to help. Apparently it is almost impossible to contact anyone outside Bamako by telephone but he has got a local agent who is organising transport and guides and he could possibly help us make contact with the man Great-Aunt Mary said would help us get to this place we are supposed to take her, which he had never heard of, by the way.'

'So?' said Will, looking at me.

'So what?' I mumbled.

'Will you go with Clemmie?'

I rubbed my face with my hands. I felt very tired and defeated and worn down by their pressure.

'I suppose so. I don't want to, but I suppose I'll have to.'

Clemmie let out a little scream and came to sit beside me and give me a hug while Will went to her fridge and took out a bottle of champagne.

'Where did you get that from?' I asked, amazed. Like most Kingsleys of our generation, Will never had any money.

'Great-Aunt Mary,' he said, beaming. 'She left me a case of it. Vintage, too!'

The cork flew out of the bottle and hit the ceiling.

'This,' said Clemmie, collecting some glasses, 'is the start of a real adventure. I know it! I really do!'

After that things moved fast. Clemmie got on with making arrangements. She called in at Trotts Travel's office in Wimbledon and found that her new best friend, Jimbo, was in a meeting. According to Clemmie, the girl manning the office and in a position to accept our cheque was in the last throes of a superiority complex so advanced that she was only just able to bring herself to lean across and take an itinerary and brochure from a filing cabinet and pass them over her desk. Clemmie said that her bored and offhand manner was in marked contrast to the vivacious way in which she took the numerous personal telephone calls that punctuated her visit. She managed to convey that not only was Clemmie her social inferior but that she had many much more important things to do than deal with our arrangements, talking to her friends being the most pressing.

'Honestly,' said Clemmie, 'you'd think she was doing us an almighty favour, not us bringing in a bit of business! She only looked about sixteen, too. I reckon her dad is owed a big favour by Jimbo and has made him take her on work experience. There can't be another reason to employ someone like that.'

Together we looked at the itinerary and brochure and I pointed out several spelling mistakes and typing errors. 'Oh, she was far too grand to bother about things like that!' explained Clemmie. We also discovered that the expedition was the first that Trotts Travel had sent to Mali, which was described as 'a country rich in archaeological and cultural interest, a land of great past empires and proud dynasties and, as yet, very little disturbed or influenced by the west'.

Our fellow travellers, Clemmie had been told, were a married couple and two singles. The couple were well known to Jimbo, having travelled widely with Trotts Travel in east Africa and South America. The other two, of undisclosed sex, although Clemmie thought they sounded like men, were an anthropologist who was completing a thesis on the Dogon tribe, and a photographer.

We were scheduled to leave London on 30 December, flying first to Paris and then on to Bamako, the capital of Mali, where we would be met at the airport by an English-speaking guide, and were provisionally booked to return with the same group two weeks later, although no one had the slightest idea how long it would take us to deliver Great-Aunt Mary's ashes to her chosen spot because as yet no one had even heard of it.

Uncle Peter had collected the ashes, which he said were a surprisingly small amount of uniform grey dust in a casket, and we argued about what receptacle they should travel in for the rest of her epic journey. It was Divinity who provided the answer, presenting us with one of her bespoke handbags in the shape of a pug dog wearing a jaunty spotty bow tie.

'Isn't it perfect?' said Clemmie admiringly, flipping the little pink felt tongue. 'Great-Aunt Mary will love it. It will remind her of Pugsy and she can travel as hand luggage. I wouldn't trust her in the hold, would you? Imagine if she got lost. She'd haunt the baggage halls for ever.'

Together we filled in forms and had passport photographs taken which made me look beefy and small-eyed and mean, and Clemmie as if she was a fairy princess. One of Jimbo's minions whisked our passports off to Brussels to the Malian embassy and they came back with full-page visas printed in magenta ink and beautiful curly foreign-looking handwriting.

Then there were the injections – yellow fever and rabies and all the others – which made my arm ache and Clemmie take to her bed for two days. It's all very well for her, I thought, as I pinned up Christmas decorations in my classroom and lost my voice rehearsing my class for the end-of-term school entertainment. In fact the whole trip was all very well for Clemmie and not for me. Will might have charmed me into it but I still did not want to go.

Then, out of the blue, I was offered a room in a house where someone had taken a year out to go travelling with her boyfriend. It was close to work and it was affordable but I couldn't move in until the New Year. I had finally cleared out the flat and left a small pile of Ted's possessions in two cardboard boxes inside the front door. I borrowed Will's car, and he and Jake, Clemmie's next brother down, who works as a chef in London, came to help me load up my stuff to take to Dorset. The cardboard boxes remained in the empty flat and I realised as I drove back to London that I would have to do something about them and that I had left them there for exactly that reason.

I could harden my heart and put the whole lot out

for the dustmen. This was an attractive option in some ways but it went against the grain to bin perfectly good stuff – CDs, some clothes and books, a set of black-and-white mugs – all of which a charity shop might be glad of. It was simple enough to take the boxes to Oxfam but I resisted, knowing in my heart that the third option was the one I favoured – to telephone Ted and ask him what he wanted me to do with his remaining things. They provided me with the perfect excuse to make contact and I so longed to hear his voice again. I still missed him with a physical pain and I clung to the hope that once the connection had been made between us, the old loving feelings would reignite. I told myself that men were notoriously lazy about working at relationships, that they were emotional cowards, that it was easier to walk away than make the effort to rebuild a love affair. It was up to me to open the possibility of a rapprochement and also to let Ted know how I felt about us breaking up. Perhaps pride was keeping him away. Perhaps he didn't want to be the first to make a move. If I told him again how much I loved and missed him, there was a chance he would fall back into my arms.

I convinced myself of all this in my more optimistic moments, and then a great douche of cold reality would sweep over me and I would know that this was a delusion and that short of being bound hand and foot and held captive in a windowless room, Ted could have contacted me if he had wanted to. After all, my mobile phone never left my side. No, if Ted had wanted me back he could have done something about it. I heaved the boxes out on to the communal landing and pulled the front door shut. I wasn't going to make any kind of decision except that from now on I didn't care what happened to Ted's things. They were no longer my responsibility.

Clemmie became obsessed with packing for our trip. Trotts Travel sent us a list of suggested clothing, including things like a set of silk long-johns and a sun hat large enough to protect the back of the neck; water bottles and purification tablets, high-grain cereal bars and gifts for the local children. Clemmie read it out to me, dressed, as usual, in one of her imaginative outfits: two layers of trailing gypsy skirts, a little fur jacket and a pair of embroidered Moroccan slippers. 'They've got to be joking!' she said. 'Four pairs of drip-dry cotton trousers. Long-sleeved safari-type shirts. Safari-style jacket with pockets – useful for camera, film, sunglasses, penknife, notebook and pen.'

'I suppose that's all very sensible,' I pointed out. 'It's hot, and the people are mostly Muslim, so we will have to cover ourselves up.'

'Yes, I understand *that*,' said Clemmie, 'but I don't see any need to go around looking like Jock of the Bushveldt.'

'Who?'

'You know what I mean! As if we are there to do some colonising, with our pockets full of mirrors and beads and postcards of the Queen.'

'Clemmie! These are *clothes* we're talking about, not foreign policy.'

'Well, I'm not going about in a pith helmet and long shorts. I think lovely loose sari-type trousers and tunics and flowing scarves are the thing. You've seen photographs of these Malian people. They have terrific style. They don't find it necessary to wear those crease-free trousers with Velcro-fastened detachable legs, so why should we?'

'Well, I'm not buying anything new,' I grumbled, although I was already mentally sorting through my wardrobe. If I accepted Clemmie's style advice, I had plenty of old hippy clothes lying around at home that would do. We would look like a couple of tinkers, Clemmie and I. All we needed was a three-legged dog on a piece of string. I wondered vaguely what our fellow travellers would make of us. The couple sounded ominously like the sort of people who strike terror in my heart. I imagined them as rich and confident, with the time and money to travel expensively. Plenty of their kind have moved into big houses in Dorset, and although they are enthusiastic about country life they are condescending and patronising towards the locals, with their loud, braying voices in the pub, their badly behaved dogs and their big new four-wheel-drive cars in which they disappear back to London.

'The boys are lending us sleeping bags,' said Clemmie. 'I've got them airing out of the window at this moment. They smelled of feet.'

'Mmm! Lovely!' I said.

'We'll be staying in guesthouse places while we are travelling with the others from Trotts Travel. It's only when we set off on our own that we'll probably be sleeping rough. According to Jimbo you can usually find someone who speaks French, so we should get along all right. Thank goodness for all those French exchanges we did as kids.'

Although I had agreed to go to Mali with her, there was still one conversation I felt we had to have.

'Okay, Clem,' I said, taking a deep breath, 'let's get

this clear from the start. If we get out there and find that we can't make contact with this man of Great-Aunt Mary's, this Salika person, then that is *it*. We find a suitable place to scatter the old girl and we call it a day. I'm not going wandering off on our own in the Sahara. You've got to know what you are doing in an environment like that and you've got to be with people you can trust. I looked up Mali on the Foreign Office travel advice page this afternoon. Look at this!' I handed her a printed sheet and waited while she skimmed through it.

'I know all this!' she said airily, handing it back. 'Will told me. But they always exaggerate, don't they? They try and put you off going anywhere but the New Forest or a coach tour of the Lake District.'

I picked up the sheet and read out, 'Because of increased risk of banditry and kidnap we advise against travel to the north of Timbuktu. Bandits and smugglers across the borders of Mali, Mauritania and Algeria constitute a real risk to travellers, especially after dark.'

Clemmie had picked up a hand mirror and was studying an imaginary spot on her face, refusing to meet my eye. Instead she said, 'Emily! Pick up that free local paper on the table. What's that on the front page? Muggings? A rape? In one week, and in this neighbourhood alone. London is a million times more dangerous than Mali, where crime levels are actually really low. It says so if you read on a bit. Anyway,' she said, putting down the mirror and looking at me brightly, 'wouldn't it be blissful to be kidnapped by those camel men? It would beat teaching, wouldn't it?'

I shook my head. Sometimes Clemmie's remarks are too silly to merit an answer. On the other hand, she was probably expressing her real opinion. It would be typical of her to think that it would be exciting to be kidnapped.

'It would be a big mistake on their part,' I said. 'Who do you think would pay the ransom? I can't see the Kingsleys forking out to get us back.'

'Isn't it sad,' said Clemmie, 'to be so superfluous?'

I considered this for a moment. Of course it wasn't true, because Clemmie was an adored only daughter and sister, and my parents had to care about me because I was their only child. What she really meant was that neither of us had a best beloved man who would move heaven and earth to get us back. Of course, if we had, we probably wouldn't be in a position to be going off to Mali anyway. We could only contemplate this trip because we were free at heart. Given Clemmie's beauty, this takes some explanation.

The Kingsleys are not a remarkable or distinguished family. For centuries the chalk hills and muddy vales of Dorset have provided the parameters for their ambitions, and those that do not farm are small-town solicitors, estate agents or brewers; ordinary, solid middle-class men who marry into the same sort of families and rear unremarkable children. However, like a thread of gold running through a dullish bolt of cloth, there occurs every now and then an aberration, a throwback to some exotic and unexpected forebear, a marauding Viking or a Saxon noble, and a Kingsley is born possessed of remarkable golden looks. My father is such a one, and Clemmie and Will are the same. Because Clemmie and I grew up together, our families living only a few miles apart, I have had plenty of time to observe the particular effect of her beauty.

As a child she was slender and so blonde that her hair seemed to float about her head in a halo of thistledown. Her skin is almost transparent with a delicate tracery of bluish veins just beneath the surface, and when she is excited or hot, the milky whiteness is touched with a doll-like pink. Her eyes are far apart and of a tender blue and her gaze is soft and lingering. Her lashes and brows are golden. Her face is a perfect oval and her mouth generous and full. There is something about the pale perfection of her face, its smoothness and openness and the serenity of her expression, that reminds me of a medieval Madonna, and that is the problem with Clemmie. Hers is not a modern beauty. She has none of the frantic sexiness of supermodels, with their voracious mouths and swollen lips, their splayed, anorexic limbs and tumbling manes of hacked-about hair. Clemmie is all silver and gold, pure and calm, shining and remote, and that has been the source of her difficulty with men.

All she has ever wanted is to be loved and loving and have a big house in the country filled with children and animals. When people asked her as a little girl what she would like to be, she used to say, 'A lady', and despite growing up on a farm, she could hardly ever be prised out of a sticky-out dress. People of both sexes fall in love with her, instantly and passionately, as if dazzled by her starriness, but with men it never lasts for very long because Clemmie remains unmoved by the attention; kind and grateful, but decidedly unmoved. Chaste is an old-fashioned word, but it is the right one for her. Cool, cold, frigid is what her nastier suitors call her when after a few weeks she doesn't fall into their arms and then their beds. Finally they give up and move away, disappointed, and Clemmie drifts on, apparently unscathed and untouched.

'I don't know what love means,' she once explained to me, 'because I've never felt it, Em. I wait for it to happen, but it never does. In the end I let them down – the men – because all I ever am is fond of them. Love just doesn't happen to me.'

Without Ted, Christmas that year was always going to be a non-event, an ordeal to be got through. School broke up on 18 December, and although the children's excitement was infectious and the carol services and nativity plays were touching and funny, the commercialism and fierce acquisitiveness of most of my class was not. I overheard a lot of bragging about expensive must-have toys and electronic games and saw the closed expressions on the faces of the poor and disadvantaged children. Ahmad, the fifth child of a refugee family from Sudan, listened in silence, as did little Calvin, whose single mother struggled to send him to school at all. Some of the others boasted along with the best of them, but I knew it was bravado and that state-provided foster arrangements, missing fathers, desperate mothers, broken families, drunkenness and abuse would be the only things that many could look forward to with any confidence.

I handed out the little presents I had got for them and in return received some touching Christmas cards. 'For Miss,' wrote Calvin in wonky capital letters on a card depicting a coach and four trotting through a snowy village of thatched cottages – a landscape as strange as the moon to my class of London kids. 'Thank you for teetch me to write good.'

'Thanks a lot, Calvin,' I said. 'It's a lovely card. Have a great holiday and I'll see you next term.'

'Yer comin' back, ain'tcha, miss?' he asked anxiously. 'We will get yer again next term?'

'Yeah!' I said. 'I'll be back.' I made it sound more like a threat and he laughed.

Even Krissie Bignall sidled up and gave me a card. 'Do yer like me, miss?' she asked, coyly.

Not much, I thought. 'Of course I do,' I said and then clapped my hands above the noise. 'Come on, class! Let's have a nice straight line. It's time to go to the hall for our last assembly!'

That night I took Janet and her children out for a meal, as a thank-you for putting up with me, and then

I loaded my belongings into a taxi and went round to Clemmie's.

There was something very final about this journey, and as I watched night-time London slide past outside the rain-streaked windows I felt that I was coming to the end of an important stage of my life. Succumbing to the awful urge to hear what would hurt me most, I had telephoned mutual friends and found out by various devious means, mostly by pretending that I didn't care, that Ted and Tatty were going skiing at Christmas, that they were getting along really well, that Tatty was looking for a new flat for them to share and that she had even told someone she wanted to have Ted's baby. Ted always did love money and it would not have escaped his notice that Tatty had a rich daddy and a trust fund at her disposal.

Clemmie was waitressing up to Christmas Eve and between Christmas and New Year, and because I wasn't keen on spending too much time at home I got myself taken on as a barmaid where she was working and slept on her sofa at night. It was the busiest, noisiest week of the year and the work was flat out and exhausting but it was what I needed. I wanted to be too busy or too tired to think.

Between shifts she insisted that I got my bag ready, ticking off items on a check list, and before we left for Christmas in Dorset our packs stood leaning against the wall, bloated and cumbersome, with our sleeping bags rolled up and neatly lashed on with bright orange baler twine. Great-Aunt Mary in her pug bag perched on top, standing guard.

Clemmie was in charge of the emergency first-aid kit and had been to her doctor for antibiotics in case we got sick. It appeared there was little in the way of health care in Mali and we would have to look after ourselves. I had contributed the little bags of sweets, the bright, sparkly hair accessories and the packs of pens and pencils to give to the children we might meet. Meanwhile we had decided on and exchanged the Christmas presents we would give each other. I had taken trouble to find Clemmie a beautiful notebook covered in pink and gold embroidered cloth which opened out flat and had smooth, inviting pages of satiny white paper. 'I'll keep a travel journal,' she said. 'I'll write down the story of the trip.'

In return she had bought me a long, soft Indian scarf in every shade of blue and grey, the colour of an English sky, and showed me how to wrap it round my head to frame my round, rosy face and make me look a bit alluring, and not like a boiled pudding in a cloth.

We argued over the daft things we both wanted to take. Clemmie put in her hot-water bottle in its teddy bear cover – 'The nights can be very, very cold in the desert,' she said – and I wanted to take the lilac silk nightie that Ted had given me for my birthday. 'It's my comforter,' I explained, holding the delicate material to my cheek. Clemmie snorted. 'Just as long as you don't try and wear it! Sensible pyjamas are the recommended nightwear on Jimbo's list.'

We got a lift down to Dorset early on Christmas morning with Will and Divinity and arrived in time to file into the little church where we had last been for Great-Aunt Mary's funeral. The weather had changed and now it was warm and wet and the church was crowded with families and smelled of damp stone and musty prayer books and the sharp green scent of the branches of holly and ivy which decorated the windowsills and pew ends.

We belted out the familiar carols and there was little Miss Timmis on the organ seat working as hard as ever to coax the wheezing beast to keep up. Afterwards we went to Clemmie's parents for lunch and there were twenty-five of us jammed down the long dining-room table and spilling off the end on to a table-tennis table covered by a white cloth. Clemmie's mother, Aunt Ellen, sailed in and out beaming and calm, at her happiest with her family all about her, while my mother glowered and glared and made cutting remarks about my father. He and Uncle Peter had got themselves outside a bottle of whisky before lunch and were both flushed and loudly cheerful. Uncle Peter carved the turkey, waving the carving knife in the air and making Miss Timmis blush with his jokes about preferences for breast or leg.

Anyone looking in the window of the low stone house at the end of the muddy lane and seeing the firelit scene, with the holly twigs jammed behind the pictures and the tatty old paper chains pinned across the ceiling, would have thought that we were a united and happy family gathered for a traditional meal, a scene little changed for centuries. I glanced at Clemmie sitting across from me with a paper crown on her golden head and thought about our coming trip that would take us so far away from these gentle green hills and this noisy, embracing family. Catching her eye, I silently lifted my glass in a secret toast. She nodded and smiled and raised hers to me, and for the first time I felt that I could share her excitement and that I was glad to be leaving everything behind me.

Will intercepted and interpreted our exchanged looks and got to his feet and banged his spoon on the table.

'Hey, everybody!' he said. 'Shut up a minute! I'm sure I don't have to remind you that Clemmie and Emily and, of course, Great-Aunt Mary are about to go on an amazing and exciting African journey. Although it seems pretty weird and wonderful to us all sitting here, it is obviously something Great-Aunt Mary had planned for years. Clemmie and Emily are doing what she requested and I think we should raise our glasses to them and wish them luck.'

All the others joined in then, the boys drumming their feet on the floor and shouting unsuitable and rude advice and my father and Uncle Peter suddenly looking as if they might burst into tears. They had forgotten that they were about to lose their only daughters to a wild corner of Africa no one had ever heard of. My mother came round to the back of my chair to hug me and, thank God, at that moment Pugsy chose to cock his leg against the pile of unopened presents under the Christmas tree. I was glad of the diversion because I had just begun to believe that I was getting over crying as a pastime.

At the other end of the table I saw Miss Timmis,

her bright little face flushed by the three glasses of sherry she had been persuaded to drink, and there was something about her expression and her rather frozen smile as she raised her glass to us that convinced me that she was keeping something back.

Beryl Timmis knew more about Great-Aunt Mary than she was prepared to tell.

Beryl Timmis

I SAW THE look that Emily gave me as Will stood up on Christmas Day to ask for a toast to the girls, and for a moment I thought she had read my mind and that I had given myself away. Fortunately at my age it is not difficult to divert attention by appearing flustered and silly. It is perfectly true what they say about becoming invisible when one is elderly, female and single, and at eighty-four nobody expects a sensible answer or a sensible explanation for anything one says or does. It is easy to be written off as dotty. Emily is sharp and observant, however, even though she is so wrapped up in herself and her unhappiness over her unsatisfactory young man. She is clever enough to be sceptical and questioning and she is not the romantic that Clemmie is. Of course she doesn't want to go to Africa on what she considers a wild-goose chase and one can hardly blame her.

As we toasted the girls someone knocked over a glass and

I dropped my napkin and there was a diversion when naughty Pugsy lifted his leg on the Christmas tree and the moment passed, which was just as well. I did not want to have to explain that the expression Emily must have noticed on my face was because I had a sudden recall of a scene from sixty-odd years ago. It's a strange trick of memory in old age that while I often can't remember what I had for breakfast, I occasionally experience a complete and vivid recall of a moment from far, far in the past. Sometimes these memories seem to spring unaided out of the wool that appears to fill my mind these days. I will be thinking about something quite mundane, hardly thinking at all in fact, with my brain in neutral, and suddenly a vivid picture will flash across it like a wonderful Technicolor scene from a film of my past.

Just yesterday I was folding linen from the airing cupboard in the cottage and thinking that so much of what Mary and I had accumulated about us was of no value to anybody any longer, although Clemmie's mother had said that her children might welcome some bed sheets and pillowcases. In my hand I had an old linen pillowcase, worn soft and fine over the years, and in the corner were embroidered the initials MB in red silk, and the next moment I was in a sun-filled sitting room in Mary's house in London. It was summer and the windows were open and I could hear the birds singing in Regent's Park above the sound of traffic. Mary was kneeling beside a large leather cabin trunk busy packing away the clothes which were neatly piled on the floor beside her. Her dark hair fell loosely about her shoulders, held back from her face by tortoiseshell combs. One would have said her hair was black, but when the sun fell across it as it did now, it shone with deep red lights. She was wearing a cotton summer frock of pale blue linen with a white collar – quite short – and her legs were bare. She had painted her toenails red and she wore red open sandals. I recalled exactly what I was wearing that day: a long, shapeless linen skirt that buttoned up the front in a colour known as 'donkey', a white blouse pinned at the throat by a brooch, and a home-knitted cardigan. I remembered the scratchiness of the wool on the skin of my arms. My fine, light brown hair was done up in a roll, pinned around the back of my head, and I could remember putting a hand up to pat at the soft wisps escaping from the pins.

Although Mary and I were the same age and from the same background, and had both just left the same school, the difference between us was marked. We remained true friends because we had shared so much as we grew up, but approaching adulthood seemed to have marked us out for separate paths. In that year, poised as we were between girlhood and becoming women, there had gathered about Mary an air of expectation, a sense that there was something exciting, even dangerous, waiting for her in adult life. Her white skin and dark hair, her vivacity, her figure, which was rounded but still slim – yes, she was good looking, but it was more than that: there was a readiness and ripeness about her, a physicality and a latent awareness that was already inviting attention. Bus conductors joked and flirted with her and men turned their heads to watch as she walked past in her school gym tunic. She hated it, she said, and stuck her tongue out and laughed at them, but both she and I realised that she was on the edge of something, of possibilities and discoveries which we were too innocent and ingenuous to imagine, but which I knew for certain would never be mine.

In my hand I held the green linen envelope embroidered with her initials which I had just given her in which to keep her stockings. I had made it myself as a little going-away gift. 'Thank you, Beryl!' she said and she looked up at me and laughed. It wasn't a mocking laugh but it seemed to ripple across the distance between us, and in that moment I knew how different our lives would be and I was both sorry and grateful. The inconsequential little present which I held in my hand spoke of a desire for a tidy and orderly future, a nervous attempt at containing and controlling, at stemming the tide of chaos. The world around us rumbled with rumours of war and civil disorder and Mary was setting off alone to travel to an outpost in Africa, and I had given her a bag in which to keep her stockings tidy. Mary looked up from packing and laughed at me and I knew at that moment, with relief and regret, that unlike her, I would live my life on the edge of things, usefully, quietly and uneventfully.

The smells of the afternoon came back to me in a rush: the soot from the grate, the jug of sweet williams on the table, the dusty carpets, Coty face powder and the lily-of-the-valley toilet water Mary's mother used. Then the memory was gone, as suddenly as it came, and I was back on the landing with the pillowcase in my hand.

The scene which came back to me on Christmas Day was triggered by the fuss surrounding the girls and their trip to Africa. I suppose it was mean-spirited of me, but they are hardly setting out into the unknown. Perhaps it is the thought of being out of range of their mobile telephones which frightens them, or not being able to have a hot shower every day. I was thinking this when I suddenly remembered seeing Mary off at Victoria station in London, and how very much more of an adventure that was than a mere aeroplane flight. I forget whether her mother was there with me, although I suppose she would have been. She hadn't wanted Mary to go and had done everything to persuade her against it. Mary was catching the boat train to Marseilles, where she was meeting her father. She stood at the ticket barrier while a porter wheeled her trunk away to the luggage van, and I remember she was wearing a pale pink duster coat, a small straw hat, wrist-length white kid gloves with small pearl buttons, and high-heeled shoes. She was nineteen years old. The world then was a quite different place and Africa seemed very far away. Travel was slow and stately and it would take her a night and a day to reach Marseilles. In her trunk were various items we had bought together in the Army and Navy store, including a mosquito net and a travel kettle. I kissed her goodbye and gave her a small corsage of rosebuds I had made up from our London garden to pin on her coat. She was excited and beautiful with her dark eyes glittering. I did not expect to see her again for two years. 'Thank you, Beryl!' she said and kissed me, and as she turned to go, tap-tapping away in her high heels, she called over her shoulder with a laugh, 'I promise I'll keep my stockings tidy!'

What happened to her after that is a trail long gone cold. There is no one left to know or care, except for me, and I am not telling. The directions in her will for the disposal of her ashes came as a great surprise to me. She had never once intimated that she had such a plan, but she was like that, you see. She liked to surround herself with a little drama and she must have enjoyed the thought that this one would be enacted after her death, as her final curtain call.

When the girls came to see me I knew that I needed to tell them enough to explain the connection, the thread, that linked Mary to that unfortunate country. I could have said nothing, but to remain silent amounted to a bare-faced lie, and I was haunted by a fear that if I gave them no information they might be prompted to make enquiries, although goodness knows what they could have found out after all these years. I gave them just enough information to satisfy them, I hope, but no more. My lips have been sealed for so many years that I am not about to start talking now. I suppose that Mary thought that after her death her extraordinary request would lift the lid on the past, but I will do what I can to protect my position. She owes me that. Fortunately, I found her letter first. I could not quite bring myself to destroy it, that would surely be a sin, but I steamed the envelope open and removed the letter but left the poem. Of course they could not understand what she meant by that. Not without the letter. It did not deter them from making this trip but at least it will make it difficult for them to go to the right places and meet the right people and, most importantly, to ask the right questions.

I have no compunction about this deceit. What is the point of stirring things up after so many years? No good can come of it. When I think of that great waste of sand and glittering sky and the hot desert wind endlessly blowing, blowing, I know that all traces of what happened so many years ago will have long since gone and that it is best left that way. What good can come of picking at bones?

Clemmie

HEATHROW WAS GRIM on the morning that we queued for our flight to Paris. Having bullied passengers to arrive three hours early, the airline did not open their departure desk until half an hour before the flight was due to leave. The restless queue snaked back on itself many times, choked with luggage trolleys and skis and pushchairs containing furious babies, and exhausted toddlers collapsed on the shoulders of their fathers, and irritable young mothers who remembered what it had been like to travel unencumbered, and shagged-out young couples who looked as if they had fallen out of bed and come straight to the airport, and anxious elderly ladies on the lookout for terrorists. Everyone seemed disgruntled and dissatisfied except the very tall and thin black man wearing a bright yellow flak jacket and carrying a broom and dustpan, who swept slowly and patiently about our feet.

Emily and I were dragging along our great backpacks, mine so large that when I experimented yanking it up on to my shoulders I staggered about with bent knees, shrieking. It was like carrying a large sheep or a small donkey on my back. I had managed to avoid the sensible utility clothing with such success that instead I veered towards the Old Vic travelling players look. It was freezing in London and so I wore my old velvet coat over the top of a long skirt and several woolly jumpers and my little grey fur waistcoat that Will had given me for Christmas. On my feet were stout jodhpur boots from my Pony Club past, which would do for camel riding. I hoped the general effect was Lady Hester Stanhope off to explore the desert. Across my chest, next to my heart, was Great-Aunt Mary in the pug bag.

Emily was wearing jeans and trainers and a padded jacket and a woolly hat. Sensible Emily. A girl of the times. She was yawning and tousled and a bit grumpy at having to get up so early to stand in a pointless queue. We took it in turns to fetch paper cups of scalding coffee and several times I saw her keying text messages and then deciding not to send them. She was still suffering from Ted withdrawal symptoms.

At last a pair of Air France employees turned up and with a marked lack of grace began to process the oversized queue, and eventually we were on our way with our two small donkeys booked all the way through to Bamako.

A couple of hours later we were at Charles de Gaulle airport waiting for the next leg of our flight to Mali, and already we could tell from our fellow passengers that we were going somewhere extraordinary. Emily and I sat side by side gawping at the parade of people gathering at the airline desk. There was a fabulous collection of black men, mostly tall and stout and shining black with beaming smiles and reverberating voices, dressed, despite the grey French wintriness outside the plate-glass windows, in a dazzling range of floor-length dresses in singing colours and with sandals on their large flat feet. They all seemed to know one another, greeting noisily and slapping shoulders, laughing and embracing. Some were accompanied by stately wives who sailed along in exotically patterned off-the-shoulder dresses with matching turbans and flashing smiles. They were so beautiful and immaculate that I felt like a travelling tramp hung about in rags by comparison. Some had babies strapped to their fronts, like the pug bag was to mine, but what a marked contrast to the mewling and puking European brats we had travelled with from London. These babies, snuggling up to wonderful enfolding bosoms, looked the picture of contentment.

And their baggage! I had never seen such parcels and crates and bags, plastered with labels, done up with string – objects which looked like washing machines and refrigerators and baby grand pianos were on the move. Drum kits and huge gourd-like stringed instruments were balanced on the top and nearly everyone carried a ghetto-blaster, and each one moved with a loose-limbed gait as if they had an insistent rhythm playing in their heads. And they were joyful, too. You could tell from the raised voices, the wonderful rich laughter, the sense of excitement that they were longing to go home to the sunshine. Emily and I sat entranced.

Amongst this fabulous and lively throng of chattering birds of paradise there were some dull grey little European hedge sparrows who stood out by virtue of their drabness. Some were rather dishevelled and anxious-looking middle-aged men, patting the pockets of their safari jackets looking for their glasses or a pen, dressed in the sort of trousers I so dislike and with Cornish pasty-shaped shoes. 'Scientists, don't you think?' said Emily. 'Anthropologists or archaeologists. Going to Mali to poke about for material for their academic papers.' I thought she was probably right.

Then there was a mustering of people from the far end of the departures hall, a stir and raised voices, and a throng emerged, led from the front by a large, fat white man in a bush hat and with a white beard shaped like a spade, holding up a placard on which was written 'Elder Tours'. Behind him, in various stages of decrepitude, came a gaggle of old people, silver-haired, bent, shuffling, on sticks, slung about with bags and glasses on chains, mostly women, I saw, as they got nearer, in neat pants suits with elasticated slacks and drip-dry tunic tops, Velcro-fastened shoes and sun visors already in place on their pearly heads. On each chest was pinned a name badge: 'Dorothy', 'Kathleen', 'Mabel'.

In a minute they had shuffled to a stop around us and were taking up position on the remaining spare seats. Emily and I shunted up to make room and I realised that these were American ladies in full travelling mode, taking on the world in their dotage and full of delight and wonder at everything they beheld. Christian ladies, we discovered, from church guilds all across the Midwestern states of America who were on their way to support Christian churches in Africa.

'Our brethren in Mali,' explained Kathleen. 'We are taking them all kinds of stuff. Hymn books because, oh boy, do they love to sing! Antibiotics too.'

'I can't believe you are going to such a faraway country!' said Emily admiringly. She meant because they were clearly so old and decrepit.

'That's the point about Elder Tours,' said Mabel cheerfully. 'It doesn't matter to anyone if we don't make it back.'

'We're kinda redundant, see! Just a whole lot of bother to our families but kinda feeling we have a whole lot left to give.'

'And receive,' corrected Mabel.

'Who is the man? The Father Christmas person?'

'That's our pastor.' Kathleen made him sound like a dish of spaghetti. 'He is our group leader and he, poor soul, has to try and keep us under control, doesn't he, hon?'

'Sure does, and we give him a helluva time. Did you take your heart pills, Kathleen? We're in a different time zone, darling, so today is, like, yesterday, remember!'

'Just you mind your own beeswax, Mabel. It wasn't me that left my spectacles in the rest room in Departures. Now what are you two girls doing going to Mali all on your ownsomes? Do you work for a charity?'

'No, we don't. We are going to scatter the ashes of our great-aunt,' I explained. 'It was in her will that she wanted us to take her there.' I patted Pug Bag, which was still slung across my chest. I was terrified that if I took it off, we would somehow leave Great-Aunt Mary at the airport. Out of the corner of my eye I could see Emily making faces at me.

The two ladies looked interested.

'Oh my!' said Kathleen.

'So you have her *with* you?'

'Well, yes,' I said, but felt reluctant to explain that she was round my neck. Mabel and Kathleen looked hard at our hand luggage. They were so near to the cremation end of life's journey themselves that it seemed tactless to have started on this conversation at all and I understood why Emily had wanted to warn me off.

Fortunately at that moment a stout woman with mauve hair and trouser suit, perhaps slightly younger than Mabel and Kathleen and with 'Gloria' on her chest, came over with a clipboard.

'Girls!' she said in a rallying tone to our two new friends. 'I need you to fill in these declaration forms for Customs. Last time, Mabel, you put purpose of visit as "the work of the Lord", and that won't do.'

'Well it is, isn't it?' said Mabel. 'At least,' she added slyly, 'that's what we have been led to believe. I could have put "to get away from my bitch of a daughter-in-law for a few weeks", but there wasn't enough room on the form.'

'That's not what they want!' said Gloria sharply. 'They're not interested in that. Vacation. That's what you put. Now let me show you. You have to put each letter of your name in a separate box, like this.'

'Oh buzz off, Gloria! We're not senile. We can still write our own names,' said Kathleen.

Gloria looked offended. She had no neck to speak of, and as her head turned from side to side, her mottled jowly face seemed to swivel on her mound of shoulders like a cross fluffed-up bird. Underneath her jacket she wore a T-shirt with the word 'TEXAS' in sparkly orange letters which spread over her large bosom like a sunset across the sky.

'Well make haste, please,' she retorted. Her little mouth pursed in a drawstring pleat of creases. 'And don't start getting prickly with me, Kathleen Reinherdt. Pastor John asked me to offer help to the less advantaged amongst us.'

'Less advantaged?' said Mabel. 'What's that? Simple-minded, you mean? Give me that ballpoint, Kathleen. Where are my spectacles, darn it?' She began to delve in the day bag at her feet. 'Have you seen my reading specs? Oh, here they are. Round my neck, as usual.' The two old ladies bent their sun-visored heads to their forms while Gloria stood over them and tapped her Biro on her clipboard.

'Somewhere amongst this lot,' said Emily to me, nodding towards the other people milling about, fussing over luggage and checking the electronic departures screens, 'must be the rest of our group.'

'I know. I've been trying to work out which they are. I've narrowed it down to that lot over there. There are four of them and they look the right age and type. A middle-aged couple and two younger blokes. Heigh-ho, Em! This could be their lucky break!'

'Oh bloody hell!' said Emily, scowling across. 'Is the tubby man really wearing Rupert Bear trousers? He's exactly the sort of person I dreaded.'

'Only two of them look like that,' I said. 'The man and the woman. She's wearing a quilted jacket and she's got a Birkin bag. I bet it's a really good fake that he brought back from a business trip to Hong Kong. They seem very chummy with the other two. The tall gangly one with glasses must be the anthropologist. He looks sort of clever but shambolic. He's got a hangover, I think. He's slumped in his seat and he's trying to close his eyes but Birkin Bag keeps talking at him. That means the other guy must be the photographer. He's wearing a baseball cap and one of those filmy-type leather jackets and he keeps putting on his sunglasses and checking his hand luggage.'

Emily groaned. 'It's as bad as I thought!' she said.

'Should we go over and introduce ourselves?' I asked. 'Take the initiative?'

'Do we have to? We're going to be forced together for long enough as it is.'

'It would be friendly, though.'

'They don't seem bothered about finding us.' Emily sat lower in her seat and closed her eyes.

'Emily!' I said. 'Sit up! Rupert Bear Trousers has spotted us. They're all looking this way. He's coming over.'

'Pretend we're with Elder Tours,' said Emily, but it was too late.

The man who approached us was short, well built and well fed. From his smooth, greying hair, swept back over a bald patch, and his healthy pink complexion to his expensive leather belt, prosperous-looking belly and polished brown loafers his appearance made a clear statement about his class and status. His manner was equally confident and his voice deep and smooth with the vowels of privilege and education when he stood in front of us and with exaggerated politeness said, 'Excuse me, girls, if I should have got this wrong, but are you by any chance travelling care of Jimbo Trott?'

Emily grunted something while I felt I had to stand up and say, 'Yes, we are. I'm Clemmie and this is Emily Kingsley, my cousin.' I was just about to introduce Great-Aunt Mary in the pug bag, but thought better of it.

'Jeremy Montague! Jimbo told us about you and your extraordinary expedition,' said the man, holding out his hand and shaking mine. I noticed he wore a chunky gold signet ring and a plaited leather bracelet round his hairy wrist like a reminder of old hippy days at university. At a guess I would say he was in his early fifties and fighting it. I could tell at once that he was a man who reacted to women in a predictable way, like awful Pugsy sniffing round bitches. His eyes travelled up and down and he didn't even bother to disguise his interest. I knew he would hate the way I was dressed in layers of clothes which made me shapeless and androgynous. Jeremy Montague would be a stockings-and-suspenders man, I was sure. His manner, as he chatted pleasantly, had a flirtatiousness that was hard to ignore. I could tell that he was used to being thought of as charming. My parents had friends like this, who felt compelled to make playful and appreciative remarks when they discovered that I wasn't still twelve with knock knees and braces.

Jeremy kept talking, asking which flight we had come on to Paris, if we were related to a Piers Kingsley, a High Court judge, which part of Dorset we came from, did we know the Cottenhams who lived near Dorchester, was Philip Kingsley, one-time Master of the Portman Hounds, a relation? It was a barrage of questions and I could imagine our answers being fed into a sort of mental social assessment department situated in the high-domed forehead. Before too long a conclusion would be reached and Jeremy Montague would decide whether Emily and I were worth bothering with or safe to ignore.

Emily was not responding well. She looked grumpy and unimpressed, hunched into her padded jacket. Good manners forced me to work a bit harder on our behalf and I managed to fit in a few questions of my own, such as had any of the others been to Mali before.

'Guy has. The photographer amongst us. He worked for a French magazine which did some shoots out there a couple of years ago. He said he promised himself that he would go back one day without the ghastly fashion people. Come on over and meet everyone!'

Jeremy began to collect our luggage and encouraged me to move with a large hand in the small of my back. He ignored Emily. He could sense her resistance.

'Hang on!' I said, turning back to Mabel and Kathleen, who were still arguing over their form-filling. They reminded me of two blue budgies I had as a child who clucked and squabbled over their mirror and bell.

'We're just going to meet the rest of our party,' I said. They looked up.

'You take care now!' said Mabel.

'We'll look out for you,' said Kathleen. 'What you two gals are doing is the most darling thing I have ever heard!'

'We'll put you on our prayer list,' said Mabel. 'You and your Great-Aunt Madge.'

'Mary,' I said.

'Yes, that's what I said.'

'No you didn't, Mabel. You said "Madge",' corrected Kathleen.

'Oh my!' sighed Mabel. 'Aren't you the smartass!'

Across the other side of the departure lounge the remaining members of Jimbo Trott's party looked up with ill-disguised lack of interest as Emily and I trooped up with Jeremy. The wife, who was introduced as Jutta, was a tall, bulky woman. She was in her mid-forties, with a discontented face and big highlighted hair. She wore a small tight T-shirt and beneath it an ample bosom spilled out of a push-up bra which gave her chest an undulating hillside effect. Her clothes had a studied casualness, and despite wearing jeans and battered cowboy boots she was clanking with gold chains and bracelets and hoop earrings and wore a whopping diamond and emerald engagement ring. She gave us a glance and evidently was not impressed by what she saw.

'Oh, hi!' she said unenthusiastically, raising one hand in a small palm-foremost greeting. She had an exaggeratedly grand voice, with just a trace of a mid-European accent, perhaps Polish or German, which would account for her name.

She turned back to Guy, the photographer, who hadn't bothered to get up to be introduced. He had one jeaned leg hooked over the other and had 'cool' almost written on his forehead and probably stamped right through his stocky body like letters through a stick of seaside rock.

'Hi!' he said languidly and gave me That Look, reserved for young blonde females, that read 'I might just be interested in you, if you are very, very lucky and play your cards right.'

Jutta was clearly extremely taken by him and almost immediately resumed an excluding conversation about someone they both knew in the magazine world, in which, I gathered, she worked as an interior designer. Her bosoms undulated and her jewellery clanked as she ran a hand through her hair in a sort of preening, courting display. I glanced at Jeremy, who didn't seem to notice or care.

The other man, Hugh, the anthropologist, creaked politely to his feet and shook hands with us both. He was about thirty, very tall and thin, with a beaky, intelligent face. He wore glasses, one side of which was stuck with Sellotape. He clearly did not want to talk, and after offering his seat to us and having it declined, sat back down and resumed his silence.

There was an immediate sense that we had been recruited into a group of which Jeremy was the dominant male, and he began to organise a trip to the duty-free shop to stock up a supply of drink for New Year's Eve.

'How about we put thirty quid each into the kitty?

Is that okay for everybody? We can get a few bottles of decent bubbly to pop wherever we are. There is a very serious possibility that booze will be hard to come by.' Everyone began scrabbling about except Emily, who spoke for the first time.

'Not me, if you don't mind. I hate champagne. I'd rather have a few beers.'

There was a shocked silence, broken by Jutta, whose incredibly affected voice seemed to come from the bridge of her nose, saying, 'Please yourself, but really, beer on New Year's Eve!'

To present a united front with Em I said, 'I think I'll opt out too, if that's okay.'

Nobody cared one way or another and after Hugh struggled to prise a wad of notes out of the back pocket of his jeans, Jeremy and Guy wandered off together, talking about champagne and comparing past epic hangovers. This left Jutta, grumpy Emily and possibly grumpy, or ill, Hugh, sitting in silence in a row. After a moment or two Jutta took out her mobile phone and began texting and making calls, some of which related to what must have been two children and a housekeeper, concerning the rescheduling of a dental appointment which sounded as important as a G8 summit. Emily made a face at me and shut her eyes and pretended to go to sleep and I got out my beautiful notebook and began to write my diary. These were my fellow travellers and I was not going to let them spoil my adventure.

Beryl Timmis

YESTERDAY, 29 DECEMBER, I moved into The Willows, or rather, Emily and Clemmie's kind fathers moved me in with my few pieces of furniture and suitcases of clothes and books and papers. As promised, I have a pleasing view at the front of the house, although not the one with the bay window which was shown to me when I looked round.

The room is small but there is space for my little armchair beside the window and the pretty rosewood writing table which came from my mother. I find the bed rather high and hard but Matron has explained that this is necessary should I ever require nursing care. I shall soon get used to it no doubt.

My room has a small bathroom to one side with a convenient basin and low-level WC and plenty of handles to hang on to should I be nervous of slipping or falling. Yesterday, my first evening, I was slightly disorientated and twice mistakenly tugged the cord for emergency help rather than the light pull, and the second time the girl who came to check on me was rather sharp, although I apologised profusely for troubling her. She is only a young girl, a slip of a thing, and it shocks me that she would speak to a woman of my age in that tone. When I was young, I respected my elders. I had been taught to do so.

The brothers made a great deal of noise when they moved me in and several of the care attendants left what they were doing and came to chat. They are local women and know the Kingsley family of old, if not in person, then by reputation. Someone brought us a tray of tea with ginger biscuits on a saucer. I noticed that they were not of the best quality but from an economy catering pack, no doubt. Another assistant took away the bunch of tightly closed daffodils – creased brown tissuey leaves over a slender hard yellow bud – that Emily's mother had given me, and put them into a glass vase. They leaned out against the glass like the green spokes of a wheel and looked naked and abashed. Perhaps today I will go into the garden and pick a little greenery to put in amongst them to make them look more comfortable.

Supper last night was served at seven o'clock: soup and macaroni cheese and then individual fruit jellies. I had no appetite and the dining room was almost empty. It seems most of the residents prefer to eat in their rooms. There was no sign of Lady Forbes. I asked about her when a girl came to take my plate away.

'Who?' she said, as if Lady Forbes was a nobody. 'Oh, her! She's in room six, down the corridor on the left.' She tapped her head then and made a face, suggesting that Lady F was not all there. I retorted that Sir Richard had been Lord Lieutenant for many years and that Lady Forbes was a woman of intelligence and education, a graduate of Girton College, Cambridge, but the girl just shrugged and said, 'Is there something wrong with the macaroni? You've hardly touched it. Picky eater, are you?'

I have to admit that my heart sank a little as I went back to my room. I could not help but long for the peace of the cottage, where I knew every tread of the stairs, every creak of a floorboard and where I had spent the last useful years of my life. I am just a relic now – passing my remaining days in a ridiculously expensive home, waiting to die. I have no family left to care about me and it makes me sad to think that the last living person who loved me was my mother, who died thirty years ago. Mary and I were friends, of course, and were very fond of each other, but that is rather different and she never completely forgave me for what happened.

However, a very pleasant older woman assistant put her head round the door after University Challenge and introduced herself as Kathy. She asked me whether I would care *for a hot drink and she brought me a cup of hot chocolate and a homemade shortbread biscuit and stopped for a moment to have a chat, and that small act of kindness cheered me up and reminded me of how lucky I am to be here.*

Now this morning I am slowly unpacking my boxes and in front of me I have the shoebox of small black-and-white snaps from before the war taken with my old box Brownie. Here I am at home in Kensal Green with my parents – my mother in a wide-brimmed hat and a fur stole and my father in a soft hat and holding a cane. They are dressed in outdoor clothes although the photograph was taken in our first-floor drawing room. I am leaning against my father with my arm through his, wearing a white frilled dress. I must have been three or four years old. All my life was in front of me and it is strange to look back on my childhood self and know that it was not to amount to very much. I have led an insignificant life, and although I went on to do useful work as an almoner in a large London hospital, in the end even that profession was done away with by one government or another and my place was taken by an ill-educated social worker.

I sift through the rest of the photographs – holidays on Canvey Island, where my father kept a boat and a large white horse. There was a photograph of me sitting up on the horse in front of him. He had one hand on the reins and the other was holding a cigarette. I can remember the smell of the smoke as it drifted past my face and the hot prickly shoulders of the horse between my bare legs. It was a pure white horse with pink nostrils and pink rims round its dark eyes, but he told me it should be called grey. There are many more photographs like this, small, faded and rather dull, and I push them to one side. Sooner or later they will be thrown away when some poor soul has to sort out my belongings, but I don't want to throw them out myself. My life feels shadowy and insubstantial enough already. Then I pick up a small transparent envelope inside which is a strip of tiny photographs. I take them out and hold them to the light.

I recognise them at once although I don't remember having seen them for sixty years. I took them the day I arrived in Africa all those years ago. My boat from Marseilles had taken five days and I had been seasick for most of them. I arrived in St Louis on the coast of Senegal crumpled and exhausted, my hair sticking to my head and sweat trickling down my back between my narrow shoulder blades. The heat was suffocating and the sunlight blinding and I felt dispirited and homesick and terrified by the deafening uproar and the crowds of black people who pressed around the quay lifting up baskets of fruit and stinking dried fish for sale. I remember so clearly how nervous and alone I felt and how grateful I was to the young French civil servant in his smart linen suit who helped me down the gangplank and into one of the horse-drawn taxis waiting to take passengers to the customs shed and then out into the town. The atmosphere was entirely French and the buildings on either side of the road were red-tiled and green-shuttered. The roads were lined with trees, their trunks painted white and their dense green canopies meeting overhead to provide a cool tunnel down which to travel.

I spent the night at the Hotel de la Poste, which was full of Europeans and where the atmosphere was wonderfully gay and carefree, although I felt lonely and awkward. There were cocktails and a piano playing in the bar and a restaurant where dark Senegalese waiters glided back and forth dressed in red waistcoats and white baggy trousers and the food was entirely French. I had come all the way from London, a great capital city, to this faraway African port and yet it was me who felt dowdy and unsophisticated in my clumpy shoes and drooping skirt. The bar was inhabited by graceful mulatto women sumptuously dressed in one-shouldered robes with matching turbans. Their coffee-coloured skin looked meltingly, moistly delicious and their low voices rose and fell seductively, and every now and then one would get up and glide across the foyer and disappear into the velvet night. Of course they were prostitutes, I realised later. I was too naïve then even to guess. I asked if I might sit near them while I waited for the dining room to open, preferring their company to sitting alone and awkward, and they all turned and laughed at me, not kindly, but mockingly, looking at my unfashionable clothes and my thin, bony chest. I remember how I blushed furiously and was so grateful when the young hotel undermanager stepped forward and asked me if I would like to sit in the residents' lounge, under a slowly moving electric fan, where he brought me a tall glass of citron pressé. *I was hardly more than a child, you see. Younger, even, than the sharp young miss who was annoyed when I pulled the wrong cord yesterday evening.*

The following day, I had to wait until midday to continue my journey, taking the train that left once a day for Dakar. As I scuttled from the dining room after breakfast I bumped into the nice young French civil servant and he offered to take me round the town to see the sights. St Louis was the most important town in French West Africa and it bustled with life. It was terribly hot, despite the umbrella over the carriage where we sat, and the poor little bony horse was dark with sweat. A black veil of flies swarmed over its eyes and nostrils and it nodded its head mechanically in a futile attempt to shake them off. Its little unshod feet turned up at the toes like Moroccan slippers.

The Frenchman told the native driver to stop on the outskirts of the town, where buildings petered out and thatched huts began, then he leant across and kissed me on the mouth and put his hand on my chest. I can remember the shock I felt as his fingers pinched my nipple and his hard, wet mouth sucked at mine. I kept my lips tightly shut but felt the thick muscle of his tongue try to force them open. Frozen with terror I could not even protest until his hand moved to push up my skirt and reach the tops of my stockings and my suspenders. I screamed then and tried to jump out of the carriage, but he caught my arm and pulled me back and laughed and said, 'Tant pis! Une petite vierge!' *The driver turned and grinned, his teeth brown and broken, and said something which made the Frenchman laugh. He left me alone after that until we got back to the hotel, where he asked me to pay the driver, which I did, thrusting a note for goodness knows what into the pink palm of his outstretched hand. I felt that he was laughing at me as well and I ran up to my room, past the lounging mulatto women, in tears.*

I did not come down until it was time to leave and the kind undermanager called a cab to take me to the station with strict instructions to the driver that I was to be put on the train by him personally. The station was a further attempt to re-create France in Africa, a huge building with 'Départ' *and* 'Arrivée' *over separate canopied entrances and a large central clock tower. The trains were French, and the coaches painted light and dark green with a red stripe. Thank goodness there was a Ladies Only couchette and I travelled to*

Bamako in the company of two nuns and two young Frenchwomen going there to work as secretaries to the colonial government department. The interminable journey – was it two days and a night? – passed in a blur. I can remember the fans in the carriage, the restaurant car where the black cook brought me an omelette, a glass of cold white wine and a fresh baguette.

The sun was a white ball in a shimmering sky that met the trembling horizon in what looked like an endless city of towering heat. The train burned, the glass too hot to touch and the air that rushed through the open window like a draught from an oven. We pulled down the blinds and outside the window stretched the endless flat brown plains on which the extraordinary baobab trees stood at intervals like large knobbly old men. The only signs of life were herds of sheep or goats, I couldn't tell the difference, that occasionally crossed the dry landscape, nibbling at wind-blown thorn trees and tended by tall natives wrapped in cloths and often standing motionless on one leg and leaning on a stick to watch the train go by.

I was exhausted, sick with fatigue, when we eventually arrived at Bamako. I was met at the station by a man sent by Mary's father, a schools inspector who would accompany me on the boat journey up the great Niger river to Ségou, then Mopti, names that I had only seen on an atlas. The inspector was a small man with a ridiculous little curly moustache, very smartly dressed in a linen suit and wearing a pith helmet. He was rather taciturn and did nothing to help me with my stumbling efforts at speaking French. I got the impression that I was a great nuisance and it was only the influence of Mary's father that had persuaded him to look after me, but I was grateful all the same to be under his care. After Mopti, I knew not what, except that at the end of it all I would find Mary. It was because of her that I had come. She was not well enough to travel home alone and there had been nobody else who could contemplate the journey. 'It will be an adventure for you, Beryl dear,' Mary's mother had said. She was always suggesting that life was passing me by. 'Mary's father will take care of you. You will have the most marvellous time.'

I think of the girls, of Clemmie and Emily flying through the grey sky outside my window towards the steaming heat of west Africa. It will take them a mere five or six hours to get from post-Christmas London with its grey streets and dreary end-of-year sales to the city I can barely remember, except for its colour and brightness and dust and noise. Of course it will have changed. I suppose the colonial buildings remain, the station, the Grand Marché, perhaps the hotel I was taken to on the banks of the river and where I slept round the clock. Great Soviet-style blocks have sprung up, built by Russian money, so Clemmie told me, and it is a city teeming with people. There will be nobody there who will remember the two English girls from so long ago. Nobody will help Clemmie and Emily discover the truth. The truth ceased to exist long, long ago.

There is no point in keeping these photographs, or those that I took on the boat as we chugged up the milk-chocolate-coloured river. The tiny lumps on the surface of the water that were hippopotami, the crocodiles, the low-flying birds, the slender curves of the fishing boats, the Bozo villages that seemed to be built on the river itself, the strange little mud mosques, turreted and crenellated like miniature Venetian palaces, none of these things are done justice in the tiny, faded snaps. I put them back in the envelope and put the envelope into the bin beside my bed. I do not wish to be reminded.

Emily

ONCE WE GOT on the plane things looked up a bit. Well, frankly, they couldn't have got worse. Our group, with the exception of Hugh, who just looked weird, was exactly what I had feared – unrelievedly ghastly. Jeremy and Jutta were just about as bad as it gets in my view, although Clemmie said that it was a good thing to have those sort of people to travel with because they have a 'take no shit from anyone' attitude and we can get sucked along in their wake. It took them only a few moments from finding their seats on the aeroplane to getting themselves moved to a bulk-head position with extra leg room. I had to laugh when a very large black woman with a whole flying ducks arrangement of babies in descending order of size, each at full volume, was then moved to sit next to them.

Guy, who as a type was horribly reminiscent of Ted,

was three or four rows in front of us and I saw him put his seat back at the first opportunity, practically into the lap of the poor old Elder Tours man with a gammy leg who was directly behind him, and promptly go to sleep. Hugh had got a window seat and craned forward eagerly like a trainspotter so as not to miss anything exciting as we took off and before we hit the cloud. He was so much the opposite of Guy – impervious to what was cool, I would say – and was either woefully shy or suffering from a migraine. So far he had managed to avoid exchanging more than a few words with Clemmie or me and was sufficiently unsociable to be left well alone by the ghastly Jutta, for which he must have been more than thankful.

Clemmie and I settled into our seats and started to absorb the cheerful atmosphere of the flight, so different from the uptight and tense first leg from Heathrow to Paris. This was more like a country bus and it was the large number of Africans that made the difference. The moment the seat-belt light went out they were up and down the aisle, calling out to friends and strangers, laughing and swaying backwards and forwards to the lavatories. The Elder Tour matched them in restless energy but were more anxious, fussing and fiddling with bags and the overhead lockers, while Pastor John and Gloria sat up front and every now and then doled out forms to be filled in or glucose sweets to be sucked. Kathleen and Mabel were further up the plane in front of us but stopped to talk on their way to the lavatories. They had taken off their trainers and were both wearing flight socks. Kathleen had the eye mask up on the top of her head ready for a nap as soon as she could get settled.

Even the air stewardesses were more pleasant and obliging and in no time Clemmie and I had double vodka and tonics and those little bags of things to nibble which aren't killer peanuts. The spare seat next to Clemmie was taken by a beautiful slender black guy with large liquid eyes the colour of Guinness, the whites a creamy yellow. He introduced himself as Denne, an architecture student studying in Paris and on his way home to get married.

'Welcome to Mali!' he kept saying. 'Welcome to my country!' all the while gazing at Clemmie in a manner which suggested that his wedding would be thrown over at the drop of a hat if she gave him any encouragement. Because he was the first proper Malian we had ever met, Clemmie lost no time in asking him questions about where we were going and he proved to be the sort of man who is bursting with statistical information and who only needs the correct button pushed to set him off. He was like a website on the subject of his home country, reeling off the area of Mali to the nearest square kilometre, the size of the population and a potted cultural history. He was also very keen that we should join him that evening at the Hogon club in Torokorobougou to hear some live Malian music.

Clemmie listened politely and said that although we would love to go with him we were unlikely to be able to because we were part of a group and were being collected at the airport and taken off to destinations unknown.

'What I'd really like to know,' she said, melting Denne with her blue eyes, 'is how we would go about finding this man.' She passed over a piece of paper with 'Salika ag Baye' written in large letters at the top. Denne looked at it and frowned.

'Ah!' he said, passing it back. 'This is Tuareg. You do not want to know Tuareg men.'

'We don't? Why?'

'Look! I am Bambara – the main people of Mali. We are modern people who look to the west and belong to this world. The Tuareg are wild men from the north – our old enemies. They sold my people as slaves. I have no love for these tribesmen and now they are disinherited – their power is gone. They are poor and without hope. They live in the dust and sand of the desert or they come to starve on the edge of our cities. I tell you, you do not want to know Tuareg men.'

'But we do!' insisted Clemmie. 'That's why we are here, you see. We are on a kind of mission to travel to the north and we need to find this man to help us.'

'Why? Why you want to go there?' demanded Denne.

'It's rather a long story,' sighed Clemmie. 'Too long for now, but believe me, we just have to. We're doing it for particular family reasons.'

The first flush of ardour was already over and Denne looked huffy and offended. He shrugged his shoulders and made the sort of fuck-off-then face that he must have learned and perfected in Paris, and lapsed into silence. His Welcome to Mali vein had run dry very quickly.

After a bit, when it was clear that Denne was fed up with us, Clemmie got out the notebook I had given her and I dozed off and thought about Ted. Even now, with so much happening around me, my thoughts kept returning to him. The first glance at Guy had given me a pang of pain because of his physical similarity to Ted – both small, stocky and sexy and terribly aware of themselves. I had also dithered over buying a small brown bear in duty free because it reminded me of Ted. Clemmie pointed out that it had short, stumpy legs and small, close-together, mean little eyes and I had put it back on the shelf.

You'll get over it, is what people say about a broken heart, and of course I knew that I would. I was not about to take the E. Barrett Browning route and expire on a sofa, but I did feel that she had a point. It was quite tempting to lie down and tell the world to go away. This expedition to scatter Great-Aunt Mary was a diversion and, as Clemmie had predicted, was helping to distract me from the heartache, but it wasn't an instant cure. I could only hope that eventually the raw pain would fade and like a blister on a heel from a new shoe, a tough skin would grow over the raw place and the shoe would begin to feel more comfortable.

I looked out of the window and saw that we were flying in a bright blue world above a ceiling of cloud which looked so thick and white and solid it was easy to imagine stepping from the plane and scooping it up in armfuls. I was reminded of Great-Aunt Mary's poem. It seemed to me that this was as near as I was ever likely to get to looking at Eternity, out there through the thick plastic window, under the glittering white sun and the deep blue sky curving towards a blue horizon. I suddenly felt very small and insignificant, and for that matter, so did Ted.

An hour or so out of Bamako, the passengers started to seethe with excitement and the troop of people in the aisle became more like a line of dancers, their feet slapping the floor, their hips swaying. They were nearly home. Denne, who had not revised his low opinion of us, began to liberally squirt his face and neck from a bottle of French cologne in preparation for the reception committee that was no doubt waiting for him at the airport.

The Elder Tour party revved up their fidgeting and fussing and Clemmie put her book away and started to wriggle out of her wintry layers of clothing until she was left in a little white T-shirt and her faded cotton skirt. With her battered old jodhpur boots she looked like a homespun heroine from *Little House on the Prairie*. She shook her long hair loose from the scrunched-up arrangement into which she had caught it, and it fell in a pale mantle over her shoulders. I saw Denne stare at her, startled by a sudden flash of her beauty, and the Guy character, on his way down the plane to the lavatory, did a double-take and stopped to chat, squatting down in the aisle and showing off his bulgy rugby-player thighs.

'Hi, girls!' he said. 'All righ'?' He had a mockney accent, just like Ted. 'Jeremy has been filling me in on your story. Pretty amazing. Your great-aunt, he said, wanted to be scattered in the desert? Wow! And you've no idea why she wanted to end up in Mali? Quite a story!' He paused and looked at Clemmie. 'Are you a model? No? I thought I'd seen you somewhere before. Tell you what, I'd like to do some photos – just a few shots, okay? There are some pretty stunning locations, you know. I've been to Mali before, on an assignment with French *Vogue* . . .'

Oh, it was so boring and predictable. I stifled a yawn and Clemmie responded with polite restraint. You could tell that she was supposed to faint with excitement.

Later my attention was caught by Hugh, who suddenly sprang up from his seat, his hair on end and his crumpled shirt half in and half out of his trousers. He bumbled past, failing to recognise or acknowledge our existence, for which I awarded him high marks, and was then headed off by the air stewardess, who told him to return to his seat because the seat-belt light was on and we were about to land. It took a moment or two for what she was saying to sink in. He looked puzzled at first and rubbed his chin and stared at her as if surprised to find that he was on an aeroplane at all. He was obviously the sort of brilliantly clever person who could win Nobel prizes but who you wouldn't send out to post a letter. After Jeremy and Guy, all supercool and full of themselves, it was rather endearing.

By now we had broken through the cloud and were circling over a parched brown plain sliced by clumps of dark green vegetation and in the distance an enormous sprawl of a city split by a great curve of silver river. There was an intake of breath so full and deep that it felt as if the sides of the plane would be sucked in, and then the wheels clanked down and the ground came racing, bumping, hurtling to meet us. Then the breath was released in a whoosh of joy and the passengers whooped and cheered and clapped. The moment the plane came to a stop they were up on their feet like exuberant children about to be let out of school.

Clemmie and I collected our hand luggage and then found ourselves swept along to the door of the plane. I stood on the top of the steps looking out at Africa for the first time, and the air was hot and wet and smelled of earth. The runway had a bodged-up look, edged with broken tarmac, and the ground on either side was rocky and dry and rubbish-strewn and the sharp-looking brown grasses rustled like paper in the hot wind. Ahead of us was a collection of low airport buildings, and in the thick wedge of their dark shade my sun-blinded eyes picked out groups of workers lolling in orange and green overalls and staring across at us with passive interest.

By the time we had walked across the tarmac, Jeremy, Jutta and Guy had worked themselves into a vanguard position and were signalling to us to join them. Somehow or other Jeremy had got hold of a trolley, and their copious hand luggage, including all the clanking bottles from duty free, was being pushed by a young black man who had sauntered out from the shade.

'Come on, you two!' called Jeremy, waving us on, in the tone of a school prefect to two fourth-form laggards. 'We want to get ahead of this lot.' He indicated the first of the Elder Tour, who were tottering across the tarmac behind us. Hugh, who I had seen helping them with hand luggage – I gave him bonus points for that – had somehow got caught up amongst them, and because he was so tall and thin and they were all shrunk and bowed, his head and shoulders stood up from the group and with his startled expression and his long, bony neck he reminded me of a lone giraffe amongst a shuffling herd of geriatric gnus.

The excited crowd of home-going Africans had jostled in front of us and were pushing and crowding and laughing their way into the building and besieging the two immigration officers who were set up to deal with Malian nationals from within two little glass booths. They looked very cross indeed and there was a lot of yelling and arm-waving before they had everybody in some sort of order and could proceed with stamping the passports that were being thrust at them from all sides. At the other end of the arrivals hall a crowd of relatives and friends and taxi-drivers carrying cardboard notices displaying passengers' names were corralled behind a rope. They bobbed and craned and waved and shouted and looked as if at any moment they might stampede.

Jeremy had located the foreign aliens desk and ushered our party forward, and thanks to his pushiness we were almost at the front of the queue. An extremely tall and fat black man arrived and squeezed himself behind the counter. His skin looked tight and shiny as if he had been inflated to bursting point by a foot pump, and with his dark glasses and unsmiling face and uniform covered in braid, he cut an imposing figure. However, he processed the line of foreign aliens quickly and efficiently, shuffling through our entry forms and bringing his green stamp down from shoulder height with a bang that made the passports jump. Jeremy and Guy and Jutta were through in no time and I could see Jeremy hurrying towards Baggage Reclaim with his trolley and black youth bringing up the rear. He had obviously worked out a strategy for being in the premier position to retrieve the luggage. It was easy to see that he was the sort of man to whom life presented a series of challenges in which every effort had to be made to outsmart the rest of the field.

Now it was Clemmie's passport that was open in front of the chief of alien immigration. Suddenly and abruptly his brisk processing routine came to a halt. He paused on the back page and studied the passport photograph. He turned the page and looked at it sideways. An index finger the size of a pork sausage traced the print and the man's breath became noisy and shallow and his broad brow furrowed with concentration. Oh God, I thought, standing behind Clemmie. What the hell was wrong? His understudy, smaller and with less gold braid, leaned over to have a look. Clemmie stood nervously on one leg and then the other. Then both men raised their heads simultaneously to stare at her and she, with one deft flick of her hand, shook out her silver hair. Megawatt smiles broke across the stern faces. Teeth flashed white and gold and the chief took off his dark glasses to reveal eyes the whites of which were the colour of egg yolks. Clemmie beamed back and I grinned with relief. The man leaned over his counter and held out his huge hand and Clemmie put her slim white one in his.

'And this is my cousin Emily!' she said in a party voice, putting my passport in front of him. He couldn't bear to tear his eyes away from her face and stamped my passport any old how, half on and half off the page, which was a bit annoying because I happen to have a childish delight in collecting passport stamps.

'Welcome, beautiful ladies!' he said in a voice which rumbled from somewhere deep within his mighty chest. 'Welcome to my country!' He called over his shoulder, 'Toto!' and a young woman official came bouncing to his side. He indicated Clemmie and me. 'Baggage!' he commanded and Toto, beaming too, indicated that we should follow her.

'Just a minute!' said Clemmie, looking back down

the congested and impatient line behind us. She scanned the long trail of the Elder Tour, patiently fanning hot faces with their hats and wilting under the weight of their hand luggage. Then she darted back and dragged out Kathleen and Mabel and shunted them up to the desk. 'Would you be a darling and help these friends of mine?'

The chief nodded and smiled and indicated that they should present their passports. I glanced back and saw the Texas sunset on Gloria's bosom swell with indignation from her command post at the front of the group where she held aloft the Elder Tour placard.

Then Toto had us racing through Arrivals and round the corner and into the luggage hall where the bags from our flight were being tossed off a cart and thrown on to the conveyor belt. It took only a few minutes to find our backpacks and drag them out and then Toto organised a man and a trolley to push them for us. Clemmie fumbled in her little sequinned purse for West African currency. Neither of us had any idea what was an appropriate tip. Toto leaned across, picked out a note and gave it to the man, who smiled broadly. Clemmie held out her purse and indicated that Toto should tip herself if she felt like it. The gesture flouted all the rules of wise tourist practice but Toto put her hand to her mouth and laughed and shook her head.

'Here,' said Clemmie, fishing about in her bag. She pulled out a small bottle of scent, something she had been given for Christmas. 'Would you like this? Lily of the valley. A nice English flower.'

Toto beamed even more brightly and stowed the bottle in one of her military-looking flapped pockets. Then we were off, whizzing back through Baggage Reclaim, twinkling past Jeremy and his gang with little cheery waves and out into the blinding sunshine and steamy heat. Beauty had won the day.

Instantly we were besieged on all sides by cripples and beggars, children, old men, blind women led by infants, who jostled at our sides with outstretched hands and pulled at our clothes to attract our attention. We looked at each other, horrified, and Clemmie began to grope for the sequinned purse. Before she could find it, the beggars melted back and a tall young man holding a sign saying 'TROTTS' stepped forward.

'Welcome!' he said. 'Missy Kingsleys? My name is Mokhtar. I am your tourist guide!' and he threw a handful of coins at the feet of the unfortunate.

Clemmie

THAT FIRST NIGHT in Mali I lay exhausted and too excited to sleep in our comfortable hotel room and waited for dawn. The room was cool and whitewashed and the simple wooden beds had thin mattresses covered with light woven blankets. Thick mosquito netting meant we had been able to leave the shutters of the window wide open on to the red-soiled vegetable garden and the night was filled with the noises of the countryside although we were only a few miles from the centre of the teeming city. Born a country girl, I am used to unearthly nocturnal animal cries as the human world sleeps, but this was something else. The hot, wet night air throbbed with an insistent rhythm of cricket and bullfrog. Dogs barked incessantly and a poor little donkey complained at being tethered too tightly under a nearby tree.

We had looked out at the garden before night had fallen. Neat rows of vegetables exploded with green from the damp dark earth, puddled by water dragged in a bucket from an irrigation ditch by two slow-moving men. From over the mud-baked walls of the plot the tops of luxuriant trees pressed inwards, jostling in the breeze, and the hot air seemed to buzz with the energy of green growth which burst out everywhere, in cascades of flowering creepers over the walls of the neighbouring houses, in the palms and ferns which pushed their way through gates and fences and the rampant weeds which buckled the paving stones of the dusty road. You could almost hear nature, like a giantess, breathing down your neck.

Our hotel was a wonderful surprise. It was so clean and comfortable and completely unlike anything we had expected. Even Emily had nothing to complain about when she saw where we were to stay the night, and not least because outside the airport building we had been separated from the other members of our group.

The appearance of Mokhtar bowled me over. He was a slim, tall, handsome man wearing a red-and-white Arsenal T-shirt and jeans, but swathed round his head and neck was a bright yellow cloth in dashing local style which gave him a swashbuckling, piratical air. He never removed his reflecting sunglasses and it was hard to judge his age but he was very self-possessed and spoke in rapid French and only a little less fluent English. While we waited for the others to emerge from Baggage Reclaim, he explained that he was in the employment of the Bamako-based tour company used by Jimbo to organise our trip and that he was afraid that because we had booked at the last minute and were not paying for a more exclusive and expensive tour it was a case of sheep and goats. He was going to accompany Jeremy and party on a tour of Bamako and take them to one of the concrete block hotels in the centre of the city where there was air-conditioning and a swimming pool, while we would go with a second driver, yet to appear, to our more humble and cheaper accommodation.

In fact it couldn't have suited us better to be separated, and when Jeremy and co emerged from collecting their luggage, they seemed as pleased as we were with this discriminatory arrangement. By then our very own driver had drawn up. He was a short older man, stout, with a grizzled beard, wearing a long dirty white robe, black town shoes, very scuffed and dusty, and a black headdress with a coiled rope round the crown holding it in place. Despite the heat, on top of the robe he wore a heavy black leather jacket. His face was dominated by beady, knowing brown eyes and a large nose, which jutted out from his headdress, giving him a snouty, hedgehog look.

He was the opposite of glamorous Mokhtar, but I liked his smiley wrinkled face and that he shook hands with us so enthusiastically. He reminded me of Sid, the cowman at home on the farm, who never once lost his temper, not even when he got kicked or a cow stood on his foot and refused to move. I knew instinctively that Emily and I would be safe with Serufi and that he would look after us beautifully.

Jeremy immediately assumed the role of spokesman and began to quiz Mokhtar about the arrangements for the rest of the trip. He especially wanted to know how likely they were to find the elusive elephants. Mokhtar dealt with him very skilfully, I thought, refusing to be bullied and shrugging his shoulders in a noncommittal way.

'These are wild animals,' he said. 'They are not in a game reserve. They roam where they want. They come; they go. We can only hope!'

It was very hot standing in the sun. The heat bounced off the concrete and our faces were becoming very pink and boiled-looking. Under the shade of a row of trees to our left I could see the Elder Tour hoisting themselves, or being heaved, on to a battered coach. Kathleen and Mabel were already aboard and waving at us out of a window.

Jutta, her big hair collapsing in the heat, and looking dishevelled and cross, chipped in.

'This all sounds very hit and miss. It's not really good enough when we have been sold the whole trip on the basis of finding the bloody elephants. Don't you know where the herd is now? There must be people with some sort of local knowledge.'

But Mokhtar was not playing ball. He could promise nothing, he said, but if the party would like to follow him across the road to where his shiny four-by-four vehicle was parked, he would show them the great capital city and the world-famous road bridge over the river Niger. Still grumbling, they did as they were told, Jeremy taking the front passenger seat and Hugh squashed in the middle of the back seat between Guy and Jutta, with his knees under his chin.

Mokhtar turned to Emily and me and explained that Serufi would take us on a short tour and then to our hotel. 'Very good, very nice, very good price,' he assured us. Serufi, he added, was a country boy and the city made him nervous. He ribbed Serufi in his own language and they scuffled a bit, good-naturedly, guffawing and back-slapping. As befitted our more lowly status, our vehicle was slightly bashed and coated with dust, but we were glad to hop on to the front seat beside Serufi, who looked across at us and grinned, and then we were off, trundling into the stream of traffic and out towards the city.

I don't know what I expected but I knew that Bamako was huge and very, very poor. Perhaps I thought that it would be grey and depressing, ground down by deprivation, but on the contrary, it was bursting with colour and vitality as we crawled along in the endless traffic congestion. On either side of the two-lane road was a hinterland of thrown-together shacks, roofed with palms and sacking, and stalls and animals and bicycles and umbrellas and patches of maize and cooking fires. We passed herds of donkeys and goats corralled under the trees, and everywhere the earth was like dark crumbs with a fringe of green pressing through the dirt. People thronged along the road, the women very tall and upright and sinuous and graceful, and the colour of their robes and head-dresses was startling and wonderful. Oranges and reds and yellows sizzled against dark skin. How could they emerge looking like this from the squalor that they moved through? Every girl over about twelve seemed to have a baby strapped to her back and every young man carried a ghetto-blaster and swung along to the rhythm of its music.

Emily and I sat in awe, silenced by the colour and glamour and energy of the place and the jolting traffic which surrounded us. Cars and lorries shunted along beside us, literally held together with string, missing doors and tailgates and crammed with people and furniture and fruit and vegetables and fridges and goats and sheep. Every now and then a top-of-the-range American four-by-four with smoked-glass windows and giant bumpers spun past, sounding its horn, cutting a swathe through the dilapidated vehicles and disappearing into the distance.

Then the slice of river gleamed through the traffic, very wide and murky with a few slender fishing boats being poled along in the shallows, which were fringed with green. On the other side was the heart of the city, high-rise modern concrete buildings and a great bulky fortress which Mokhtar told us the next day was the headquarters of a bank. Serufi spoke no English and had only a few words of French, and because we had found no guidebook that dealt in any detail with Mali, we just sat and gazed in silence.

Eventually Serufi swung off the main road and to our relief we realised that we were not heading into the concrete centre but had diverted into a sprawling, meandering suburb of large houses and villas. Vegetation erupted violently along the pot-holed road, donkeys and chickens and semi-naked children wandered at will and every side street deteriorated into dust and straw and sacking shacks. Every other house had a guard asleep in the shade of the wall, or lounging outside the dilapidated gates on a plastic chair with a gun resting on his knees. It looked like the Hampstead of Bamako. 'Many foreigners!' Serufi explained, and then turned off to park alongside a sign painted on a white wall saying 'Embassy Guest House'.

He jumped out and hauled our bags up to a heavily barred door and rang the bell. We waited ages while a crowd of curious children gathered and a pregnant ginger cat wound round our legs. One of the children carried a black kitten with milky blue eyes, so tiny it could have fitted in a teacup. Then the door was opened by a smart young man in a white shirt and red waistcoat and we were ushered in. Serufi did a lot of garrulous explaining and the young man turned to us and said in good English, 'He says he will collect you at seven thirty tomorrow morning for the start of your long journey.' We nodded and smiled and Serufi shook our hands and disappeared.

We stood in a cool marble hall while the young man consulted a book behind a desk and a large ceiling fan turned above our heads and wafted our hair gently from our wet necks. Everything seemed unexpectedly stylish and spick and span and then a middle-aged white woman appeared from an office behind the desk, wearing black harem trousers and a T-shirt. She was plump and looked hot and flustered.

'Oh hi!' she greeted us in an American accent and introduced herself as Gail, the owner of the hotel, which she explained was brand new and in its first year of opening. She had come to Mali twelve years earlier to work on an NGO project funded by the United States and had decided to stay and open a guesthouse for the increasing number of visitors.

She seemed very limp and exhausted and kept sighing and fanning herself with the paper in her hand. 'Things are chaotic!' she said. 'Well, this *is* Mali, after all. Tonight is the opening of the restaurant here, but of course nothing has gone to plan. At the moment we have no oven and no cook! You see it's very, very hard to set up a business catering for the European or American community while employing hopeless

Malian staff or relying on local suppliers. Really, they can't be trusted to do anything properly!' All the time the young receptionist, who had greeted us so graciously, stood politely to one side, holding our luggage in each hand, waiting to take us to our room. I started to hate Gail and wished she would shut up. 'We'll have great music, though,' she said. 'We've got some fantastic musicians coming to play! That's one of the things they really can do here.'

I loved our simple whitewashed bedroom and the view over the garden, and after a shower and a peaceful rest on our beds, darkness suddenly fell like a curtain drawn across the sky. Emily and I were both starving by then and longing for a cold beer so we dressed and went downstairs and found a terrific hullabaloo raging. There was no encouraging smell of cooking from the kitchen but we learned that the oven had just arrived and was at this moment being connected to the electricity supply. Various key workers lounged around the lobby or peered through the kitchen door until they were herded up and set to work by a frantic Gail, who kept stopping to pat her beaded forehead with a folded tissue. The activity was only sporadic, and as soon as she had flurried off they resumed their idling and grinned at us. Enormous and roughly hewn string instruments were being manhandled through the front door and were left propped against bits of furniture in the foyer.

Eventually, nearly fainting with hunger, we managed to waylay the helpful receptionist and got him to bring us some beers and he obligingly came back with French bread and olives as well. By then guests had begun to arrive, all smartly dressed in cocktail outfits, milling around together while we sat and watched for as long as we could stay awake and then sneaked off up to our room, nearly blind with tiredness. We must have gone straight to sleep because it seemed hours later that we were woken by a loud bang on our door.

'Shit!' said Em, sitting bolt upright. 'What the hell's that?'

I fumbled for the bedside light and knocked it over with a crash. 'Who is it?' I called, getting out of bed and wrapping myself in the bedspread, which was the only thing I could find in the dark. I hovered nervously by the door.

'Hameed! I bring you super dinner!'

I opened the door a crack and our receptionist friend was standing outside with a tray in his hands. He pushed the door open gently and came in, making a great show of not looking at us, Emily in bed and me wearing the bedspread.

'You've brought us some supper? That's so kind of you!' I said, and he smiled happily over our heads and addressed the far corner of the room.

'You're welcome!'

When he had gone, Emily groaned and put the pillow over her head but I lifted the paper napkin spread over the food and found a plate of garlicky beans and six hard-boiled eggs. I ate two, without salt or pepper, and then felt my throat furring up. From downstairs I could hear the twanging of the mighty instruments and the sound of voices. The party seemed to be going with a swing but I guessed from the food that the cook was still missing, and as the opening of dining rooms go, perhaps the evening was a bit of a let-down. I hoped for Hameed's sake that Gail was not disappointed.

I lay back on my bed and stared into the darkness and listened to the party and the noises of the night and knew that I was not going to sleep again. From the top of the chest of drawers Great-Aunt Mary's pug bag surveyed the room. I thought I could see the beady black eyes winking in the darkness and the little pink felt tongue sticking out in a lively fashion. Great-Aunt Mary seemed to be enjoying herself.

* * *

The following morning Emily and I got up as soon as it was light and watched a perfect pink dawn polish the sky over the vegetable garden. The cockerels had been hard at it for hours, but just before light filtered through the blackness of the night there was a strange hush. Even the frogs fell silent, as if they were holding their breath before the new day. I swear that I hadn't slept a wink all night, as our gran often used to claim, and my eyelids felt weighted down with tiredness, but now that it was time to get up I could have slept anywhere. A cold shower woke me up and then Em and I rootled about in our backpacks and rearranged our stuff and lost things and found them again and repacked. This was to become the recurring ritual of the trip, when items of our belongings disappeared and then resurfaced just after we had given them up for lost.

We discussed the weighty question of what to wear. We were going to be travelling all day as far as we knew and it would be hot and sticky. In the end I put on a white T-shirt and a long sun-ray-pleated silk skirt I had found in Oxfam in Yeovil. It was too big round the waist and a bit tattered and frayed, but it had faded to a pink the colour of the sky and was so swirly that it swooshed round my legs and always made me feel in a dancing, carefree mood. I bound the waist with a red Indian cotton scarf and that was that. I couldn't hope to match the sizzling style of the women we had seen yesterday in their fabulous one-shouldered dresses and matching turbans, but at least I wasn't wearing khaki shorts.

Emily made her usual determined effort not to dress up and wore her jeans from yesterday with an old kaftan top that was loose and light and pretty and, although discreet, showed off her proper, womanly bosoms.

We went down to breakfast through the sleeping guesthouse. There was nobody about and in the foyer the huge musical instruments lay abandoned on their sides like ships run aground amongst a clutter of empty glasses and dirty plates. The kitchen was quiet although the oven was there all right, standing on its own in the middle of the floor. The prospects for food did not look good until Emily opened sliding doors on to the garden and found that on a pretty shady patio a collection of tables was set for breakfast.

We sat in the shade and waited and watched brightly coloured birds flitting through the trees and fat lizards sunning on the steps. After a bit there was a clattering from the kitchen and Hameed appeared, smart in a pressed white shirt, smiling as usual and bearing a jug of fresh orange juice and then a basket of croissants and a pot of coffee.

'This poor guy seems to do everything,' said Emily. 'Do you think Gail has noticed? She spent enough time yesterday slagging off her staff.'

We ate ravenously and then, when we thought we had finished, Hameed brought out a platter of fruit and we began all over again.

It was a perfect breakfast, and as we sat there it seemed to me that it was one of those rare moments when I felt entirely happy and at peace, and then I wondered if this was shameful, to be made so completely contented by something as simple as sunshine and delicious food.

Emily, being a good teacher, started to look at her watch in a responsible way, and fret that we would not be ready when Serufi arrived to collect us, and so we went upstairs and stuffed the last things into the packs and manhandled them down into the foyer just as there was a brisk knocking on the door. It was Serufi, grinning, wearing yesterday's outfit and keen to shake our hands and get us loaded up into his truck. There was no sign of Gail to say goodbye to or to thank and I hoped that she was having a lie-in after her party and would be in a better mood when she got up.

We shook hands with Hameed, of whom we were now very fond, and Emily gave him a large note from our collection of paper money and he came out to see us off. Mokhtar was outside in the road, busily engaged in lashing luggage to the roofrack of his smart Toyota. He stopped what he was doing to greet us and shake our hands. We could see Jeremy in the front seat and Jutta looking us up and down from the back.

I went over and said good morning through the window. 'Have you had a good time?' I asked. 'What was Bamako like?' They hardly bothered to reply and I got the impression that they were already hot and annoyed about something. They didn't ask how Emily and I had got on, but started a discussion about seating arrangements in the two vehicles. Then Hugh got out of the other side. He was wearing an old checked flannel shirt like my dad wears to market in the winter and a pair of battered jeans and hiking boots. Round his shoulders he had a red-and-white Arab scarf and he was wearing his ordinary glasses with a pair of sunglasses on the top. He looked very peculiar.

'Is it okay,' he said, 'if I travel with you?'

Beryl Timmis

I HAVE PASSED my first Sunday at The Willows. It is now evening and the house is quiet. A roast lunch is served in the dining room and then the kitchens close for the day and the staff go home. A light supper is available from a trolley during the evening – cheese and biscuits, fruit and yoghurt and so on, and most residents choose to eat in their rooms. I am settling in and getting used to the routine and have already decided which of the staff I like, those who are patient and kind, and those to avoid.

I don't much care about food these days and so it did not matter that lunch was poor – the lamb very tough and fatty and the vegetables overcooked. The other ladies and gentlemen seem to eat whatever is put before them and there was very little effort to make conversation. On the whole I prefer this to the residents who seem unable to stop talking. Because I am new, they single me out as a fresh victim and I have learned to keep out of their way. An exception is a tall old gentleman with a shock of snowy white hair. He seems a little confused and never recognises me when we meet in the corridor or in the residents' lounge. His eyes are very blue and he must have once been a handsome man. His one topic of conversation appears to be foxhounds, on the subject of which he is quite lucid. Yesterday he accosted me in the passage and said, 'Did I ever tell you that it was Bluebell *who was Champion Bitch at Peterborough in 1968, not Custard, who was Supreme Champion at Builth Wells the same year?' I assured him that he hadn't, and then he moved on to a full history of Bluebell's offspring, only faltering occasionally to say, 'Or was it* Parsnip *who went to the Flint and Denbigh? Dear me, I shall forget my own name soon.' I saw him yesterday being collected by his daughter, who was taking him home for lunch. 'Here's your daughter, Colonel,' said Pat, the assistant on duty, and he looked up vaguely. His daughter was a good-looking woman in a well-cut coat and expensive shoes. 'How are you, Dad?' she said, kissing him and taking his arm. 'Ah! You've come to take me home,' he said. 'I have been very well looked after here but,' and he lowered his voice, 'they don't know very much about* hounds. *It was Ramble, you know, my dear,' I heard him say as they went out to the car. 'I think I might have told you it was Rascal who went to the Quorn in '54.'*

I am ashamed to admit that my spirits are a little low this evening although I do not need to be reminded how fortunate I am to be here in The Willows. I am well cared for, warm and comfortable and I know that this is not the case for so many of the world's population, old or young, and indeed I am grateful. It is Mary I have to thank for making these arrangements for me should she happen to die first. She had no intention of ever coming here herself. She always said that she would see to it that she never reached the stage of needing to be looked after and I suppose that she intended to take her own life when she felt that it had become a burden.

My thoughts keep returning to Mary, but not to the recent past or the years I spent as her companion; rather to days of our girlhood. I can't deny that I have been unsettled by Clemmie and Emily's trip to the desert and I realise that I feel upset that Mary thought to arrange it so deviously through the instrument of her will. What did she hope to achieve by reviving the past, which matters nothing, nothing to anyone still living, except me? Everyone else who played any part is long dead and it is not as if the girls are even blood relations.

What she chose to do so secretly has forced me to be evasive. No, worse than that, she has made it necessary for me to lie and this is deeply distressing to me. My upbringing, my parents, everything I have believed in all my life, rise to condemn me, and although I am convinced that I had no option, I can't drive it from my mind. My sleep is disturbed and fitful and I have begun to dream of the Sahara. Last night I dreamed that I was in Kidal, staying at the residence in the mud fort carved out of the desert sand. Of course Mary was there too, and we were in the little dusty courtyard under the palm trees where someone was trying to grow vegetables. We were engaged in an argument and she was accusing me of, I can't remember what, and then it suddenly began to rain and we looked up at the hard blue sky in amazement. 'There,' she said. 'I told you it would be all right.'

Then one morning last week, Kathy came into my room to run her hoover round the carpet and dust the furniture. She was about to empty my waste basket into a black bin bag when her hand dived in and she drew something out and said, 'Oh, you don't want to throw these out, do you?' and I saw that she was holding up the old envelope containing the photographs.

'Yes, yes,' I said. 'I don't want them. They were taken far too long ago. They are of no interest any more.'

'You should keep them then,' said Kathy. 'They're history, they are. Can I have a peep?' How could I stop her? Then she was full of how interesting it was that I had been to

Africa. 'You're a proper traveller, you are!' she said. 'Oh my! Look at you here with these camels! Listen,' she said. 'Tell you what, my son-in-law can get these blown up for you. Printed up nice and big so you can see they proper.' She wouldn't take no for an answer and went off with them in the pocket of her overall.

It feels as if the past has come back to haunt me.

Emily

WE DROVE OUT of Bamako, Clemmie and I sitting side by side on the front seat next to Serufi, Great-Aunt Mary in her pug bag between us, and Hugh silent in the back. He had got a notebook out of his pack and sat with it on his knees, a pen in his hand, staring out of the window.

'Did you sleep well?' Clemmie asked him in a conversational tone.

'Yes. Yes thank you,' he said but did not offer any other information or ask us how we had got on. Clemmie would not leave it there. She saw his reticence as a challenge and launched into an account of our evening and the party that never was, making a funny story of it. I nudged her to shut up but she chatted on relentlessly. There was no sound from the back, not even listening-type noises. Hugh merely looked out of the window and appeared to ignore the flow of talk.

'And so,' finished Clemmie with a little laugh, 'that was that! No cook, no food!'

Silence.

By now we were out of the main part of the city, following a dead-straight road which disappeared into the shimmering distance. On either side there remained a dwindling strip of roadside stalls and knots of people, donkeys and goats under the shade of banana and mango trees. A drift of the beautiful women, dressed like queens, glided serenely amongst them, but by now I realised that despite all the vibrancy and colour there was a desperate edge and that what we were admiring was the sight of very poor people engaged in trying to flog recycled bits and pieces, which at home would be chucked on rubbish tips, to other equally poor people.

Gradually the countryside changed and the people and stalls thinned out and then we were passing through a sparse forest which went on for mile after mile. It was getting very hot sitting in the front seat in the full sun even though Serufi drove with his window open and a warm wind blew on our faces. Every now and then huge lorries roared past the other way with a blast on their horns. There was only just room for two vehicles to pass and the tarmac of the road was raised a foot or so above the land which fell away on either side. Any loss of nerve or giving ground on Serufi's part would have meant a wheel over the edge and we would have rolled over. Occasionally we passed vehicles which had done exactly that, lying upside down on the brown grass surrounded by groups of motionless, sad-shouldered people, like mourners at a funeral.

It was a relief that Serufi drove so well, calmly and cautiously, slowing down when he saw that ahead a gang of donkeys was intending to cross the road or a child was running alongside trying to turn back a herd of frisky goats which threatened to break away. Mokhtar was much more of a boy racer, with his flash dark glasses and his shiny Toyota. He had long since disappeared up front and I thought how pleased Jeremy would be at getting wherever it was first.

Suddenly Hugh spoke. We were so accustomed to his silence that it made us both jump, and Clemmie banged her head against the window. He wasn't talking to us though; he was addressing Serufi in an unrecognisable language and Serufi was gabbling back and looking in his rear-view mirror to make eye contact.

Clemmie turned in her seat to look at this new, talking Hugh.

'Goodness!' she said. 'Whatever language is that you're speaking?'

'Bambara,' he said. He had a learned, precise sort of voice and spoke very fast, as if to get what he had to say over with. 'It's the majority language of Mali. I don't speak it very well. Actually, I've just asked Serufi where he comes from, and he is Tuareg, from Tamnarasset in Algeria, so his own language is Tamashek, which I also speak a little.'

'A Tuareg!' breathed Clemmie, delighted to have found one at last. She didn't seem to mind that Serufi was a small and stout specimen, and not exactly like the glamorous men she had been so smitten by in the photographs. She turned to give him one of her special smiles, which distracted him so much he nearly drove off the road.

'So is Mokhtar,' said Hugh. 'He comes from Gao, up north where you are heading.'

Serufi had registered Clemmie's enthusiasm and smiled and nodded at us before firing something off at Hugh.

'He wants to know if you are married,' said Hugh.

'No, of course we're not. Why? Does he want to

marry us?' asked Clemmie, amused. 'Because if he does, I would think about it very seriously, he is so sweet.'

'Yes, I think he probably does.'

I turned round in my seat to give Hugh a look. He seemed to have slept on his hair in a funny way and it was standing up on one side of his head, but apart from that his face was serious.

'He's a widower. He thinks either of you would make a good wife, but I have just told him that you are too old and set in your ways.' I snorted and looked at him again to see if he was joking and saw that he meant it. Then I suppose he thought we might be offended, because he added, 'Tamashek wives should be young and strong and skilled in desert traditions. It's a very hard life, you know.'

'But Emily and I could be a kind of "buy one, get one free" offer,' teased Clemmie.

Hugh glanced at her, bemused. I guessed he was the sort of man who shopped in a daze. I could just imagine him going round a supermarket buying the same things every week regardless, impervious to clever merchandising.

'Tuareg these days are monogamous. Their women are considered to be the most beautiful in Africa,' he added.

'So they wouldn't fancy us!' sighed Clemmie.

'I don't think they find pale skins and hair attractive. They are genetically predisposed to prefer women who will survive in one of the harshest environments in the world. However, Mokhtar was telling me last night that European women are thought of as rich prizes because of their comparative wealth. I believe a number of French women come to look for husbands amongst the Tuareg nobility but I don't know what the success rate is.'

'I never thought anyone would want to marry me for my money,' said Clemmie.

'It's all comparative. Any westerner is rich by the standards of nomadic people,' said Hugh, answering her seriously. Not for a second had he acknowledged the pulling power of Clemmie's beauty, and because this was a novelty for her I could tell that she was amused.

She began to scrabble in her bag, looking for her piece of paper with the name 'Salika ag Baye' on it. She held it out to Hugh. 'Please ask him if he knows this man.'

Hugh took it and spoke to Serufi again. Serufi gave a long reply, taking a hand off the wheel to shake in the air over his head.

'He knows the family,' reported Hugh. 'There aren't that many Tuareg in the country. Only about ten per cent of the population are Tuareg or Moor, and because it is a tribal system they tend to at least know *of* one another. He thinks that Mokhtar has already made enquiries on your behalf. Apparently we are leaving you at some sort of crossroads, where you are going to be met by Tuareg from the area you want to travel to.'

Clemmie's eyes were shining. 'That's wonderful!' she said. 'Did you hear that, Em?'

'Bloody hell!' I retorted. 'It doesn't sound a very satisfactory arrangement to me. I tell you, Clemmie, I'm not going to get dumped at a bloody roadside like an old fridge. No way!'

But Clemmie wasn't listening. She was gazing out of the window at the landscape, which had changed to rolling grasslands scattered with stands of large stately trees.

'Oh, do look, Em!' she said. 'It's like Windsor Great Park!'

We stopped for lunch at Ségou, which Hugh explained was Mali's second city and was once an important river port and a crossroads. Nowadays lorries en route from Burkino Faso to Bamako stop there to go through Customs. We drove down a road lined with what Hugh said were balanzan or shea trees. On either side were ramshackle colonial villas with exploding vegetation in their gardens and on the left we caught glimpses of the grey slide of the Niger river at the end of each shady road. 'It's Henley-on-Thames, isn't it?' said Clemmie, continuing her Home Counties theme. Unfortunately the attractive part of town did not last for long and we left behind the shady trees and began to pass through an ugly concrete sprawl, dominated by a huge football stadium built for the African World Cup. Bloody football. There was no getting away from it, although it seemed unlikely that the Tuareg we had seen photographs of on their camels would dismount to kick a ball about in the sand. They looked too noble for that.

We pulled over to stop in front of the Independence Hotel, outside which the Toyota was already parked. By now it was extremely hot and I felt bloated and red-faced and sweaty although Serufi was still wearing his leather jacket. Our truck was immediately surrounded by children clamouring for attention with outstretched hands until Mokhtar appeared and shooed them away. He explained that he and Serufi would go and fill the vehicles with diesel while we had lunch, so we piled out of the truck and went into the building, grateful for the sudden shade.

Inside there was a long empty bar and doors open at the back on to a pretty, shady courtyard garden where tables and chairs were set under the trees and sheltered by awnings. It looked cool and green and inviting. Jeremy and Guy and Jutta were sitting at the only occupied table, drinking beer and eating French bread and olives. Jeremy looked over and said in a satisfied voice, 'Where on earth have you lot been? We've been here half an hour. We've already ordered and we're on our second beers!'

He was wearing his checked trousers and a panama hat. Jutta had exchanged her jeans for khaki bush trousers with a lot of leg pockets. She also wore a bush hat and a well-pressed white shirt. They looked, I had to admit, very colonial and *Out of Africa*, whereas Clemmie and I looked like dishevelled hippies, and Hugh just looked weird. Occupying the cool corner was Guy, in a loose linen shirt and drawstring trousers and aviator shades and with artfully gelled hair. Jutta had one bare foot propped on a chair in front of her. There was a large sticking plaster on her big toe. The sole of her foot was yellow and looked unattractively like the rind of a Dutch cheese. I chose to ignore the injury but Clemmie, ever kind, said, 'Oh dear! That looks sore. What have you done?'

'Bloody swimming pool at the hotel!' she said crossly. 'All the tiles were coming up and I stubbed my toe. They can't do anything properly in Africa.'

'Where on earth is our food?' asked Jeremy loudly, signalling to the waiters, who lolled under a tree and watched us with a marked lack of interest. They stirred themselves a little, changed their positions and then settled down again. Waiting was obviously the name of the game.

Hugh and I sat at the end of the table and Clemmie went back inside to find the loo. She was gone a long time, and when she re-emerged and stepped into the dappled sunshine the pink skirt shimmered about her legs, and her hair, which she had loosened, floated round her shoulders in a shining, lifting wave. She looked as if she was walking through a cloud of golden dust. Behind her came a little troop of waiters bearing trays on which balanced beer bottles filmed with cold, glasses, plates, knives, baskets of bread and finally omelettes and bowls of golden chips. It was like the entrance of the Queen of Sheba.

'I ordered for us!' she explained to Hugh and me.

'I hope an omelette was all right for you, Hugh? It seemed the quickest and easiest thing.'

'Oh yeah! Thanks. Fine,' he said vaguely. He obviously didn't care what he ate. Which of his senses were in proper working order? I wondered.

At the other end of the table I could see Jeremy bristle. He got to his feet. 'This is ridiculous!' he exclaimed. 'We ordered half an hour before you! Here!' he called to one of the waiters. 'Food? Where is our food?' He spoke deliberately and loudly and tapped his watch with a finger.

'Do you mind if we start?' I said. 'It seems a shame to let this get cold. Here, Jutta, would you like a chip?'

After we had finished our omelettes, some fried chicken and bowls of rice arrived for the others. Jutta took bottles of soy, Tabasco and Worcester Sauce from her bag and put them on the table. 'I always travel with these,' she explained. 'Jeremy calls them "culinary anaesthetic". They help to make impossible food edible.' However, the chicken, which swam in thick yellow oil, was evidently extremely tough. It was built like an athlete, with no breast and enormous sinewy legs. 'Honestly!' she said impatiently. 'You'd think that they could at least cook chicken!'

She pushed it aside and liberally splashed soy sauce on to her rice.

Jeremy and Guy were having one of those beer conversations so beloved of men, and it seemed that the local Castel which we were drinking was considered okay. Hugh took a book out of his backpack and began to read. It was called *Redefining Animism in the Light of the Colonial Experience.*

After the others had finished eating they began to discuss the rest of the trip, having gleaned more information from Mokhtar on the journey from Bamako.

'This afternoon we go on to a place called Sévaré,' said Jeremy to us all, in a company chairman voice, 'where we stay the night. I gather that from there it's basically left to Timbuktu and right to the Dogon country and straight on to the elephants and where these two girls are wanting to go, so we've got a slight conflict of interests. Old Guy here wants to hang a left to photograph some of the mud mosques along the river, and Hugh, presumably you want to get into the Dogon country as quickly as possible? Mokhtar suggests that you should explore along the Bandiagara escarpment which is the site of the ancient cliff dwellings. Meanwhile Jutta and I are extremely keen to track down these elephants. We may or may not be lucky. It would be a tremendous coup to get some photographs of them because they are the most elusive and mysterious herd in Africa.'

He paused. Whatever came next would somehow work out to his and Jutta's advantage, I knew that much.

'So, what I suggest is that tomorrow we split up. You boys take Serufi and do your thing, and the girls and Jutta and I will press on northwards with Mokhtar. He reckons that from Sévaré, it's half a day's drive to Gourma, where the elephants are most likely to be. They come for water, you see, and that is where the rains create these large temporary lakes. The place where the girls are supposed to leave us, according to Mokhtar, is along that stretch of road, so we can drop them off as we go by. If we are lucky and catch up with the herd, then Guy can come on and join us.' He smiled round the table. 'Doesn't that seem to make sense to everyone?' We all nodded, not feeling up to making any objections.

Serufi and Mokhtar reappeared. Mokhtar had removed his yellow headdress and without it he looked altogether less exotic and imposing. His black hair was very short, like a woolly cap, and threaded with springs of silver. He was older than I had thought at first. He and Jeremy and Guy were now very chummy and there was a lot of joshing.

'This is a good man,' said Guy admiringly, giving Mokhtar one of his cigarettes. 'You should have heard some of his stories on the way up here. He was a rebel in the Tuareg wars. He used to be a smuggler across the Algerian border.'

Mokhtar shrugged modestly.

'Mokhtar,' I said, not liking the sound of any of this, 'Clemmie and I need to talk to you about our arrangements. I'm not at all happy with this idea of leaving us at the roadside. Who is it exactly that we are supposed to be meeting tomorrow?'

'A cousin,' said Mokhtar airily. 'No worries, ladies. Ahmada is my cousin. He is from Kidal, in the desert. He takes you there, pronto. He is important man. He knows all Tuareg in Kidal. He will help you. It is his pleasure.'

I had to be satisfied with that.

Later, as we drove through the outskirts of Ségou, Clemmie and I were surprised to spot the Elder Tour coach pulled up outside Hotel Dogon – 'Drop in for Antiquities' – and the last few passengers being shipped aboard. Gloria, unwisely wearing square-legged three-quarter-length trousers and a smock top which made her even more of a breeze-block, was standing at the door with her clipboard. The last person up the steps was a small elderly man in danger of tottering backwards under the weight of a very large carved wooden female figure with long pendulous breasts. I had the feeling he might come to think of it as a mistake when he eventually wrestled it back to Arkansas. There was no sign of Kathleen or Mabel and I hoped that they were all right and holding up in the heat.

'I wonder where on earth they can be heading?' said Clemmie.

'There are Christian churches between Ségou and Sévaré which are supported by American Protestants,' said Hugh, and at that moment we saw one, standing back from the road in a patch of green, like a sudden view of New England: a white-painted church with a tin roof and a steeple on which there was a wooden cross.

This time Hugh was sitting next to Serufi, with Clemmie, me and Great-Aunt Mary in the back. Serufi was much more animated now he had someone he could talk to and we were also able to ask him questions through Hugh as an interpreter. It turned out that he was not a nomadic Tuareg at all and didn't much like camels. He lived in a mud house in a desert town in Algeria and earned his living driving tourists about.

'But there can't be that many tourists in the Sahara,' I said.

'Enough, I think. Quite a few anthropologists and archaeologists want to be taken to see the cave paintings in the mountains. It's a bit easier now the civil war is over in Algeria and the fighting has stopped in Mali. Also the few travellers in the Sahara would be mad to consider crossing the desert without a guide. It's much too dangerous.'

'So is he an exception? That he's not leading a traditional nomadic life, I mean?'

'I don't think he's that's untypical,' said Hugh. 'You see, the Tuaregs came off very badly when their traditional territories were carved into countries by the French. They now find themselves spread across Niger, Mali, Algeria, Burkina Faso and Libya. Traditionally they would have crossed and recrossed these borders to trade.'

He asked Serufi a question and there was another long reply.

'Serufi says that when he was a boy his tribe used to take animals across to Algeria to sell and brought back all the things that they needed to survive in the desert – like flour and dates, sugar and tea. Luxuries too, like carpets and cloth, if they were well off. Nowadays they are prevented by the military and Customs and they are expected to pay taxes and this is very hard for them to accept when they get nothing from the government in return.'

Serufi, fascinated by this translation of his words, looked across at Hugh and nodded, and added something. His comical face was grave.

'He says it is a poor outlook for nomadic people clinging to their traditional way of life in the desert. There have been years of droughts and they have virtually no help from the government, which controls foreign aid. The most desperate are forced to drift to towns to survive. They then have to buy firewood and water – which are all free in the desert. He says he is an exception. He is lucky to have made the transition and to get work with tourists. On the whole, the urban Tuareg is not a happy man.'

'What about these people that you are studying? These Dogons? Are they very different? They're not nomads, are they?'

'No, they're a completely different people. Tuaregs are Berber in origin, I think, whereas the Dogons probably came from the Nile valley and are pastoralists.

They live in one particular area, an isolated hundred-and-twenty-five-mile escarpment, and their ancient inbred way of life has resulted in a unique animist culture. Of course, after colonisation they became a magnet to French anthropologists, and now, unfortunately, to tourists. You must have seen photographs of Dogons – their stilt-dancers and their extraordinary masks are well known.'

'I saw them on websites when I was looking up Mali,' said Clemmie. 'They look amazing. What are animists anyway?'

'They attribute a living soul to all natural objects – trees, boulders, clouds, thunderstorms and so on.'

Clemmie looked entranced. 'Oh Hugh! That's so lovely! I must be an animist then. I had no idea that there was an actual religion that believed all of that. I've always felt natural objects have a spirit of their own. I've known for ages that I am not a born Church of England person, not with that hairy archbishop who looks as if he came from the rare breeds shop.'

Hugh looked at her blankly and then fell silent.

'What is the subject of your research?' I asked.

'I don't think you'd be interested,' he said diffidently.

'I am. Really.'

'Well, I'm studying the recurring myth of men who

can fly. The Dogons believe that they flew to the Bandiagara escarpment. It is a myth that is repeated in many other primitive cultures across the world and I am trying to establish if there is any common ground between them.'

'The Dogons *are* just like us, Em!' cried Clemmie. 'We always hoped to fly when we were little. Look, Hugh, here!' and she pushed her hair away from her white forehead. Hugh turned his head to look. 'See this?' she said, tracing a thin silvery line that ran down her brow from her hairline. 'It's a scar,' she said. 'When we were eight, Emily and I tried to fly. I was so sure I could do it that I jumped out of a hay loft on the farm. I had to have fourteen stitches. I really think that I must have been a Dogon in a previous incarnation, don't you?'

Hugh stared at her incredulously and rubbed a hand across his face. He could not find the words to answer.

The afternoon sweltered past. Hugh dozed in the front with his Arab scarf wrapped round his head to prevent it knocking against the passenger side window. Serufi put on the radio and listened to softly playing Arabic music. Clemmie curled up and slept, her hair spread over her face, her golden lashes fluttering. I watched the country flying past, the road a straight line through flat brown fields and occasional villages in which camp-fires burned outside mud and straw huts. Goats and sheep crowded in the shade under the trees. Naked children chased chickens and dogs and snatches of their screams came drifting through the open window. Women pounded millet, turning the chore into a graceful parabola of movement. Tall men rode very small and sprightly donkeys laden with wood at a smart trot along the dirt track beside the road.

I realised that I hadn't thought of Ted all day.

Clemmie

IT WAS DARK when we reached Sévaré. We knew we were coming into a town when huts and shacks began to crowd alongside the road, lit by lamps and campfires, and then concrete and mud-brick buildings loomed out of the dark. The sky was vast and black, studded with stars, unlike the lurid yellow of a night over any English town. We sat up and stretched. It had been a very long day and we had only stopped twice to pee, Emily and I squatting side by side behind a scant thorn bush, the burning sun striking our bare bottoms, both terrified that the huge ants and beetley things, as large as a thumbnail, which scuttled away across the parched brown earth would regroup and come back and bite us.

Serufi had driven uncomplainingly, as cautiously and carefully as he had begun that morning, hours earlier. As the sun went down he pulled over and stopped and got out, took his prayer mat out of his bag and without a word trotted a little way off to pray. We got out to stretch our legs and watched him without speaking – a small kneeling figure bowing down to the ground, dark against a huge fiery sky. I thought of what Hugh had told us about animism and I could see that you would have to believe in something in this country where the natural world was so vast and powerful and showy. The lazy, don't care, not-for-me attitude to religion that prevailed amongst most of my friends in England would not stand you in good stead out here. I thought of Great-Aunt Mary on the back seat of the jeep, travelling to her final resting place, and already this strange journey started to feel like something else – like a sort of pilgrimage.

At last we pulled up towards the centre of the ramshackle town, which stretched out in low buildings on either side of the broad road. Serufi negotiated his way through a set of double gates into a small parking area outside what appeared to be a hotel. The Toyota was already there, being washed down by a man with a striped plastic bucket. Out in the road, beyond the gates, a clamour of street vendors jostled and called,

'Missee! Come see! Silver! Jewellery! Carpets! Come see! Very fine antiquities!'

Serufi indicated that we should go inside while he unloaded the truck. There was no sign of the others but the man behind the desk seemed to know who we were. He put down two room keys on the counter and showed us that we should follow a boy who was staggering through the door with the backpacks. The hotel seemed to be of two storeys and built round a large courtyard in which tall trees were strung with fairy lights. Our boy climbed some stairs and then took us along an outside passage past a row of battered metal doors. He stopped at one and unlocked it for Hugh, and then took us on to another where he dropped our bags and fitted the key in the lock. The door swung back to reveal a bare concrete room with two wooden beds and a chair. He reached for the light switch, which had come away from the wall and was dangling by its wires. Sparks shot out but a strip light covered in wire mesh, like in a butcher's shop, stuttered brightly with a buzzing noise. In the centre of the ceiling hung an enormous fan, like an aeroplane propeller, and the boy showed us how to work it from controls on the wall. I was quite ready for him to be electrocuted but instead the huge blades began to move slowly and a roaring started in the background. When the fan was up to speed the noise was like a large diesel lorry labouring up a hill and we had to shout above it to make ourselves heard.

'Are there any towels?' yelled Emily, looking over at the bare beds. 'Or sheets, or pillows?'

The boy shook his head. 'Hotel full,' he shouted back sadly. 'No towels, no sheets.'

'Bloody hell!' said Emily, but I pointed out that we could sleep in our sleeping bags and we both had small towels in our packs. I gave the boy a handful of change and he backed out. When he had gone we looked about us and even Emily laughed.

'It's a bit like an abattoir, isn't it?' I shouted. 'Only noisier. Would you rather switch this thing off and boil?'

'Yeah!' shouted Emily. 'Much!' I didn't dare touch the switch, not after the sparks, but I remembered that you had to be earthed to get a shock, so I pushed the bed close enough for me to flick the switch in mid-air as I jumped off. This took several tries to synchronise properly and by then Emily was doubled up with laughter. The engine noise died and the fan slowed down and stopped. The silence was thick and heavy and buzzed with heat.

'I could open these,' said Emily, pointing to the heavy wooden shutters over the window. She began to wrestle with the rusty metal bolt and then banged at the shutters with her hands. They were stuck. She tried again with more force and the handle flew off and clattered on to the floor and then the right-hand shutter, which had creaked open, fell to pieces and dropped into a banana tree outside the window.

We rolled on our beds, weak with laughing.

'We'll catch something awful from these mattresses,' I said when I could talk. 'Look at them. They're all stained and disgusting.'

'Yuck! And look at the bloody beetles!' said Emily. There was an orderly line of them, like a well-drilled black army, along the base of the far wall.

'Where are they going?'

'Into a hole, thank God. They must be getting out the other side or they would be banking up, wouldn't they?'

I rolled off the bed and tiptoed over the concrete floor to look at the shower room. There was a lavatory without a seat and a pipe sticking out of the wall at head height, above a wonky tap.

'It's bliss!' I reported. 'A sit-down lav.' The water which trickled from the tap was stone cold.

'It's New Year's Eve!' called Emily from the bedroom. 'I'd forgotten. Isn't it lovely to be here and not having to force the jollity at some gruesome get-together at home?'

I wondered whether she was thinking about Ted and what he was doing. I was glad, though, that she had admitted it was lovely.

'It would be even worse to be a Scot, spending the evening in a tartan sash, carrying a lump of coal and a bit of cake called a bannock. Isn't that what they do? First-footing or something?'

'I was sick in someone's handbag once,' confessed Emily, 'as the clock struck midnight.'

'Emily! That's disgraceful! Don't listen, Great-Aunt Mary!' Pug Bag was on the floor between our beds, bright-eyed and pink-tongued as ever.

We were working ourselves up to being childish and giggly. We lay on our beds and laughed, amusing ourselves in exactly the way we had done since we were small. Then Emily went to have a shower and emerged naked, toothbrush in hand, to tell me that she had forgotten she should not have used water from the tap to clean her teeth.

'Do you think I'll get dysentery or some other water-borne disease?' she asked. 'The one where worms eat through your eyeballs?'

'I expect you will,' I assured her.

She reappeared with her big toe wrapped in a wad of lavatory paper. 'Who am I?' she said with a bad-smell look on her face, which set me off laughing again.

There was a bang on our metal door, and through the wide gap between it and the floor we could see a pair of deck shoes and a few inches of yellow trouser leg. Emily grabbed her towel, which was far too small to cover any part of her very adequately, and we snorted with laughter. There was no door to the shower room and nowhere to hide.

'Who is it?' I called unnecessarily. I bet there was only one pair of Rupert Bear trousers in Sévaré on that or any other night.

'Jeremy!'

'Just a minute!' Emily was hopping up and down, tossing clothes out of her backpack, searching for something to wrap herself in.

I opened the door a crack. Jeremy was standing outside looking very smooth and groomed, with his hair wet and combed back, and wearing a pressed pale blue shirt. He looked in curiously, and following his gaze I saw that Emily, as a last resort, had got into her sleeping bag.

'Aren't you a bit hot in that?' he said. 'We managed to get ourselves moved into a room with air con. What a dump this is!'

'We love it,' I said. In actual fact, I really did. I couldn't have loved it more if I had tried. He looked at me as if I was mad.

'Anyway, we obviously can't get a decent meal here tonight. Mokhtar has agreed to take us to Mopti, where there are some quite good fish restaurants, so we've been told. Do you girls want to come? We're leaving in ten minutes or so.'

Emily and I looked at one another.

'It's very kind of you,' she said, 'but we think we'll stay here, don't we, Clem? We've had enough of sitting in a car.'

'Please yourselves,' said Jeremy, shrugging. He had another peer at Emily, who was looking quite fetching with her wet hair round her shoulders, holding the bag up against her breasts. 'Shame, though! New Year's Eve and all that!' and off he went along the passage.

When Emily and I eventually pulled ourselves together we realised that there was a lot of activity in the courtyard below, and then suddenly the fairy lights twinkled on and hanging out of the window we saw that there were tables set amongst the trees. Then there was a loud bang and the lights went out and after a lot of scuffling about in the dark the waiters started to put candles on the tables instead.

'Look!' said Emily. 'They are making a party for us!'

We got dressed and went downstairs. By now there were several tables occupied and the waiters were wearing tall silver paper cones, like upturned cornets, on their heads and looking very festive. We were shown to a table, beautifully laid with red-and-white paper cloths and napkins, and given a 'Menu du Reveillon'. We ordered beer and had a look at the other diners, who seemed to be small French tour parties with the air of weary travellers. Some of the women were wearing shorts, especially the ones with the most unfortunate legs. I was glad that Em and I had dressed up in floaty, sparkly things, to give the waiters a bit of encouragement.

Over by the wall we could see our fallen shutter lodged in the banana tree, but fortunately there was no table underneath. Next to us was a young man eating on his own, looking very solitary and miserable, and so, fired with New Year bonhomie, I asked him if he would like to join us. '*Non merci!*' he cried, looking most alarmed, and then bolted his meal and rushed out. I had obviously wrecked his evening and Emily said that he must have thought we were voracious women who were intending to drug him and force him to perform unnatural sex acts. I couldn't think of anything worse on such a hot night, but then a Frenchwoman at the next table explained that he was a madman from Lyons who was bicycling across the Sahara on his own.

We ate pumpkin soup and a bony capitaine fish from the river and duck and tinned peas and a slice of coffee gateau, and it was all delicious. Afterwards we went and got our torches and did an arm-in-arm race down the road outside the hotel to have a look at the town. The road was pitch black and full of potholes and pools of water and there were a lot of people about, sitting outside the shops on those white plastic picnic chairs which by now must be found in every corner of the earth, or lounging round fires. We were chased by a little crowd of vendors and men pleading with us to go to a nightclub. There was nothing to see except ramshackle bars and shops selling sacks of flour and tins of condensed milk, so we ran back again.

This time Emily stopped to look at the coolie-like hats that were hung about a very tall man with dazzling tombstone teeth who said that his name was Bill. Hugh had explained to us that these were the hats worn by the Peul people, another of Mali's ethnic groups, who are semi-nomadic and herd cattle and goats. The hats are conical and made of leather and woven grasses and are very strange and beautiful. Bill had the finest example on his own head. He wore it on top of his black headcloth and it looked very stylish indeed, really rather Audrey Hepburn by Cecil Beaton for *Vogue*. Emily and I tried some on and the crowd around us grew, with men pressing us to buy their jewellery or cigarettes or keyrings or hideous nylon blankets made in Taiwan. They thought we were very amusing and cracked up at the sight of us in the hats, especially me. I was the biggest joke of all and I had never before seen people actually slapping their thighs while they hooted with laughter. They wanted to touch my hair and the boldest of them put out their hands to stroke it. Rather a smart know-all teenager who spoke English tried to persuade us to go to a Dogon festival with him the next day. He annoyed Emily by calling her 'mama' and me 'missy'. He said that the men were laughing because at first they had thought I was a ghost. They did not know how I could be so pale and still be alive. I could see that we were going to have the hardest time extricating ourselves, especially from

Bill, who was very insistent that we should buy his hats and kept offering us ever lower bargain prices. Eventually we just had to make a run for it, but not before Emily did a deal with him and promised that she would come back in the morning when she had some money with her. That made the parting a little less painful for him but he still stood as close as he could get to the hotel gate, waving us off.

It was a relief to get back inside the compound and we stopped to check the time. It was still only eleven o'clock. Very loud disco music had started up and we followed the sound to a large concrete room with tables and chairs stacked in the corners. It was entirely empty except for two of the youngest waiters, about fourteen years old, who were dancing to 'You Sexy Thing', still wearing their pointy silver hats. Emily and I couldn't resist joining in, which they found hilarious. Their dancing got ever more wonderful and we whirled and stomped and leaped about until just before midnight, when we asked them to get us some beers so that we could drink to the New Year. We sat on one of the tables and swung our legs and swigged the beer and watched the second hand of Emily's watch. When it reached midnight we clinked the bottles and drank to each other and Em made a speech about our family and friends and what we wished for them for the coming year. It went on and on because she had to work through all my brothers, and we toasted each one with a clash of our bottles. Our two waiters listened open-mouthed and then we toasted them and showed them how to join hands to sing 'Auld Lang Syne'.

It was the nicest New Year's Eve I had ever had.

Back in the courtyard garden some of the French groups were celebrating in a fairly gloomy way and we waved to them on our way past to bed. We wondered how the rest of our party were getting on in Mopti. I couldn't believe, even with their duty-free champagne, that they could have had a better time than us.

The following morning we woke when it got light. Emily was grumpy again and sat up in bed and counted the bites she had acquired during the night and made me write down the number in my diary. She wanted her suffering to be documented and said that she had now probably got malaria as well as the disease contracted from the water. I swear that I hadn't slept at all but I suppose I must have done. The bed was very hard and my neck was stiff. The morning was not yet warm and the thought of the icy shower was not all that appealing, but we forced ourselves and felt better when we had ducked under the tap.

We had been told that we had an early start, and because I was ready long before Em, who was searching in her bag for the antihistamine cream, I went on down to breakfast and found the tables had been set in the room where we had danced the night before. There was no sign of the rest of our party, just a few of the French travellers complaining about the bad coffee and the stale bread. I sat down, and after a bit a large, unsmiling woman, her bare feet slapping on the concrete floor, brought me a tin jug of watery coffee and a basket of bread. I had my journal with me, and as I ate I began to write down the events of the previous day.

I looked up a few minutes later when I sensed a change in the atmosphere. It was like those experiments in school physics lessons when an electrical charge is activated and sparks begin to fly across a space between two electrodes. The cause of this sudden reaction was an extraordinary figure crossing the room, dressed in a swirling dark red robe, the face entirely veiled in an indigo head cloth wrapped round and round to form a turban. As it came closer I saw dark eyes flash through a narrow slit in the cloth. The figure paused. I knew it had to be a man because of its height and breadth of shoulder, but he was lissome and graceful as a dancer. He looked round and then came on, all energy and movement, drawing the colour from the rest of the room and stirring the torpid atmosphere so that the lazy, slow-moving waitress started forward to prepare a table and the French parties went quiet and followed him with their eyes.

He stopped at a table next to mine and sat down and I saw that his clothes were dusty and travel-worn and realised that the extraordinary outfit was normal everyday wear. I felt totally overwhelmed by his presence and did not look across at him but kept my eyes on my book, only peeping under my lashes when I dared. I saw him reach inside the robe and draw out a stubby revolver, which he placed on the table in front of him as if it was the most ordinary thing in the world, and then take out a packet of cigarettes. Between the folds of cloth his eyes took in the room and then rested on me. I felt I could hardly breathe. His gaze was bold and unwavering and because his face was hidden it was impossible to tell if the stare was friendly or hostile. The dark eyes glittered and the beautiful fine-boned hand played with the cigarette packet. Then the moment of suspense was broken and he looked away from me to call the waitress. His voice was deep and resonant, and she shouted back and hurried from the kitchen with coffee and bread, and he turned away to smoke and eat so that his face was shielded from the room. He was noisy and restless, gathering staff round him, exchanging news, I imagined, draining his cup, calling for more, and all the time I felt he was conscious of the effect he created and was enjoying it. He glanced at me from time to time and I tried to pretend that I was absorbed in my journal, but the whole performance was mesmerising and I hoped so much that Emily would show up before it was over. Of course I realised that he was a Tuareg, but he was the first I had seen who made no concessions to the west, unlike Serufi and Mokhtar, and all the words that I had read to describe Tuareg men – mysterious, proud, aristocratic, imperious – were those that now came to mind.

He sat at the table for perhaps ten electrifying minutes and then he was on his feet, the revolver tucked into a belt, some coins thrown on the table, more shouting and he was off, whirling between the tables. At the last moment Emily came through the door and they met head on. I nearly cheered and clapped, her entrance was so perfectly timed. I saw her stare, her eyes wide, taking in the full apparition, until he stepped back politely with a little bow and then was gone. Emily looked after him and then across the room at me and made a 'wow!' kind of face.

Through the long windows I could see the man swing out across the car park to a battered, dusty pick-up, exactly like the one belonging to Emily's father that had taken Great-Aunt Mary to the crematorium. Then, just as he was climbing into the driver's seat, there was more shouting and he got out again. I was intrigued to see that it was Serufi and Mokhtar whom he got out to greet and it looked as if they were his oldest and dearest friends.

Emily, who had missed all this, came across the room and sat down opposite me. I saw that she was carrying a Peul hat.

'My God!' she said. 'Who the hell was that?'

'Look!' I pointed out of the window. 'He knows our men. We'll have to ask them. But he's a Tuareg, Em! A proper Tuareg! Wasn't he fabulous? God, those eyes! I am just terribly disappointed that there wasn't a camel waiting for him outside. He's got an old Ford pick-up like your dad's.'

Emily stared out of the window. 'I've never seen

anyone have quite that effect,' she said. 'I mean, he's obviously tall and slim, which helps, but the get-up is just unbelievable. It's such a strange concept – a veiled man – but it's so alluring. I always think of veiled women as being oppressed, but the opposite is true when you see a man wrapped up like that. It seems to enhance his physical presence. He seemed so, well, *powerful*. Phew!' She fanned her face with her hand.

Outside the matiness was continuing and I saw Mokhtar say something and then all three men turned to stare through the window to where we sat in the dining room. 'They're talking about us!' I said to Emily, and because it seemed rude not to acknowledge them, I gave a little wave. Serufi and Mokhtar grinned and waved back, and to my delight the veiled man lifted one long brown hand in salute. There was a little ripple around the breakfast tables. The French women in their shorts, with their manly haircuts and big Velcro explorers' sandals, missed nothing. They turned to stare. They recognised me as the girl who had terrified the cyclist the night before.

'Look,' said Emily, breaking into a hard, crumbly roll. 'I've got the hat. Bill was out there waiting for me.' She put it on the table and together we admired the painstaking workmanship, the decorated leather and the tiny stitches that held the woven grasses in place.

'It's really beautiful,' she said, 'but I don't know why I bought it. Whatever will I do with it when I get it home? I don't even have anywhere permanent to live! I'll be wearing it sitting in a cardboard box.'

'You had to buy it,' I said. 'It was meant for you. It doesn't have to have a function. It's just a lovely thing to have. Anyway, you couldn't have disappointed poor old Bill.'

Jutta's ringing tones could suddenly be heard across the room and then she and Jeremy, followed by Hugh and Guy, came to join us. She was carrying her own jar of Nescafé and was dressed, as yesterday, in proper safari gear.

'Good morning, you two!' said Jeremy pleasantly, leaning across to kiss us both. 'Happy New Year!' He smelled of fresh aftershave. Guy followed his example while Hugh managed to drop some cutlery and disappeared under the table. I asked them how they had got on in Mopti. Apparently they had been disappointed because when they got there the town was in darkness and it wasn't possible to see the river. They had to content themselves with the sound of the water slapping against the harbour and the smell of rotting fish. They had had a reasonable dinner but it had been a long way to drive and the champagne was warm and shaken up.

We told them about our evening while Jutta began organising the waitress, sending back the bread as stale and trying to get hot water for her coffee. Eventually she got up and went into the kitchen to sort it out and we could hear her explaining what she wanted very loudly and clearly. Hugh said nothing and stared into space and Jeremy and Guy talked about the women they had seen in Mopti and discussed whether they were sexy and what exactly made them so. Emily glared.

Jutta came back with a jug of hot water and said, 'Would you believe it? They have nothing but UHT or tinned milk, and in a country stuffed with bloody cows!'

'One in particular!' said Emily distinctly. Hugh's head shot up to give her a look but the others did not seem to hear, although perhaps Jutta did, because the next moment she spotted Emily's hat hanging by its leather string on the back of her chair.

'You didn't buy one of those things, did you?' she asked in an incredulous voice.

'Hmmm!' said Emily.

'What? From one of those men hanging around outside?'

'Yes.'

'What did you pay for it?'

Emily told her and Jeremy did a quick calculation.

'Ten pounds? You must be completely mad,' he said. 'You could have got that for a couple of quid. You have to bargain with these people, you know. It's what they expect. Ten pounds was way too much. Way too much. You was robbed, my dear.'

'I don't think so,' said Emily stubbornly, but Jutta was getting up a head of steam.

'This country will be ruined, you know, if tourists start paying those sort of prices,' she said in a preachy voice. 'It will soon be more profitable to hang around these wretched hotels trying to flog rubbish to foreigners than it is to do a proper job. Then what happens is that they keep their children out of school to beg. Ten pounds is what they probably *live on* for six months!' She started to butter her bread and slapped on a layer of jam.

'I paid what the hat was worth to me!' said Emily fiercely. Her face had gone very red. 'I don't care if I could have beaten him down to fifty pence. People like you make me sick, boasting about how cheaply you've managed to buy things from really, really poor people, proud of the wonderful bargains you strike. It's obscene, coming from people who have everything. You think the whole bloody world is yours to get at a knock-down price.'

A chill silence fell on our table. Jutta stopped chewing. Even Hugh looked up.

'Don't be silly!' said Jutta, as if she was talking to a difficult child. 'All I was saying . . . Jeremy, back me up on this . . . is that while we were in Kenya last year—'

'I don't want to hear, thank you,' said Emily, getting up and holding her hat in both hands in front of her like a shield. 'I've finished my breakfast. I'm going to wait outside.'

After she had gone Jutta said, 'Well! I never thought she'd fly off the handle like that!' She looked round the table for reinforcement.

Jeremy laughed. 'Girls! What are they like! Wrong time of the month, I expect!' Guy sniggered. I got up and followed Emily.

I found her sitting in the sun on a low wall where the jeeps and minibuses were being loaded by their drivers. She still looked red in the face – exactly as she used to when we had a bust-up when we were children. Emily can be very fierce. She's a Taurean and is true to type. In fact she is exactly like a bull we had on the farm called Homer. He was a peaceful old thing as a rule but every now and then he went on the rampage. Once he galloped straight through six wire fences and broke two gates.

Jutta didn't know Emily well enough to recognise the telltale signs, but I had seen her shaking her head and pawing the ground and knew that if further provoked she would get dangerous.

We sat in silence for a bit and watched the French groups sorting themselves out and climbing into their buses. Quite a few of them had bought Peul hats, which were proving difficult to stow away. I hoped that Bill had made a killing.

When Mokhtar appeared, cigarette in hand and with his head wrapped in his lovely yellow scarf, I asked him about the man we had seen at breakfast. He laughed, showing his perfect, very white teeth.

'This man is cousin. His name is Tayen. He lives between here and Burkino Faso. He is a customs officer but he comes from the north. His grandfather has many, many camels. We tell him of your journey and he is impressed – two beautiful young ladies who travel alone in the desert. He wishes to accompany you!'

Goodness, I thought. Yes please. But I could see that it was said in a joking way. It seemed that Mokhtar had a lot of cousins and I hoped that the one who was to meet us on the road would be as wonderful.

Mokhtar noticed Emily's hat and I held my breath as he examined it and asked her how much she had paid. I thought she might say 'mind your own business', but when she told him he said, 'This is fair price. Many, many hours of work to make this hat.' Emily beamed.

At that moment Hugh appeared. He had wrapped his head in a similar style to Mokhtar and had applied thick white sun cream to his bony nose. I was glad that he arrived in time to hear Mokhtar's comment, because he nodded and said, 'You were quite right back there,' in his funny quiet, academic voice. 'These hats are beautifully crafted. They are not tourist rubbish. Each one is a work of art.'

'You might have bloody well said so,' said Emily, but I could tell that she was pleased.

'Look!' I said, pointing to the crowd gathered round the gate. 'There's that pushy boy who wanted us to go to his Dogon party!'

Hugh pricked his ears up at that and shot off to find out more while Emily and I were taken by

Mokhtar to a bazaar-like shop to buy lengths of cotton muslin for headdresses which we were told were called *chech* in Arabic and *tagelmoust* in Tamashek. I bought a lavender-coloured length and Emily bought blue, the colour of the Mali sky. Mokhtar told us that in Tuareg society the more material a man had wrapped round his head, the more important he was.

When we got back to the hotel it was time to leave. Hugh was very excited by what he had found out from the teenager and was going off with him in a very ancient taxi. Apparently the ceremony was one he had always wanted to see and certainly was not to be missed. He could hardly bear to delay in order to say goodbye, but he managed to shake our hands and wish us luck in a distracted way before he rushed off.

Guy kissed us both on both cheeks and said he hoped that we would catch up later and we bade goodbye to dear little Serufi. He was amused that we had bought ourselves the cheches, and he insisted on wrapping us up in them, round and round and then under our chins so that we both looked like Sister Annunciata who was the terror of our convent school.

Eventually Jeremy and Jutta appeared. Jutta and Emily pointedly ignored one another. Mokhtar sorted out their luggage while Jutta fussed over the whereabouts of an insulated cold bag containing a lump of foie gras which she had brought with her from France and which she and Jeremy wanted to have for lunch. Foie gras in the middle of Africa! I could hardly believe my ears but I knew that Great-Aunt Mary would have been pleased.

Beryl Timmis

NEW YEAR'S EVE was, thankfully, a non-event at The Willows. I felt sorry for the staff who had to be on duty and imagined that they would have much rather been at home or at a party with friends, but when I commiserated with Kathy she told me that she preferred to be at work. It saved her from having to go 'down the Legion' with her husband, who I gather is a drinker. With any luck, she said, by the time she got home he'd be out for the count. Of course the Christmas decorations are still up and there was a glass of sherry for those who wanted it before dinner at seven o'clock. There was only a handful of us to enjoy it, most of the other residents choosing to eat in their rooms and some already in bed.

I looked at the small glass of sweet sherry in my hand and thought of Mary, who would have taken a dim view of it. The moment the clock in the hall chimed six, she used to say, 'Sun's over the yardarm, Beryl. Time for a drink!' She would heave herself out of her chair – she wouldn't allow me to make her gin cocktail – and stump out to the kitchen. She always made sure there was ice and lemon and she was particular about the glass. It had to be a heavy lead crystal tumbler. Gin, Italian vermouth and a dash of Angostura Bitters – not something I could drink myself. It had a kick like a mule, Mary said. She was fussy about the gin, too. She said it was daylight robbery that a well-known brand sneakily reduced the alcohol content to below forty per cent. She went through all the bottles in the supermarket until she found one that was up to strength.

I don't believe that she drank for the pleasure of it. What she looked forward to each evening was the deadening of the senses that alcohol brings. Three stiff gins down the line and the world seemed a better place. Five o'clock was the worst hour of the day, she said, neither one thing nor the other, but as soon as the clock struck six and she had the glass in her hand, she was better. Now she has gone and I have all the time to think about the past, about her life and mine, I wonder how things might have been different for her. Children would have changed things. If Mary had had a family she would not have become the selfish, disappointed woman that she turned into. That sounds critical and unkind, but it is true. Too much time to think about oneself is not good for anyone, and I include myself in that category. I think she would have wanted children. She had a natural way with them, and although she could be sharp she enjoyed their company. She never had to play the part as I have always had to do. Children frighten me with their direct and unpredictable questions, their uninhibited behaviour. I think that they are judging me and finding me wanting and I hear myself adopting a false, bright tone. Big grown girls like Emily and Clemmie are also frightening in a different way. Quite without meaning to, they make me feel insignificant and my life pointless. I feel as if I am the living example of what they and all other modern girls have a fear of becoming – an old maid.

After Mary got back from Africa and had recovered her health, she told me that she couldn't have children. It was hard to know whether she minded, she was so strange at that time. After that she embarked on what was then a fast life – dating servicemen, sleeping with them, throwing them over and moving on. It was a relief when she settled down with Tim Kingsley, a dull but kind man. The evening that they got engaged they had a party in a London hotel. Tim looked as if he did not know what had hit him. He was not a sophisticated man – the son of a Dorset farmer – but he had done well in the army and looked dashing in uniform. He was no taller than Mary; a square man with a countryman's rough red cheeks and wavy brown hair. Mary looked beautiful although she was still too thin and wearing a pale blue crêpe dress which did not suit her sallow skin. Her long dark hair was dressed in a thick roll, secured with two combs. She laughed and smoked and drank and dragged Tim round by the hand to talk to their friends. I remember that when I congratulated her she pulled me into the powder room. 'Don't congratulate me,' she said. 'I don't want your congratulations. In many ways this is the worst day of my life.' I can't remember what I said. I don't think I would have been brave enough to suggest that if she felt like that she should not be marrying Tim. 'I would rather be dead,' she said.

I enjoyed the sherry, and John Fellowes, one of the presentable and compos mentis *male residents of The Willows and who is therefore much in demand, persuaded me to have another. This seemed to upset Susan Clifford-Jones, a stout widow with over-permed white hair and a large broken-veined face, who seems to consider him her property. She glared at me and made a point of excluding me from the conversation, so I talked instead to the foxhound colonel. He was very down in the mouth, poor old thing. Kathy said that he had believed he was going home for good, and that he had been distressed when he was delivered back to The Willows. He has a lot of falls and there is such a length of him to topple over, like a great tree bringing everything down in its path. He had fallen out of bed and cut his forehead and had spent Christmas Eve in Casualty in Yeovil hospital waiting to have it stitched. 'I'm a damn nuisance,' he said to me. 'Damn nuisance, that's what I am. Just another thing for Caroline to worry about.' He was so downcast that he didn't even want to talk about hounds. His lower lip trembled and his huge liver-spotted hands plucked at the legs of his trousers as we sat in the drawing room waiting for dinner. He was such a fine old gentleman that I could not believe anyone would find him a nuisance and his impeccable manners never deserted him even if his mind wandered. Kathy said the staff all loved him. I would have liked to tell him this but didn't feel that I knew him well enough, and not with Susan Clifford-Jones listening. She is not a woman I care for very much. She has assured me that she is only staying while she recovers from a hip replacement operation and I don't like the way she refers to some of the residents as senile within their hearing.*

Dinner was roast pork. It was perfectly all right, but the crackling was like strips of orange rubber and the roast potatoes were pale and flabby. What Mary would have thought of it does not bear repeating. The colonel tucked his napkin into his trousers, like an apron, and ate very fast. When he had finished he sat back like a schoolboy waiting to be congratulated on having a clean plate. For pudding there was chocolate mousse in small plastic tubs with a squirt of foam cream on the top. The colonel picked up his tub and rapidly spooned the mousse into his mouth from under his chin.

When we got up to go into the lounge for coffee, he fumbled with the buttons of his tweed jacket and did it up wrongly, all skewwhiff. The pointed end of the napkin, which was still tucked into his trousers, hung down beneath the jacket like a strange sort of sporran. I saw Mrs C-J glance at it and make a disapproving face but there was nothing I could do – the front of the colonel's trousers being an area to which I felt I could not draw attention. One of the young assistants came in with the coffee tray, and although she is just a girl, a teenager, she laughed and said, 'Look at you, Colonel! What's this you've got here?' and pulled at the napkin and did his jacket up again. Her naturalness was such a relief. I am such a fool, you see, a silly old spinster, and I could tell that Mrs C-J was laughing at me. She said something under her breath to Mr Fellowes and he looked across at me and smiled, not at me, but at my old-maidish prudery.

After coffee there was the showing of a video on the large television, something about an unlikely group of Yorkshire ladies taking off their clothes for a calendar. Mrs Clifford-Jones thought it was hilarious and laughed out loud, clutching

Mr Fellowes' arm, and I managed to find my way out and go to my room without drawing attention to myself.

It's pleasant to sit here in the light of my little desk lamp and listen to my wireless. Kathy has tuned it in to Radio 4 and I am looking forward to the classic serial – Adam Bede *– which is on tonight. Today I asked Kathy if she could find me my old world atlas. I wanted to look up French Sudan and to remind myself of the country where Emily and Clemmie will have travelled today. She couldn't find it and now I wonder when I last saw it and realise it might have been years ago, before I even went to live with Mary in Dorset. That's what happens as you get older: memory plays tricks on you.*

Clemmie told me that they were travelling by road, whereas I went by boat as far as Gao. In those days it was the most usual way to travel upcountry unless one could get a ride in a light aircraft. The French had a good mail service to all the far-flung forts in the Sahara, but few passenger flights.

The schools inspector who accompanied me was on his way to the interior of the country to assess the possibility of opening native schools attached to the military outposts. On board the boat he spent the day in a deckchair in what little shade there was, drinking Pernod. The further we travelled up the river, the more depressed and taciturn he became.

He seemed to view the native population as being too

primitive to educate at all. It was a waste of time and he blamed the Frenchwomen – wives of army officers – for interfering and causing trouble. 'This is not a country for women!' he said sternly, at the same time as ogling some young French radio-telegraphists who were sunbathing on deck, their heads thrown back, their eyes closed behind their sunglasses and with their stockings rolled down to their ankles.

The boat was huge, slow and dirty, the lower decks packed with Senegalese soldiers and cargo, the upper deck reserved for paying passengers. On either side the river stretched, pale brown and soupy, fringed on the far shores with reeds and trees and the occasional village of thatched huts. The sky was white and trembling on the horizon and the terrible heat beat down.

My cabin was on the wrong side of the hull. The sun turned it into an oven a few hours after dawn and it was stifling all night. In the end I followed the example of the young Frenchwomen and dragged my mattress out on to the deck. I asked them if I could join them and they shrugged dismissively, looking me up and down, despising me for my unfashionable clothes and awkwardness. One of them, the prettiest one, was sleeping with the captain, disappearing after it had got dark, sometimes bringing cigarettes and bottles of wine back for her friends.

Ségou was our first stop and I was taken by the schools

inspector to spend a night in a small hotel on the river run by Lebanese brothers. I had my clothes washed and ate a simple supper in my room, grateful for the electric fan which stirred the hot wet air.

When we returned to the boat the French girls had vanished and I was too nervous to sleep alone on deck. The boat was less crowded now and I insisted on being moved to a different, cooler cabin. I had to give the steward an enormous tip and he leered at me unpleasantly. Four days later we arrived in Mopti. I saw the town on the horizon long before we got there, a clot of green trees, waterfront buildings, a busy port, a crane loading and unloading. Somewhere among the reeds the great river had divided and I was told that we were now chugging along on the Bani. We docked alongside a rusty old cargo boat filled with slabs of salt brought from Timbuktu. Smaller boats, slender as canoes, were mounded high with silver fish or huge pale green melons. Alongside the harbour were market stalls and pressing throngs of people, brightly dressed, some with flat baskets on their heads, these too heaped with fruit or fish or round bread. The brown flashes I saw in the water were children, jumping naked from the quayside, and then I realised that the shallows were crowded with naked people, men and women, quite openly washing themselves, the men's genitalia bobbing in the water, the women's flat breasts floating. Above them a restaurant was built out on piers over the water and I could see well-dressed Europeans and French army officers drinking and eating at tables with crisp white cloths.

It was early evening and the light was fading over the river while an enormous red sun floated on the horizon. By the time we disembarked it had vanished and night had fallen as if a black velvet curtain had been drawn across the sky. I was taken to a hotel near the river. The roads were beaten dirt and beggars crowded round our horse-drawn taxi. I suppose I stayed there one night, I can't remember now. I was to continue alone on the boat to Gao a further four days up the river. The schools inspector told me that French administrators loathed having to travel further north. Civilisation stopped in Mopti, where there was the possibility of a proper meal and a decent bottle of French wine and some interesting shooting on the marshes. The river teemed with hippopotami and crocodiles.

Further north was for the desert diehards, the peculiar men who could stand the isolation, the climate and the difficulty of dealing with the legendary blue men of the desert, the fearsome veiled Tuareg, who were notoriously rebellious. I gathered that there was some consolation for the men forced to serve there. Certain outposts had 'gone native' – the army officers mixing freely with the Tuareg women, who were rated as very beautiful. He spoke to me of harems. I did not know what to think. Surely Mary's father, the distinguished governor of this whole area, would not allow such a thing? It seemed very un-British, but what did one expect of the French?

When I came down for breakfast the next morning there was a telegram waiting for me. It was from Mary's father. I took it back to my room to read. He was going to meet me in Gao, where he was due to inspect the fort and where there was a residence, but Mary was not with him. She was too unwell to travel, he said, but he did not tell me what was the matter with her. He would try to make arrangements for me to go to her. My heart sank. This journey was proving too much for me and the thought of the long return trip overcame me. I remember feeling utterly desolate and unequal to the task. I was frightened of everything – of travelling alone on the boat, of meeting the eye of the insolent steward, who had started to brush past me on the narrow walkways, smirking as he pushed against me. I was frightened of eating on my own, of the mixed-race crew, whom I felt were always watching me, of the French captain, who stank of garlic and spoke to me in rapid French in an accent I did not understand. I was frightened of where I had been and where I was going. I was terrified of the throngs of native people, especially the women, who seemed so huge, their bodies gigantic barrels of blood and bone and muscle and glossy black skin, so confident and unconcerned as they shoved and pushed and shouted and laughed, their great red mouths open to reveal sharp white teeth. I felt small and shrivelled and horribly pale – a little dried-up moth, an empty papery husk.

I had a little cry, and then gave myself a talking-to and prayed on my knees beside my bed for the strength to continue. Prayer has been a comfort to me all my life. Afterwards I washed my face and went back down for breakfast. I asked the boy in the lobby to buy me some cigarettes and a lighter. If I smoked I would feel somehow older and more sophisticated – more like those knowing French girls who had got off the boat at Ségou. All my life I have had to pretend to be something other than myself. In my heart I know that I am not meek and quiet little Miss Timmis. That is a part I have learned to play – protective colouring to disguise the fact that I am really a rather nasty and selfish person.

I sit here in the pool of light thinking about that time so long ago and it distresses me to find that the memories are still so acute. I haven't thought about that journey for, oh, fifty years at least, but now the peace of my little room is disturbed by the return of those feelings of inadequacy. Mary has forced this on me. She must have known how little I want to revisit the past and she must have known that the journey she planned for Emily and Clemmie would make it impossible for me to escape. It was cruel of her. I am here at The Willows thanks to her generosity, but she has robbed me of my peace of mind.

Emily

THE PUG BAG was making life difficult for Clemmie. Every time we went anywhere, even got out of the jeep for a moment, it attracted attention. No one had ever seen anything like it before, the cult of ironic hand-made bags not having reached west Africa, although now we were in Dogon country it fitted in quite well with their weird tribal masks and talismans. Children clamoured to touch it, to pull the pink tongue, to pat its head, and worst of all to see what was inside. From what I had learned about Dogons, I gathered that they posted their dead into little square-cut caves way up the face of their sheer escarpment, which can't have been an easy task, and so they might have understood the nature of our journey and why it was so important – to Clemmie at least.

Clemmie did not dare take the pug bag off for one

moment, fearing that it would be stolen if she put it by her chair while she ate, or left it alone in a hotel room. It had to always be around her neck, like the bloody albatross, its beady black eyes ever watchful and its tummy plump and round with the remains of Great-Aunt Mary.

For my part, I thought it would be a good thing if it did get stolen. It would save us a lot of bother, and the longer this journey went on, the more clearly I understood just how far we were going and how absurd it was. I noticed at the hotel in Sévaré how our men talked to other drivers, and when they explained that we were travelling far into the north of the country there was a lot of teeth-sucking and head-shaking. No one but the foolhardy went that way. For a start there was nothing there except desert, and it was dangerous country where bandits trafficked over the Algerian border and eccentric Europeans trying to drive across the Sahara were kidnapped and worse. No wonder the customs officer had been excited about us – we were a pair of exotic sitting ducks.

Much as I felt at odds with Jutta and Jeremy, I had a strong sense that we were safe with them, and if they deposited us today on some desolate stretch of road then anything could happen. At the back of my mind

I wondered whether I could appeal to Jeremy, explain how worried I was about our expedition and ask him to have a go at dissuading Clemmie from setting off on our own. I nursed a hope that when we met this cousin of Mokhtar's we might hand over Great-Aunt Mary and pay him to go and scatter her on our behalf. When I looked out of the window at the endless featureless plains, growing ever more sandy and dry, I could not see why it mattered where she came to rest. One place was so very like another.

The passing traffic was now few and far between as we headed away from the tourist areas of Timbuktu and the Dogon country. Every now and then an overloaded lorry appeared as a black dot in the distance, growing larger and larger until it hurtled past with a blast on its horn, but mostly we bowled along on an empty road. This was cattle country, and although my father would have said there was no keep to speak of, we passed herds of glossy zebu cattle, hump-backed, deep-chested, wide-horned, being taken to water holes to drink. They were fine-looking beasts in very good condition. Any Dorset beef farmer would have been proud of them. I remarked on this to Mokhtar and he said, 'This has been a good year for rain. It is not always so.' Following the herds were small family groups, travelling on donkeys, carrying rolled-up tents and sacks of rice, the men wearing their Peul hats against the beating sun. They stared at us as we passed. Sometimes the children waved.

We came to a stop to let a huge herd of bulls cross the road – hundreds of them, tossing their heads and bellowing, driven by tall, rangy stockmen who raced about on foot with sticks in their hands. 'They're taking them to the Ivory Coast to sell,' explained Mokhtar. 'It will take them two weeks to walk from here.' I thought of my dad, who grumbled about loading our beef cattle to drive them to Taunton market thirty miles away.

Up ahead, in the shimmering distance, the flat brown plains were distorted in the heat and I thought I saw a great peak rising abruptly into the sky, and then another, like a sudden jagged alpine range. I watched until my eyes ached and I realised that they had not deceived me. A stranger outcrop I had never seen, rising high and sheer from the brown plain and glowing pink in the heat.

'Fatima's Hand!' said Mokhtar, pointing, and I saw what looked like rocky fingers and a flat palm held up against the pale, trembling sky.

'Extraordinary!' said Jeremy, hanging out of the

window to take photographs. 'Sandstone I'd guess, from the colour.'

'Very holy place,' said Mokhtar. 'The home of powerful spirits. No one may approach without permission of the village chief. The highest peak is seven hundred and thirty metres.'

We had driven in silence most of the way, but now Jeremy wanted to stop to take photographs of men making red mud bricks beside the road, amongst pools of water. He got out and walked a little way from the jeep but the men stopped working and stood in hostile little groups. 'Good morning, my friends!' he called cheerfully. '*Bonjour, mes amis*,' but the men glared and started to shout and throw stones.

'Wow!' he said, hopping back in and slamming the door. 'What was that about?'

Mokhtar shrugged. 'They think that you steal from them. The image of them in your camera is a theft.'

'Amazing, isn't it?' said Jutta. 'To be that primitive?' She looked at her watch. 'I'm bloody parched and starving. Can we stop somewhere soon, Mokhtar? We've been driving over four hours.'

'Certainly!' said Mokhtar obligingly. 'I look for a place,' and the next moment he had plunged the jeep off the road and set off across the dusty plain towards a thicket of spindly thorn trees amongst which a herd of goats scattered.

'Look!' said Clemmie to me. 'Aren't the goats perfect?' Each one was neatly divided into black and white squares, front half white and rear end black, or the other way round. 'They're Chanel goats. I adore them!' I saw Jutta raise her eyebrows at Jeremy and make a 'spare me' sort of face.

Mokhtar came to a stop under a tree, and when we climbed out we realised that a stiff hot wind had got up and the surface of the ground was on the move in little drifting waves of dust and sand.

'This wind is called *adu* in Tamashek' explained Mokhtar, sniffing the air like a dog. 'It blows always from east to west.' He busied himself at once, throwing mattresses down from the roof rack and inviting us to lie on them in a patch of shade beneath the tree while he collected grey and twisted thornwood to make a fire. I began to help him and wandered off to where there seemed to be a better supply lying under the next group of bony trees.

'I shouldn't do that if I was you!' called Jutta from her mattress. 'Unless you want to get bitten by a scorpion!'

'Oh, but I do,' I said under my breath. She was like the worst sort of school prefect.

Clemmie came over to join me and we walked off to find a suitable place to have a pee. There seemed to be low-lying water in the distance, grey and shimmering in the hard light, and the ground was pitted by the little cloven hooves of hundreds of sheep and goats. There was no sign of the goatherders so we squatted where we were, watching with fascination as our pee disappeared into the dry ground. Flies immediately buzzed about us, settling on our lips and eyes. All around us the ground was scattered with little hard round turds.

'Can you remember the dung fights we used to have?' asked Clemmie, rolling them about with a twig. It had been one of our favourite activities, collecting dried sheep and horse turds and lobbing them at one another like hand grenades. A full pitched battle amongst the eight of us was quite something. I gave her a wink and put some little dry goat pellets in my pocket. They were the shape and size and colour of black olives.

Back at the camp, Mokhtar's fire was burning brightly and he had a kettle wedged on the flames and a teapot set on the ground. He poured the water from a great height into the teapot. Our gran would have said he should have let it draw, but he poured it at once from shoulder height into five little glasses and then tipped them all back into the pot. This was repeated several times. It was as much of a rigmarole as having afternoon tea with Gran used to be, what with her strainer and teaspoons and sugar tongs and kettle of hot water to top up and wobbly old hand shaking the cups in their saucers. It's funny how often I'm reminded of her and how much I still miss her, and I know Clemmie does too.

Jeremy and Jutta had opened a bottle of red wine and were drinking it from pewter beakers, the sort people take to the races for smart picnics. I saw Jeremy move the bottle and put it behind him. I realised that he didn't want to have to offer us a drink. Jutta had unpacked her pâté de foie gras, which sat on a piece of crumpled waxed paper in a sweating grey lump. Somehow she must have acquired a stick of French bread from Sévaré, which she chopped now into rounds and spread on a plastic bag beside it. Meanwhile the breeze blew dust and sand in every direction and she tried to position herself to act as a windbreak

'Jeremy?' she said. 'Shall I do you one?' She slapped a wodge of pâté on to a bit of bread. The pâté was grey on the outside but a gentle pink in the middle. Jeremy wolfed it hungrily and slurped some wine. He lay back on one elbow and adjusted his panama hat. Beyond him two goatherders had appeared shyly from the trees and were standing watching.

'Would you two like some?' said Jutta to us in a slightly grudging tone.

'No thanks,' Clemmie and I replied in unison.

'Well there's far too much for Jeremy and me!' she said, annoyed. I suppose she thought we should have been grateful. 'It won't keep in this heat.'

Mokhtar passed us our little glasses of tea, which was strong and very, very sweet. The goatherders crept a little closer. One of them stood on one leg, leaning on an enormous rifle. The other was wearing a beautiful dark blue and yellow outfit with yellow plastic shoes and was carrying a hefty axe. I wondered if they intended to murder us, but they looked much too timid. Mokhtar began to assemble lunch in a large tin bowl. He peeled a mound of cold cooked potatoes and added onions, green peppers, a tin of sweetcorn, a jar of black olives and six hardboiled eggs. A jar of French dressing went over the lot and he gave it to us to help ourselves. I took what I wanted and passed the bowl on, but before I did, I reached into my pocket for the little black turds and rolled them on to the mattress by Clemmie's feet. She began to snort with laughter. The temptation to drop them on to Jutta's plate was almost too much.

The two herdsmen were now standing almost beside us and Mokhtar addressed them in an offhand, lordly manner. He thought himself a bit too wonderful, I decided, with his sunglasses and his gold watch. I much preferred our modest little Serufi. In fact Mokhtar had got more and more pleased with himself and Jeremy made it worse by encouraging him.

When we had finished, Mokhtar tipped the remains of our delicious lunch on to a plastic plate and gave it to the two men, who scuttled off a little way to eat hungrily, scooping the mess up with their fingers. When they crept back he took the gun and made a show of shooting amongst the trees, knocking twigs off the ends of branches. Each time the shot echoed and reverberated and flocks of water birds got up in a clamour from the distant water.

This was the signal for Jeremy to talk loudly and authoritatively about shooting and guns, which was obviously one of his specialist subjects. He got up and went to the jeep to fetch a copy of *Shooting Times* from his bag and started to show the puzzled herdsmen pictures of pheasant shoots in Yorkshire. They both studied the photographs closely, breathing noisily, their heads bent together.

Then Jeremy wanted a go with the gun and set up a tin can some way off on a little pile of stones. He missed several times before knocking the can into the air and looking pleased with himself. Clemmie drifted over and said she would like to try. Jeremy thought she was teasing but she set the can even further away and took the heavy gun on to her shoulder. He started to give her instructions, explaining about the sights and how she should aim and that she should be aware of the kick-back effect. This involved putting his arms around her and pressing up close behind. Jutta, on her mattress, looked distinctly annoyed, or maybe she'd eaten rather too much pâté.

Clemmie raised the gun and took careful aim. The herdsmen watched solemnly. With a single shot the can leapt into the air and Clemmie handed the gun back, smiling. I wasn't in the least surprised. She had owned a rifle since she was about ten and was the best shot in the family, known to bring down a brace of pheasants with a left and a right. It is one of her surprising accomplishments. As children we spent hours shooting squirrels and rabbits out of our bedroom windows. My dad used to give us fifty pence per rabbit until Clemmie got so deadly that he said he couldn't afford it any more.

Smiling sweetly, she gave the gun back.

'Holy shit!' said Jeremy in frank admiration. 'That was bloody good. You never told me you could shoot. You don't look at all the type. Did you see, Jutta?'

'No!' she snapped. 'For heaven's sake, Jeremy, stop messing about with that gun, making that dreadful noise. I've already got a headache.'

Mokhtar handed the men little glasses of tea and they squatted by the fire, answering deferentially when he spoke to them.

'These men are Songhai,' he explained to us loftily. 'They are poor herdsmen. I will give them money for the cartridges that we have used.'

'Please tell him that I love his beautiful yellow shoes,' said Clemmie. Jutta sighed theatrically. Mokhtar translated and the man's face lit up and he looked down lovingly at his feet. Clemmie had said exactly the right thing.

'Why are they carrying that great rifle about?' I asked. 'I mean, they're just goatherds, aren't they?' Mokhtar passed on the question and the men gave a long explanation.

'There are two man-eating crocodiles in the water,' said Mokhtar eventually, pointing in the direction in which we had wandered. 'They take many animals and people too.'

'My God!' whispered Clemmie, looking over her shoulder. 'Just imagine, Em! We might have been eaten back there. We could have been foie gras ourselves.'

Jeremy and Jutta finished off the bottle of wine and slumped on their mattress looking rather red in the face. Clemmie and I sat under the tree and she combed out her hair, which floated and fanned on the wind, while Mokhtar and the men gazed at her adoringly. The pages of the *Shooting Times* flicked over in the wind and time seemed to stand still while Fatima's Hand shimmered in the distance, pointing to heaven. I tried half-heartedly to think about Ted but I couldn't even remember what he looked like. Instead I worried about the next stage of our journey and wondered how I could find the opportunity to talk to Jeremy without Clemmie overhearing.

I must have dozed off, because when I woke up I was lying on the mattress, leaning against Clemmie, who was also asleep. At least, she had her eyes shut. I lay for a while looking at the pale, molten sky through the thorn branches above my head and listened to Jutta telling Mokhtar about her twins, and how although they were only thirteen they had already been all over the world. She droned on about her family's schloss in Austria, salmon-fishing in Chile, riding in Costa Rica, an elephant farm in Botswana, a beach house in South Africa where two of the four servants had AIDS. I felt sorry for Mokhtar, who could have done with a bit of peace and quiet after all that driving but was too polite to lie down and close his eyes.

Eventually it was time to move and we stood up and gathered our things. Clemmie adjusted the old faded kikoy she had tied round her waist. One of the brothers had brought it back from Kenya for her years ago and it was among her favourite possessions.

'Is that from Kenya?' asked Jutta, pointing.

'Yes,' said Clemmie, smoothing it down over her hips. 'Don't you love it? It's like a painting – giraffes in the sunset.'

'You see that pattern all over Kenya,' Jutta informed her. 'It's actually a very common and cheap curtain material.'

I made a face at Clemmie and we shook with laughter.

'What is so funny?' demanded Jutta. 'Oh, *honestly*! You two are like silly children.'

My sense of dread increased as we got back on to the road and headed northwards. This time Clemmie and

I were sitting in the front and I quizzed Mokhtar about his cousin and our approaching handover.

'How far will we get tonight, Mokhtar?' I asked.

'Gao,' he said. 'My home! My cousin he take you there. This road stops at Gao. It is only ten years that it has been built. After that, all is sand.'

'And after Gao?'

'One day more to Kidal. My cousin is from Kidal, he will help you. He is important man – a nobleman. You stay with him in Kidal. It is arranged. Afterwards you take the camels.'

'Okay,' I said, thinking aloud. 'And how will we keep in touch with you? To get us back to Bamako again?'

'My cousin has telephone.'

'But you don't.'

'We arrange a day and I come back for you. No problem. Look, we have arrived.'

Up ahead I could see some roadside shacks and a swinging sign, 'Motel Homberi', and some straggly trees. A few minutes later we were bumping off the road and coming to a stop.

'This is it!' I said to Clemmie.

Three men leaned against the back wall of the nearest shack in the shade of a rickety veranda. A fourth man lay curled up asleep on a plastic mat at their feet. The motel sign banged in the hot wind, but apart from that, nothing stirred.

'Is this where you leave us, girls?' asked Jeremy, peering out of the window as Mokhtar jumped out and began to manhandle our bags off the roof of the jeep. 'God! Rather you than me!'

He and Jutta climbed out to say goodbye to us and then he reached into his bag for a copy of their itinerary and a sketch map. 'Look,' he said kindly. 'We are going on here, to Gourma, near where the elephants are supposed to be. We'll be there a couple of days, I should think, and then we are heading back to Dogon country to join the other two. If you need to get a message to us, you could telephone this hotel where we are staying for four nights.' He tore off the telephone number and gave it to me. 'Just in case,' he said. For a moment I felt quite fond of him.

Mokhtar leaned our packs against the wall and came back to shake our hands.

'But where's your cousin?' I asked.

He laughed. 'No worries. He will be here.' He gestured with his arm. 'Go in!' he said. 'Sit in the shade. Ahmada will not be long.'

'Can't you wait?' I pleaded. 'What happens if he does not come?'

He laughed again. 'He will come. But this is motel. You can stay here and when we come back on this road in one day or two, we will see if you are still waiting!'

So that was that. We watched as they got back in the jeep and reversed on to the road. In a few minutes they were disappearing in the shimmering distance. The men leaning against the wall did not move and we stepped over the sleeping man to sit at a table in the shade. Little brown birds flew busily in and out of the open windows and the hot wind blew gusts of sand and set balls of dry weeds bowling along the empty road. It was the most desolate place I had ever seen.

Clemmie

IT WAS OBVIOUS that waiting at Homberi was a low moment for Emily. She sat slumped on a plastic chair and made holes in the paper tablecloth with her fingernail and looked very down in the mouth. I tried to think of something to cheer her up but couldn't. It was best to say nothing. We sat in silence and watched the birds, while the lounging men watched us. Eventually I got up and went inside and found a sort of bar. One of the men levered himself off the wall and followed me in and I managed to buy two cold Castel beers and took them back out to Emily, who was now tapping her foot and looking at her watch every two minutes.

I got out my journal and began to write. When I got to the bottom of the page, I told myself, Ahmada would have arrived, but he hadn't. The road was utterly empty in both directions. If it hadn't been for Emily, tapping away, I would have been perfectly happy and without a moment of anxiety. I felt quite safe and completely unworried. Ahmada would arrive and all would be well, or Ahmada would not arrive and all would be well, but in a different sort of way. I felt a great sense of peace. The cold beer, the sleeping man, the banging sign were somehow utterly familiar and comforting. Nothing seemed to matter very much and I could have sat there for ever.

Emily finished her beer and began pacing up and down, which woke the sleeping man who very slowly got up from his plastic mat and went inside. She walked down to the edge of the road and looked both ways. She walked back again. She sat down and drummed her fingers and looked at her watch. She glowered at the lounging men, who grinned back lazily. They were very, very black, wearing T-shirts and ragged trousers and necklaces of bright beads.

After a while I got up to look for a loo. The inner courtyard of the motel was of bumpy, beaten-down dirt and a spindly tree grew in the middle. The low buildings were made of mud with open latticed windows through which the little brown birds swooped and dived. I found a room in which a lavatory pan stood in a corner with no seat, and apparently not plumbed in. The outlet pipe reappeared on the other side of the outer wall beneath the window. The slope beyond was dotted with excrement, all dried up and odourless. Opposite the lavatory was a tap but there didn't seem to be any water. I sat on the rim of the bowl, glad that I had wet wipes, designed for babies' bottoms, in my bag. The little birds flew in and out and I realised that they were flycatchers. It was peaceful sitting there in the cool with the fretted mud triangles of window to look out of and a breeze blowing through. I noticed that whoever had fashioned the window had thought to embellish it with a curly decorated arch which reminded me of Picasso or Matisse. For some reason this made me very happy. Anyone who bothered to create such a design had to be happy too.

There was a chain to pull, and when I did so a cistern emptied into the bowl and I saw that there was a striped plastic bucket to refill the cistern, but it was empty and the tap was dry.

When I went back through the bar to where I had left Emily she was no longer there and neither were any of the idle men, and our packs had gone. I had one moment of panic and then I saw that an excited group had gathered under the trees and that a vehicle had arrived and that Emily was waving to me. I stepped off the shaded veranda and into the glaring sun and was temporarily blinded. I could not distinguish between the figures under the tree until I was nearly up to them, and then I saw that Emily was beaming and that one of the men, wearing his distinctive dark red robe and indigo chech, was Tayen, our customs officer from Sévaré. The man accompanying him was very tall and broad and dressed in a dark blue robe with a huge pale blue chech wrapped around his head. His skin was the colour of milky coffee and he had large, gentle brown eyes and a trimmed moustache. Both men had pulled the material away from their faces so that their mouths were half visible and they were talking and laughing and the men from the bar were now all loose-limbed animation as they clustered round them.

'Clemmie!' cried Emily. 'This is Ahmada! He's arrived!' and the tall man stepped forward and bent his head over my hand.

'Welcome,' he said in English. 'You are welcome to my country. I am your servant!' and then he straightened up and looked into my eyes and instantly I knew that we could trust him and that I would follow him anywhere.

'And Tayen!' said Emily. 'Can you believe it? He has come with Ahmada. He has arranged to go with us to Kidal!' and Tayen darted forward and kissed my hand and bowed. 'They are all the same family or tribe or something,' she explained. 'They say they are all cousins. It seems that Tayen was so struck by what he heard from Mohktar about our trip that he decided to divert and wait for Ahmada to come by to collect us.'

Ahmada stood to one side watching me gravely. 'When you are ready,' he said, 'we will go. We have many miles in front!'

Tayen was busy unwrapping a flat cloth revealing waxy yellow layers of something unrecognisable. The men gathered round and began to unpeel the layers with their fingers and stuff them into their mouths with much satisfaction.

'This is very special cheese,' explained Ahmada, inviting Emily and me to try. 'It is made from the first milk in the stomach of a newborn kid.'

'My God!' said Emily. 'Colostrum cheese!' but we tried it all the same. Farmers' daughters that we are, we are not squeamish about things like that. As children we used to lie underneath Barbara, the Jersey cow, and squirt the warm milk straight into our mouths from her udder. Most of our friends thought it was disgusting. The cheese tasted fine, a bit like mild cheddar.

'We are ready?' asked Ahmada. 'Niggler!' and he opened the rear door of the Toyota Landcruiser.

'Niggler!' we said, taking it to mean 'Let's go!' and climbed in.

The rest of that day's journey was wonderful. Emily and I sat in the back gazing at the broad shoulders and turbaned heads in front of us and nudging each other in a state of high spirits and partial disbelief.

'I wish Ted could see you now!' I whispered.

Ahmada's long brown hands rested on the wheel and his eyes sought ours in the driver's mirror from time to time as he answered our questions and explained about life among his people. Tayen, who had little English but spoke rapid French, fidgeted about, lighting cigarettes, pressing buttons on the dashboard, opening and shutting the windows. He and Ahmada seemed the best of friends and when Ahmada was not talking to us they spoke together in Tamachek and there was a lot of quiet laughing and amusement, exactly like it is between Em and me.

'Tayen is very, very good camel man,' said Ahmada. 'He wishes to accompany you into the desert. You will ride the camels of his father – the finest camels in the Sahara. It is arranged.'

The next question had to be asked and I did not know quite how to introduce the subject. In the end I just came out with it, which made Emily stuff her chech in her mouth to stop herself laughing.

'Ahmada, are you and Tayen married? I mean, are you both married men?'

'Oh yes! We are both married men,' he said. 'I have wife in Kidal, who you will meet, and three children. I am a happy man. Tayen is also married but he is a wild man!' He translated this for Tayen, and they both cracked up.

'Why are you ladies not married?' Ahmada asked, his beautiful brown eyes seeking mine in the mirror. 'This is very strange to us.'

'It's rather strange to us too,' I said, 'but in England it is quite normal.'

'Normal? How can this be?'

'We are waiting for the right man.'

'Ah!' He still seemed puzzled but we left it at that.

We learned that Ahmada had been to university in Algeria, where he studied to be a water engineer before returning to his home town. He now lived in a house but still felt that he was a nomad and every so often would pack his family up and set off on camels into the desert for several weeks at a time. Tayen was the first of his family to move away from the desert and work for the government. Ahmada told us that this was only possible after the civil war had ended and the government made some concessions to the Tuaregs. Whenever he could, he returned to his father's lands in the desert and resumed traditional Tuareg life.

'Ahmada,' I said, 'this man, this Salika ag Baye, whose name was given to us. Do you know him?'

'My goodness, I know him,' he said, 'but he has been dead many years. Twenty maybe. Maybe more.'

I stared at Emily in dismay. 'Oh no! We were instructed to find him. We were even given an address. We were told that he would be able to take us to this special place where our great-aunt wanted her ashes to be scattered.'

'He has family,' said Ahmada, 'but not in Kidal. They live in the mountains of the north between Algeria, Mali and Niger. He has many sons. The eldest is the Lion of Temesna.'

'The what?'

'The Lion of Temesna. He is Tuareg nobleman, once very rich, very powerful, but no more. Life is now very hard in the desert. We have many droughts and the government want money for taxes, but we have no money. We exchange and barter goods but no longer can we move about our land to trade. We are prevented by borders. In return for our taxes we get nothing – no hospitals, no schools, no aid. All remains in the south.' We had heard this before. It was exactly what Hugh had told us.

'The Lion of Temesna!' I said quietly to Emily. 'Have you ever heard of anything so romantic? Do you think there's a Lioness?'

Emily had thoroughly cheered up by now. I could tell that she felt much happier about the whole trip. For a start it was an exhilarating experience to be in the care of two such very attractive men. Any girl would have felt the same. They were older than us, probably in their late thirties, and Ahmada was such a confidence-inspiring guy. It made things much less complicated that he was married. How lucky his wife was, I thought, imagining what it would be like to lie in his arms with his long fingers stroking my skin. Tayen was a much more tricky proposition and would be quite a handful, I would guess, but I was glad that he was coming with us on the camels. It would be a bit like following a really good field master out hunting at home: you could be sure that he knew the country and would keep you out of trouble, but he would take you over the most exciting fences and give you a wonderful day.

'Do you know the place where we have to go?' asked Emily. 'So far nobody has heard of it.'

I scrabbled about looking for the piece of paper and then spelled it out to Ahmada. 'It's called Timadjlalen. I don't know how to pronounce it, but that's where we have to take our great-aunt's ashes.'

Ahmada and Tayen exchanged glances and spoke rapidly to one another in Tamachek.

'My goodness!' Ahmada said to us. 'We know this place. It is far off. A long ride for you, but all is possible.'

'You do! That's wonderful. Is it a very special place or something?'

'It is beautiful place, beloved of the Tuareg, but we have a big question. Why did your ancestor wish to be there in death? How did she know of this place? It is very strange to us.'

'Ahmada,' I said, 'I wish we knew. It's a mystery. All we know is that she was out here in Mali before the war. World War Two, that is, when she was just a girl. Her father was French and was something to do with colonial administration.'

Ahmada transalated this for Tayen and there followed

a long discussion between them. Eventually he said to us, 'The French, yes, they were in Fort Kidal. The fort is still there in the desert. It is possible that your ancestor visited, but relations between Tuareg and French were not so good. There was much fighting and sometimes this was a dangerous place for Frenchmen. We do not know why your ancestor would wish to lie here in death.'

No more did we, and puzzled silence fell between us. Emily got a tin of travel sweets out of her bag and passed them round. They were very comfortingly homely. My mother used to make us suck them when we were driving to France to go on holiday and we complained of feeling sick five minutes after leaving home. Once she gave us raisins instead but one of my brothers stuck one up his nose and couldn't get it out. He had to have it surgically removed in Dorchester hospital and we missed the ferry.

Ahmada and Tayen were very keen on the sweets and ate three straight off, and would have had more had Emily not decided that they would have to be rationed if they were so popular.

We bowled along through the scrubby landscape and every now and then I saw flashes of the great Niger river in the distance on the left. The sky lost its blinding glare and the shadows lengthened and the road stretched on, a deep purple line in the evening light until it melted in the distance into the purple sky and the desert on either side like a purple ocean. 'This is *sahel*,' said Ahmada. 'It is the edge of the desert. The desert advances every year and drives the people further afield for water and food for their animals. Soon we will cross the river to Gao. After that we are in the desert, the land of the Tuareg. To cross the river for us is to go home.'

Then up ahead we saw a big dark car parked on the side of the road and a very large man in sunglasses standing beside it. Ahmada pulled over and stopped and the man came to the window. He was wearing an Australian bush hat and a checked shirt and his enormous fingers were chunky with gold rings. He seemed very pleased to see us and greeted Ahmada and Tayen like old friends. There was much talk and hand-shaking and some discussion about Emily and me. The man had a good look at us and shot his hand through the window to shake ours and I saw that as well as the rings he wore a huge gold watch.

Tayen got out and climbed on to the roof of our vehicle and threw down a length of rope and then attached it to the black Mercedes saloon. The man had run out of petrol and we were going to give him a tow into Gao.

'Whoever is he?' asked Emily as we drew slowly away and the rope tightened and the great black car gathered speed behind us.

'He is important man,' said Ahmada. 'The deputy mayor of Gao. He owns a hotel and a nightclub.'

'The Peter Stringfellow of Gao,' said Emily, and it seemed that the world over there are opportunities for men of that sort to make money, even in this most unlikely place.

I could see that we were getting closer and closer to the river, and the road which had been straight all day now curved towards a group of shacks, sheltered beneath a sandy cliff. On the opposite bank there was a shock of bright green vegetation, vivid in the evening sun.

'Rice!' said Ahmada, and I could see that amongst the green, tall white wading birds ducked their heads as they stalked along the water's edge.

Halfway across the river, a rusty old orange ferry churned its way towards us, the brown water boiling in its wake. The tarmac road petered out into a dirt track and we came to a stop by the shacks while Peter Stringfellow leaned out of the window of his car and waved his hat in the air. Immediately we stopped, our jeep was surrounded by spindly children with the swollen bellies of malnutrition, trying to sell us water lilies and clamouring for our attention. Little hands shot through the open windows. '*Cadeau? Cadeau?*' they pleaded.

Emily and I emptied our purses of change, but still they plucked at our sleeves and begged. One little girl of about seven, her head bristling with pigtails and with a big snotty-nosed baby in her arms, was pushed to the back by the others.

'Stop that!' said Emily fiercely, in her teacher voice, but the children took no notice until Tayen shouted at them and they slunk away.

'That poor little girl didn't get anything,' said Emily, upset. She got out and slammed the door and marched towards the children, who were scuffling about by the water's edge. I saw her single out the little girl, but the minute she looked as if she was going to give her something, the bigger boys were there, pushing her aside. Emily turned on them and wagged her finger fiercely and reluctantly they dropped back. I saw the delight on the little girl's face as she pocketed the coin Emily gave her and then scuttled off towards the shacks, the stonking great baby hoisted on her bony little hip.

They'll have the money off her, I thought, the minute Emily's back is turned, and I was grateful that the ferry arrived and we drove up the creaking ramp behind a lorry carrying wood. Somehow Mr Stringfellow had managed to get hold of some petrol for his car. We saw some men filling the tank by sucking petrol from a tin can with their mouths.

On the other side of the river there was no road, just crisscrossing vehicle tracks through the drifts of sand and in the distance a blur of low red mud buildings standing amongst palm trees. As we got closer I realised that this was the beginning of the town, where the sand roads between the buildings were wide and littered feet deep on either side with rubbish. The buildings themselves looked crumbling and mean, with heavy barred doors on to the street but no windows. They were interspersed with grass huts and shacks, amongst which goats and donkeys roamed and cooking fires smouldered. Knots of men lounged on corners staring unsmiling at us as we passed. It was a strange, uncomfortable place where the poverty and squalor looked unremitting and the people sullen, lifeless and resentful. I was glad that we were travelling with men who knew what they were doing and would take care of us.

Then, as so often happens when one makes an instant judgement, I had to revise my opinion. We slowed down and Tayen jumped out to open a high metal gate and we turned into a courtyard, and all at once we were in a haven of green and order. There was a garden of bright flowering creepers and trees with chairs and tables set out beneath them and two robed Tuareg men coming forward, smiling and gracious.

'Welcome, my friends,' said Ahmada. 'Welcome to Sahara Passion Hotel.'

The hotel was simple. It consisted of a corridor of bedrooms with roughly made wooden furniture and a shower room at the end, and an outside lavatory in a mud hut open to the skies. After we had showered and changed Emily and I went to sit outside in the garden. It was now quite dark but strings of lights hung between the trees.

'This is a lovely place, Ahmada,' I said when he came to join us.

'It is an old building,' he said, 'dating from French colonial time. It was once the residence of the colonial administrator. It is made into a hotel by a Frenchwoman and her husband, a Tuareg. We stay here amongst friends.'

'A colonial building!' I said. 'So it might have been where Great-Aunt Mary stayed. Do you realise that, Em? She might have sat here in this very garden.' I looked about us, trying to imagine the scene, but it was too hard to think of our great-aunt as anyone other than the person we knew who would have hated the place: the wonky beds with thin mattresses, the outside lavatory, the filthy street.

She would have enjoyed the dinner we ate later, brochettes of capitaine fish from the river and a tomato salad. Emily seemed to think that we shouldn't eat raw vegetables but it was too delicious to resist. Tayen had disappeared the moment we arrived. 'He goes to buy our provisions,' explained Ahmada. 'From tomorrow we have no more opportunities. Now I take you to visit the nightclub?'

We walked with him through the dark streets, trying not to fall in a gutter or one of the many holes. There were more people about now that it was cooler and the women were as beautiful as we had seen before. I had the feeling that many were prostitutes, dressed in tight skirts and high heels, leaning dreamily in doorways or crowded in dimly lit rooms where there were lots of men and a thick ceiling of smoke. Ahmada said that they were Songhai people, Fulani or Peul, or Bozo, that the river brought people of many tribes to Gao in the hope of work. There were hundreds of children about, bare-footed, half-clothed, many with botched-up protruding navels or squint eyes. Down by the river they were diving into the water off the harbour, mostly naked, among them well-developed pubescent girls with beautiful young breasts, apparently unselfconscious of their nudity.

It was a strange, uneasy place; louche and decadent, indolent and decaying yet still with a beauty I find hard to explain. If these people had fallen from the Garden of Eden into this desperate stew of poverty, they still had a sort of innocence clinging to them. They were the poorest people I had ever seen but there was laughter and happiness too, and all the toddling babies seemed to be loved, scooped to their mothers' breasts or passed like parcels amongst their relatives, while the old people lay on bundles of rags in the shacks of their families.

I thought of the lush green villages of home and the little stone churches where mean-mouthed, squabbling Kingsleys got down on their knees every Sunday. If I was God, I knew which people I would love best, but this was a pointless train of thought. I had grappled with that sort of thing when I was going through a religious phase at our convent school and had been terrified that I might be called by God to become a nun. Thankfully, the more I thought about it the less I believed. He was making a good job of things and I was let off the hook, so to speak.

I did not enjoy being a sightseer and neither did Emily. With nothing to offer, nothing to give, we were just gawpers from another world.

Ahmada made stately progress through the streets, standing head and shoulders taller than the crowd, and we followed close on each side while people turned to stare. He stopped to pick up a small naked boy, crying in the dirt, and set him on his feet. He gave out a coin here and there, mostly to the old, the blind or the crippled.

'Are there aid agencies here to help these people?' asked Emily in a troubled voice.

'Yes,' said Ahmada. 'They come for a few years when they are funded by the United Nations or other countries. They open clinics for the children, help with blindness or polio, but then the money is gone. These people mostly have to help themselves.'

We walked away from the crowded streets along the river, past the old mud-brick French fort, which was now a run-down hotel. A few tourist minibuses were parked under the palm trees and I tried to imagine Great-Aunt Mary as a young woman, pulling up outside in an open army jeep. Why had she never *told* us about any of this, about this extraordinary country and the time she spent here? Why had she kept it a secret until after she had died? Now we were here and seeing it with our own eyes, her silence became even more of a mystery.

A few minutes further on Ahmada pushed open a metal door in a high mud wall and motioned to us to go in. Inside there was a dark courtyard lit from the opposite end by a green neon sign which read 'Casablanca Bar'. On a shelf behind the bar was a row of prestigious-label bottles, London gin, Glenmorangie whisky, Pernod, Cointreau, but they were all dusty and empty. There did not seem to be anybody about or anything else to drink, but then Peter Stringfellow himself appeared, beaming, still in his bush hat and dark glasses, and motioned us to go through to the room behind the bar where there was a large chest freezer. He opened the lid and inside, standing in pools of water, were bottles of Castel beer. He took some out and then invited us to admire his music system which he had rigged up with speakers on either end of the bar. His only music was a scuffed tape of a country-and-western singer called Moe Bandy. We sat in the dark on plastic chairs and listened to Moe, whose plaintive, lonesome cowboy voice and lyrics about loving and losing his girl seemed perfectly matched to our mood.

We sipped our beer from the bottle while Ahmada and Stringfellow engaged in a low, murmured conversation which rose and fell, backwards and forwards between them, in a gentle, soothing cadence. The hot wind clattered through the branches of the palm trees over the wall and Moe's sad voice floated up into the vast black starry heavens.

We woke very early the next morning, before the sun had spread even a little light into the sky. Directly outside our shutters a donkey brayed and the cocks began to crow, and Em and I ventured to the loo, our torch catching the tail-ends of skittering, scuttling night-time creatures as they darted away. There was a dear little toad in the lavatory and we ushered him outside.

On the way back to our room the beam of my torch hit the mud wall beside the door, and there, quite clearly, I saw that someone had scratched a heart with an arrow through it. I traced the heart with my finger. It was more than just a scratch. Whoever had made it had spent a long time etching it deep into the brick. On either end of the arrow there must have once been the initials of the lovers but these had been deliberately scraped away and were indecipherable. I looked at it for a long time. How sad, I thought, that something had happened to alter that confident declaration of love into a denial. I decided not to show it to Emily.

Beryl Timmis

I THINK IT took about ten days to travel on that boat from Bamako to Gao. By the time I arrived I was exhausted by the strain of it all, by the heat, by the wrenching stomach cramps I suffered and the terrible explosions that followed. I felt weak and listless and often wept in my cabin knowing that I was so far from home and so alone. Mary's father would be waiting for me but I did not know him well enough to feel comfortable with him and the knowledge that Mary was not there dismayed me. What was the matter with her and where was she? In a week or two we should be making this journey together, but in the opposite direction, thank the Lord, back to the safety of France and then England.

I can remember the boat docking in Gao and how I was struck by the desolation of the place. This was not like bustling, lively Mopti, but a small town of low red mud buildings under the shade of palms and nothing else but sand and blistering sky. The harbour was guarded by the Senegalese riflemen I had seen before, wearing baggy white trousers and high round hats. There were a few military vehicles drawn up but the rest of the traffic was mule carts and donkeys and even one or two camels, the first I had seen.

A young French captain met me and took me to an open jeep where a driver waited. A few minutes later we arrived at the low one-storey residency, over which a French flag flew. There were guards at the gate who saluted as we passed through into an inner courtyard where there were flowers and trees. I was helped out of the jeep and through an office where a young soldier was busy on a radio transmitter. My escort knocked at an inner door and then showed me into a dim room furnished simply in French style and with a fine carpet on the floor. Electric fans whirled in the ceiling and sitting on a sofa in a white suit, his long, elegant legs crossed, was Mary's father.

He stood up to greet me and kissed me on both cheeks. 'Beryl!' he said, holding both my hands in his. He spoke English with hardly a trace of an accent. 'I cannot thank you enough for coming all this way. It is an experience, no? To travel through western Sudan is an experience in itself and I hope that you were not too uncomfortable? I am afraid this is a terrible place – terrible. I would have preferred to meet you in Bamako or St Louis, but I am afraid that I am sometimes required to come into the north – and here I am, but not for long, I hope. A cup of tea, perhaps?' His eyes crinkled. 'It is the right time for English tea, I think, but unfortunately I cannot promise cucumber sandwiches! Lieutenant!' he called to the young soldier. 'Tea, please, for the young lady! Now, Beryl, come and sit by me here. But I am forgetting, you will want to wash after your journey. I am afraid that we have very limited accommodation but I hope that you will not be too inconvenienced.'

He led me across the room and into a corridor off which there were several doors. He opened the furthest to show me a simple bedroom with a low travelling bed covered by a mosquito net, and a washstand, a chair and an armoire. My luggage was on the floor beside the bed, waiting for me. There was a tall shuttered window looking on to the courtyard. It was like a piece of rural France, although the floor and walls were of mud.

'There is a bathroom of sorts at the end,' he said, 'but you will find there is water for washing here in this jug. When you are ready, come and join me.'

When he had gone I sat on the bed and took off my sandals. My feet were filthy. I caught a glimpse of myself in the glass of the armoire. My hair was flat to my head and I looked exhausted, with dark rings under my eyes. My linen dress was crumpled and shapeless and heavily stained under the arms. I looked a perfect sight. I took off my dress and threw it on the floor and stepped out of the slip I wore beneath. I stood there in my bodice and drawers and looked at my flat chest and my skinny arms and legs and felt, once again, unequal to the task. I wanted to be elegant and womanly in the company of Mary's father, but instead I was a gawky, travel-stained schoolgirl.

I did what I could to tidy myself. I remember the joy of the bowl of water and the cake of French soap and the thick white towel. I washed all over and put on a clean cotton dress, blue with a white collar, and my string of pearls, and combed my hair. I powdered my nose – pointless in that heat – and splashed on some toilet water my mother had given me and went back to join Colonel Barthelot.

The young lieutenant had produced a tray with a tall silver teapot, cups and saucers and a plate of little French biscuits.

'Ah!' said the colonel when I came in, looking me up and down. 'Charming, my dear,' and I felt shy and tongue-tied. I had said virtually nothing since I arrived and did not know how to begin. I had not seen Mary's father for some years and there was the awkwardness of his failed marriage and the fact that I knew more than perhaps I should have done of the reasons why. My mother was not a discreet woman and relished the details passed on to her by Mary's

mother. The colonel was a man who did not understand what it was to be faithful, I learned. He was certainly good looking and charming, with his groomed moustache and slicked-back greying hair.

I balanced the tea cup on my lap. The tea was too strong and I was not offered any milk and the biscuits were hard and dry.

'Please,' I began, 'tell me about Mary. You know that her mother asked me to come out here to accompany her home? She is most terribly anxious about her. In England there is growing talk of war, you see, and now you tell me that Mary is unwell and that she isn't here with you, and I don't understand . . .' My voice trailed off.

Colonel Barthelot offered me a cigarette and then lit one himself. He leaned back and blew smoke through his nose.

'I understand,' he said, 'and Marie's mother is right to be concerned. This is why I welcome you, Beryl, and thank you sincerely for the sacrifice you have made for your friend. You are brave to travel so far on your own when I think that perhaps, unlike Marie, you are a little timid? This, in a way, is the problem with Marie. You know she is head-strong and courageous and this I admire, but it can cause difficulties.'

'But what is it? What is the matter with her? Where is she?'

The colonel drew on his cigarette. 'She is in the north. Two, three days' drive from here. These desert territories are arranged into subdivisions and she is in the Kidal subdivision, where there is a small outpost of colonial cavalry. Perhaps I am at fault that I allowed her to accompany me there. It is dangerous country where we have to constantly be watchful of attack by rebel Tuareg, but at the moment we have peace. The outpost is in the care of a young lieutenant. He is a good man and has done well, but there is a degree of fraternisation, which is causing a little concern. Young men, you know, without the company of women, it is only natural, and this lieutenant has taken for himself a Tuareg "wife" – maybe more than one. Tuareg women are very beautiful, you know. It is important in these delicate situations that the position of chef de poste *is not undermined. We have only a handful of French troops posted there and rely on Senegalese riflemen and* goumiers *– troops recruited from amongst the local tribesmen. It is a situation which can easily become dangerous.*

'In my position of governor of these territories I try to visit far-flung and desolate outposts at least once every two years, and it was time to call on young Lieutenant Charpentier. Marie and I and some of my staff, including a medical officer, flew up from Mopti. Of course Charpentier had warning of our visit, which is only fair, and the place

was cleaned up and ready for us. There was no sign of his "harem" but there was plenty to suggest that women lived on the fort. Flowers and vegetables were cultivated, there were pet animals, including a young lion, captured in the desert, and evidence of children living there. I decided to leave my aide-de-camp and the medical officer at the fort for a few further weeks. My ADC was not at all happy with the idea and begged to be excused, but I insisted. The doctor had plenty to concern himself with. The soldiers rarely have the opportunity to get routine complaints treated and he intended to run a clinic for mothers and children of the nomadic tribes. We do what we can in these situations and it helps to further better relations.

'Marie meanwhile had fallen in love with the desert. Each morning, before it became too hot, she went out exercising with the cavalry and Lieutenant Charpentier took her on expeditions to the Tuareg camps. She rode camels and went hunting for oryx and mouflon, the wild goat of the region. She begged me to allow her to remain. She said that she had a little medical training and would like to help the doctor. She asked to return with him when the aeroplane came to collect him in a few weeks.'

'But she didn't?' I asked, not understanding. 'So is she still there?'

The colonel looked at me solemnly and sighed. 'Alas, it

is more complicated than that. The time I speak of was last year, ten months ago. I have only seen Marie once in that time and much has happened since.'

'What?' I asked. 'Please tell me what has happened to her.'

The colonel sighed. 'My dear Beryl,' he said, 'I am sorry to tell you that Marie is married.'

Emily

SOMETHING WAS HAPPENING to Clemmie. Since we began travelling with Tayen and Ahmada, her happiness was such that she smiled even when she was dozing in the back of the jeep, and when we stopped along the way she raised her arms wide above her head as if to embrace everything she saw. She said that she loved it all, the rolling sands across which we surfed, skewing sideways, wheels spinning, the flat plains over which we raced, the herds of loose camels, the scattering of desolate mud villages, blasted by the sun and the wind.

We stopped at a stock market in a village and she loved that too. Donkeys, cattle and camels were herded together while Fulani and Taureg men, all tall and veiled, discussed prices and slapped each other's palms when agreement was reached.

'Wouldn't your dad feel at home?' Clemmie said to me, eyes shining. 'He'd love it! It's just like Taunton market! I so want to buy a camel. That beautiful white one. How much will she cost me, Ahmada? Look, Em, she's so beautiful and gentle. Look at her eyelashes!'

'A good riding camel is expensive. Three thousand euros, perhaps. Very special camels can be worth one hundred thousand. Tuareg camels are very fine, very well bred,' said Ahmada.

'Three thousand euros! I could afford that, Em. I could put it on a credit card! How could I get her home? Do you think I could, or would it be cruel?'

She babbled on like this, drifting about amongst the animals with her Tuareg scarf draped over her head in a Virgin Mary style and her trailing gypsy skirt, and stopped everyone in their tracks with her ethereal beauty. Women and children called to her to come and talk to them and I noticed that there was no begging amongst these people; instead they wanted to give us something, pressing a camel tooth bead into our hands, or a few dusty nuts. The women were boldly and brightly dressed with beautiful jewellery, their headscarves decorated with gold coins, and they were confident and outgoing, teasing Tayen and Ahmada, laughing amongst themselves.

'My goodness, yes!' said Ahmada when I commented on this. 'Tuareg women are very strong. They own their own property. They marry who they want and divorce if they are not happy. It is women who decide big issues. The lineage of Tuareg comes through the mothers.'

'How sensible! They all look well, don't they, Em? Strong and healthy. What do these people eat, Ahmada?'

'Much milk, cheese, butter, dates, a little cereal, a little meat. But there is hunger when the droughts are bad. Tuareg live to old age – eighty or ninety years. The family size is small. Four children, maybe. More cannot be raised when times are hard.'

'It's all so civilised. You can tell that the Tuareg are a superior sort of people, can't you, Em? It's not just that they look so noble.' She was like an overexcited child at a party who had been fed too many E numbers.

A bit further on along the road, Ahmada stopped by a well where an enormous herd of camels was being watered. I counted to two hundred and gave up. They were magnificent beasts, of every colour, many with young. Ahmada and Tayen got out and asked us if we would like to go with them.

'These people are Arabs,' announced Ahmada. 'We are going to buy camel milk from them. Camel milk is a perfect diet. With dates, it is possible to live and be healthy on nothing else. Camel milk is for Tuareg men, goat for children and cow for women.'

We walked over the hard-trodden glittering sand to where the tall beasts were milling around beside a hand-pumped well. A man came to greet us in a dirty white robe with a black headdress. He was very dark and swarthy and stared at Clemmie and me with undisguised curiosity. Ahmada and Tayen greeted him and there followed a long discussion during which a younger man was sent off with a tin bowl to milk a female camel. Ahmada went back to our vehicle and returned with a box of pills in his hand.

'These are antibiotics,' he explained. 'This man has children who suffer with tonsillitis. It kills many children here because they have no drugs and no money to buy them. These will help a little but not enough.' He gave the pills to the man, who stared reverently at the box in his hand.

The younger man came back with the full bowl, which Ahmada offered to us first. We both tasted the warm milk, which was clean and light, and passed it back. Ahmada and Tayen then drained the bowl between them, two or three pints each, after which they appeared very refreshed.

'They're like my dad, stopping off for a couple of pints at the Trooper before lunch,' said Clemmie.

'Let's go!' said Ahmada, wiping his mouth.

'Niggler!' said Clemmie.

We stopped again at one o'clock when Ahmada veered off course and pulled up under a thorn tree. When we climbed out it was very, very hot, the featureless distance like a shimmering sea. It was utterly silent.

'We eat lunch down a tree,' explained Ahmada, and he and Tayen set about unpacking what we needed, including the mattresses for us to lie on in the little bit of shade. After a short time they had a fire going and Tayen was making lunch in a bowl like the one we had had the previous day. Ahmada boiled up green tea from the decorated pouch that he wore round his neck, adding sugar from a sort of leather stocking.

'These pouches are traditional for Tuareg,' he explained to us. 'They would normally hang from the saddle of the camel. Tea and sugar are very valuable in the desert.'

All four of us ate from the bowl and the men pulled meat off some cold cooked lamb bones and ate it hungrily with their fingers.

'We are meaty, milky men,' said Ahmada, which was evidently true. He sighed with satisfaction.

After we had eaten our fill, Ahmada commanded us to rest. We both settled down on the mattresses and Tayen, with the greatest gentleness, pulled off Clemmie's boots. 'It is more comfortable,' he said in French. Then he and Ahmada took a striped plastic kettle of water and went off to wash and pray.

Clemmie, lying on her side, her glimmering hair spread out about her, said dreamily, 'That was the most lovely thing a man has ever done for me – pulling off my boots like that. Don't you think so, Em?'

'Clemmie, he's married,' I said and turned over.

I woke with a start and lay for a moment absorbing the heat. When I stretched my arm above my head, the heat of the wind on my skin was like opening an oven door. After a bit I was aware of a faint throbbing sound in the distance. I sat up and looked around us. Tayen and Ahmada were both stretched out, sleeping peacefully. They looked so strange and stately in repose, both dressed in their traditional robes and loose trousers, their cheches wrapped around their heads, their long slender hands clasped over their chests. Clemmie lay between them, the shade of the tree dappling over her, her delicate white feet curled up to one side. It made such an extraordinary picture that I reached for my bag to get out my camera. I would take a photograph while they slept. Nobody at home would believe it.

The throbbing sound had got louder, and as I put my camera away I saw a black dot in the distance travelling towards us over the sand. I thought immediately of the Foreign Office warnings of the dangers of travelling in the north of Mali. What if these were bandits approaching? Ahmada and Tayen slept on. I stood up and shaded my eyes to see better and to my relief Ahmada stirred and raised himself on one elbow.

'Emily!' he said. 'Everything is well, my friend?'

'Look, Ahmada,' I said, pointing. 'There is someone coming.'

He glanced over and smiled. 'This is a lorry,' he said, 'transporting dates from Algeria. Over there is main road between Algeria and the south.'

'It is?' I said. 'But there isn't a road. There's nothing but sand!'

He smiled. 'Ah, but it is there. The eyes of desert people can see the road. Often it gets blown away and moves a little here or there, but we can still see the way.'

We watched the lorry lumber past, so overloaded that its chassis barely cleared the ground. Atop the mountain of sacks several men were perched. They waved to us cheerfully. What it must have been like up there, lurching about in the full sun all day, did not bear thinking about.

'Ahmada,' I said, 'our government gives a warning to tourists about travelling in the north of Mali. It is supposed to be dangerous. People have been kidnapped and murdered.'

Ahmada looked grave. 'God save us!' he said. 'This is true. These things have happened and we regret them very much. There are two things I say to you. These tourists are unwise to travel alone in desert and become lost, and second, these bandits are few.'

'But are we safe?' Are we safe here, for instance – miles from anywhere in an expensive jeep and obviously carrying money?'

Ahmada looked shocked and affronted. 'But you are in the care of Tuareg,' he said simply. 'Here you are the safest person in the world. This is our land.'

In the afternoon we drove on and on through the endless Tilemsi valley, sometimes sandy, sometimes rocky, but always scattered with donkeys, sheep, goats and camels. Clemmie sat and smiled dreamily out of the window, sometimes singing softly to herself. I was glad that she hadn't heard my conversation with Ahmada. She would have been furious with me. However, it came forcibly back to me when a cloud of dust and sand coming very fast in the opposite direction revealed itself to be a sinister-looking black truck with smoked-glass windows. The driver waved at us to stop and I realised that what I could see poking out of the windows were rifles.

We slewed to a standstill and Ahmada and Tayen began a nervous conversation before getting out and slamming the doors. Some very scary-looking men, very black, all wearing sunglasses and elaborate army uniforms, got out of the other vehicle. They were strung about with bullet belts and God knows what other firearms.

'Bloody hell, Clemmie,' I whispered. 'What's this about? Don't look. Pull your scarf over your face. Don't let them see that we're Europeans.' Even Clemmie had the good sense to look nervous. We sat in the back of the jeep holding hands, stuffing our scarves in our mouths in fear.

The next moment the door on my side of the jeep was wrenched open and a large black hand gestured that we should get out. With shaking knees we complied. Ahmada and Tayen were over on the other side by the black truck, surrounded by the soldiers, leaving us at the mercy of an enormous man whose uniform was covered in gold braid and stars and medals. He reminded me horribly of Idi Amin or some other African dictator best known for his prisons and sophisticated methods of torture.

It took me a moment or two to realise that he was smiling, beaming in fact, and that he wanted to shake our hands, and then shake them again, and finally to kiss them.

'David Beckham!' he said joyfully. 'Michael Owen!'

'Yes! Yes!' we cried in relief.

'Chelsea! Liverpool!'

'Oh, yes.'

'Manchester United, Leeds, Tottenham Spurs!'

'Oh,' said Clemmie, searching for inspiration. 'Um . . . how about Everton? And Newcastle?' After that the conversation dried up and we were saved by Ahmada hurrying over to introduce us.

'This is the colonel who makes for disarmament and demilitarisation of the Tuareg. He is very important man and friend.'

Just as well, I thought.

After saying fond farewells we got under way again and I asked Ahmada to explain what the colonel's job entailed.

'After the end of the civil war it has taken time to disband Tuareg resistance. Kidal was centre of rebel country and there stays behind hostility and suspicion between the people of the south and the Tuareg. Mali now has Tuareg prime minister, yes, so things are better, but there are still many problems. The nomadic authorities, the local mayors, must look for taxes and this is very hard. How can it be possible to tax people who have no money? How can you tax them when they get nothing back from the government?'

'But he is a good man, is he, this colonel?' I asked.

'Yes, he is good and fair.'

'I thought he was lovely,' said Clemmie, 'but I think we were a bit of a disappointment because we couldn't talk to him very much about football.'

The afternoon wore on and the light went from the sky, which faded through orange to pink to violet. Ahmada drove steadily, flying across the empty flat sands, following tracks which sometimes disappeared entirely, and then dropping to crawling speed to steer through deep, treacherous gullies which pitched the jeep from side to side so violently that we banged our heads against the roof. Every now and then we came to a sudden halt in banks of soft sand, and reversed hurriedly to seek a firmer footing. The important thing was not to get stuck. Occasionally we passed the skeleton of a donkey or a camel, the bones bleached by the sun, or the remains of a broken truck, stripped to its rusting chassis.

Once, far off to the right, we passed an ancient lorry, so heavily laden that it had sunk deep into the sand. A crowd of desolate-looking men surrounded it, some digging frantically around the wheels, others just standing, their shoulders stooped despairingly.

'From Nigeria,' said Ahmada, looking across and shaking his head. 'They try to leave Africa. Many die trying to cross the Sahara to Morocco and then to Europe.' I realised that the lorry was laden with pitiful possessions, bundles and suitcases and oil drums, piled high into a mountain and tied on by an old net. How bad things must be at home to make these men attempt such a journey, and with such a frail hope of ever reaching their destination.

'Can't we help them?' asked Clemmie, distressed.

'They are plenty. They will dig all night. They do not wish help because they cross illegally. No, we stay away.'

It was too dreadful to contemplate.

I looked at the pug bag on Clemmie's lap and touched the pink tongue with my finger.

'It's so strange, Clemmie,' I said quietly. 'This journey, these amazing people, and thinking that Great-Aunt Mary has been here before us all those years ago. What can it have been like then?'

'The landscape won't have changed,' said Clemmie, looking out of the window. 'It must have looked just like this, and the people won't have changed much either. A few more vehicles, I suppose, and getting here must have taken a lot longer. What I can't get my head round is that she wanted to be brought back. The further we go on this journey, the more unlikely it seems and the less I understand it, especially as she never talked about it, never mentioned it to anyone.'

'But you're still determined to do it, aren't you?' I said. 'To take her to this extraordinary place? She has had to rely on you because I wouldn't have done, no way, not if you hadn't forced me.'

'I knew I had to,' said Clemmie simply. 'I just knew that I must.'

We were both dozing and it was pitch dark when the jeep came to an abrupt halt. We had arrived at a roadblock of oil drums set across the sandy track where it threaded between two rocky outcrops. A nervous-looking young soldier came forward carrying a machine gun and a torch, which he shone into the jeep at each of our faces, blinding us in turn. There followed a murmured exchange before he rolled the barrels to one side and waved us through.

'What was that about, Ahmada?' I asked.

'We have to tell him who we are,' he explained. 'Kidal is still a place of suspicion.'

'Have we arrived then?'

'Yes, we are arriving.'

We peered out of the window but there was little to see. This was a town that the desert seemed to threaten to take back. There were the now-familiar red mud buildings and wide streets but these were sifted with sand. Lights glowed softly from some open doorways, but it was very quiet. We turned this way and that, through the cross-work of streets, before pulling up outside a metal gate in a high wall. Tayen got out to open it and Ahmada drove through into a courtyard and turned off the engine.

He turned to us. 'Welcome,' he said. 'Welcome to my home!'

Clemmie

WHEN WE ARRIVED in Kidal, Emily and I were both very tired and would gladly have gone straight to bed, but our arrival caused a stir and the large mud house was full of visitors and confusing comings and goings. Once more Tayen disappeared into the night. He was off to organise the camels for the next morning and also to try to discover the whereabouts of the ag Baye family, who might provide the clue to the Great-Aunt Mary mystery.

Emily and I were invited to use a proper tiled washroom with a tap and a big plastic bowl and then sit in a large windowless ground-floor room where there was a beautiful carpet but little furniture except for decorated camel saddles to lean on, set at intervals around the walls. It was as near to a tent as you could get indoors.

It was the first time we had seen a real Tuareg saddle and these were works of art, made out of wood and brightly coloured tooled leather in reds and vivid greens. They were shaped a bit like a milking stool and the front was decorated with a high, narrow carved wooden cross about as long as my forearm, angled forward and sticking out like the bowsprit of a ship. The back was also high and carved in intricate designs, like a narrow wooden chair back. Ahmada came in and explained that there is a legend that the cross is a Christian symbol dating back to the time before the Tuareg were converted to Islam around the ninth century. Now it is purely for decoration and is not robust enough to be used as a handhold or something to hang on to in emergencies.

Visitors of both sexes came to the door to look at us and then withdrew. Ahmada's wife, NouNou, very pretty and gentle, bustled about, rounding up numerous children, who were too scared to come and meet us until Emily produced a little tub of that liquid soap stuff and blew fountains of bubbles into the air. They came then, entranced, and she invited them to try to blow for themselves and they chased the bubbles and clapped their hands and squealed with laughter.

Then Ahmada invited us to mount the outside

stairs on to the roof, which had a low wall around it, and there were the white plastic picnic chairs waiting for us and a tray of coffee was brought and a bowl of dates. We sat there alone, looking up at the bright stars and feeling the warm wind blow through our hair, and enjoying a few moments when we were not being objects of interest. 'What a nuisance we are!' said Emily. 'I feel really sorry for poor NouNou, having us dumped on her like this. I'd be furious if it was me.'

'It's part of the culture to be hospitable to strangers,' I said. 'Unlike ours, which is to keep the chain on the door and lie flat on the floor so that unexpected callers will think we're out.'

Ahmada reappeared up the stairs with four of his male friends, courteous, aloof men who sat on mats, talking and drinking tea and evidently discussing our expedition. The pug bag was pointed out, where it sat on my lap, and the tone of the discussion seemed to be reverent and serious, as though what we were embarking on was an expedition that was understood and held in high regard.

Then NouNou and some other women staggered up the stairs with trays of food. She set a huge dish of steaming couscous and a platter of grilled meat in front of us and delivered the rest to the men and then went back down the stairs.

Emily and I looked at one another, sharing the same thought. Neither of us felt like tackling a large meal but we had to do our best. The meat was so tough that it was impossible to chew, let alone swallow. I got a lump of it going round my mouth from one side to the other and chewed and chewed to no avail. Emily had a quick look over the wall behind us. 'It's a sort of garden!' she whispered, and she took the lump out of her mouth and lobbed it over. Fortunately it very dark and the men had remained in their corner and were tucking into their meal and not taking any notice of us, and we managed to dispose of enough meat to look as if we had enjoyed it. When we had finished Emily said, 'I'm so knackered, Clem. I'm going to ask Ahmada if I can go to bed. I don't care if it's a breach of etiquette.'

It turned out that if we wished we could sleep on our mattresses on the roof where it was cooler, so we muddled about in a dark corner, sorting through our stuff by torchlight, going back down into the house to clean our teeth and put on pyjamas then creeping back upstairs and into our sleeping bags. The group of men took no notice of us and I lay there listening to the rise and fall of their voices, waiting for sleep.

Some hope, as it turned out. To begin with we were too hot and flapped our sleeping bags open and tossed about. Then, just as the night began to cool and the desert wind to blow, some very amplified and beginner's Grade 1 electric guitar music began from somewhere close by in the town. It was interspersed with commentary and sounded as if it was coming from a youth club where everyone was clamouring to have a go, both on the guitar and on the microphone. In competition, Arab disco music began blasting out from somewhere else. It went on and on with only a few pauses, during which I thought that at last they had gone home to bed, only for it to begin all over again.

Ahmada's visitors had left long ago except for two who were sleeping where they lay, oblivious to the noise. For Emily and me it was like trying to sleep on the floor of a nightclub.

We tried everything: Em's homeopathic sleeping pills, cotton wool ear plugs, winding our scarves round our heads and putting them in our sleeping bags, but the music was so loud that the roof beneath us reverberated. We tossed and turned and Em grumbled and said it was fucking ridiculous to travel to the furthest point from civilisation and then be kept awake by disco music. I tried to cheer her up by telling her to think of First World War trenches and the poor men who slept on their feet with bombs falling round them. At last the music stopped and in the sudden and startling silence we could hear the mosquitoes zooming in and then cutting out as they homed in to bite.

We had to sit up and scrabble to find a torch to search for the insect repellent and smear it on before we lay down again. In between all of this we kept wanting to go to the loo, which meant shuffling down the stairs trying not to wake the whole house. At about three o'clock the cockerels started up and then the donkeys and the goats and the sheep and finally the blasting sun.

'I haven't slept at all. Not the entire night!' said Emily, sitting up, and she did indeed look rough. Her eyes were slits in a face swollen by tiredness, her hair on end, and she had definitely been bitten. There was a red bump on her cheek and two on the rim of her ear. I didn't look much better but the day was beginning and the men were scratching and yawning and getting up out of their nests of blankets – all fully dressed, refreshed and ready to go.

Emily and I managed a cold all-over wash using the tap and washing-up bowl in the bathroom, and got dressed. Ahmada appeared and said that he had sent out to the baker for bread for our breakfast and that as soon as we had eaten he was going to take us into the town to buy some suitable clothes in which to ride camels. Emily asked him about the music from the night before and he said that the youth of the town had been given musical equipment as part of a French charity's effort to foster traditional Tuareg music amongst the young.

'Ha!' said Emily, looking cross. It wasn't difficult to see what she thought about it, but then the bread arrived and that was French too – lovely long crispy baguettes – so I suppose we had something to thank them for.

The shop Ahmada took us to was on a dusty street crowded with market stalls selling dates and onions and flour and millet and striped plastic buckets and beautiful leather flip-flops. We dived into a doorway and found ourselves in a dark room in which robe and trouser ensembles were displayed high up on hangers strung from the ceiling. Some were very grand and formal with gathers over the shoulders and embroidery in stiff and shiny material – big-occasion, mother-of-the-bride stuff – and others were ordinary everyday wear. Emily chose a simple combination in dark blue and I got the same in pale blue. The trousers were easy to adjust because they came in an enormous wide T-shape and you simply caught up the ends of the waist and tied them in a knot. The shopkeeper, who was very tall and gaunt, grinned at us, allowing just a glimpse of his mouth and one long brown tooth.

'You realise that this is men's gear we have bought,' said Emily, looking down at herself. 'That's why he's so amused. He thinks that we're a couple of cross-dressers. He's never seen anything like it.'

Small boys had started to peer inside, pushing each other and giggling. Unlike their fathers they wore ordinary cotton trousers and ragged T-shirts and most were bare-footed. One in particular, about six years old, was lovely, with curly brown hair and large brown eyes. I held him by the hand and smiled at him and he smiled shyly back.

'Look at this one I've caught, Em. Wouldn't he make a perfect page boy? Can't you see him in a little velvet suit following me up the aisle in Sherborne Abbey?'

Emily just sighed and raised her eyes to heaven.

We walked back through the town with Ahmada, along one sandy broken-down street after another, and most people we met seemed to know him and greeted him enthusiastically.

'This Tuareg caste system,' said Emily as we trotted along beside him. 'Can you explain it, please . . . you know, the slaves and so on?'

'My goodness. There is no longer this hierarchy as in the far old days,' said Ahmada, rather wistfully I thought, 'but the traces of the system remain. Some noble families are now very poor, but by their lineage they remain always noble. Old times, a noble family would have vassal family to care for animals, and also slaves to do hard work, and blacksmith caste to do ironwork.'

'It's exactly like home, Emily, if you think about it,' I pointed out. 'Lord Digby at the top, then all the tenant farmers, then the farmworkers and the tradesmen. And we have impoverished nobility too. There's that charity that always used to make us laugh, the one for Distressed Gentlefolk.'

Emily looked at me scornfully. 'I don't think Dad would like to be described as a vassal,' she said. 'Or Neil a slave.'

'But it *was* like it not so long ago!' I said. 'Remember that verse we're not allowed to sing in "All Things Bright and Beautiful", the one about the rich man in his castle, the poor man at his gate, He made them high and lowly, and ordered their estate?'

'That was a Victorian idea. Things *have* changed, thank God!' said Emily sharply.

It took a long time to pack up Ahmada's jeep with all that we would need on the camel trip, but at last we were ready. An extremely black-skinned Tuareg had appeared, who was very lively and energetic and had a wonderful high pealing laugh. He was introduced as Cassini, our cook. He wore a white chech and a pale blue robe and a big red ski jacket, despite the heat.

We went to change into our outfits and amused one another very much by how we looked – which was a cross between Lawrence of Arabia and a fortune-teller. We reorganised our packs and stowed away in the bottom all the things we wouldn't need on the camels. On the top we put our fleeces and warm socks and sweaters and woolly hats because Ahmada said that it would be very cold at night.

When we emerged, decked out in our Tuareg robes, we were greeted with delighted laughter. Of course Emily was quite right and we were dressed as men, and so probably we were as funny as pantomime dames in England. We said goodbye to NouNou, who appeared with a baby in her arms to see us off.

'How can we thank her?' said Emily. 'It's really

embarrassing to just breeze in and out like this. Treating the place like a hotel, my mum would say.'

'Do you think she'd like my little sheepskin waistcoat?' I asked. 'It's the nicest thing I've got and it gets cold at night in the winter.'

I opened my bag and delved down to the bottom to pull it out. I loved it so much but I couldn't think of anyone I'd rather give it to or a nicer home in which to spend its days, and I knew that Will, who had given it to me, would approve. I held it out to NouNou and she took it shyly.

'Try it on!' I suggested, and she handed Ahmada the baby and slipped the jacket over her vivid navy and white robe which she wore with an orange, yellow and red cloak affair. It looked wonderful. She would create a sensation in Bond Street with her dark beauty and grace. She laughed and held the fur to her face.

'She loves it,' said Emily. 'That was a brainwave, Clem!' I was quite glad to hear her acknowledge that I had a brain at all.

Ahmada kissed his children and embraced NouNou very tenderly and it charmed me to see how open and loving he was with his family. Perhaps Tuareg men had always been like this, or maybe they had their own version of our New Man. Then we piled into the jeep with Cassini and off we went.

'Where are we going, Ahmada?' I asked.

'Maybe twenty minutes. We go to meet Tayen with the camels. He brings them to the start of the desert.'

'How many camels will there be?'

'Six riding camels and two for baggage. We are a proper camel train.'

I went quiet after that. To be truthful I was a bit apprehensive about the camel part of this adventure. So far, all we had had to do was sit in the back of an air-conditioned jeep and be transported here and there. The next stage would be quite different. For a start we would be out in the full glare of the desert sun all day and I had no idea how Emily and I would cope. I knew that we had to slap on sun cream at every opportunity and drink litres of water to avoid dehydration. We had seen Ahmada load up with a crate of bottled water, which was a relief. He said that the camels would drink from wells and that the men would take their water in goatskins which hung from the saddles.

I was also nervous about the camels. The ones we had seen were very tall indeed, standing perhaps eight feet high, and there was all the business of getting on and off which I had heard was precarious until you got the hang of it. Falling off a horse was one thing, but falling off a camel would be like toppling from a ladder. People had also warned me that they were vicious and bad-tempered beasts and that riding them was extremely uncomfortable and sometimes made you feel seasick.

I looked across at Emily, who had gone very quiet. She looked tired, with dark smudges under her eyes. I remembered that at the end of all this she would be flying home to start the new term at her London school and I felt a pang of conscience. This trip was not turning out to be strong on rest and relaxation. I wondered if, like me, she was apprehensive about the camel-riding. She hadn't said anything, and we were so physically adventurous and foolhardy as children that to admit to being nervous now was totally out of character.

I leaned across and touched her hand and she turned to look at me.

'Okay?' I said.

'Yeah.' She managed a small smile.

'This is what it must feel like to be a jockey milling around at the start of the Grand National,' I said. 'You know, you've done all the preparation and finally there you are waiting for the signal to go, but now you are wondering what the hell made you do it, and it's too late to pull out.'

'Yeah,' she said. 'I suppose it must.'

We were driving through scrubby desert on no apparent track, weaving amongst thorn trees and making any goats and sheep run for cover, and then up ahead we saw a rough block building and a flagpole.

'This is the first school for nomadic children,' explained Ahmada. 'The teacher here is a friend of mine and he looks after our vehicle while we make our journey.'

This news brightened Emily up and she started to take a professional interest in the school and what it taught, and then wanted to know about the Tamachek alphabet. Ahmada told her that later on he would write it out for her. There were very few children in the school at the moment, he explained, because the herds had moved away to where there was grazing.

We could now see a tall man waiting beside the building and Ahmada pulled up to let him climb in beside me.

'This is Abed,' he introduced us, and off we went again.

Although he was a Tuareg, Abed was wearing western clothes. I guessed that he thought it was more modern and suitable for a teacher. You wouldn't expect a Scotsman to turn up to teach in a kilt with a dagger in his sock, or a Welsh woman to wear one of those pointy hats and a shawl. He seemed rather solemn and shy and could hardly bring himself to even look at us. Emily quizzed him in French on curriculum and teachery sort of things, but since he replied very briefly, they did not make much progress. We gathered that the school was an important government initiative and was seen as a gesture of reconciliation towards the Tuareg people after the bitterness of the civil war. I could imagine Emily getting home and starting up a twinning project to send the school pencils and teaching materials, although I couldn't see that many of her London children, with their mobile phones and designer trainers, would be that keen on doing an exchange visit.

As we drove on you could tell that Cassini and Ahmada were getting more and more excited at the prospect of the camel trip. They had begun to talk loudly and Cassini's wonderful laugh kept spilling out and made us laugh as well. He spoke no French and so we didn't have the slightest idea what he was saying but it was infectiously funny all the same. We were now bouncing across a flat wide plain, thick with coarse bushes and dotted with the occasional thorn tree. Ahmada and Cassini peered out of the windows to the left and right. They were looking for the camels. Eventually we pulled up under a tree and Ahmada switched off the engine. As the sound died away a silence fell which seemed to press down from the hard blue sky above. We got out and stood under the tree. The thorns were at least three inches long. It was very, very hot and I could feel a trickle of sweat between my breasts and shoulder blades. Absolutely nothing moved and there was nothing to see except more of the same in every direction. Emily leaned against the trunk and closed her eyes. The men began to unpack the jeep, piling the stuff under the tree.

Cassini collected sticks for a fire and soon he was boiling a kettle and making tea. It was always the right time for a cup of tea and I thought how Gran would have approved. The men hunkered down to drink and smoke. Now we were out in the desert their voices were subdued. The huge silence and emptiness seemed to require it.

I lost track of how long we were there before Ahmada stood up and shaded his eyes and said, 'They come! The camels arrive!'

Emily and I stood up too. There was a dark smudge on the horizon, barely distinguishable from the horizon itself, and then I could make out small dots moving up and down, swaying rhythmically. I saw that these were the heads of the camels, travelling abreast. Our men began to yodel long cries of greeting and then we heard faint replies, and as they got nearer we saw that the camels were coming at a fast trot, their necks outstretched. The bright colours of the saddle blankets and the swinging tassels and decorated saddle bags were dancing splodges of colour in the distance. As they got closer we could make out two veiled riders perched on the tall saddles, the reins held high in one hand, their bare feet resting on the necks of their mounts. Each one led a string of three camels behind him. They rode with perfect, effortless balance, sitting tall and proud, and now they started to swirl the ends of the long reins above their heads and their cries were the long ululating calls that I had heard on the disc that Will had given me. Out of the simmering heat of the desert, out of the monochrome landscape which seemed petrified by the silver plate of the sun, out of the pounding silence they came galloping with their fearsome cries and their flashing colours.

Half terrified, half enthralled, Emily and I stood

rooted, side by side. My heart was racing and the heat was making my head throb. I felt weird and spaced out and as if I was drifting away from reality. I found Emily's hand and closed my fingers round hers. 'Goodness, Em!' I whispered. She didn't answer but dug her nails into my palm.

The leading camel, very tall and pure white, now seemed to be coming straight at us, the rider's face hidden behind the folds of his white chech. 'Hold hard, Clem!' muttered Emily and we instinctively knew we had to stand our ground. It was like when Emily's dad used to make us stand in a gateway to head off a bull. The great camel reared its head back and came to a stop only a few feet in front of us. The veiled rider kicked with his heels on its neck and it dropped to its knees, protesting loudly, and then folded its back legs, lowering itself on to its belly. Swiftly the man threw his leg over the high cross at the front of the saddle and leapt to the ground. Standing in front of us in a magnificent lime-green robe, the figure reached out to take our hands. It was Tayen.

Beryl Timmis

THIS MORNING KATHY brought back the photographs. She was anxious that I should have a look at them there and then, and even though I was reluctant, she had been so kind that I could hardly refuse.

It is distressing for me to relive these times, and as much as I try to block them out and think only of the present, my mind is undisciplined and keeps returning to French Sudan. It is as if I am being forced to confront what happened. For all this time I have hardly given it a thought. It was something that occurred when I was a girl. I did what I knew to be right, what Colonel Barthelot knew to be right, and I had no regrets. Have no regrets. So why is my sleep disturbed and my heart heavy, and why do memories, long forgotten, force themselves to the surface of my mind? Of course, I know why. It is because of Mary's mischievous request in her will. Almost as if she guessed the truth, she has disturbed the peace of my remaining days.

But I can't blame it all on Mary. It isn't her fault that I can't enjoy the novel I have chosen from the library, or doze peacefully in the afternoons after lunch. It is, I realise now, because something has shifted inside me. Doubts that I hadn't entertained before have crept into my heart like ivy into brickwork, and are now forcing it to break open and release feelings that I have denied all these years. I resist them with all my might. Why should I be made to feel guilty? None of it was my fault. I was the innocent in this sorry tale.

But was I? I am eighty-four years old and death cannot be far away. All my life my faith has been a comfort to me, but now it torments me. When I die I believe that I will meet my Maker and must account for my actions. How will I make Him understand that I did what I did because I thought it was right? Does a sin committed in good faith remain a sin? Is it too late to seek forgiveness? We are taught that it is never too late, but to be forgiven I must admit my guilt and confess that I sinned grievously against Mary, and this I cannot do, ever, because I still believe that what I did was right. Colonel Barthelot assured me of this at the time. He told me that I was courageous. He held my hand and kissed me. He kissed me. I remember the prickle of his moustache as his lips pressed against mine and how glad it made me that I had pleased him. He was such a distinguished man, too good for Mary's mother, whom I had always considered a silly woman. So my mind goes round and round and I find little peace.

I think of those two girls out in the desert and I am reassured that they will find nothing. It is too long ago. No one will remember. This is a comfort to me but also a burden, because the secret that now weighs so heavily will go with me to the grave. I find myself quite weak and trembling as Kathy hands me the packet of photographs. I tell her it is my heart, that I must rest for a moment, and I sit back in my chair and close my eyes. She is frightened and asks if she should ring the bell for assistance. I am all right, I am all right, I try to say, but my mouth is dry and the words are faint. What if it is *death that has come knocking? What if I die without forgiveness? That rash and inappropriate kiss from Mary's father, which has sustained me all these years; was my silence bought at too great a price? I am weak and feeble and tears slide down my cheeks.*

Poor Kathy pats my hand. 'There, there,' she says, 'you'll be all right, love.'

With a great effort I pull myself together. I am not ready to die yet. I struggle to sit up and search for the handkerchief tucked into my sleeve. I wipe my eyes behind my spectacles.

'I am perfectly all right, Kathy,' I say. 'Perfectly. Please

don't fuss!' To reassure her I open the photographs which are on my lap. They are grained and blurred and faded to sepia. The enlarging process has distorted them a little but the subjects are perfectly recognisable: the snaps of colonial Bamako taken from the horse-drawn taxi, the views of the river as dull as I remember – the flat water, the featureless shore. There are some I don't recognise, taken in Gao, of the residency and the mosque, the extraordinary mud building built in 1495 that was tomb to the prophet Askia. Kathy tells me that I had written this on the back of the tiny photograph. She says that she and her husband have recently seen a travel programme on the television about the mud mosques of Mali. She tells me that she can't believe that I got there first, all those years ago. 'You'd think he'd discovered them!' she says of the television traveller. 'You'd think no one had been there before him!'

There is a photograph of me standing beside the aeroplane that took me from Gao to Kidal; a high-wing monoplane sitting on the sand where it had landed, with a little cabin and a row of windows. The pilot is next to me in a long leather flying coat and a leather helmet. I suddenly remember walking over the sand to meet him. I was unsuitably dressed in a long linen skirt when trousers would have been much more practical, but my mother would not allow me to wear trousers and I haven't to this day.

I remember the young soldier carrying my suitcases and the colonel holding my arm. Then he took the camera from me and insisted on taking that photograph although, in my shyness, I protested. 'But you will want to show your young man!' he said, laughing. 'You will want to show him evidence of your great adventure!'

The hem of my skirt had collected some tiny prickly burrs from brushing against a desert bush. They were almost impossible to pull off and extremely irritating to the skin. The colonel bent to help me, and as he did so his fingers brushed my bare leg. No, it was more than that. He stroked my leg, quite deliberately, and smiled up at me. I carried that moment for a long time and wondered what he had meant by it. Was I a child in his eyes, or was his action something different? Could he really have seen me as an attractive young woman despite my unstylish clothes and my schoolgirl manner? Krim-krim, that was what the burrs were called. I haven't thought of that word for over sixty years. Krim-krim.

Kathy is talking all the time, passing the photographs, demanding my attention. The next one is of Kidal, that lonely and desperate outpost. I took it from the garden that had been created around the three-room residency, looking over towards the block house where the soldiers lived. The next is of the line of horses used by the cavalry, small and tough, accustomed to the terrible punishing heat, and then there is one of the camels, hobbled in a corral. The next is of Lieutenant Charpentier lounging on the steps of the residency. He is wearing a white pith helmet and loose white trousers. Sprawled over his knees is the young lion that he kept as a pet. 'Pato', Kathy is telling me. The lion's name was Pato. I had written it on the photograph. I remembered how it had roared at night when the wolves howled. How horrible it had been. How savage. It was a cruel and desperate place.

Colonel Barthelot had been right about the women. Charpentier and the young radio-telegrapher lived openly with Tuareg girls. They bathed in a tin bath under the trees and flaunted their nakedness while the Frenchmen lounged in the shade, smoking. I had never seen a completely naked woman and was shocked by the full breasts and luxurious pubic hair. The girls laughed and splashed each other and their sliding eyes were mocking.

Of course Charpentier had nothing to fear from anything I might report to the colonel. He was made confident because of Mary. He knew that the colonel's hands were tied. It was as if there was an unspoken understanding between the two men, and I remember thinking how wrong it was of Mary to put her father in this position. I felt angry with her on his behalf, although he himself had shown more sorrow than anger.

Charpentier was helpful, to an extent. As soon as a supply plane could be sent, it would take me to Mary and fly us both back in various stages to Senegal, where we would pick up the boat to Marseilles. Meanwhile I had to wait. I passed the days sitting in the shade, reading. The hours seemed endless, from when the sun rose in the pale sky to when it set in a ball of fire. Meanwhile the terrible wind blew endlessly, banging doors and shutters and whipping sand into spirals that raced each other across the compound. It got everywhere. My scalp prickled with it, the corners of my eyes became crusted, my mouth was full of grit. I woke with a cough that I shared with everyone else at the fort. I heard the men hawking and spitting in the mornings when the thin bugle call floated from the barracks.

Someone had evidently been moved out to allow me a small square room with a high shuttered window and a narrow camp bed. I asked to take my meals in my room but Charpentier insisted I join him and the young wireless operator in the evenings when they dined under a vine outside the residence. The Senegalese cook had been trained by the French and the food was passable. We ate couscous and roast meat, goat and sheep and the occasional antelope shot in the desert. The bread was plentiful and good. The men drank quantities of red wine.

I don't remember how long I was there. Perhaps two days,

or maybe three, but it seemed endless and I felt utterly alone. I longed to see Mary again and it tormented me that I couldn't go straight to her. Charpentier said that the over-land trip by camel was too far and too dangerous. I had to wait for the plane. At last he received news that, weather permitting, it would come the next day, bringing supplies and mail. 'Prepare to leave,' he said. 'Your stay with us is nearly over!'

Kathy is telling me how she rode a camel when she was on holiday in Morocco. She says it was a dirty great beast and that she was scared stiff. She tells me that she will bring a photograph to show me. Thank goodness, she gathers my own photographs and puts them back in the packet.

'I'll leave these here,' she says, propping them on the table by my chair. 'You can have another little look later on. You'll enjoy that, won't you, love?'

When she has gone I close my eyes. Was it murder? I ask myself. Was it murder that I committed all those years ago?

Emily

MY CAMEL WAS called Absau. He was eight years old and a pretty, pale dun colour. A cappuccino camel. Officially he is termed *jaune*. Ahmada told me that there are five possible colours in the camel range – *rouge*, *blanc*, *jaune*, *noir* and *azarghaf*, which in Tamachek means coloured, either brown or black and white. It is hard to imagine a piebald camel, but they do exist.

Absau was beautiful and gentle with large dark eyes and a thick fringe of eyelashes. He had a soft, tufty forelock, and as I rode I could reach out with my bare toes and bury them in his short blond mane. His round furry ears twitched back and forth as I talked to him and occasionally he would turn his head right round and look back at me as if he was asking me a question.

Getting up on him for the first time was bloody terrifying. Baba, who was introduced as Tayen's younger brother, and who was beautiful, with dark skin and slanting eyes, came and stood at his head and took hold of the plaited leather rein which was attached to a small ring through the right nostril and passed under the neck. He spoke quite good French and told me to take off my trainers, which he tied by their laces on to the front of the saddle.

'No shoes on Tuareg camel,' he explained. 'Tuareg ride with feet.'

Absau was lying down with his legs jack-knifed neatly beneath him, and Baba put a foot on his knee to discourage him from rising before I was properly in the saddle. Everything seemed to be done from the left side, as with a horse. Then he indicated that I should get up into the saddle, which I could see at once was much easier said than done. The saddle sat on a thickly folded brightly coloured blanket, high up on the withers of the camel, just in front of the hump. The seat was covered by another folded blanket, and to mount I had to lift my right leg right up and over this saddle, which, on the back of the couched camel, was a good three and a half feet up. Without using the cross at the front as a handhold, I had to hop like a monkey on to the seat. It was much harder than vaulting on to a horse and I dreaded making a fool of myself. Somehow or other I managed to scramble into place, glad of the baggy trousers and the long robe to hide my awkwardness. Then Baba, still standing on Absau's bent knee, asked if I was ready. I gripped the base of the cross with one hand and put my feet in position on Absau's neck and nodded, too nervous to speak. At Baba's command, Absau, complaining loudly, unfolded his hind legs and rose up suddenly from behind and I was pitched up and violently forward. Then the forelegs came up and I was thrown back and then forward again as he came upright, and there I was, mounted on a camel.

Baba passed me the rein and Ahmada hurried over to see how I was getting on. I looked down on him from what seemed a very great height. 'Very, very camel man!' he said approvingly. He was beaming and excited and I realised that this was a moment that he had been looking forward to. He clearly loved being back in the desert and even more so because this was such an unusual trip.

The seat of the saddle was small and narrow, not much wider than that of an old-fashioned bicycle, and perched as it was high up on Absau's withers, I felt very insecure. To make matters worse, the surface of the folded rug on which I sat felt extremely slippery under my bottom. Unlike riding astride a horse, where you have a lot of animal directly between your legs and the option of gripping with your calves to keep your balance, as well as a good long shoulder in front to save you if you pitch forward, sitting on a Tuareg saddle was a much more precarious business. On either side there was a sheer drop, eight feet to the ground, with nothing to hang on to or break my fall if I found myself slipping one way or the other. In front of the cross of the saddle there was only the dip of Absau's slender neck, way beyond reach except when I stretched out my bare feet. Baba showed me how to place them, one behind the other, like a ballet dancer, and how to use them to keep my balance on the saddle. This was just about possible when we were stationary, but when we moved off I knew I would feel terribly insecure.

I hardly dared to turn my head to look for Clemmie, but I realised she was already up on her tall white camel, her feet resting on his neck, and had taken up the rein in her right hand. She looked beautiful, of course, and confident, but when she caught my eye she made a terrified face and I knew that she was as scared as I was.

The men leapt up into their saddles, their camels grumbling loudly to one another, and there was much shouting of last-minute instructions and farewells as Abed climbed into the driver's seat of the jeep in order to take it back to the schoolhouse. It was time to go.

'Are we ready?' cried Ahmada, whirling the end of his rein above his head. 'Niggler! Let's go!' and pressing his heels on to his camel's neck he moved off. I had no option but to fall in behind because it was Absau who was making all the arrangements. His action was slow and swaying and I had to concentrate hard on balancing, using my feet to keep me in position and holding on to the base of the cross with my free hand. It felt very peculiar and unsafe. Shit, I thought. We've got a hundred miles to do like this.

For perhaps the first couple of hours we rode on flattish, featureless ground of white sand and scrubby bushes, and Absau's neck was steady and I began to feel more confident, but then the country changed and the sand rose and fell like a lumpy sea. The moment Absau negotiated a bank or a dune and dropped his neck accordingly and maybe broke into a few steps of a trot on the downhill side, my feet slipped off his neck and I could only remain in position by trying, desperately, to keep my balance on the narrow, pitching saddle. It was possible to half turn and hang on to the back with one hand, but this was uncomfortable and meant that my weight shifted to one side or the other, which in turn felt precarious.

It was utterly hair-raising and I hadn't got enough nerve to look round at Clemmie until, thank God, we hit a smoother, easier stretch. She was riding two behind me and I noticed now that the beast she had been mounted on was huge, the biggest by far, and pure white, with a very proud and disdainful stare. Eventually she was able to come alongside me and she told me that his name was Badoush, and that he was the personal camel of Baba and Tayen's father, who was the head of the tribe of Imrad. Along the curve of his haughty nose there were three little bobbles in a row, which was the mark of a very well-bred camel. When he was born the skin had been nicked and twisted into these knots, as a permanent reminder of his noble lineage. Clemmie said she had been told that he was a dancing camel. 'Isn't he perfect, Em? Baba has told me that the Tuareg train their very best and most beautiful camels to do a sort of wonderful musical ride, like dressage, only much more exciting because it's with guns, I think, or swords maybe, and the camels actually dance!'

With Pug Bag still round her neck, she looked graceful and completely at home with her white feet resting on Badoush's white neck, but she said that she felt as insecure as I did.

'I shall fall straight off if he does anything but walk!' she confessed. 'I'm only just managing to sit here at all. If I look down I get vertigo.'

'Stop it, Clem! Don't make me laugh!' I pleaded, turning to hang on to the back of my saddle.

Our little camel train had sorted itself out by now, with Tayen and Cassini, who rode like demons, their bare feet working away at the necks of their camels, in the lead. They kept galloping ahead and cavorting about in a showing-off way and I was terrified that their antics would set our camels off, but to my relief they plodded along in a stately fashion as if they knew they were looking after us.

Behind them came Ahmada, who looked like a city man out for a weekend ride, and who complained loudly that his saddle was too small and therefore very uncomfortable. Without understanding a word, it was easy to follow the gist of the conversation, which ran on totally predictable lines, exploring the inevitable consequences of having his manly tackle squashed.

The camel train came to a halt and Cassini and

Ahmada got off and tried to readjust the saddle. There was a lot of ribald laughter and then Ahmada got on again, squawking in a high-pitched voice as his camel began to rise. Cassini laughed so much that he fell over on to the sand on his hands and knees and Clemmie and I shrieked and struggled to hang on like two terrified monkeys on a cliff face.

Behind us was Baba, leading the pack animals and riding quietly. Every now and then he came alongside to encourage us or show us how to use our feet to guide our camels. We had to unlearn the impulse to use our heels as a sign to go faster as in horse-riding, because a few sharp little kicks was the signal for the camel to go down. Instead, to urge your mount on you used a heel-to-toe pressure on the neck and made a soft huffing sound as if you were blowing on to a pair of glasses before you polished them.

'It's the gentlest command you could think of,' said Clemmie. 'They really love their camels, don't they? Do you see that they don't carry sticks or wear spurs or put barbaric bits in their mouths, and did you notice the care they took when they saddled up? They took ages adjusting the saddles and the packs to make sure that the camels don't get saddle sore. I love them for it, I really do, and look at the wonderful condition the animals are in. They'd win Best in Show at the Bath and West, wouldn't they, if there was such a thing as a class for camels?'

Ahmada, who had come to ride alongside us, explained that indeed the Tuareg do love their camels and that when a boy is given his first riding camel it grows up with him so that he knows it as well as if it was his brother or sister. Clemmie's eyes shone. It was the sort of thing that really appealed to her because she was always devoted to her animals at home, weeping for days when a dog had to be put down or her old pony, Blazer, dispatched. She still couldn't say his name without tears welling in her eyes.

'Tell us about Cassini,' I said to Ahmada. 'Is he a nomad or a townie?'

'He lives in an encampment,' said Ahmada, 'but he is not a true nomad. He no longer moves with a herd of animals although every year he goes with camels into the far desert to fetch salt from the mines in Taoudenni. Fifteen days each way.'

'Why is salt so important?'

'It is needed for the health of camels and all other animals. Salt is necessary for life.'

'He is a wonderful rider!'

'Yes. He wins many camel races.'

'Is he married?'

Ahmada laughed. 'My goodness! Six times! He has nine children. He gets divorced and passes on his wife and takes a new one.'

'What do you mean, passes on his wife? You make her sound like a parcel.'

'I mean she is free to marry another man.'

'Oh, I see. Who looks after the children?'

'They stay with their mothers when they are young. Later they choose to go with their mother or their father. A divorce is often a celebration. It is no problem. To be married is not always to be happy. Because Tuareg women own tent and animals, they do not need a no-good husband. Goodbye, they say, and he must leave. Or if the Tuareg wife is not pleasing to her husband, then he will leave her, but she keeps all that is hers.'

It sounded a very sensible arrangement and made me think of my mother and father and the mess they had got into. My father would enjoy some aspects of being a Tuareg, and maybe my mother would too.

'How can he afford to keep so many children?'

'Ah!' said Ahmada. 'That I do not know, but maybe it is that Allah must provide!'

No wonder Cassini had prayed so devoutly at noon.

'What about beautiful Baba?' asked Clemmie. 'He is just like a film star, isn't he, Em?'

'Baba is engaged to marry for two years but he cannot because he is too poor. He must buy his wife and he has no money, no animal of his own, except his camel.'

'Oh no!' cried Clemmie. 'Poor Baba! How dreadful to be in love and have to wait. I wonder how much money he needs?' I knew what she was thinking. In a moment she would suggest that we sponsor him.

The sun beat down and Clemmie and I pulled our cheches across our faces to protect them. The camels' pace felt more regular now and we had both relaxed enough to find the swaying movement soothing and hypnotic. As the afternoon wore on a heavy silence fell over our little group. I looked at my watch once and then looked again and found that an hour had passed like a minute. The landscape hardly changed although every now and then we climbed to the top of a ridge and there was a new valley spread out below. We saw no one and nothing moved. The sky was a clear, high dome of blue across which no bird flew. From time to time I saw on the horizon what looked like a flat stretch of water with trees reflected in it, disappearing into a blue and gold drifting fog, and knew that it was a mirage. Behind us Baba began to sing in a low, gentle voice. The rhythm of his song was the rhythm of the camels' feet.

I tried to think about Ted. It seemed a long time since I had last turned it all over in my mind. Out of habit I wanted to revisit the pain of what I had been through, like the compulsion to pick at a scab. My relationship with him had been such an important part of my life for so long that I needed to continually reassess what he had meant to me and what losing him had made me become. I had been defined by him, and with him gone I was scared of confronting the bit of me that was left behind. I dreaded finding that I was less than half a person with less than half a life. At least if I thought about him, obsessed about him, he was still occupying my emotions and shaping my identity. I was still Emily in relation to Ted. I might be dumped, angry and bitter and fuelled by a lot of rage and regrets, but my life had a meaning and a context. Emily with no Ted, emptied of feelings for him, was another, more frightening, matter.

The overwhelming peace of the desert, the scoured landscape, the silence, the steady plod of the camels had an insidious calming effect. Why did I do it? I found myself thinking. Why all this agonising about him? Why didn't I just let it go, let it all slip away? What bound me to Ted was a chain of my own making, hammered out of hurt and lies and deceit and self-deception. Why should I drag it about with me? I could just loosen my hold and let it fall away. When Ted had dropped out of sight, the view that would open up would be of the true and enduring landscape of my life, stripped bare, clean, undistorted. Then I could begin again. I could make a fresh start with a clear sense of myself and who I really was.

Gradually the light faded and on one side the sky changed from vermilion to violet to the palest green. On the other, where the sun was going down, everything was pink, the closer to the rim of the earth, the deeper the pink, and as the pink rose higher into the heavens it paled and became yellow and then green and then melted into the colours of the other side. Cassini jumped down from his camel and began to gather brush for a fire. By the time we halted and Absau dropped obediently to his knees, the light had all but gone and the first stars glittered in the vastness of the heavens.

We had stopped in a shallow bowl of land with a featureless edge, empty in all directions except to the north, where there was a line of rocks, black blocks against the last glimmer of light. Cassini got the fire going and a pot of something on to boil, while Baba and Tayen unsaddled the camels and hobbled them loosely before turning them away to find what they could to eat.

Ahmada sorted out the bedding and untied our packs from the saddles, which he lined up together and covered with blankets. Clemmie and I had a quiet discussion about where we should sleep. Much as we liked and trusted the men, we did not want to behave inappropriately or give the wrong signals. So far there had been no problem at all and we wanted to keep it that way.

'You see, they don't find us at all attractive,' Clemmie explained. 'We're much too big and white – like those two Large White sows that Grandpa had in the orchard!' Of course, this was miles from the truth, at least in Clemmie's case. It was easy to see that Tayen and Baba had fallen under her spell. I had the feeling that Tayen's dashing displays of camel-riding were to attract her attention. He behaved like the boys in the village who rode about on bikes with their feet on the handlebars to make the girls, giggling on the bench by the war memorial, take notice.

'Well let's go on the opposite side of the campfire,'

I said. 'They seem to have put all their blankets over there.' I pointed to the line of camel saddles.

We began to unpack our bags, scrabbling about for what we needed. It was now quite dark and we had to use our torches, but Cassini wanted to borrow a light to shine on his cooking pot, so we were reduced to one between us. We kept putting things down in the sand and then losing them. We located our sponge bags and, taking a bottle of water, sloped off to find a place to wash. We limited ourselves to a mug of water each, and it wasn't as hard as it sounds to clean one's teeth and wash one's face and hands and other key areas in such a small amount. It seemed that as we got accustomed to the heat of the desert we sweated very little and were generally un-smelly, even at the end of a long day. Our feet felt fine and papery to touch and the skin of our shins was silvery. We were drying up in the heat.

It was wonderful to take off all our clothes in the dark and feel the desert wind, which had risen as the sun went down, blow over our bare damp skin. Clemmie had brought green-tea-scented talcum powder and body lotion and we slathered this on before we put on our pyjamas. We loosened our hair and brushed it with drops of rosemary oil. The dry atmosphere had made my wavy hair go completely straight and smooth, exactly as I had always wanted it. Straight hair made me feel a different person, more sophisticated and thinner. Clemmie's hair shone silver in the starlight.

Slipping on our flip-flops, we shuffled back to the fire, where the men were gathered, half their faces lit golden by the flames, the other half in shadow. They were talking quietly, laughing softly, pouring tea into little glasses, and they looked up as they heard us approach. Cassini and Baba gazed open-mouthed at Clemmie. It was the first time they had seen her hair. She hunkered down beside them, resting her hand lightly on Ahmada's shoulder, and a silver curtain fell forward across her face. I was struck by how at home and natural she was amongst this gang of tribesmen, and then I remembered that she had grown up like this, surrounded by adoring brothers, and that was the difference between us. Or one of them, at least. She put up a hand and carelessly tucked the wing of hair behind her ear and then twisted the whole silky mass of it into a hank and tucked it into the neck of her pyjama jacket.

The spell was broken. The men moved over to allow us to sit on a blanket and passed us glasses of tea. Cassini was stirring a pot over the flames and breaking up a flat circle of bread and adding it to the stew. Ahmada passed him some tin bowls and he slopped spoonfuls into each one and then handed them round. The contents tasted strange but wholesome. There were carrots and onions in a dark gravy and some pieces of meat. The bread had swelled into stodgy lumps. Cassini passed round an old tin filled with sheep butter which the men added to their stew, where it swam in oily yellow globules on the surface. Clemmie and I declined but we cleared our bowls and even had a second helping. We hadn't realised how hungry we were. Cassini was pleased and laughed his high, pealing laugh. It was so dark I could hardly see his face, just his white teeth and his quick hands as he stirred the pan.

'Gran would have thought this was highly indigestible, wouldn't she?' said Clemmie to me, poking with her spoon into her bowl. 'All this doughy bread. She'd have said it would keep her awake all night! Up and down, she would have said, looking for the Rennies.'

'I think she'd have a point.' It made us smile to remember our grandmother, who had hardly ever left Dorset in her long life, and what she would think if she could see us now.

'Do you think she's got her eye on us?' asked Clemmie, looking up at the sky. 'She'll be saying, "Whatever are those two girls up to now? Look at the pair of them down there with those wild desert men!"'

Now we had eaten I was overcome with tiredness, and although it was only half past seven, Clemmie and I began to sort out our sleeping bags. Time, as observed in our ordinary lives, like so much else, did not apply here. The wind had grown quite chilly, so we wrapped ourselves up in our scarves, put on warm socks, organised our packs beside us so that they were like bedside tables, and put the torch somewhere we could find it in the dark. We were sure to have to go off into the night for a pee. The pug bag sat on the sand between us, his little black glass eyes keeping watch. Great-Aunt Mary, I thought, just look where you have brought us, you old witch. We climbed into our sleeping bags and I snuggled down while Clemmie put on her night cream. She is a stickler for skin care, whereas I am far too lazy to bother.

'You really should,' she chided me. 'Just think how dry and wrinkled you will get in this climate.'

She passed over the jar and then we lay back and watched Cassini cleaning the dinner bowls with a piece of stick and wiping them with a sack. The men had made a nest of blankets behind the row of camel saddles, which acted as an efficient wind break, and they were already settling down. Within a few minutes they appeared to be asleep, and Clemmie and I lay for a while watching shooting stars travelling across the brilliant night sky as if drawn by a silver fingertip. The wind moaned softly and the fire hissed a little as the embers shifted and fell. From far off a coyote howled, and then another. Somewhere out there in the dark our camels were foraging; otherwise we were entirely alone.

'Good night, Em,' whispered Clemmie.

'Good night.'

'Do you know what I'm thinking?'

'I can't begin to guess.'

'"I saw Eternity the other night,"' said Clemmie, raising her arms to the huge night sky.

'"Like a great ring of pure and endless light, All calm as it was bright!" This is it, Em, isn't it? This is what she meant. This is what she wanted us to see.'

Clemmie

THE NEXT DAY did not start well. I woke at dawn, conscious of someone stirring, and saw Cassini poking the fire into life and putting the kettle on for tea. The other men had not moved from the pile of blankets and while it was still dark it seemed a good time for Emily and me to get dressed. Emily was cross at being woken and it was bitterly cold peeling off our pyjamas and tugging on our clothes. We both had congested sinuses and sniffed loudly and repeatedly and Emily said that her eyes were bunged up. She complained that she was constipated and that she hadn't had a proper crap for five days and was annoyed that I had.

'It's not exactly a competition,' I said. 'Anyway, I'll give you something for it. I've got some laxatives in the medical kit.'

'Yeah! And then I'll get the runs, which will be great, stuck on a camel all day!'

We went back to the fire as Cassini woke the other men, who groaned and stretched and scratched. They seemed to have the same early-morning sniff and cough as we did. We could hear them at it, snuffling and hawking away as they folded up their blankets. As dawn broke and streaked the sky with pale yellow light they shuffled off with their mats to pray, their murmuring voices drifting across to us where we sat in silence, hunched into our fleece jackets, our heads wrapped up against the cold.

Then Baba was sent off to look for the camels while we drank our tea and ate some of the unleavened bread from the night before and a handful of hard dry dates. We were all subdued by the early hour and the cold. The magic of the night before had evaporated.

Emily complained that she had a headache and I gave her some paracetamol. Cassini and Ahmada both said that they also had bad heads and I gave them some as well. They seemed terribly keen on pills and wanted to know what I had got for bad stomachs and sore throats. They explained their ailments with grave faces, and eagerly took whatever I prescribed and instantly cheered up when they had swallowed the dose.

'Don't you have natural medicines?' I asked Ahmada. 'Plants and herbs and things like that?'

'Oh my goodness, yes!' he said. 'We divide illness between the bottom and top half of the body. The top half is hot and the bottom half is cold.' He explained that ailments of a hot nature had to be treated with cold cures, and cold ailments with hot. All foods and plants fell in to one or other category. For instance, cow milk is cold, while camel, sheep and goat milk is hot. He pointed out a fleshy plant which grew in the sand. 'This is colquinte,' he said. 'It is a hot plant. It is poisonous but is used for cold illnesses of the stomach. It causes vomiting and then the fever passes.'

'You can see the attraction of the pills,' muttered Emily.

She was still cross because of the constipation. I persuaded her to take two laxative tablets. She insisted on reading the directions, which promised her a 'gentle evacuation', including all the possible contraindications, before she agreed to swallow them. Ahmada hovered around and said that he would like some as well but I fobbed him off with a little tub of Johnson's baby powder for his saddle sores. He showed the little plastic drum to Cassini and shook some powder out on to the palm of his hand. Cassini sniffed it suspiciously and, licking a finger, gave it a taste.

It was still very cold and windy and the sun was just a white glare in a grey sky. We sat and waited, and then Cassini and Tayen went to look for Baba. They were gone a long time. Eventually Cassini reappeared and told Ahmada that Baba and Tayen were following the tracks of the camels, who, despite being hobbled, had started for home when they had been let loose the night before and had gone a long distance back the way we had come.

Emily and I were familiar with this strong homing instinct in livestock. Whenever we moved the sheep they managed to find a way to get out and go back to where they had come from, and the cattle were nearly as bad, charging through the village and cutting up the verges and always making for the grand lawn at the Old Rectory. It was rather endearing to hear that camels were the same.

After a long time we heard a far-off yodelling cry and then we saw the camels coming at a fast trot with Tayen and Baba riding bareback. When they pulled up, we learned that it was naughty Badoush who had led the rest away, and he looked particularly superior and offhand.

The camels were couched and saddled and the two baggage camels carefully loaded and then we were ready to go. Tayen came to help me mount Badoush and getting on was easier this time. When I was ready in the saddle, Badoush lurched up on to his feet, protesting mildly. Tayen passed me the rein and without couching his own camel somehow leapt up into the saddle and we were off.

It was cold for the first hour or so and my bare feet froze on Badoush's neck. Emily had discovered that Absau had got ticks and she was convinced she would get bitten, although the men assured her that camel ticks didn't attach themselves to humans. I made the mistake of reminding her to drink frequently from the bottle of water we each carried in our saddlebag and she nearly fell off trying to reach it.

Tayen and Ahmada argued about the way, stopping and pointing and then taking off in another direction, and I held things up again by asking to get down from Badoush the moment I saw a suitable rock to go behind, which made Emily glare jealously. By midday the landscape had changed and the sand had given way to hills of bare rock and boulders and loose shale and it was difficult for the camels to find a path. Their flat, spreading feet were unsuitable for negotiating the sharp, broken ground and we made slow progress. Badoush stopped every few steps to complain and riding was uncomfortable and scary. As our camels slid and stumbled, Emily and I hung on grimly to the backs of our saddles while the wind howled between the high rocks and spun stinging sand into our faces.

When the sun came out it thumped off the rocks and we were both hot and cold at the same time. The heat seemed to sear my lungs with each breath. It was like swallowing a blowtorch. It was a desolate, horrible place and it stretched as far as the eye could see into the distance. There was nothing for it but to shut up and plod on.

By two o'clock it was extremely hot and we had not had a break. The men seemed tense, Tayen and Ahmada still arguing quietly. One of the baggage camels cut its foot and Baba jumped off and tried to bind it. It took fright and jumped sideways and a bag of rice spilled from the sack that hung from its side. Cassini looked back and shouted angrily at Baba, which upset Emily and me, who could see that it wasn't his fault. The atmosphere was strained and uncomfortable. When we got going again I spoke to Baba to try to show him that we were on his side, but he did not reply and pretended that he hadn't heard, his face dark and sulky.

Emily grumbled from behind me. The saddle was rubbing her and she had a collection of sharp little burrs, which Baba said were called krim-krim, along the hem of her robe. They were working their way into her skin, and she still had a cracking headache. 'On and bloody on!' she muttered. 'We've been riding for three fucking hours and there's no end to this horrible place.'

Slowly, as the afternoon drew on, we moved across the high rocky plateau and descended on to a sandy plain, where at last Ahmada called a halt. Badoush dropped to the ground without being told and I had to grab at the cross on the front of my saddle to stop myself falling. Thank God it didn't snap off in my hand. It was then that I noticed, with an awful lurch of purest panic, that I no longer had Pug Bag around my neck.

Beryl Timmis

THIS MORNING I took communion. We are fortunate here at The Willows that the matron arranges for a local priest to call once a fortnight to administer the sacraments to any of the residents who wish to partake of them. We gather in the lounge, those of us who are able, one or two on Zimmer frames, and receive communion together. It is not always without incident. Last time there was a medical emergency. Muriel Fry had one of her turns and had to be stretchered out. There are often spectacles lost down the backs of chairs, or malfunctioning hearing aids, or mix-ups over sticks and handbags. Some of the staff, such as Kathy, join us, and are as helpful as they can be, but nevertheless for those of us who are a little more compos mentis, *it can be distracting.*

Although Matron puts a notice on the door as a reminder to the residents that there is a service taking place, both times

I have attended there have been interruptions. At some point the door was pushed open and a loud voice demanded, 'What's going on in here?' before one of the staff bundled the intruder, protesting, out into the corridor.

This morning the service was conducted by a woman priest. She was perfectly pleasant although I find it hard to come to terms with the idea of a woman administering the sacraments and she struck me as rather patronising towards us. She used the tone of a primary school teacher, bright and jolly, and spoke slowly and clearly as if we were all hard of understanding. Lady Forbes was helped into the room by Kathy. She walked very slowly and leaned heavily on her stick but she is still an imposing-looking woman. Her craggy face is highly coloured and her hair very white. Kathy has told me that she does what she can to make it tidy, but this morning it looked particularly unkempt. She is often dressed eccentrically and today was wearing a tweed skirt and what looked like a quilted bed jacket. Kathy brought her over to sit next to me on the sofa, which has a high, firm seat. She looked at me, quite without recognition.

'It's Beryl Timmis, Lady Forbes,' I said gently.

'Who?' she said in her booming voice, turning right round to stare at me.

'Beryl Timmis.'

'Have we met?'

Kathy made a face at me as if to say that there was no point in continuing this conversation, so I just said, 'Yes, we have.' I had spoken to her in the corridor several times already and had reminded her that I used to help with the Lifeboat collection which she once organised. I noticed that she had become very thin. She sat with her legs wide apart, the tweed skirt sagging between them. She wore no stockings and the skin of her stick-like legs was mottled blue and purple and veiny like old marble. I remembered how very smart she used to look dressed in her WRVS uniform, laying a wreath at the war memorial in Sherborne on Armistice Sunday. Her photograph was in the local paper each year. I thought how sad it was that old age can rob the most distinguished person of dignity.

The lady vicar began the service by introducing herself as the Reverend Pauline Cook and looking round with a bright smile. Lady Forbes turned to me. 'Who is this woman?' she demanded in a very loud voice. The room went quiet and then the Reverend Pauline began again, addressing herself to us personally this time.

'I don't understand a word she's saying!' interrupted Lady Forbes. 'Is she the chiropodist?'

Kathy managed to shush her and the Reverend Pauline wisely pressed on. I particularly wanted to have time to think about the words of the communion, especially the admission of sins and the absolution. Of course we were using a modern version with garbled, incomprehensible language, but I had read my old Book of Common Prayer in my room beforehand. 'We acknowledge and bewail our manifold sins and wickedness, which we from time to time have most grievously committed . . . the remembrance of them is grievous unto us; the burden of them is intolerable . . . forgive us all that is past . . . Have mercy upon us. Have mercy upon us.' I read on. 'Almighty God . . . who of his great mercy hath promised forgiveness of sins to all them that with hearty repentance and true faith turn unto him . . .' Hearty repentance. That was what I needed to think about. Unless I heartily repented I could not ask for, or expect, forgiveness.

Looking round the room, I didn't imagine that the sins accumulated there amounted to very much. At our age there wasn't the scope. Pettiness, greed, impatience, intolerance perhaps. It is as hard to love one's fellow man at eighty as it is at any other age. These were the sins of which I could repent. The other thing that troubled me and had weighed me down since Mary died I would push away and do my best to forget.

The Reverend Pauline rattled through the service in a singsong voice and then began to administer the host. She complicated matters by asking each of us our name, our Christian name. Of course we were taken by surprise, unused to this personal approach, and some of the communicants became flustered. When she reached us I was ready with 'Beryl', but Lady Forbes glared and said, 'What did you say?'

'What is your Christian name, dear?' said Reverend Pauline gently, holding the wafer high in one hand as if she were training a dog.

'What do you want to know for?' boomed Lady Forbes suspiciously. She looked round for Kathy. 'What does this woman want to know my name for?'

Kathy did her best to soothe her, but it turned into what we call an 'incident' and Lady Frobes had to be led from the room. Of course this was most distracting and quite took my mind off my personal prayers and what I wanted to reflect upon. I waited a little time after the service had ended and considered asking the Reverend Pauline if I could speak to her, but she was the wrong person and it was the wrong place and she was already chatting to the staff and busy wrapping up the chalice and the wafers and putting them into a shopping bag as if they were the leftovers of a picnic.

I went back to my room and sat in my armchair. In a short time morning coffee would come round and I decided I would take both milk and sugar because I felt a little shaky. On the table by my chair was the bright yellow packet of photographs. I looked at it for some time before reaching for it and holding it in my lap. When Kathy had her day off I could give it to the girl who came round to empty our waste-paper baskets into a black bin bag, and that would be the end of it. I could tell Kathy I had mislaid the packet and by then the bag would be long gone. I was certainly not going to look at them again. I pushed the packet down the side of the chair, out of sight.

I have lost count of how many days the girls have been gone and have not the slightest idea where they will be by now, but I doubt very much that they will have reached the fastness of the desert where I travelled. That savage land will always be a bare and empty place. They won't have the protection of the French army as I did, and of course Mary's father made everything as easy as possible for me. He was so grateful, you see, that I had come to take Mary home.

When the aeroplane arrived, landing in the sand outside the fort, it was flown by the same pilot who had brought me from Gao to Kidal. It was a regular commercial flight, operating a mail service to these isolated outposts in the desert, and there was usually room for one or two passengers. The colonel had arranged that I be flown to Mary and that the pilot go on to refuel at the large French fort at Bourem and then come back for us the next day. Charpentier had sent men on by camel to mark out a makeshift runway in the sand, so Mary knew I was coming.

Her father had explained that it might be difficult to persuade her to come away with me, especially because she was now married and it would mean leaving her husband, but he insisted that she must be got out of the country before it became too difficult to travel. 'I am afraid that of late Mary and I have not enjoyed a good relationship – certainly not when I learned that she had married so unwisely and without my consent. There is going to be a war,' he had said gloomily. 'It is imperative that she return to England with you while it is still possible and this is what you must persuade her to do. She will listen to you. You were her best friend in England and she will value you for your good sense, my dear, of which I can see you have enough for both of you.'

I blushed with pleasure. I had never been special in any way before. I was more accustomed to being invisible and overlooked, and I can see now that in a small and self-important way I felt that he was right, that he had looked into me and seen my worth as no one else had done.

'But what is the matter with her? You said that she was unwell?'

The colonel threw up his shoulders. 'A woman's problem,' he said vaguely, 'and also,' his voice dropped confidentially, 'I tell you, Beryl, what I do not admit to others. Marie is suffering from what we call desert fever. Her mind has become confused, weakened by the sun and the isolation of where she has been living. Let me put it like this: she is not herself. But do not be alarmed, my dear. You, with your common sense, your sensitivity, will understand. You will do what is necessary.'

I nodded, pleased and flattered by his confidence in me, but I didn't know what he meant at all. I had no idea of what condition he was referring to. All I knew was that Mary would be glad to see me and would be counting the hours until my arrival. I was confident of that. In this dreadful wild place the familiar face of an old friend from home would surely be a source of joy.

The flight was rough. The wind buffeted the little plane, which lurched and bucked alarmingly, but the pilot, a taciturn man who did not address me once – and I was to be glad of this later – appeared unconcerned. We flew low over endless sand and stony plains and then a great rocky ridge of sharp red boulders. It was the most desolate place I had ever seen. After an hour or so he turned to me and shouted something I could not catch, the noise of the engine and the vibration were so great, and pointed ahead through the cockpit window. Then I saw in the distance a line of painted oil drums in the sand. The landing strip. We were nearly there. God willing, I should soon see Mary again.

There is a sudden knock on the door, and I start in my chair as the girl comes in with my coffee.

'You all right, love?' she says. 'You look as if you've seen a ghost.'

A ghost! Why had the girl used that word? I search her face as she puts down my cup of coffee. She is a lardy girl with full pink cheeks and a thick band of fat under her chin. Her brown hair is braided in that curious way, in row upon row of tight ridges all over her scalp. Her expression is mild and gentle and indifferent. What could she know anyway?

There is not a person living who could suspect that I am a murderess.

Emily

I HEARD CLEMMIE gasp with horror and turned to see what was wrong. I was bloody fed-up, feeling really quite ill with an awful headache and stomach pains, and the journey had been tough. Everyone seemed on edge, and as we worked our way through the godforsaken landscape I had felt a growing sense of resentment. What a ridiculous thing this was that we were doing. What a pointless waste of time and effort. A selfish old woman had manipulated us into fulfilling her crazy last wish – or rather, had worked on Clemmie's romantic silliness, and she in turn had worked on me.

One look at Clemmie's face was enough to warn me of what was coming.

'The pug bag!' she cried. 'Where is it? It's gone!'

My first reaction was fury. I wanted to hit her. If

she was joking, it wasn't funny. In fact it was the last straw. She began to search frantically amongst the bags attached to her saddle. 'It was round my neck all the time!' she whimpered. 'I never took it off!'

'It can't have gone,' I said. 'Don't be so fucking stupid. It can't have gone if you never took it off.'

Clemmie stopped scrabbling about, fell to her knees beside Badoush and burst into loud tears. 'I did!' she wailed. 'I remember now. I took it off when I stopped to go to the loo. I took it off and put it on a rock!' She covered her face with her hands, sobbing loudly.

The men gathered round, greatly alarmed.

'What is the matter?' said Ahmada. 'Oh my goodness, what has happened?'

I felt my own tears threatening, hot behind my eyes.

'She's lost it!' I cried. 'She's bloody well gone and lost Great-Aunt Mary. She put Pug Bag on a rock miles and miles back when she asked to stop. Remember?' I threw my arm out in the direction from which we had come. I was still furious, without a shred of compassion for Clemmie's misery, and I marched off to sit in the scant, unmoving shade of a thorn tree. I wanted nothing to do with it.

Ahmada hunkered down next to Clemmie.

'You have lost your beloved relative?' he asked gently.

'Yes,' sobbed Clemmie.

'Do you know where?'

'Yes, I think so. Like Emily said, way back where you stopped for me. Before the rocky bit, near the beginning of our ride.'

Ahmada said nothing. He got up and went to Tayen, who was busy unloading the pack camels. They had a low conversation. Baba joined them and they began to argue with a lot of hand gestures and arm-waving.

Clemmie looked across to me, her face contorted with misery. 'I'm sorry, Emily. I'm so, so sorry! I've been so careful. It was the one thing I knew I had to be so careful about – I've never taken off the bag before.'

I sniffed and didn't answer. She wanted me to be nice about it and I couldn't. I was too angry and felt too ill and was too thoroughly pissed off.

'I'll have to go back,' she said. 'I'll have to. I can't leave Great-Aunt Mary on a rock.'

'Oh yeah!' I said furiously. 'Do that! Ride back into the desert. Go on! That would be fucking sensible, wouldn't it?'

Ahmada and Tayen came back to Clemmie with the air of a delegation.

'No worries!' announced Ahmada. I couldn't believe

how kind and calm he was. 'Tayen will go back. He will rest his camel and go back tomorrow morning very early. We will continue slowly to the well, half a day from here. We will water our camels and wait for him to join us.'

Clemmie stood up. Her headscarf had slipped down and she flicked her hair so that it hung loose. Consciously or not, she was weaving her magic.

'He can't go on his own! What if something happens to him? What if he can't find it? I must go with him!'

'He will travel fast if he is on his own. He remembers the place and he can read the tracks of our camels. He is Tuareg!'

Tayen, standing beside him, looked even more lofty and noble than usual. He was glad to have been singled out to do something special for Clemmie.

'I am so, so sorry. Tayen, I am so sorry!' Clemmie turned to him and reached out and took his hand. They looked at one another for a long moment. Tayen lifted his free hand and gently stroked her hair. He said something to Ahmada.

'What is he saying?' asked Clemmie.

'He says your hair is like moonlight on the sand. He says a man does anything for this beauty.'

That was it. I had had enough. I stood up. I knew

that I was not beautiful, that my face was hot and red and I was shaking with anger.

'Now just a minute,' I shouted. My voice was harsh and ugly with emotion. 'Just wait a minute. Clemmie, I need to talk to you.' I marched over and roughly grabbed her arm and turned her away from the men.

'It's so sweet of Tayen—' she started to say.

'Shut up,' I snapped, 'and listen to me. The further we go on this wild-goose chase the more I know it's madness. You've become completely fucking obsessed by it. We've got Great-Aunt Mary's ashes to Mali, which is more than most people would have done, and we've got them as far as this, and that's far enough. Look around you, for God's sake. What is there? It's nothing but bloody desert. Sand, rock. There's nothing fucking well *here*, Clemmie. One place is exactly like another. You can't ask Tayen to ride back a whole day's journey to look for the pug bag. You can't do it. It's too much. We can rest here tonight and all go back tomorrow and find the bag and scatter the ashes under a thorn tree or something. Have a ceremony, whatever you want. But this is it. We've gone far enough!'

Clemmie looked at me aghast. Her blue eyes filled with tears.

'Don't say that, Em!' she pleaded. 'We must go on.

We've got to. The further *I* go, the more *sure* I am. I know it's a lot to ask Tayen, I feel just dreadful about it, but these men understand how important it is. If we just say, oh dear, well we might as well call it a day and scatter Great-Aunt Mary back where I lost her, that just wrecks everything. Don't you see? It makes our journey seem trivial, just a trip, a bit of fun. These men understand how important it is for her to rest in this special place. Why do you think Tayen decided to join us? They see it as an honour that this old English lady loved their country so much she wanted to come back here. They understand about travelling and hardship and belonging somewhere!'

'Clemmie, you're just romancing. They're *nomads*. They don't have a sense of home in that way. They're keen to help us because they know we'll pay them well and they're poor. Anyway, you don't even have a fucking idea why she wanted to come back here. She was a old senile woman. I mean, Clemmie, look around you! What *is* there, for fuck's sake?'

Clemmie's face was suddenly flushed. She was breathing lightly and rapidly. She caught my arm and dug her sharp nails into it. 'How dare you!' she breathed. 'How dare you say that about these men! You can be so horrible, Emily. You can be so . . .' She struggled to find the word that best condemned me. *'Base!'*

'No, I'm just realistic and that's what you can't stand. Let me go! Look what you've done!' I shoved my arm out at her so that she could see the red half-moon marks her nails had made. 'You don't bloody care about Tayen and his camel, do you? That will be four days without water. I'd be more concerned with the living than the dead if I was you!'

That stung her, as I knew it would. She bit her lip and flinging her hair over one shoulder went back to Ahmada, who was watching us anxiously. She put her arm through his and drew him aside, their heads bowed close as she spoke to him confidentially. She was at it again, weaving her spell, enchanting, getting her own way. Just watching her made me feel larger, hotter, redder in the face and more furious. I sat down under the tree again and watched the men, who were calmly going about their tasks, but there was something about their studied indifference which told me they were very aware of the battle raging between Clemmie and me.

Tayen was already stretched out, resting, like an effigy on a tomb, his chech wrapped over his face. That's what he is, I thought: a knight pledged to do his lady's bidding. Cassini had unloaded some firewood from the pack camels and had started a fire. Baba was hobbling the camels, tighter this time. I tried to calm myself, breathe deeply, but self-righteousness raged and I couldn't quell my anger. All around me the desert quivered and burned in the terrible drumming heat of the afternoon. The loosed camels went a little way off and knelt in the sand and then settled down to rest, lowering their heads and stretching their necks to lean on their chins.

Cassini had the kettle on to boil and had taken a carcass out of a sack and was chopping at the bones with a knife. The shreds of meat hanging from the ribs were almost black. He threw them into a pan with some onions. My guts churned and gripped and churned again and my head banged. I closed my eyes and only opened them when Ahmada came to stand above me.

'Emily,' he said solemnly. 'No worries! Camels can be one month without water in cold season. This is cold season. Tayen's camel is strong and well. He will drink and feed tomorrow. This journey is nothing for a Tuareg.'

What could I do but look up at him and shrug? So be it. Clemmie had got her way, as usual.

* * *

That night was terrible. The cold wind rose again and howled all night and there was no way of sheltering from its stinging onslaught. My stomach dissolved and I had to get up every few minutes to struggle away and squat in the sand. I felt weak and dirty and ill and miserable. Throughout the night Clemmie wiped my face and held my hand and insisted I sip water, and although I knew she was right, I didn't want to accept anything from her. I was still too angry.

The men stirred before dawn, and through sand-crusted eyelids I watched Cassini stoke up the fire while Tayen saddled his camel. He drank a glass of tea and took a lump of unleavened bread and some dates and wrapped them in a cloth. He lashed a skin of water on to his saddle. It was still dark when he left. Clemmie had got up and gone to him. I saw her white arms glimmer in the light from the fire as she put them round his neck. I suppose she kissed him, I don't know. The next moment he was gone without a sound, his camel a pale, swift shadow disappearing into the dark.

I still felt weak and ill, although my stomach had at last given up its constant grinding and churning. Now it was reduced to the occasional cramps. Clemmie brought me over some tea but the outside of the glass was sticky and the sweetness of the tea made me feel sick. I longed for proper English tea in a mug, scalding hot, unsweetened, with a splash of milk, and then a bath. A long, hot, deep bath.

Clemmie sat beside me. 'Poor Em,' she whispered. 'What a dreadful night you had. Do you still feel awful?'

I couldn't summon the energy to go on being angry, but I didn't answer either.

'How is your head? I don't think I should give you anything for it until your stomach has settled, but I can bung you up with Immodium.'

'Implodium more like,' I corrected weakly.

'Poor old thing,' she said again. 'But just think how thin you will have got.' She had the good sense not to mention our fight or the lost pug bag. 'At least that horrible wind has gone, although it's still freezing.' She climbed back into her sleeping bag, sitting up with it held round her neck.

Cassini began to stir something in a pot and then Ahmada and Baba rose as the dark sky faded into the palest primrose and green and the morning stars shone brightly until they were extinguished one by one. Apart from the scuffling of the men near at hand, the world was utterly silent now the wind had dropped. I lay back and looked up into the great arch of sky which curved over my head and melted into the empty horizon, and experienced a rare moment of complete calm. My anger, my anxieties, my headache, everything about *me*, seemed to dissolve into the vastness and I thought again of Great-Aunt Mary's poem and knew that at some time she must have felt the same.

This great sense of emptiness and peace did not last for long. It was as if, like the poet, I had had a glimpse of Eternity that was soon knocked out of the way by ordinary mortal goings-on. As soon as we were up and about Clemmie and I started sniffing and coughing; the men hawked and spat and grumbled. Cassini clashed his pots and one of the camels yelled complaints when Baba caught it and brought it back to the camp.

The men went to pray while the sky was yellow, still pale, but already fierce-looking, with a forewarning of the thumping blue that was to come when the sun got up. By the time we were sitting round the fire to eat breakfast, it was hot. Cassini passed round bread and dates and more tea but the thought of eating made me feel ill. Clemmie explained to Ahmada, and Cassini started to prepare me a special brew of dried herbs and grasses which smelled like silage.

'You've got to drink it, Em,' instructed Clemmie. 'A bad stomach is a cold complaint and so it needs a hot cure. They are going to get you camel milk as soon as we reach the well, where there will be a lot of livestock.'

'Please!' I groaned. I sipped the foul-smelling brew, which tasted vile and bitter but surprisingly did not make me gag.

'Are you going to be all right to ride?' asked Clemmie. 'It's only a few hours to the well where we are going to wait for Tayen. You can have a good rest when we get there.'

While the men broke camp and saddled up, Clemmie took me off with a cup of water and made me sit down while she washed my face and hands and combed my hair. I felt too weak to even hold a brush. 'I am sorry about what I said, Em. Calling you whatever it was,' she said.

'It's okay.'

'Your hair is so beautiful here in the desert,' she went on. 'It's the colour of a new penny, almost red.' She insisted I put on moisturiser and sun block and then she took each of my feet in turn and smoothed cream on them with her cool pale hands. Even if she can be completely infuriating at times, you can understand why everyone loves her. 'You need to be looked after today,' she said fussily, and I felt pathetically grateful, like you do when you are ill as a child and your mother tucks you up in bed with a hot-water bottle and a warm Ribena drink.

Somehow or other I managed to get up on Absau, and for the whole morning dear Baba rode alongside me and tried to teach me Tamachek words for camels in a valiant attempt to keep my spirits up. A male was *amali*, a female *telant* and a baby *aladiod*. The rein was called the *tarant*, the ring through the nose the *teajempt,* the saddle the *terrick*, the girth the *achaife*. He told me, I think, that the camel gestation period was twelve months and that the young were usually born in August. He explained that Absau was his camel and that he had reared him from a baby and that he was very fast and obedient and he would live to be, perhaps, twenty-five years old. I didn't dare ask what happened to old camels. I guessed that they were probably slaughtered and put in the pot.

It was much easier going than the day before. Although it was very, very hot there was enough of a breeze to make it bearable. The sand was firm and white and the country gently undulating and my spirits began to lift. The Immodium was keeping my guts under control, and if I felt them moving I clenched my bottom and sat down firmly on any potential explosion. We stopped twice, once when Baba jumped down to kill a snake that he had spotted near some rocks. It looked innocent enough but Ahmada said it was a deadly horned viper. The second time was to lead our camels across a deep wadi. Each side was grown with thick bushes and thorns and Baba gave me his sandals to wear and took me by the hand to help me down and up the other side. Ahmada picked up Clemmie and carried her, laughing and protesting.

At about midday I noticed that the sand in every direction was pitted and marked with the footprints of many animals. At about the same time Absau started to get excited, exactly like a horse when it hears hounds. His head went up and he flicked his ears and began to whiffle through his nose and sniff at the air. The other camels were the same and soon they were all jogging. I tightened my hold on the rein and realised I had no idea how to stop a camel and felt sure that Absau was about to run off in a direction of his choice. I held on to the back of my saddle and tried to relax into the stride as you do when riding a horse without stirrups. Before long we were all trotting fast, and although it was terrifying and I felt extremely insecure, it was also thrilling. Baba and Ahmada were laughing and shouting encouragement.

'Very, very good camel men!' cried Ahmada over his shoulder as we flew along. Cassini went in front, twirling his rein above his head and shrieking with laughter. Clemmie was alongside me, sitting straight and graceful on her beautiful white Badoush, her scarf flying behind her, the red tassels of the saddle cloth dancing.

Thank goodness this dash was short-lived. The track we were following turned a rocky corner and in the distance we saw a great herd of livestock in a wide, flat-bottomed valley. There were about fifty donkeys gathered round a well and further on a hundred or more camels around another. There was a scattering of tents and a big gathering of people. It was extraordinary, having not seen another living soul since we left Kidal, to suddenly come across a hubbub of human activity. It was like coming into town.

Our arrival brought the whole place to a standstill, and as we raced into the midst, I felt as if Clemmie and I were captive white women brought in by slave-traders. We came five abreast, with Ahmada, Cassini and Baba riding by our sides. They had raised their cheches to veil their faces and had caught their mounts up, 'nagging' we'd call it with a horse, the rein held aloft in the right hand, so that the camels showed themselves off proudly, lifting their heads haughtily and throwing out their legs as they moved. Clemmie and I did our best to match their style. Weak and feeble as I was, I didn't want to spoil the picture.

After that brief moment of glory when all eyes were on us, things started to go downhill. The knots of men on either side shouted out greetings and each one had to be replied to formally and at length by Ahmada. Backwards and forwards the greetings went. It was a proper 'how's your father' as Grandpa would have said, with strings of enquiries about the health of near and distant relatives, politely exchanged. This brought our progress to a complete standstill, and meanwhile the sun beat down and Absau fidgeted. My head started to swim and my hands and knees trembled.

At last Clemmie managed to get a word in edgeways and asked if we could move on out of the sun, and Ahmada suggested that Baba took us and our camels off to an even further well to give them water. He couldn't bear to drag himself away from his friends, he was so enjoying the chance to be sociable. I suppose it isn't often that real desert Tuareg, being so scattered, get the chance of a good catch-up.

When we got to it, the well was a wide, deep hole, the sandy rim marked by a low edge of branches. The method of getting the water was to let down a goatskin attached to a rope on the other end of which was a small boy on a donkey. When the skin reached the bottom and filled with water, the boy beat his donkey with a stick to make it trot away and the skin came bumping up to the surface, where it was caught by an old man and emptied into a battered oil drum cut in half which was pushed up close to the edge of the well.

Our camels smelled the water and pushed forward, whiffling their noses in anticipation.

'Shit, Clemmie,' I said. 'We should have got off first,' but it was too late now. The first skinful of water was being hauled over the edge, spilling as it came, the old man leaning over to catch it and empty it into the drum. Absau and Badoush jostled forward, bumping together in their eagerness. Simultaneously they lowered their heads to drink and at the same moment bent a little at the knee, suddenly pitching Clemmie and me forward so we clung perilously to our tiny slippery saddles, poised in mid-air, with nothing to hold on to. The well gaped below us, a bottomless dark hole, and Clemmie began to giggle helplessly.

'I'm going to fall off!' she wailed. 'I'll fall straight down the well and I'll take the bucket, the donkey, the little boy and the old man with me.'

'Don't!' I pleaded. 'Don't make me laugh,' but it was too late and I was too exhausted to control myself.

'Don't look down!' she cried. 'Just don't! Baba, please! Where are you? Baba, come and save us!'

Baba came running over and had to haul our reluctant, bellowing camels away from the water and make them couch so that we could get off. As Absau bent his knees and came down, I fell forwards and slid sideways off the saddle, landing on the sand, stuck on my back like a sheep. Clemmie staggered over and pulled me the right way up, and clasping each other we lay where we were, our dirty faces streaked with tears of laughter.

'What would our parents have put in the local paper?' I giggled. 'Emily and Clemmie Kingsley, dearly loved cousins, tragically, down a well.'

In a few moments we were surrounded by curious children. 'They've come to see the Large White sows taking a dust bath,' snorted Clemmie. 'They've never seen anything like us before, Em! We're not really very, very good camel men at all, are we? In fact we've wrecked Ahmada's fly-past! He so wanted to show us off to his friends!'

At last we pulled ourselves together and followed Baba, who had finished watering our camels and led them over to a little stand of acacia trees which grew on the side of the valley. There were no tents here, just a scattering of goats and sheep tended by the children, and it was a peaceful place to rest. We helped him unsaddle and then collapsed in the shifting shade, watched from a distance by the circle of silent, staring children. I stretched out on my mattress feeling light-headed with laughter and exhaustion. I would have given a lot to have a wash, but our bottles were empty and Baba was busy filling the water skins and arranging for some feed for the camels, so we made do with baby wipes and a squirt of Clemmie's scent. We unwrapped our heads and brushed our hair and the children stared at Clemmie as she fanned out her silver mane over her shoulders. The boldest of them crept forward and we held out our hands encouragingly and I searched my backpack for some sweets to give them.

They were skinny, dusty-looking children ranging from about five to thirteen years old, olive-skinned and dark-eyed. They were barefoot, the girls wearing coloured cotton skirts and tops, the boys in ragged trousers and T-shirts. The girls had long dark hair, some tied back in scarves. They squatted down close to us as I tempted them with the sweets. Eventually the oldest nervously took one and the others followed suit. They held the wrapped sweets in the palms of their hands, looking at them in wonder. I realised that they had never seen such a thing before and I showed them how to remove the paper and put the sweets in their mouths. They copied me and began to smile. Their teeth were very white and even. That's what a sweet-free childhood does for you.

Clemmie found the packs of sparkly hair accessories that I had brought with us and gave them to the girls. She showed them how to put the slides and combs in their thick, stiff hair and passed round her little make-up mirror and they gazed into it, transfixed by their own reflections while the boys watched, envious of the attention. I remembered that I had pencils and notebooks in my bag and I got them out and gave them to the boys and encouraged them to draw me pictures – of themselves, of their camels and their other animals. They took the pencils and held them awkwardly at first but they soon got the idea and began to make squiggles and then shapes on the paper. I showed them my own version of a camel and they laughed in recognition and then started to draw their own, and made stick figures to accompany them.

Despite feeling ill, it was the happiest way to spend an afternoon. These children would be ranked as amongst the poorest in the world, but when I thought of some of the kids I taught in London, deprived of security and love and a sense of belonging, it seemed to me that it was they who were the poorer and their spirits scarred and damaged.

Baba arrived then and shooed the children away and they scuttled off, clutching their presents. In his hands he carried a metal jug that he offered to me with one of his most tender smiles.

'Camel milk,' he said. 'To make you well, Emily.' He handed it to me to drink and his long brown fingers brushed against mine. I wasn't accustomed to being looked after by a man. It was something I'd always felt uncomfortable with, but I had to admit that it made a nice change.

Clemmie

ALL THE AFTERNOON I worried about Tayen and whether he had found Pug Bag on the rock. What if he hadn't? I kept thinking. What then? Emily would insist on chucking it in and going back, and I couldn't argue with her, but I knew that I would have a sense of incomplete business and would be very reluctant to return home having failed Great-Aunt Mary, and even worse, mislaid her.

Since I had been in the desert, during the long hours in which we rode in silence, I had tried every now and then to visualise home but increasingly found that I couldn't. I couldn't conjure up a field of green summer grass and fat black-and-white cows. I couldn't picture the lane which twisted and turned along our little valley between the hills to the long, low farmhouse where I grew up. I tried to take an imaginary journey through the house, opening doors and passing through the rooms that were so familiar, but even if I began the tour, I couldn't finish. My mind drifted away to something else. In a panic, I tried to see my parents' faces, to hear their voices, but they had been wiped away. It was as if a part of my conscious memory had been sealed off. It wasn't that I wanted to forget home or my family, but it seemed that even these few days in the desert had burnt away the connections that joined me to home and that the searing sky and huge empty landscape had taken me over. I knew with certainty that I wasn't ready to go back.

We didn't see anything of Ahmada or Cassini the whole long afternoon. Dear, kind Baba brought us some flat bread and milk and dates but Emily didn't want to eat anything. She said with satisfaction that she could feel her hip bones for the first time in seven years. We lay on our mattresses and dozed, listening to the sighing of the wind and watching the wide blue sky above our heads, pierced by the thorns of the acacia. Our camels were couched near us, each one with a sack of barley to eat. Their great jaws worked from side to side and their magnificent eyelashes drooped sleepily and they looked very contented. From time to time one would lift his tail and a few small, hard droppings the colour and size of very dried-up prunes would roll away on the sand. Camels had proved to be the least smelly animals in the world, contrary to what everyone had told me. Compared, for instance, to the cows at home with their great, steaming streams of stinky green muck, they are very clean and economical beasts.

Just when I had been feeling so disconnected from home, I found that looking at the sacks in which the camels had buried their noses reminded me suddenly and unexpectedly of parties when we were children.

'Do you remember Georgina Bradley Paxman?' I asked Emily.

'What on earth made you think of her?' she answered sleepily. 'I haven't thought of her for twenty years! She was at junior school with us, wasn't she? And rather a princess? Didn't she come from Poole or somewhere?'

'Yes! Her father owned lots of garages and she wore high heels to school when we all had lace-up shoes, and she was the first to have a bra.'

'I remember her birthday parties. Everyone nearly died with anxiety that they might not get invited. We all had to pretend to be her best friend for weeks.'

'That's exactly what I was thinking of. Her birthday parties. She lived in a house on Canford Cliffs and the drive had electric gates and when she was about eight she had a disco and catered food and everything.'

'Yes, I remember now. Did we hate it?'

'I expect we were jealous. Mrs Bradley Paxman had big whooshed-up blonde hair and a face the colour of tandoori chicken.'

'Her father was the same. But what's made you think of Georgina all of a sudden?'

'It's those sacks the camels are eating out of. Do you remember that then *we* had a party and it was the usual old children's thing, with races on the lawn, including sack races, and your dad had chucked us some old feed sacks from the farm and they were full of crud, quite horrible and mouldy, and it stuck to Georgina's party dress and made her cry.'

Emily chuckled. 'We were fairly horrible ourselves, because of being brought up with the boys. I expect we gave her the worst sack on purpose.'

'I expect we did. I wonder what she is doing now.'

'I can guarantee that she won't be lying on a mattress in the Sahara,' said Emily faintly, 'feeling ill.'

'She won't be worried about losing the remains of her great-aunt, either.'

'No, I think we can be fairly confident on both those counts.'

Although we were clearly a great curiosity, the people who had gathered at the wells left us alone. Women and men passed by for a while and stared from a polite distance. I tried to write in my diary but I felt too listless and hot and Emily was too queasy to want to engage in our childhood pastime when we had nothing better to do, of trying to decide on our best all-time meal, three courses of our very favourite food. I kept thinking I could hear ice chinking in a tall glass of vodka and tonic and wondered if I was getting alcohol withdrawal symptoms or suffering from too much sun. Every now and then I sat up on my elbow to see if there was any sign of Tayen, but the horizon was always empty.

When the afternoon sun was at its hottest, the goats retreated to lie in the shade of the sparse groups of bony trees and the herds of little donkeys dropped their heads and closed their eyes, ears back, resting their hind legs, and everything slept. The whole world seemed to hum with towering heat. Baba stretched out asleep beside Emily, his chech pulled over his face, his chest just visibly rising and falling. Goodness knows where Cassini and Ahmada had got to.

I watched a black beetle labour through the sand and idly knocked him over with a thorn. He lay on his back waving his legs for a few moments and when he had managed to struggle to his feet set off resolutely once again. He had a clear idea of where he wanted to be and nothing was going to stop him. Even the interference of my thorn, like a dreadful instrument of fate, didn't put him off.

As the afternoon wore on, the heat diminished very slightly and lost the edge of its stunning, knock-out intensity. A tiny breeze stirred the trees and breathed gently on my hot face. The camels rose to their knees and stood up, shaking the sand from their flanks, then moved off slowly to pull at the thorny bushes. A few men began collecting the goats, calling to one another, and further up the valley women appeared at the entrances to the low black tents that we had passed on our way, and busied themselves with fires and cooking pots. I began my housekeeping – sorting out my backpack and looking for my torch, which I hadn't been able to find since our last stop. Emily was still asleep, curled up on her mattress with her scarf draped over her head. She looked peaceful and I hoped that when she woke up she would feel better. Maybe the camel milk would do the trick.

I scanned the distance again, shielding my eyes with my hands. It seemed as empty as before but then, as I watched, I thought I saw a tiny spurt of dust and a dark dot. After a few moments I was sure that there was something coming. For ages I couldn't tell exactly what it was, but it was moving fast and looked like a single camel coming in our direction. I got to my feet. Please, I prayed, please let it be him. Emily stirred and sat up.

'What is it, Clem?' she asked, seeing me looking. 'Is it him?'

'I don't know. I can't tell. But it's just one camel and the man has a dark robe and chech. He looks in a hurry.'

Emily came to stand beside me, peering where I pointed. Then we heard a faint cry, a high-pitched ululating cry which carried on the shimmering air, and the goat men turned to look, shading their eyes. Baba stirred, yawned and got to his feet to stand beside us. We could see now that it was a fine, tall camel and that the rider was leaning forward as he galloped, his long rein whirling above his head. His face was hidden behind his veil. He was a terrifying sight. He cried again, and this time the call was echoed by the men of the wells, and the women too, who had come out of the tents and stood together, some clapping their hands or beating cooking pots with spoons.

Then I saw something that made my heart leap. Unmistakably, around the neck of the camel-rider, was Pug Bag. Great-Aunt Mary was coming back to us.

That night there was a celebration. We moved camp a little way from the wells and away from the trampled ground fouled by the animals, to where there was a scoop of sand encircled by rocks. The men set about building a big fire. Ahmada had bargained for a brown-and-white kid which was brought, bleating piteously, slung across the withers of a small donkey ridden by a beautiful young woman. Cassini cradled it in his arms and then took it a little way off and slit its throat.

It was a good thing that Em and I are farmers' daughters or we might have found it very distressing. Instead we knew that the kid had been well cared for all its life and that its swift end was part of the traditional and delicate balance achieved by people who live amongst animals. A few minutes later it had been decapitated and skinned and its carcass was strung in a tree while Cassini got ready his sharp knives to do the butchering.

Tayen was drinking tea, lounging on his side, very

lively and proud of himself. His camel, unsaddled and resting, stood behind him, every now and then dipping its head to touch his shoulder, as if the adventure had brought them close together and now they couldn't bear to be parted.

Tayen had lowered his chech so that his beautiful mobile face was visible, and told his story with much laughter, his dark eyes flashing. I had kissed him, I couldn't help it, when he had jumped down from his camel and put the pug bag round my neck, and I felt his hard body against mine and thought, God, what a man this is.

His story, which he was clearly embellishing for the delight of Ahmada and the others, was simple enough. He had retraced our steps and found Pug Bag with no difficulty, exactly as he said he would. He started back immediately and then stopped in the rocky wilderness to sit out the heat of the day in the sheltering shadow of a little cliff. While he was there he had met two other travellers. He had watched them as they toiled across the stony plateau. They were two riders and a baggage camel, loaded with salt. He had the advantage of them, for they hadn't seen him, and when he was sure, he hailed them and they came over and shared tea and tobacco with him. They were

Tuareg, from the northern mountains, and he told them our story and asked them about the family of Salika ag Baye. They weren't sure where the family was living – somewhere in the desert, with their herds – but they said they would pass on the message that we had come from England with the name of their family on our lips.

'That's so wonderful!' I cried. 'It's just amazing. If I hadn't lost Great-Aunt Mary and Tayen hadn't had to go back for her, he would never have met these men and we would never have been able to let the ag Baye family know what we are doing here. It's as if she somehow led those men to us!' This made Emily sigh and roll her eyes, but I really did feel that there was a guiding hand somewhere in all of this.

Cassini was busy with his cooking and there was a sense of excitement because he was preparing freshly slaughtered meat, which was a rare treat. He knocked the sticks of the fire to one side, revealing a hearth of red-hot stones. He packed some of these into the stomach of the kid along with its chopped-up entrails, kidneys and heart. The bag of stomach was twisted closed and it swelled up like a small bomb and hissed alarmingly as he rolled it in his hands from side to side and back and forth. The heat from the stones was cooking the contents. I told Emily not to look, given the delicate condition of her own stomach.

Meanwhile the pieces of raw kid were buried under the hearth and Cassini relit the fire on top. While the meat was cooking, he offered us *melfouf*, little pieces of the liver grilled on sharpened wooden twigs. We picked at it politely, but when he emptied out the little stomach bomb on to a tin plate, chopped it roughly and passed it to us, we looked in horror at the steaming, glistening bits and pieces, the greyish tubes and little flaps of what looked like bright green carpet.

'This is *tarfa*,' said Ahmada. 'The lining of the stomach is green. Very, very good! Please eat!'

Fortunately, because the dish was communal, we could take tiny pieces and exclaim at how delicious it was, and after the men had politely held back to allow us what we wanted, they tucked in themselves and soon the plate was clean.

Various men well known to Ahmada and the others had been invited to join us to eat, and the talk round the fire seemed to include a lot of discussion about us. The strange men turned to stare, not rudely, but out of curiosity. Ahmada passed round the tub of Johnson's baby powder, each man studying it carefully and shaking a little out to smell and rub into the palm of his hand. When I had stowed it in my backpack in London, I had no idea what a huge success it would prove to be. Sore bums from uncomfortable saddles seemed to be as common a problem for the Tuareg as it was amongst the hard riders of the Blackmore Vale.

When the talk became animated, Emily and I were able to sit back and watch and listen. One of the men was particularly scary-looking, very dark and fierce, with a cruel, hard face, and he had the most to say, using his hands as he talked, his voice rising dramatically.

'What is he saying?' I whispered to Ahmada, glad that he was sitting close beside me, because the anger and intensity of this man alarmed me.

'It is about politics,' sighed Ahmada. 'He fought in the war and he believes that things have not improved for the Tuareg and that they should fight again.'

I couldn't imagine anything more terrifying, on even a less than dark night, than this veiled man coming at you on a galloping camel. He looked as if he could cut your throat just as easily as he was angrily sticking his dagger into the ground, and make a good job of it.

Meanwhile, Cassini had dug up the roast kid meat

and brushed off the sand and chopped it into rough pieces and put them on the plate. Emily was by now looking very pale and she moved away, explaining to Ahmada that her stomach was still sick. This passed the social burden to me, but at least this was meat and not intestines, and when I tasted it I found it was tender and delicious.

When everyone had finished eating and the men were leaning back on their elbows around the fire, Ahmada said, 'If you would like to meet the women of this tribe, they are at their tents a little way off. They will give Emily milk for her stomach.' I wondered if this was a polite way of saying that it was now time for the men to be alone to talk men's talk. Anyway, we both wanted very much to meet the women and Emily said that she felt well enough to take a short walk, so we collected some little presents from our packs, left Pug Bag sitting safely on top of our belongings and followed Ahmada through the soft green evening light to where the valley floor opened out on to a scrubby plain and where we could see the light of the camp.

A group of ten or twelve women were gathered about the campfire with the younger children. They wore black headscarves and beautiful silver bracelets and rings and some had kohl around their eyes. The oldest, perhaps in her seventies, had henna patterns on the back of each hand. They sat cross-legged with straight backs and stared at us in amazement. I could see that they had been busy repairing a tent, sewing the animal skins neatly together. Ahmada explained that the Tuareg tents were the property of the women and they made and repaired them in the dry months in preparation for the rains. The skins were cured and waterproofed by rubbing in a mixture of earth and sheep butter. When they were new they were a rich ochre colour and they became black with age. They were about a metre and a half high at the centre and the wooden poles which held them up were beautifully carved. Both ends could be opened, or closed to shut out the rain or the sun and the dust. They took about a day to put up, Ahmada told us, and were carried on donkeys when the family followed their herds to find grazing.

'These are very poor people,' he explained. 'Of the old vassal tribe of Imrad. They are good people.' He passed the women packets of tea and sugar, and a portion of meat he had carried with him in a sack. The old woman thanked him graciously and shuffled off to put the gifts away.

'I leave you here!' he said, clearly longing to get back to the real fun of the evening. He was like one of my brothers choosing between a girlie night in or a session in the pub with his mates. No contest.

The women gestured to us to sit down with them, and we did, hoping that our smiles said enough to convince them that we appreciated their hospitality. They stared at us quite openly and talked amongst themselves, giggling. The young woman sitting next to me leaned over and ran her finger along my arm. I suppose that she wanted to feel my skin because it looked so strange and mushroom pale next to her own. She gestured that we should take off our scarves because they would like to see our hair, and when we did there was a sharp intake of breath and then peals of laughter. The old woman, the granny of the family, signalled that I should go over to her so that she could place her gnarled old hand on my head and said something to the others, who all smiled. Another young woman stroked Emily's hair and seemed to say that she thought it was beautiful. Then she pointed out that we both had coloured varnish on our toenails, which interested and amused them. I wished that I had thought to bring some bottles of polish with me from England. They would probably have been as great a success as the baby powder was amongst the men.

One of the older women gestured that we should help with the sewing and Emily had a go but was hopeless, unable to push the blunt bone needle and leather thread through the skin. They laughed uproariously at this and tried to help her, and then wanted me to have a go. The fact that we were so inept entertained them hugely. The girl next to me took my hand in hers. Her palm was very hard and warm, the skin rough and dry as an autumn leaf. It was hard to tell how old she was, in her twenties perhaps, about my age. A small, ragged toddler of indeterminate sex leaned against her shoulder, twiddling her hair, her finger in her mouth. The girl turned my hand over and studied my palm, moving her finger along the lines as if she could read something there. The granny brewed tea and passed us the familiar little glasses and Emily got out our cereal bars and handed them round. They were accepted with the same grace as the presents from Ahmada. The granny said something to one of the younger women, who went off and returned with a scrap of dusty black plastic, the tattered remnant of what had once been a bag, in which there was a handful of jojoba nuts which she gave to us.

It was beautiful to sit by their fire as the light drained

from the fiery orange sky, which was full of soft, pigeon-coloured clouds like fat satin cushions. I felt completely at home although we did not have a single word of common language. The girl with the toddler, who had held my hand, now leaned against me, the child drowsy on her lap, and rested her elbow on my knee as she talked and laughed with the others. It was such an accepting and open-hearted gesture that I felt really moved, and tears welled in my eyes. I looked round at the strong, handsome faces, lit by the fire, at the big-eyed children who snuggled up to the women's sides, at a baby at her mother's breast. Just as I had loved Tayen with all my heart as he galloped into camp with Great-Aunt Mary, I was moved by a huge love for these women too, and touched by their simplicity and goodness.

There was still a vermilion glow on the violet horizon, but above our heads the huge sky was fading to an aquarium green and the first stars were shining brightly. From amongst the scrubby grass and bushes the goats bleated and a far-off camel yelled, but all about us the great silence of the night was gathering. It seemed as if the little bright fire was the only light on the curve of the earth.

One of the women fetched a lute and began to play

and sing in a strong, thrilling voice and the others joined in, using the heels of their palms to drum against anything within reach. My new friend took one of my flip-flops to beat against a cooking pot. The music was strange and unearthly to our ears, but I knew it was about love and friendship and loss and sorrow.

Emily

LOOKING BACK, I can read the signs, but then I just thought it was typical of Clemmie to be so swept away by everything and everyone. I could understand that she was affected by the desert and the people, it was hard not to be, but where I saw grinding poverty and helplessness, she saw an enviable way of life and simple, noble people. Where I saw the Tuareg wars as a last convulsion of a defeated nation, she saw them as an honourable crusade against a cruel oppressor.

'Em!' she whispered to me as we sat round the campfire that night and Ahmada told us what the angry man had said as he stabbed the ground with his knife. 'I'd fight for them. I really would. I'd fight for the Tuareg!'

She would, too. I just hoped that they would never

let her get on the other end of a gun. She would be lethal.

Later, when we went to visit the women and sat with them while the sky went dark and listened to the music of the lute and their wonderful, evocative songs, I saw that she was crying. Silver trails ran down her face which she did not brush away. The pale wings of her hair fell forward and the Tuareg girl who was leaning against her occasionally reached up to touch the moonlit hair as she sang.

Before we left, the same girl gave Clemmie a plaited leather necklace affair which she had hanging around her neck and which Clemmie had admired. It was a strange thing, more like a little breastplate or shield, with tasselled decorations. Clemmie put it on at once and the women were delighted and laughed and clapped their hands. When we got back to our camp, Ahmada told her that it was called *edoran* and was a marriage token, worn by brides or by young women who were betrothed.

'But why did she give it to me?' asked Clemmie.

Ahmada shrugged. 'If you say you like, so the women give to you. It is the custom. When I take you to them they ask me if you are married, and when I tell them no, they are sorry and wish for you a good man!'

Clemmie listened solemnly but did not reply and we hardly talked as we got ready for bed. Something was happening, something momentous, and as yet I did not know what it was, but we both sensed it, like an approaching thunderstorm on the air.

Beryl Timmis

LAST NIGHT I had a terrible dream and woke with a thudding heart and a sense of dread which is still with me. I lay and stared into the darkness and could not remember where I was. In fact, here at The Willows it is not dark at all, ever. We are not allowed the comfort of the dark because we are old and lights must be left on at all times. My room is lit with a dim orange glow from the emergency nightlight in the corner, and the blaze from the corridor is a bright strip beneath the door.

We must be kept in the light, like battery chickens, because we are old and we fall and stumble, fumble and totter, and our eyes are dim. We are denied the dark in case we wake in the night and think we are dead.

Yesterday Mrs Clifford-Jones had a heart attack. It happened after lunch as she was returning to her room for a little zizz, as she called it. She had eaten rather a lot of lunch. Chicken pie and mashed potatoes and peas. I watched her fork going backwards and forwards to her mouth, which was painted pink. It looked like a sea anemone, opening and closing. Between mouthfuls she dabbed at the corners with a paper napkin. For pudding there was a mincemeat tart and ice cream and she had two helpings. She laughed about it at the time, nudging Mr Fellowes and saying something about men liking a good handful of woman. I said nothing. I never have been able to join in this sort of talk and I was conscious all through the meal of a feeling of dislike and, I am sorry to say, of superiority that I have developed for her. I realise that I allowed myself to believe that I was a better person than Susan Clifford-Jones, that she was vulgar and rather stupid.

Then, as lunch came to an end, she turned to me and said, 'Beryl, would you like to come to my room later on for a cup of tea? The afternoons drag so and my daughter has brought me some shortbread biscuits.' I was surprised and confused and flustered, in my usual silly fashion, as I thanked her and tried to excuse myself. It was an act of kindness on her part but I turned it down. Five minutes later she was dead, collapsed over the Zimmer frame she used to walk from one room to another as her hip healed.

It was a terrible shock to us all, and although the staff have been anxious to keep us calm and prevent any hysteria, and immediately brought cups of tea to those of us who were involved, several of the ladies are deeply upset and Mr Fellowes is looking decidedly shaken. Once or twice Susan Clifford-Jones had suggested to me that there was something between them, a romance I suppose, and she was certainly a flirtatious woman who enjoyed the company of men, and whom men liked in return.

As for me, I feel regretful that I hadn't immediately accepted her kind invitation, because that was what it was. She was being kind to me because she knew I have no family and that I do not have any regular visitors. Her last words spoken on this earth were kindly and her last thoughts were charitable. I should be glad that, in a way, I allowed her that opportunity. I have prayed for her this afternoon, prayed for her soul as it begins its journey from this earth. I am sure that she was a good person. I can't believe that she ever committed a real sin, and certainly not a crime. When she comes before the judgment seat, there will not be a serious mark against her name.

This afternoon my hands are trembling and I find I cannot read or think about anything else. Death will come to us all, and here at The Willows it will be sooner rather than later. The dear old colonel, who was so confused by the drama at lunchtime and stood in the corridor suggesting that they carry Mrs Clifford-Jones home on a field gate, as if she'd had a hunting accident, told me the other day that he is looking forward to death. 'It's high time,' he said, his old blue eyes watering. 'You'd put down an old horse or a hound, but they won't do it to us when we're past it. I'm more than ready for the bullet. It would be the kindest thing, my dear, the kindest thing!'

What has upset me is that I am not *ready to die. I am frightened of dying because I am frightened of the rack and the torment. Condemnation is very real to me and I don't believe that hell is just a story. My thoughts keep returning to the desert and that is what I dreamed about last night.*

I dreamed that I was back there with Mary. I suppose we were young women, but that didn't matter or seem to be important. I told her that her father had sent me to take her home and she laughed. She was wearing red nail varnish and she lit a cigarette and laughed again. 'Oh Beryl!' she said. 'You don't think for one moment that I'll agree to that! Look around you! Why should I want to go?' I saw then that she was not living in a tent but in a very comfortable flat, quite high up, and that although the desert was outside, the room was cool and furnished in a normal way. In fact it looked very like the interior of her London home.

'I have everything!' she said. 'All the things you will never have! I have children and grandchildren and I am very happy here, so you will have to run along and go home without me.'

Her tone was light and teasing but I knew that she meant what she said. She was standing with her back to the window, which opened on to the desert below, and the next moment I started forward and gave her a sharp push, and taken by surprise she took a step back and toppled out of the window. I knew instantly that she had fallen to her death and that I had killed her. It was this terrible truth which woke me and remained with me long after I had realised where I was and that it was only a dream.

Clemmie

WE BROKE CAMP early the next morning. The sky was still bright with stars when Cassini stirred up the embers of last night's fire and the sparks showered like little fireworks in the dark. Emily was fast asleep but I shook her awake. She had slept soundly all night long – I could hear her even breathing – whereas I had lain awake for hours, from time to time lifting my bare arms to the sky and feeling the cool wind blow across my hot skin. From far away I could hear the sound of wolves howling. I tossed and turned and whenever I laid my head on my pack to try to sleep, the blood pounded in my ears and my eyes sprang open and I felt alert and watchful. It was such a beautiful night and I didn't want to miss it.

Perhaps because of the wolves, the camels stayed close to our camp and I could make out the ghostly shadow of my white Badoush as he couched near where I lay. Pug Bag was beside me and in the bright moonlight I could see his little red tongue and beady eyes. 'You're nearly there!' I told Great-Aunt Mary. 'Tomorrow we will arrive at your chosen place and lay you to rest. Then it will all be over.'

I shook Em's shoulder again and she stretched and sat up. 'Bloody hell!' she said. 'What's the matter? It's still pitch dark. It's the middle of the night!'

'No it's not. Cassini has made the tea already. He's baking bread this morning. He's set it to cook in the sand under the fire.'

'Shit!' said Emily. She lay back down while I collected my stuff and went off to wash and get dressed. I had worn the same outfit for the whole trip and I loved not having to think about what I was going to wear. When I came back to the camp the men were getting up, rolling their blankets and packing their camel bags, while Emily had gone back to sleep in their midst. She was making up for the bad night she had had when she was ill.

I went to sit by the fire and Cassini silently passed me a glass of tea. The early morning was so beautiful when the moon was a big pale disc and everything was hushed and the men spoke in low voices and the sky was streaked with yellow and pink before the sun came over the horizon.

The men went off to pray, and when they came back they hunkered by the fire without talking and drank tea. Cassini dug up his big round of flat bread and brushed the sand off before breaking it up and passing it round. It was hot and heavy and sank into my stomach like a comforting stone.

At last I got Emily up and she made the men laugh because she was slow and grumpy and kept yawning. I doled them each out a Rennies indigestion tablet and a vitamin C pill, just to keep them happy, and then we saddled our camels and were ready to go. I must make the most of every moment of today, I kept telling myself, because soon it will all be over. Badoush was refreshed by the water and food and moved up the line of camels until I was riding alongside Tayen at the front, and he grinned at me with a flash of his white teeth and we trotted together, side by side, and suddenly trotting was easy and comfortable and I lost my fear of falling off. We flew along and I cheered Badoush and twirled my rein above my head and he flicked back his ears at the sound of my voice.

At noon we stopped in a dry stream bed where there was something for the camels to eat amongst the thorns and acacias, and while Cassini made a fire and brewed tea, Ahmada and Tayen took Emily and me to climb amongst the rocks and showed us where there were prehistoric paintings of elephants and giraffes and lions. We stood and looked at them in wonder and took photographs. Once this desert valley had been flowing with water and was home to all these animals and the men who had left us their drawings of them.

There was meat again for lunch in a soupy stew with macaroni, and Cassini produced a tin of Del Monte fruit salad for Em and me, which we ate off a plate with a teaspoon. After lunch we had more tea and then stretched out on the sand to sleep out the fierce heat.

We started off again while the sun was still high, but Ahmada wanted us to make Timadjlalen, Great-Aunt Mary's special place, and it was a long ride. Cassini and Baba collected wood for the fire as we went along and Baba narrowly missed being bitten by a scorpion which hid beneath a branch. This reminded me of Jutta, whom I hadn't thought about for days, and by now I found I had quite fond feelings for her, of the 'good old Jutta' variety. She had been right about scorpions and we should have listened to her. I asked

Baba what would have happened if he *had* been bitten and he said that everyone in the desert was bitten at some time or other and that it was nothing. He would have cut an X over the sting and tied a tourniquet above and let it bleed, and then later put a small stone over the bite and bound it in place.

It was impossible to tell what Timadjlalen was like because we arrived in the dark when we were stiff and tired. I had no sense of the place at all, except that we had climbed up a slope from a valley floor and were camping amongst enormous Hovis-shaped rocks as big as transit vans and the sand was fine and without stones. A wind blew gently and tonight the brightness of the stars and the moon turned the night sky a deep watery green. It looked as if the moon was a ship at sea and the stars her milky spangled wake.

Emily and I scuffled about trying to organise our things. We put our mattresses alongside some smaller flat rocks which were low enough to be used as bedroom furniture, a bedside table for our water bottle and torch and chairs to drape our clothes over. It seemed a great treat to have our stuff out of the sand for once.

I put Pug Bag in a good position to look over the dark well of the valley so that when the day dawned

Great-Aunt Mary would know that she had arrived and that Emily and I had so nearly completed the task she had set us.

We were too tired for a proper supper. Cassini brewed tea and we ate some dates and bread and then climbed into our sleeping bags and lay side by side, conscious of each other, although we did not talk. I could not make out what caused the sudden heaviness of my heart. I should have felt excited and joyful that we had arrived but instead I felt swept by sadness and full of a nameless longing. I suppose in my heart I was frightened that in the morning Emily would be proved right and there would be nothing here to explain why we had made this journey.

When I woke, the sun was already climbing into the sky and in the pink morning light I sat up and saw Timadjlalen for the first time. Emily was also stirring and she propped herself up on her elbow to have a look at where we were, and I was glad because I wanted to share this moment with her. This was it. This was where Great-Aunt Mary had wanted to be for all eternity.

We saw that we had camped on a gentle slope on the side of a wide valley which was home to a small collection of distant Tuareg tents. Gathered about the tents were many animals: sheep, goats, donkeys, a few camels, and as we watched a man rode out from the tents on a black horse with a long dog running in front. It was the first horse we had seen in the desert and even from this distance we could see that it was beautiful, quite small and finely made but full of fire, with an arched neck and a plume of tail. The man wore an indigo robe and a white chech which streamed behind him. The dog was even more exciting. It was long and lean and graceful – a desert Salugi, the ancestor of our greyhounds.

Four or five children were herding the goats and moving them down to the tents where three women began to catch them and rope them together, head to tail, in order to milk them. From where we sat we could hear voices and the sound of their laughter. Every now and then they stopped what they were doing to turn and look up at us, strangers who had arrived in the night.

The valley bottom was quite well covered in short clumps of dry tough grass and low-growing bushes and I saw that our camels had not needed to go far to find food. They were standing and lying in a group just below us, their jaws working, with the pink morning sun warming their coats. It was a beautiful, serene place and it seemed strangely familiar, a bit like a Saharan Blackmore Vale, where man and beast lived in harmony with the landscape. It was easily the most homely sort of place that we had travelled through, but it still didn't make any sense why Great-Aunt Mary had wanted us to bring her here. She never liked the country, so none of the things that I loved about the scene we had woken to would have appealed to her.

I turned to Emily. 'So this is it, Em!' She shrugged. It didn't add up to her either, I could see that.

'I still think Harrods Food Hall would have been a better choice,' she said. 'I can see it's a beautiful place, but God knows why we had to bring her all this way.'

'Well we did, and we have. I suppose we've got to decide how and where we do it – the scattering bit. We ought to make a ceremony of it. Perhaps we should build a little cairn of stones to mark the place.'

'When shall we do it? The sooner the better, really, because we've got a hell of a trek back again.'

'After breakfast, maybe.' For some reason, now that we were nearly done, I was reluctant to complete our task. 'Great-Aunt Mary always thought food was important.'

'Not Cassini's bread,' said Emily. 'She wouldn't have thought much of that.'

'Do you know what day it is?' I said, suddenly remembering. 'It's Will's birthday!'

It was a happy coincidence because he, in his way, had a lot to do with us being here at all. If it hadn't been for his powers of persuasion, I doubted that Emily would ever have agreed, and I knew that I would never have come without her. Dear Will, the kindest and best of my brothers. Emily loved him as much as I did, and we sat and looked at Great-Aunt Mary's lovely valley and thought fondly of him.

Our men had gone down towards the tents to speak to the women and came back with camel milk and honey, which we ate with dates and bread for breakfast. Whatever Emily said, it was delicious.

We were still sitting round the fire, well wrapped up because the morning air was cold, when Tayen pointed out two camels riding up the valley. I had honey on my fingers and licked them one by one and I took little notice until Tayen reported that the camel-riders had stopped at the tents and were now coming in our direction. I stood up then and shaded my eyes. I had grown accustomed to the sight of Tuareg camels but these two were covered with brightly decorated saddle bags, woven green-and-red saddle cloths, fringed reins and great dangling swathes of tassels. Round their necks were skeins of fine black leather from which dangled copper-coloured drinking bowls. The men looked especially got up as well. One wore an emerald-green outfit with a red crossover sash, tightly waisted, and a black chech pulled up over his face. The other was all in white with the same red sash. These were men dressed for an occasion.

Emily and I watched them cantering up the slope, the camels' labouring feet kicking up a cloud of sand, and the next minute they had arrived and Tayen and Ahmada went forward to welcome them and the exchange of polite greetings began.

The men jumped down from the camels, which Baba took away to unsaddle, and the strangers were invited to our fire. Cassini began wiping out the tea glasses and boiling the kettle. The two men came forward to shake us by the hand, keeping their faces well covered, as was proper, but I could see that one was older, perhaps in his fifties, while the younger one in emerald green was tall and broad and his eyes were brown and full of animation. It's hard to tell if someone is smiling when their mouth is covered but these eyes shone with humour and warmth.

The tea party began and I found myself sitting next

to the tall young man and gazing at his long, thin brown feet which he had slipped into leather sandals. There is something so uniformly horrid about male English feet, so white and hairy-toed and misshapen from spending their lives crammed into shoes. These feet were perfect, the palest coffee colour and dusted with fine sand from the journey. The toenails were creamy and smooth, not yellow and thickened, and I longed to put out one finger and run it along the high arch of the foot, where there was a tracery of fine veins beneath the skin. It reminded me of getting told off when I was a teenager visiting the Rodin museum in Paris, when I couldn't resist touching one of the sculptures.

The talk had clearly moved to us and Ahmada had a lot to say, pointing to Pug Bag, which was safely round my neck. Both the men turned to stare at it and then at us, and a torrent of talking broke out. Tayen became very excited and jumped up and embraced the men.

'What is it, Ahmada?' I asked. 'What's going on?'

Ahmada turned to us, beaming. 'This is very big news, ladies!' he said. 'These men are from the family of Salika ag Baye. The men who Tayen met on his journey passed on the message that you were travelling here with your ancestor. They have come, riding night and day, to meet you. This man is Sidi ag Amar and this man,' he indicated the younger, 'is his nephew, Chamba, the Lion of Temesna.'

Emily and I stared. The Lion of Temesna. The descendant of the mysterious man named in Great-Aunt Mary's will. I remembered where I had first heard that name, Salika ag Baye, sitting in Mr Godfrey's freezing car at the funeral. A world away.

Now he turned to us, or rather his descendant did, and speaking in excellent French he told us of the surprise he had felt on hearing that two English girls were travelling across the desert on a special mission.

'What I have come to ask you,' he said, 'is where you heard the name of my great-grandfather, Salika ag Baye. This I have come to ask you.'

'Ah,' said Emily. 'That is quite a long story. Come on, Clemmie, where do we begin?'

Gradually, and with much backtracking and interrupting of each other, stumbling sometimes when we couldn't find the right word in French, we told our tale. 'And so,' I concluded, 'that is why we are here. We have come to Mali to return the ashes of our great-aunt. This is where she wanted to be, and not just anywhere, but *here*, Timadjlalen. Her will was quite specific about it.'

'But,' said Emily, 'we have no idea why. It is still a mystery to us and there was no one at home who could tell us, not even her closest friend.'

Then the tall young Chamba began to talk. His voice was low and gentle, and now that his chech was loosened we could see more of his handsome face. He had high cheek bones and a long aristocratic nose. He was older than I had first thought. I saw now that his moustache was flecked with grey. He had very good, even white teeth.

'This is my story,' he said. 'I am born thirty years ago to my mother Momo and father Attahar. I am the eldest of four boys and a sister. My father died three years ago but my mother still lives. We come from the north, between Kidal and Algeria, and our ancestral lands are from there to Niger. Now we have little. We are poor people, made the poorer because of the droughts that have ruined our grazing grounds and the wars about which you will have heard that have brought so much suffering to my people.

'My father, born under French rule, was sent by the French to school in Bamako. It was their policy to educate the eldest sons of Tuareg nobles. This way my father learns French history and language and, it was hoped, comes to think like a Frenchman. It takes him many days to travel from the desert to Gao to go by boat to Bamako, and always he wished to be home in the desert.

'My father is born of Tehama and a woman who is half French. Her name is Celeste – not a Tuareg name. There are many stories of her birth and it is known that she was born here at Timadjlalen. When she was just a few days old, her mother, a Frenchwoman, left in an aeroplane in the company of a young English friend, abandoning her baby, who was brought up by the women of the tribe and by her father, Salika, my great-grandfather, also the Lion of Temesna. The mother of Celeste was never seen again and my great-grandfather carried with him for the rest of his life a great and lasting grief, for he loved this woman dearly.'

Emily and I looked at each other. Nothing made sense. Was Great-Aunt Mary out here with this Frenchwoman who had a baby? Was that the connection?

'Why did the mother abandon the baby?' I said. 'Whatever made her do that? It seems so unnatural.'

Chamba shrugged and made an open gesture with his hands. 'Who knows?' he said. 'It was a long time ago and the world was a troubled place. The second great war was about to begin, and many things change. Who knows what happened to her? But she loved the baby, my great-grandmother. That we know.'

'How do you know that?' asked Emily. 'It doesn't seem very loving to fly off and leave her baby behind. Why didn't she take her with her?'

Chamba shrugged again. 'The story is told that she was sick. The aeroplane came to take her away, but she left something for her baby in her tent. It was treasured by my grandmother and has been in my family ever since.'

Chamba reached into his saddle bag and brought out a book-sized packet wrapped in an oiled cloth. Carefully he took it out and laid it before us. It was a small green linen envelope, painstakingly stitched in coloured silks. The initials 'MB' were embroidered on the front. It looked completely familiar to me, the sort of old-fashioned thing that you see in bric-à-brac shops in English country towns. Our gran would have kept her handkerchiefs in something like this, or her stockings. Chamba slid his hand inside and brought out a fold of paper on which there was some writing, a lock of dark hair tied with a thread, and a gold charm bracelet.

He handed me the paper and I unfolded it carefully. The writing was in pencil, and a bit shaky.

'"I saw Eternity the other night,"' I read, but could not go on. Suddenly I knew the rest. A lump came into my throat and my eyes welled with tears. Now I understood. It had taken me so long to get there, for the pieces to fall into place, but now I knew Great-Aunt Mary's secret.

Emily leaned across and took the paper from me. 'There's a letter too,' she said, and began to read. '"My darling baby Celeste, I am frightened that I am ill and I do not know what will happen to me, but I want you to know how much your mother loves you. You are the most beautiful baby, with your father's lovely dark eyes. I also want you to know how much I love him and how happy I have been this last year of my life and that you and he are the best part of it . . . if anything happens to me . . . just so that you will grow up knowing. Your ever loving mother, Mary."' The writing was faint and Emily's voice faltered.

We sat in silence, looking at one another. We were both choked with threatening tears. Emily brushed her eyes with the back of her hand.

'Is it a happy ending or not?' she asked with a sniff. 'I can't make up my mind.'

'I don't know,' I said. I thought of Great-Aunt Mary at the end of her life, huge and misshapen, with her swollen ankles and her fierce manner, her cigarettes and her gin. I remembered what Miss Timmis had said about her when she got back from Africa, how ill and withdrawn she had been.

She had left her heart here.

Beryl Timmis

OF COURSE IT was nothing like my dream. When I stepped out of that aeroplane and stood on the dazzling sand I saw that we had landed on a wide valley floor, scattered with sparse vegetation. On either side, gentle hills rose to a jumble of large square rocks, as if a giant child had thrown down its building blocks. In the distance I could see a collection of low black tents and many animals, goats and camels and a dog or two. It took us twenty minutes to walk across, the pilot rather unwilling to accompany me but nevertheless lugging my suitcase, our feet sinking into the soft sand and dragging on our progress.

It was terribly hot. I could feel sweat trickling down my back and my hair was wet on my neck beneath my hat. I couldn't believe that this was where Mary was living. It was a profound shock to me and I agreed wholeheartedly with her father that she must have lost her mind. Nobody who was quite sane would choose to stay in such a dreadful, inhospitable place.

As we drew closer there were no men to be seen, only women and children peering terrified from the tents, and I remembered that Lieutenant Charpentier had told me that he had called the men away on a desert exercise, which he did from time to time. When at last we were quite close, a young woman appeared, dressed in long black clothes with a scarf over her head, and I thought for a moment that it must be Mary, grown stouter, but it wasn't. Instead, this young woman had come to take me to her.

I found her in one of the black-skinned tents that was hung with decorated woven curtains across the entrance. I had to bend to enter, and stepping out of the sun into the shady interior blinded me for a moment. Then I saw that the floor of the tent was covered in beautiful glowing carpets and that the sides were bright with decorative wall hangings, some of which glinted with silver discs or tiny pieces of mirrored glass. Towards the back, leaning on round floor cushions, was a girl with large dark eyes in a pale face. Her long black hair was loose round her shoulders and she wore a pale pink shift.

'Beryl!' she said, and stretched out an arm to me, and it wasn't until she spoke that I realised that it was Mary. 'I can't get up to hug you,' she said, 'because I'm not very

well. I've had a baby, Beryl! A baby girl. Just two days ago. I lost a lot of blood.'

I knelt beside her and put my arm round her and kissed her forehead, but all I could think about was what she had just told me. A baby! Was that what the colonel meant when he said that Mary was unwell, or did he not know that he had a grandchild born in this terrible situation? Either way, it was far worse than I had guessed. Then I saw it, the baby, a tiny yellow wizened thing wrapped tight in cloth lying on the cushions beside her.

'She came early. She was born the day before yesterday, a few weeks premature, I think,' said Mary, tracing the baby's cheek with a finger. 'But she's beautiful, isn't she? I'm going to call her Celeste.'

'Mary!' I said. I couldn't bring myself to look at the hideous baby, which seemed listless and half-dead. 'I've come to help you. To do what I can.'

'You are so sweet to have come all this way!' she said dreamily, leaning back. 'I'd have loved to have you here when I was in labour. Now it's over, I'm amazed the human race survives, the whole thing was so ghastly. The women here thought I made the most awful fuss. They drop their babies like rabbits. Anyway, they're very kind to me. They feed Celeste when I'm too weak. I think I have a high temperature, or maybe it's just so hot . . .' Her voice trailed off.

'Your father is worried about you. He never said anything about a baby. Mary, does he know?'

'No. We haven't spoken much over the last few months. We argued terribly about me being here.' She closed her eyes again for a few moments before she went on. It was an effort for her to talk, but I needed to know. I needed to understand. 'Charpentier,' she said. 'He might have told him I wasn't well, but I made him promise not to say anything more.' She waved a listless hand about her. 'You can understand why. Papa would have insisted that I was flown out, and I didn't want to leave.'

And of course the colonel would have been right. Anyone could see that. Any sensible person.

'Where is your husband?' I could hardly bring myself to say the word, and I thought of what her father had told me, that a tribal marriage of this kind would not be legally binding and certainly not recognised in civilised society. She turned her head to me and smiled. 'My darling Salika? He is away for a few days with his men. He works with the French occasionally when they have a convoy or a camel train that needs protection.'

'Your father told me. Mary, you must know that he is terribly distressed by your marriage.'

She was so still that I thought she was dozing, but then she whispered, 'Wait till you see him, Beryl! Wait till you meet him before you judge. He is a Tuareg noble. He speaks French. He is the best man I have ever met.'

'But how can you live like this? In the desert? In a tent, with these savage people?' I was so distressed that I felt tears in my eyes.

'I love them!' she said simply. 'They are my people now.' She closed her eyes and I put my hand on her forehead. It was terribly hot but her hands felt cold. I had no doubt that she was quite seriously ill. I had so little experience, but I had heard of post-partum fever. To give birth in a filthy tent must have exposed her to inevitable infection.

'I must get you to a doctor, to a hospital. The aeroplane is coming back. Your father has arranged it all.'

There was a long silence. Then Mary said, 'I don't want to die, Beryl. I am frightened of dying.' When she turned to me again, her face was wet with tears.

'Of course you won't die. Not if we can get you to a doctor.' Although I tried to be strong, I felt so frightened and inadequate that I started to cry as well. We were so young – just girls – and so inexperienced. In my heart I thought she really might die. I thought that she might die there in that tent.

'I don't want to die now and leave Celeste and Salika. He hasn't seen her yet. He doesn't know that she has been born. I have so much love, Beryl. So much love.'

I can't remember exactly what happened next, but I slept beside her that night. The women of the tribe came with food and milk for the baby. They dipped a rag in sweetened camel milk for it to suck. It was a terrible baby – a yellow rag doll. It was clearly going to die. It hardly cried, and when they unwrapped it from the cloth which bound it, its little freed arms waved feebly in the air and it made a mewing noise like a kitten. Its tiny hands had long curled fingers like the transparent legs of a hermit crab. It had trailing wisps of long black hair, and when it opened its eyes they were black and gummy. I wouldn't touch it and turned away when they tried to pass it to me.

Mary's condition became worse. She drifted in and out of consciousness. I knew that she needed medical help if her life was to be saved. I felt trapped in that terrible hot tent, unable to do anything but wash her burning body and insist that they bring me boiled water for her to sip. Every now and then I stood outside in the sun and listened for the sound of the returning aeroplane. I thought I would go mad if it didn't come soon.

At last, on the evening of the second day, I heard the throb of an engine and rushed out to see a dark dot in the sky. The women and children and goats scattered for cover but I ran out to wave my arms above my head. I can remember the relief I felt as the plane circled and came in to land on the makeshift airstrip.

After that the taciturn pilot took charge and Mary was carried in a sling between two poles to where the plane sat in the sand, and I followed, holding the baby for the first time. The women were wailing, keening, as if they knew that there was death in the air, but the pilot shooed them away. They were terrified of the aeroplane and ran back across the sand to the tents, their skirts bunched in their hands. The pilot carried Mary in his arms and climbed up into the hold of the plane. 'We'll make her as comfortable as possible,' he said. 'We'll be in Gao in two hours. Keep your fingers crossed that she'll make it. You'd better hand me up your luggage and we'll get off.'

I put the baby down and struggled to pass up my case and Mary's trunk. The pilot hauled them in and then moved up to the cockpit to check his instruments.

At the last moment I decided. I left the baby. I left it lying in the sand in the blaze of the sun.

That was what I did. I climbed up into the plane and took my place beside Mary.

'Everything in?' asked the pilot, coming back to slam the door.

'Yes,' I said.

The next moment the propeller was turning and the plane was bumping along the makeshift runway. I looked back and the baby was just a little bundle on the ground, then a little rock, then a stone, then uneven sand, then gone for ever.

Emily

WE SCATTERED GREAT-AUNT Mary amongst the high rocks overlooking the valley where she had been so in love, and made a little pile of stones to mark the place. All of us climbed up the slope as if we were in a procession, Clemmie carrying the pug bag leading the way, me behind and Chamba next because, after all, she was his great-grandmother, and then the others following silently.

It wasn't hard to find the right place. We both knew when the sand path between the great boulders widened and then became straight, like the aisle of a great cathedral, and then the rocks stopped altogether and we realised that we had arrived. Turning to look back the way we had come, we could see the whole valley spread out below, the tents and the animals now in miniature and the great sweep of horizon and sky on all sides. The sun was a silver plate high in the heavens, and then I realised that the moon was there too, sailing aloft. It's like Great-Aunt Mary's poem, I thought. Eternity. The rocks, the sand, the sky, the sun and the moon, all untouched by earthly years, and now Great-Aunt Mary was to float off on the clear air and become part of it all, at peace at last.

Clemmie unzipped the pug bag and gestured to me and Chamba to scoop up the fine grey dust. I had the inappropriate thought that it was like emptying a Hoover bag, but this was what we had come for and so I did as I was told, and soon the fine ashes were drifting through the blue air and floating away.

Ahmada and Baba, Cassini and Tayen, who we had to thank for everything, stood and watched solemnly, their faces still and serious, their cheches wrapped formally so that only their watchful eyes showed. When we had finished they moved silently away as if they sensed that we might want to be alone.

'Perhaps we should say some prayers,' I said, brushing my hands on my robe. Neither of us could think of anything suitable except the 'Our Father', and then we sang 'The Lord's My Shepherd' in harmony, as we had done in the choir at school. The words seemed just right as we looked at the far-off tents and the sheep and goats. As Clemmie put it, Jesus would have been very at home here.

Then we filled Pug Bag with sand and left him there on a little pile of stones to keep Great-Aunt Mary company, although Chamba told us that the valley was never lonely because it was a favoured place for the Tuareg, there being two wells in the area, and in the springtime it was full of tender grass and flowers.

On our way back down, I saw that the Lion had caught hold of Clemmie's hand to help her on the places where the path was steep, and I thought with a pang that it was ever thus, and I would be left to get down by myself, but he turned to hold out his other hand to me, and I knew I could have loved him myself. It was evident that Clemmie already did.

She had been half in love before she even met him. I had seen it happen all along the way as she got starrier and happier and more elated. She had loved everything: the camels, the desert, the men, the sun, the moon, the wind, even Cassini's disgusting bread. She was waiting for Chamba to happen. Now her face was flushed with a mixture of emotions, sadness and happiness. Her scarf had slipped to her shoulders and I saw Chamba gazing at her beautiful face and the fall of her silvery hair. They were hopelessly in love within a few hours, minutes even. Chamba followed her with his tender brown eyes and she became ever more graceful and lovely, and I remembered Great-Aunt Mary's observation that Clemmie was destined for a man who bore arms and loved women.

We rode back three days across the desert and Chamba and Sidi came with us, and Chamba and Clemmie rode side by side, like a lord and his lady, and I could see that Tayen was jealous. He either showed off with his camel antics or sulked and rode to one side on his own. He had my every sympathy. I felt exactly the same. Love like theirs is very excluding because it fills the air about it with a heady atmosphere that makes everyone else sick that it is not they who are so blessed. Even Baba moped a bit and I guessed that he was thinking about his girl whom he could not afford to marry. Only Cassini and Ahmada seemed unaffected.

Now that we had fulfilled Great-Aunt Mary's wishes, Clemmie seemed to have forgotten all about her, so engrossed was she in her own love story, but I couldn't get her out of my mind. There were gaps in the story which I couldn't make out, and as we rode I turned it over in my mind. I could understand that Mary had been airlifted out of the desert because she was ill, and that she thought it was better that she left her baby behind. What I couldn't understand was that she had never attempted to come back and claim her. Why? The war might have made such a thing impossible, but after the war?

By then she had remarried, or married properly, because I don't suppose that a Tuareg marriage counts, so what had happened to the love that she spoke of so movingly in the letter she left behind? Had she just given up on her Tuareg husband and daughter? Perhaps back in London, back in civilisation, her impulsive affair in French Sudan had seemed something to be denied and put firmly behind her. It certainly sounded as if that was what her mother had decided she should do. Mary had gone on to marry Great-Uncle Timothy, for God's sake, who was, if all accounts are true, one of the dullest men around.

This seemed the most obvious explanation, but what troubled me was that it was so unlike the Great-Aunt Mary I had known, who was firm and consistent in all her opinions. One thing she was not was a quitter.

What was it that Miss Timmis had said? Mary may have had a sort of breakdown and would never talk about what had happened to her in French Sudan, and when she recovered she went off the rails, or so

Miss T implied, and slept around before netting the most boring man in Britain. And who, I kept wondering, was the *friend* who had been with her in the aeroplane? And why, if Mary had so determinedly denied to everyone, herself included, that any of these things had happened to her, did she want us to bring her back here for eternity?

There were no answers to be had, at least not until we were back in England. I still had the vague feeling that Miss Timmis was keeping something from us and I intended to go to see her and ask some questions.

The other thing that I thought about, watching poor old Tayen's lovesick performance, was how I felt about Ted. However hard I tried to revisit and inspect my old feelings of hurt and betrayal, they seemed to have disappeared. The painful little barbs that had hooked me back so often to dwell on the past had become blunt. To my intense relief, I found that I was cured. I discovered that the wrong Ted had done me no longer hurt, and I could think about him in a nostalgic way about good times we had shared. He couldn't get to me any more. The desert had cured me, seared me, scraped me clean. Thanks to Great-Aunt Mary, I had seen Eternity, and realised that Ted wasn't part of it.

* * *

When at last we arrived back at the little nomad school, there was Ahmada's vehicle waiting for us under the tree in the yard, glinting blindingly in the dappled sunlight. Someone had washed and polished it while we were away. This was the moment that I dreaded, because it was time to say goodbye to Baba, to Chamba and Sidi and the camels. Painfully, Clemmie and I would have to shake off the desert, brush off the sand and climb into the jeep which would drive us back towards the real world.

In my heart I must have known what might happen. I hugged Baba and thanked him again for the care he had taken of me, remembering how he had ridden alongside me and patiently taught me Tuareg words when I would rather have been left somewhere to die. When no one was watching, I emptied all the spare money I had into his hand. I hoped that it might help him pay for his bride. I promised that I would never, ever forget him and I fed Absau dates and stroked his soft, furry face.

I looked round for Clemmie, who I knew would be feeling very tearful. She and Chamba had dawdled away from the rest of us and I saw that they were deep in discussion. Their heads were bowed together and then Chamba turned Clemmie towards him and put out a hand to stroke her hair back from her face. I saw Sidi watching them from where he was busy reorganising the camel baggage and then he glanced across at me and we exchanged a look of understanding.

I collected my backpack and went to stow it in the jeep, and then climbed into the vehicle to get out of the sun and to wait. We had a very long drive in front of us and I hoped for Ahmada's sake that Clemmie would not delay us. He had to get us back to meet up with the rest of our party and to catch our plane. Already I found myself checking my watch and making mental calculations of how long everything would take. The spell and enchantment of the desert was wearing off. I noticed how filthy my clothes were. The hem of my robe was grey and the front stained and grubby. My hair, although wonderfully straight, felt clumpy with dirt and sweat. Sitting in the truck, I realised that I smelled strongly of camel. I longed for a shower and then an ice-cold Castel beer. Or two. Come on, Clem, I thought. Get it over with.

Then she and Chamba came back to where we waited. They were holding hands and Clemmie was smiling radiantly, although I could tell from her face that she had been crying. She came straight over to the truck and got into the other side and turned to me and took my hands in hers.

'Emily!' she said. 'I know this will be a shock, but I'm not coming back. I'm staying here, Em. I'm staying with Chamba. I've made up my mind.'

I stared at her.

'What? Are you mad? You can't do that!'

'I can! Why should I go back? I don't want to, and I've got nothing to go back for. My visa is for six months, so I'm staying.' She sounded absolutely emphatic. 'I'm sorry to leave you to go back on your own and everything, but I know you'll understand. I'm in love, Em. Totally and utterly. For the first time in my life. I want to stay here for ever. I want to marry Chamba.'

'Clemmie, you don't know him. You've only just met. Don't be so silly!'

'I do know him. I know him better than I've ever known a man. I adore him with my whole heart. You know, before we met we were like two of those shooting stars in the desert sky, travelling in a rush towards one another. Chamba says so too. It was destiny, Em, that's what it was!'

'How can you stay? In a place like this? You don't

have enough stuff with you. What about all the things you'll need, things that you can't live without?'

'There's nothing I need more than I need him.'

'What about money? What about . . .' I went on and on, but she wasn't listening. There was a sort of madness in her eyes. She was like someone high on drugs. She was wild with love.

Eventually I started to cry. I felt exhausted and utterly torn between what I thought was my duty as a responsible cousin, and what Clemmie was insisting on doing. If she refused to come with me there was nothing I could do to make her. I imagined standing in the kitchen of the farmhouse in Dorset, explaining to my uncle and aunt that I had left their beloved only daughter in the desert with the Lion of Temesna, whom she intended to marry. It would be beyond their comprehension.

'I love you, Emily. You've always been the best. I'm sorry to do this to you, I really am, but I know I must stay. You see, don't you, that Chamba is special? Tell Mum, will you, that he passes the Blazer test. I love him more, you know, more even than Blazer.' She leaned forward to kiss me.

'Wait, Clemmie. You've got to tell me where you will be, where we can get in touch with you. You must see that. You can't just go off the screen for everyone.'

'There will be ways of keeping in touch. I am riding back with Chamba now to his tribal lands, to his tents, but he has a house in Algeria, in Tamnarassat, with a satellite telephone! He's writing out the number and addresses and everything for you. I am going to be useful, Em, in clinics and schools and things. I want to help his people. Their plight is desperate but nobody in the west knows about them and they are too proud to beg. I won't let the world forget them.'

I closed my eyes. I suppose I'm cynical, but to me it was typical Clemmie in Wonderland stuff. Reluctantly I pulled my pack out of the jeep and sorted out all the stuff I would leave with her, even down to my dirty knickers. 'You can wash them,' I pointed out, 'because I don't imagine you'll be near an M&S for the time being.'

'You'd better have this,' said Clemmie, handing me her hot-water bottle in its furry cover. 'I don't think I'll need it now.'

'Keep it. It can be freezing out here. But you had better have this,' and I gave her Ted's silk nightie. She held it to her face and then we hugged one another, rocking back and forth and trying not to cry.

I had to be brave about it. I had to be a Kingsley and tough it out and kiss Chamba and make him promise to take care of Clemmie. He held my hand and looked into my eyes and gave me his word, and I believed that he would. He was a man of honour. From round his neck he took a silver and bronze medal on a leather lace. It had four points, shaped like a star, with an intricate pattern engraved on the silver.

'This is for you, Emily,' he said, putting it round my neck. 'This is Tuareg. Wherever you may roam, to the four corners of the earth, you will never be alone. See these little marks here, they are for the camels of a camel train, this here is water and this the sun and this the moon – all things beloved of Tuareg.'

Somehow or other I took photographs of Chamba and Clemmie standing side by side, her arm through his. I have the photograph on the mantelpiece at home and people always pick it up and look at it, intrigued. It shows a tall, magnificent and mysterious man in emerald-green Tuareg robes, a dagger in his red crossed sash, his black chech pulled high to cover his face, and next to him a very beautiful young woman, also robed, with a scarf over her head, her silver hair loose on her shoulders, her face transformed with joy. Round her neck, on a long leather cord, she is wearing an ornamental tribal marriage talisman. I have given a copy to Uncle Peter and Aunt Ellen. It is the nearest thing they'll ever have to a bridal photograph of their daughter.

The other men were tactfully occupying themselves with the baggage and packing up the sacks of unused feed and provisions for Baba to take away with him. Beautiful Badoush had been hitched behind Absau and then came the string of other camels. He looked very disdainful of the arrangement. Clemmie went and laid her head against his white flank and stroked his shoulder while he stared haughtily into the distance. I could tell that she was crying and I sniffed myself, wiping my nose with the back of my hand. I didn't know how I was going to part from her. I didn't know how I could bear to leave her here. A hand fell on my shoulder and I half turned, my eyes swimming, and then I felt arms circling me and a strong stout body to lean against. Dear, kind Ahmada understood.

By now Baba had couched Absau and climbed up on to his saddle and gathered up the rein. He pulled his chech to cover his face and the next moment Absau was climbing up from his knees and the camel train began to move slowly off, the lazy beasts at the back unwilling and protesting. We called our goodbyes and waved and waved.

Chamba went to stand beside Clemmie as if he was sheltering her in his shadow.

'What about Clemmie?' I asked Ahmada. 'She doesn't have a camel now Badoush has gone.' It had only just occurred to me that Chamba and Clemmie and Sidi, the big wallflower, were not going in the same direction as Baba.

'Ah! You will see. She travels like a Tuareg wife.'

Sidi and Chamba were now ready to leave and Sidi mounted his camel and sat waiting, his face impassive behind his chech. He gave nothing away of his feelings about Clemmie. He simply seemed to accept that she was staying. Clemmie came to hug me again while the men embraced one another in a completely open and unabashed way.

'Emily!' Clemmie said through her streaming tears. 'Every day and night I'll think of you, my best and dearest friend on earth!'

'Please go,' I said. 'I can't bear this.'

Chamba's great brown camel was ready and he mounted swiftly and then indicated that Clemmie should climb up behind the saddle, sitting sideways with her arms round his waist. The camel's back was broad and wide and I hoped that she would be comfortable, because Ahmada said that she had a long way to travel.

Then Tayen dashed forward and knelt beside the animal and showed Clemmie that she should use his knee as a step and took her hand in his to help her. It was a lovely forgiving gesture, as if to say that although she had broken his heart he wished her well. Clemmie rewarded him with one of her most radiant smiles and in a princessy way placed her white foot on his bended leg. She seemed weightless as she rose up gracefully and settled herself behind Chamba and put her arms tight round his waist and rested her cheek against his back. Then his camel lumbered and swayed to its feet and there she was, perched high above my head, smiling, although tears rushed down her cheeks.

Sidi was ready too, and so we stood and watched them go, Ahmada, Tayen, Cassini and I, and Clemmie turned and waved for as long as she could and that was my last view of her, riding into the infinite sandy distance behind her Lion.

We dropped Cassini back in Kidal and said hallo and goodbye to NouNou and Ahmada's children. Ahmada explained to NouNou why we no longer had Clemmie with us and she looked at me with wide, startled eyes as if she was as frightened for Clemmie as I was. Hanging in the hallway was Clemmie's little sheepskin waistcoat, and I could hardly bear to look at it, thinking of her on a cold desert night when she might have been very glad of something so light and warm. I just had to believe that Chamba would look after her as he had promised.

Then began the endless drive to Gao. We hardly talked on the way back. Ahmada and Tayen took it in turns to drive and I sat in the back on my own with my head and heart too full of what had happened to be able to think of anything else.

The following day we rose at dawn and crossed the river, this time without the mayor and his Mercedes in tow. How long ago all that seemed, and how strangely flat was the yellow water of the great river and how colourless the horizon, as if all the vitality and excitement we had experienced on our outward journey had been washed away.

By midday we reached the little shanty stop at Motel Homberi, where the sign still swung in the wind and the men slept on the veranda. Today the patron was about, a tall man in a striped yellow-and-black robe and a baseball cap, who greeted Ahmada and Tayen with great affection. He brought two tins of peas to our table for inspection and invited me to read the labels, as if they were bottles of vintage wine, and when I was satisfied he carried them off to the kitchen with movements as graceful and languorous as a ballet dancer. Under the table at my feet was a mangy yellow bitch, also fast asleep. Her extended teats flopped over to one side as she lay snoring. We ate peas and rice and peanut sauce for lunch and then Ahmada and Tayen stretched out on the veranda to sleep and I sat in the shade and felt incredibly lonely without Clemmie, and whenever I thought about her there was a fullness in my throat and I couldn't swallow.

At about four o'clock, when the shadows were just starting to lengthen, a truck appeared in the distance and when it pulled over I saw that it was dear Serufi, smiling and waving, and Hugh sitting beside him, wrapped in his Arab headcloth, come to collect me. Ahmada and Tayen woke up and they had a terrific catch-up with Serufi, but I couldn't put what had happened into words to tell Hugh, who came and sat beside me. He looked exactly the same and was wearing the same clothes he had had on when we said goodbye to him and still had a stripe of white sun cream down his nose. I just sat with my chin in my hands, too choked to speak.

He was really very sweet and went inside and came out with two beers and said, 'I think this should probably be brandy or something stronger,' and as I sipped I slowly told him what had happened. He didn't say anything, just looked thoughtful, and when I had finished he said, 'When we arrived and I realised you were on your own, I thought something terrible had happened to Clemmie, an accident or something, so it's actually a relief to hear that she is all right.'

'How can you call it all right?' I asked. 'It doesn't seem very all right to me.'

'It is, in the sense that Clemmie sounds extremely happy and as if she knows what she is doing. She struck me as being the sort of girl who needs something extraordinary in her life.'

'She did?' I was surprised that he was interested enough to have come to any sort of conclusions about either Clemmie or me.

'Oh yes! There is something quite steely under that fey exterior. I'm sure she will be all right, Emily. She'll have the Lion eating out of her hand by now.'

'He is already!'

'There you are then. I know it's easy for me to say

don't worry, but I really shouldn't if I were you. Not too much. I would have been much more concerned if it had been you who was left behind.'

This surprised me so much that I stared at him. Surely he realised that I was the practical, sensible one? 'Why?' I asked. It is a horrid truth that most people find themselves fascinating, and I certainly admit that I do.

'You're a much less single-minded person, I would have thought. And less robust, in a way. I think you would have found it very hard to lead a desert life. The harshness, the poverty, the injustice would have done for you.'

'And it won't for Clemmie?' Clemmie, who was all silver and gold and fine as a piece of bone china.

'I think she will make it romantic somehow. She'll see it in her own special way and make it beautiful. She'll certainly make everyone she meets feel better. That's her particular gift. But look, don't listen to me, I hardly know you,' he finished diffidently.

We finished our beers in silence and I thought about what he had said. I was beginning to see that I had misjudged Hugh, writing him off, in a smug way, as being totally unaware of everything around him. In fact he was very observant and acute, and of course if I had bothered to think about it, I would have realised that to be an anthropologist you had to be interested in how people behaved.

Ahmada had already put my backpack in Serufi's truck and it looked as if we were ready to leave. I had already paid him what we owed him, a modest amount for all that he had done for us, and I felt humbled when he was reluctant to accept the money, remembering how I had maligned him in that respect. I hated saying goodbye to him, who was the best of the lot of them in my view. A truly good man. I hugged him very hard until he held up his arms in mock discomfort and I made him promise me that he would look out for Clemmie as best as he could, even though she would be miles away from where he lived.

'You will come back,' he said. 'You will come back to see your friends. You have a place always in our hearts.' He turned to Hugh. 'Emily is very, very good camel man!' he said. 'Brave as a Tuareg,' and I felt ridiculously touched and pleased.

Then I had to say goodbye to beautiful, wild Tayen. I loved him too, for his gaiety and courage. We hugged each other and he kissed me on both cheeks and his brown eyes brimmed with emotion. 'Chamba is a good man,' he said. 'He will look after your friend. She is more valuable to him than diamonds or a thousand camels.'

I gave them my tin of travel sweets, the last thing I had to give, and then stood out in the road and waved goodbye until there was only a little cloud of dust on the horizon.

Clemmie

IT WAS THE hardest thing I've ever done, saying goodbye to Em and leaving her to go home alone. My heart felt as if it had swelled to fill my chest and press against my ribs, but as much as I loved her and as much as her arguments about causing concern for my parents and brothers struck me as true, I had no hesitation in staying with Chamba. My love for him was so overpowering that everything else faded away. Even if he hadn't loved me back I think I would have stayed and begged to be allowed to follow him, like a handmaiden, a member of his tribe. The fact that he loved me too was the most wonderful gift in the whole world and I felt as if I had spun off to orbit a new sun and that my life would forever be measured from this moment – before and after Chamba. The time before, my childhood and growing up in Dorset with my loving parents and my brothers, I can only think of as a sort of preparation for the time that was to come, when Chamba rode his camel across the desert and into my life.

He is a beautiful man, tall and well made, strong and lithe. Of course this is what first attracted me, I can't pretend it didn't. The fact that he is utterly without vanity, unlike most good-looking men I have met, was the second thing I noticed and appreciated. He laughs a lot but is also serious and carries with him a weight of responsibility for his people, and mixed up in my love is a big measure of appreciation of this. He is a man of real worth. When I try to describe him I use all these old-fashioned adjectives like honourable and chivalrous and courteous and gentle – words you hardly hear used any more because they aren't qualities that are appreciated much at home, where everyone strives to be hip and cool and successful. He is a man from another age. That is the man he is.

Our lovemaking I can't find the words for, and he wouldn't want me to share what we mean to each other, but afterwards, lying in his arms, watching the night sky full of shooting stars, is to feel utterly safe and secure and so loved that tears wet my cheeks and he wipes them away with my hair.

Although I am so far away from everyone I know and love and in a country that couldn't be more different from dear Dorset with its gentle green hills and lush river valleys, I feel utterly at home because I have found in Chamba the thing that was missing from my life. He is my other half, the man who makes me whole.

I don't think about the future. I know that there will be problems and difficulties, that the life ahead of me will often be hard. I can tell that Sidi wonders if Chamba knows what he has let himself in for, and poor Emily drove away and left me with a heavy heart, but I don't think about any of this, because none of it matters compared with what I have found. I live for every moment of every day that Chamba and I are together, and for every second of every night that I lie in his arms.

Of course I think of Great-Aunt Mary who brought me out here in the first place and who must have shared exactly what I feel. I remind myself that she followed her heart and found love in this most unexpected of places, and how brave she was to turn her back on what the rest of the world must have thought. And then she lost it all, or had it all snatched from her. No wonder she wanted to come back here, to be forever in the place where she had loved so much and where she had left her tiny daughter. Great-Aunt Mary, thank you. You brought me here and you gave me Chamba. You showed me the way to fall in love.

Emily

THE BACK OF Serufi's truck was loaded with sacks of stuff that Hugh was taking home for carbon-testing. He had had a wonderful time with the Dogons and was returning with stacks of material, notes and photographs. I realised that one of the reasons he was so much more animated than on the outward journey was because he was lit up with success. The gathering of material for his research was a painfully slow business and he told me that the good old Dogons had provided him with exactly what he needed to complete his thesis.

The boy from the motel in Sévaré had proved to be the key player in all of this. He had taken Hugh to a fertility ceremony rarely witnessed by westerners and had then invited him to stay in his village, where he was introduced to shamans and magic men, astronomers and medicine men. Hugh had taken copious notes and made many recordings, had partaken of so many hallucinatory drugs and drunk so much home-brewed alcohol that he said his eyeballs were still spinning, and altogether had had a rare old time.

'And the flying men?' I asked.

'Oh yes!' he said. 'I've got some amazing evidence about them. I sometimes thought I could fly myself. I suddenly remembered what Clemmie told me about you two when you were children. You know, jumping out of hay lofts.'

'Except we weren't under the influence,' I reminded him. 'It was just that Clemmie had decided that we could do it.'

Hearing him talk, I realised that for Hugh this trip had been like a whirlwind and his perceptions were complicated by layer upon layer of new and vivid and sometimes contradictory experiences, all mixed up, like looking through a kaleidoscope. It was as if he was going home with a tangled ball of multicoloured wool which he would have to unravel before he could start knitting something useful. I suggested this to him and he agreed and said it was a good analogy, although he found it hard to imagine himself knitting, but on second thoughts he had once been forced to make a pot-holder at primary school.

'Field work can be incredibly monotonous,' he said, 'and then suddenly you hit on something like this.' He indicated his bags in the back. 'Then the whole thing becomes tremendously stimulating and exciting, like striking gold. It's so easy to get bogged down in the academic, scientific side of anthropology and forget that it's real people one is studying.'

In contrast, I was beginning to see that for Clemmie and me, our time in the desert was something completely different. Instead of standing outside, as an observer, as Hugh had been, we had been drawn into the lives of our desert men, and instead of bringing back complicated data about them, it felt as if we had learned about ourselves. Out there in the silence and emptiness of the desert, our lives had been stripped to the bone and we had discovered some simple truths.

'Have you seen anything of the others?' I asked. 'I wonder how they've got on.'

'Oh yes! I was with them last night at the hotel in Mopti. They've had a wonderful time as well. Guy has taken some great photographs and Jeremy and Jutta found their elephants. The herd was rampaging through a village somewhere not far from where they dropped you off. It was brave of them to get up so close to them. They were huge apparently – much bigger than those in east Africa, and known to be very unpredictable. So all in all everyone seems to have managed to achieve what they most wanted.'

'Where are they now?'

'They've gone on ahead with Mokhtar. We are going to meet them at the airport.' He paused. 'We were talking about you two last night. They said that they'd been worried about leaving you in some godforsaken place on your own.'

'Oh yeah!' I snorted derisively. 'They couldn't wait to get shot of us!'

'I don't think that's true. They might not be people of much imagination, but they're kind-hearted.'

'Hmm!' I was not convinced.

It was a very long drive. We stopped twice and Hugh moved into the front passenger seat to sit next to Serufi and to chat with him and keep him awake. I sat in the back and thought about Clemmie and wondered where she was. She and Chamba would have struck camp long ago, before it got dark, and perhaps they were now asleep or talking quietly, lying in each other's arms under the stars. Thinking of that made me feel lonely, partly because of my own single state and partly because of how much I would miss

Clemmie, not just on the rest of our journey home, but always.

The road between Ségou and Bamako was long and straight. It was a strange and lovely experience to drive through the velvety dark with the windows rolled down, the smell of the African night, the hot earth and the cooking fires wafting on the warm wind and the flames lighting up the dark villages. Between each village the road was utterly black without a single light to be seen on either side, the beam of our headlights sometimes pinpointing the glowing orange eyes of an animal wandering near the verge. Serufi drove very carefully, frequently sounding his horn.

'He says it's very dangerous,' Hugh told me. 'There are a lot of night-time accidents when vehicles strike stock on the road. Apparently the animals like to lie on the warm tarmac.'

There was very little traffic to begin with, but as we got nearer to Bamako it became busier and the occasional lorry came like a roaring beast out of the dark, with blasting horn. We could see the headlights from miles away, and then there was the clamour and the suck and rush of wind as the monster raced past. Serufi's square hands rested lightly on the wheel and his brow furrowed with concentration.

I nodded in and out of sleep in the back but was awake to watch the approaching lights of a huge truck, their yellow beam flashing across the scrubby trees on either side of the road. It wasn't until the very last moment that I realised there wasn't enough room for us to pass. I saw Serufi's hands gripping the wheel and suddenly wrenching it round and heard Hugh cry out. To avoid us all being killed outright, our truck swerved sharply and a front wheel went over the edge of the tarmac. The next few moments were chaotic as we rolled over like a ball before coming to rest on our side in a maize field. The engine was still running and our headlights were pointing up into the high branches of thorn trees. The lorry had vanished into the night.

Miraculously we were all unhurt, and after this was established, Hugh's first concern was for his artefacts.

'Shit!' he said, trying to climb sideways over the seat. 'My stuff has been thrown all over the place.'

We pulled ourselves out and looked at the damage. It was obvious that there was no way that the vehicle could be righted and get us to the airport and poor little Serufi was as upset as if he had lost a member of his family. He walked round and round his truck, sighing and shaking his head, before he began to pull out our bags. I found my torch and helped

Hugh reassemble his stuff, his masks and spears and headdresses.

'What can we do?' I said, looking at my watch. 'We'll miss the plane.' I felt strangely calm and unworried although I had probably only just escaped with my life.

Hugh spoke to Serufi and then said, 'He says that we should try to hitch a lift. He will stay here and wait for Mokhtar to come back and help him. He says there is nothing else that we can do.'

That was how we came to be standing on the edge of the road, waving our torches and sticking out our thumbs in a hopeful fashion to any passing traffic, when the Elder Tour coach came by on its way to the airport.

Mabel and Kathleen happened to be sitting in the front, in the command position, the Pastor and Gloria having been struck down by terrible diarrhoea almost from the beginning of the tour. They spotted us and insisted that the coach stop and back up to where we were standing and we climbed aboard with all our luggage. It was the greatest piece of luck.

Mabel and Kathleen were on flying form and had had the time of their lives. They looked as chirpy as ever and their hair was still as pastel-hued and tightly permed as when they had set out. Their Stay-Prest pants suits were uncreased and their blouses crisp. They were like a pair of pearly but elderly guardian angels.

'So that beautiful friend of yours isn't going home with you?' marvelled Kathleeen. 'Listen, darling, I don't blame her one little bit. I love it here myself. I'd stay too if I could have my time over.'

'Honey, we slept like babies on mattresses in tin huts,' said Mabel.

'You might have done, sweetheart. Someone not a million miles from here snored the whole night long!' retorted Kathleen.

'The people of our sister churches were just darling. They brought the Lord to us when all the time we thought we were bringing Him to them!'

What was more, no one had died in their party, which I thought was pretty remarkable and against all the odds, and no one had been too ill either, apart from Gloria and the Pastor, who had overdone the goat curry, and an old gentleman who had a snake drop on his head from the roof of a hut and had passed out from shock.

We made it to the airport in good time, checked in and went to look for the others. Strangely, now that we had arrived safely in a busy, brightly lit departure hall and there were shops selling tourist rubbish and duty free, and other Europeans milling about, all looking hot and crumpled and creased, I suddenly started to shake. My knees actually trembled and I realised that my shoulder ached dully and that I hadn't just walked away from the accident unscathed.

'What we need is a stiff drink,' said Hugh, who I now saw had a bruise on his cheek and the beginnings of a black eye. We went to find a bar and there, inevitably, were the others.

I heard Jutta's voice before I saw them. She was telling someone not to have ice in their drink and explaining that it was a common cause of stomach upsets. 'They make it from tap water, you see,' she was saying. 'They don't understand that it should be sterilised. As if freezing makes it safe!'

They were looking slightly travel-weary. Jutta's big hair had entirely deflated and was now scraped back into a small tuft of ponytail. Her large sunglasses were sitting on the top of her head. She was still wearing a fair amount of clanking gold jewellery but mixed in amongst it was a lot of native stuff, big beads and leather thongs and painted discs. The front of her white shirt was marked with a large, rather disgusting-looking brown stain. Jeremy was wearing khaki safari shorts and his short white legs, furred with wiry hair, were stuck out in front of him as he lounged on a small plastic chair. His face was sunburned and looked raw and red. Guy, wearing an indigo Tuareg chech draped round his shoulders and a string of Dogon beads on a leather cord round his neck, was busy sorting through his camera bags.

They looked up as we arrived and Guy and Jeremy got up to kiss me with a fair degree of enthusiasm and a welcome that verged on being warm.

'Fantastic! You've got here! We were just getting worried. We're longing to hear how you got on . . . Where's Clemmie?'

'It's a long story,' I said.

'What do you mean?' demanded Jutta, like a hound picking up the scent. 'Isn't she with you?'

Hugh gave my arm a little squeeze as he drew Mokhtar to one side and began to explain about the accident and where Serufi was waiting to be rescued. His recounting of our accident deflected the interest of Guy and Jeremy and I heard 'You two are bloody lucky to be alive!' and 'Peasant mentality! They shouldn't be allowed to drive anything but a fucking donkey and cart,' and other similar remarks.

Jutta listened, aghast, as I sketched out what had happened to Clemmie and me and why she had decided to stay.

'But this is so absurd!' she cried when I had finished. 'How does she think she can live in a country like this?'

I shrugged. I now found myself in the position of defending Clemmie. 'It was her decision,' I said simply. 'I think she knows what she is doing.'

'But it is madness. Couldn't you have stopped her? Jeremy! Listen to this!' Wearily, I had to retell my story for the benefit of Jeremy and Guy.

Jeremy implied that he was entirely unsurprised by Clemmie's behaviour. 'She struck me as being incredibly impulsive. And naïve.' He made her sound retarded.

'What good does she possibly think she can do?' demanded Jutta in a challenging tone. 'It is utterly irresponsible. She'll be another mouth to feed, a drain on a community which is already struggling to survive. She'll then have to be rescued by the Foreign Office. A great friend of ours who is very high up in the FO told us that girls who behave like this, you know, think that they have fallen in love when they are somewhere exotic on holiday, are a complete nightmare. They are always having to bring them home when things go wrong.'

All this was hard to argue with, so I just shrugged my shoulders and sighed, and after that they became quite sympathetic towards me and drew me into their group in an embracing way, as if now that I was on my own I was one of them and it had been Clemmie's presence that had separated us before. Jutta found some arnica for my bruised shoulder and Jeremy bought us double brandies and Guy kept giving me reassuring little hugs.

I was too tired to resist their advances, but I was glad that I had Hugh there. Because he had offered a different view of Clemmie, and also because of our shared accident, he felt like an ally. When Jutta stood up I was satisfied to see that she hadn't lost any weight, whereas my jeans had become extremely loose, and I learned that the stain on her shirt was from her bottle of Worcester Sauce which had leaked in her luggage.

Mokhtar was anxious to say goodbye and organise the rescue of Serufi, and I was glad that they all thanked him so warmly and Jeremy took him to one side and passed him a thick wad of notes.

'He was a wonderful driver and guide,' said Jutta approvingly. 'He not only found the elephants for us but also we stayed in comfortable hotels, unlike that terrible place on the first night. You see, unless these people understand the standards expected by western travellers, their tourist industry is never going to get off the ground.'

I thought of Hugh happily stoned out of his skull in a Dogon village and Clemmie and me sleeping on the sand under the stars and washing out of a mug, and the Elder Tour in their tin huts, and knew that although she was probably right, what we had experienced was something much more wonderful.

My last memory of Mali was the wet heat of the tropical night as we trekked across the tarmac to the aeroplane. Looking out of the window as we took off, Bamako was a jumble of lights and then there was nothing but empty blackness stretching to the very horizon. On the empty seat next to me I put Bill's beautiful Peul hat to keep me company. As we flew north, I rubbed at the scarred plastic window and peered out. Somewhere down there was Clemmie. I wished very hard that she might look up and see the tiny coloured wing lights and think of me. Then I slept.

When we arrived in London it was early morning and bitterly cold. We had flown over frozen grey fields and then the vast grey city and the silver coil of the

Thames. We were a shuffling, yawning, silent group who stood round waiting for our luggage, and I found that I had already developed a sense of dread. Outside the airport, ordinary life awaited me. Soon I would have to explain to the family that I had left Clemmie behind, and then I had to move into a new flat and go back to work, none of which were at all appealing.

At last my scruffy old backpack came round on the conveyor belt and I found myself as pleased to see it as if it was an old friend. I hauled it off and said goodbye to the others and we exchanged addresses and promises of keeping in touch.

'How do you go from here?' asked Hugh.

'Airport bus, then train.'

'I'll wait for the bus with you. I'm not in a hurry.'

We bought ourselves great sticky buns and mugs of coffee in the arrivals hall and then stood at the bus stop, companionable but not talking. Our eyes, grown accustomed to the vivid colours of Africa, watered in the cold wind and smarted at the drab greyness of the morning, the concrete buildings, the people hunched into coats, their faces pinched closed with cold, the sky the colour of granite.

It occurred to me that Hugh seemed reluctant to say goodbye and it reminded me of Tayen and his camel, who had grown close after their trip together. When you have shared something you know to be life-changing, you are loath to part from your companion, as if, once separated, you might lose the magic of whatever it was that had been so important.

I felt the same. I didn't want to part from him because it meant setting off on my own and returning to the company of people who, however hard they tried, could not imagine what it had all been like. I felt hollow with tiredness but knew that I must go straight to Uncle Peter and Aunt Ellen to give them the news of Clemmie, and after that I was going to see Miss Timmis.

Beryl Timmis

*F*OR THE LAST *few days I have been unwell and confined to my bed. The staff here became anxious about me because I have lost my appetite and someone reported that my mind was wandering when I did not remember meal times. They tell me that I am confused, and perhaps I am. Kathy has been very kind and sometimes sits with me with a cup of coffee and chats to me about her family. She seems to have a lot of bother with her daughter-in-law, whom she calls 'a right bitch, excuse my French'. I am relieved that she hasn't noticed that the photographs have gone. It is easy to think, when you are old, that your concerns are important to other people, when of course they are not at all. Kathy has plenty of other things to worry about.*

This afternoon Emily's mother came to see me. It was an unexpected visit but she told me that Matron had telephoned to say that she was concerned about me. She brought me some snowdrops from the garden of the old cottage, which was a kind thought. She seemed less unhappy than she had been at Christmas and told me, in a rush, that although she and Emily's father had been through 'a bad patch', things were now better and they were planning to have a holiday. 'Together!' she said with emphasis. 'And nothing to do with farming. Not to Perth for the bull sales, or to Poland to look at potatoes. No, we're going to Greece in May. I can't wait! In fact,' she added confidentially, 'we are getting on better than we have for years.'

She also brought news of the girls. 'They're due home tomorrow,' she said. 'Ellen and I can't wait to see them and hear all about it. Tell me,' she added, lowering her tone. 'You knew Mary well; what is it all about, Beryl? Why Mali? Why the desert? There's got to be a reason.'

At that point I lay back on my pillows and closed my eyes and she thought that she must have tired me out because after a few minutes she patted my hand and collected her bag and scarf and gloves and crept out.

So, I thought, it was all over. By now the girls would have left Mary's ashes somewhere in the desert and it would be finished and this dreadful chapter closed. When they were safely home I would be able to put aside these troubling thoughts. But for now they wouldn't leave me, and as the pale winter light faded from my room I remembered that when I got Mary to the hospital in Gao she was seen by a French doctor, who tutted gloomily and shook his head. She was too ill to move, he pronounced, but Mary's father would have none of it. He came to the hospital and shouted at everyone and within the day it was arranged that Mary and I were to be flown to St Louis and on the next ship to Marseilles and from there to Tilbury.

He insisted on taking me out to dinner, although I was unwilling to leave Mary's bedside. He persuaded me that I must have a rest or I would exhaust myself and that he needed to tell me how grateful he was for what I had done in bringing Mary out of the desert. He wanted to know exactly what had happened and it became clear to me that when he had sent me to her he had not known that she was expecting a baby. Even now he never asked about the child and I realised that he thought that Mary had had a miscarriage. It was as if that terrible baby had never existed.

After dinner he took me back to his suite of rooms at the residency. I had drunk more wine than I was accustomed to and he gave me a brandy and it was only then that I broke down and started to weep. He came to sit beside me on the sofa and held me in his arms and I told him everything. He was shocked, I imagine. He must have been, but he called me a poor girl, a poor sweet girl, and he kissed me. He said that there was no need for anyone to know, that it was our secret, that what I had done was quite right. He said I had done the best thing for Mary, for everyone. He moved my hair away from my hot face and held my hands and kissed me again. His words and those kisses I have never forgotten.

I did not see him again.

On the voyage home Mary was confined to the hospital ward of the ship and I remember that she was put on a drip and was given frequent injections of morphine which kept her permanently drugged.

She did not know about the baby until we were several days out at sea. I sat by her bed and held her hand as I told her that her baby had died before we left the desert and had been buried in the valley near the tents. She turned her head away and wept and the noise was dreadful, dreadful, like a wounded animal, and they came and gave her another injection and then she slept.

When at last the ship docked at Tilbury, her mother met us in a cab and whisked her home and I became redundant. In fact I was kept away from her as if I were an unpleasant reminder of what had happened and as if the dreadful series of events were somehow my fault. She was ill for a long time. She had lost interest in everything, her mother said, especially when she had one letter from her father, the last letter she would ever receive from him, in which she learned that Lieutenant Charpentier had passed on the news that her 'husband', Salika, had taken another wife, who was already expecting a baby.

I dreamed about the baby again last night. Its little hands were scrabbling pathetically against the side of a zinc bucket as I drowned it like a kitten. I could hear the soft scrape, scrape, scrape until all went quiet.

I am a murderess.

I am a murderess.

Emily

BREAKING THE NEWS wasn't as bad as it might have been. I telephoned Will from the train and explained what had happened and, recognising a crisis, he said he would get off work and drive down to Dorset to give me moral support.

There was no one at home when I arrived by taxi from the station. My mother was at work and my father was God knows where. His pick-up was gone from the yard, which looked brushed and tidy. It was very cold and the water in the cattle trough was frozen, crusted with a fur of white ice. Only the calves in the barn crowded to the rails to welcome me home, their grassy-scented breath floating above their heads in a cloud, their rubbery pink noses twitching. I let myself in the back door and made a cup of proper tea and then leaned on the Aga and waited for Will. Bill's Peul hat sat on my backpack in the middle of the kitchen floor, the only piece of exotic evidence that I had ever been away, apart from Chamba's necklace, still around my neck.

The clock ticked, the day's newspaper with its headlines about a terrorist plot uncovered in Ruislip lay folded on the table, the fridge switched itself off and on in the background. Everything was neat and orderly and unchanged. It was hard to believe that yesterday I had escaped death in a car accident and that the day before I had parted from Clemmie and that she had ridden off on a camel to start a new life.

Will arrived not long after and we sat at the table and drank tea and I tried to explain as best I could what had happened. He listened in silence and then said, 'In a way it doesn't surprise me, and I agree with this Hugh friend of yours that she'll be all right. Clemmie is strong, we all know that. She looks as if a puff of wind would carry her off, but she's tough. She always was the most determined of any of us. You think that she really loves this man?'

'Totally and utterly. Like one possessed. They are both mad about each other. He could hardly bear to let her out of his sight from the moment he first saw her, and she was like . . .' I struggled to find the words to explain, 'she was like a flower opening in the sun.'

Will sighed. 'Is he really a good man, do you think? Will he look after her?'

'Yes. I'm sure of that. It's the practical, everyday things that I worry about. How will she survive in such a hostile place? What if she gets ill? Gets appendicitis, for instance? Gets pregnant? Runs out of money?'

'We all take risks every day of our lives, no matter where we live.' He tapped the paper with its terror headline. 'I don't suppose she is in any more danger there than here. But Christ, Em,' he said. 'How we're going to miss her.'

We found Aunt Ellen in the kitchen making bread. She's that sort of person. Uncle Peter was in the pub, which was also fairly true to form. I couldn't avoid telling Aunt Ellen at once, because if I'd made her wait until we yanked Uncle Peter off his bar stool, she would have imagined the worst, that Clemmie was dead or taken hostage or something. So I told her, watching her strong red hands kneading the dough, the little pile of her rings set to one side and covered in flour. She went on kneading as if she had to, but heaved one or two heavy sighs which made the front of her apron rise and fall with emotion. Maybe she was seeing a dream of Clemmie in a big white dress coming down the aisle of Sherborne Abbey fading away for ever.

'Clemmie was always destined for something different,' she said finally. 'I just pray that she will be safe and healthy and happy. A life like you describe is beyond my comprehension. He sounds a wonderful man!'

I was filled with admiration. To love your child so much that you could let them go seemed to me to be pretty marvellous.

'Will she get tired of it, do you think?' she asked. 'Will the glamour wear off and she'll want to come home for a bath? Like at the end of Pony Club camp?'

'No, I don't think so. She really is in love.'

'Then I have to be glad for her.' She put her floury hands round me and hugged me hard. 'Thank you, Emily,' she said. 'Thank you for doing what you could. Now we must concentrate on the practical things like trying to keep in touch. After all, we'll be able to visit her. That should be possible, shouldn't it?'

Will put his arms round his mother and kissed her on the forehead, and I thought, there, Aunt Ellen, that is your just desert – children who adore you.

'There was something else,' I remembered. 'She wanted me to tell you that Chamba passes the Blazer test. He's the first man who ever has.'

'Oh, Clemmie!' said Aunt Ellen, her eyes shining with tears. 'She must love him then. She really must.'

When I got back home, my mother's reaction was very different. She had cheered up considerably since Christmas and was wearing a ra-ra skirt and cowboy boots. It seemed that she and Dad had made it up and I had the greatest difficulty in preventing her from giving me the details. The great thing, though, was that she was happy, which made her an altogether nicer person.

When I told her the news, she immediately started on about telephoning the Foreign Office, saying that Clemmie had clearly been drugged and taken advantage of and now all her things would be stolen and the money would go to fund Al-Qaeda, who, she was sure she had read somewhere, operated in the Sahara Desert.

'Calm down, Mum!' I pleaded. 'It's not a bit like that. Clemmie is totally and utterly in love with this man. In love with everything about his people and his country, in fact!'

'It was like that with the Moonies,' said my mother, 'in the sixties. They gave them this love drug . . .' and she was off again. It was impossible to explain to her what Mali had been like for Clemmie and me. She would never understand. She went to look for my father, clomping across the yard in her boots and little twirly skirt, like a middle-aged cowgirl. I just hoped that she wouldn't catch him on his mobile phone talking to one of his girlfriends.

The next morning Will came with me to see Miss Timmis. They had been a little worried about her, the staff said. Although she had settled in very well at first, the last couple of weeks she had grown rather quiet and distant and had stopped eating. They were glad we had come to see her. A visit would maybe cheer her up, bring her out of herself.

We knocked on the door and heard a faint 'Come in!'

Miss Timmis was sitting in her armchair by the window. The room was hot but she had a rug over her knees. I was shocked to see how frail she looked. The last time I had seen her she had been bright and lively, but now her eyes were sunk in yellow sockets and her skin had a blueish, waxy colour.

She stirred when she saw us and held out a little skeletal hand.

'My dears!' she said. 'How nice! How very kind! Come and sit down. Oh, where can you sit? Emily, is that chair too hard for you? Will, you will have to sit on the bed. Oh, this is so kind!'

'Miss Timmis,' I said, 'I am just back from Mali. I had to come and see you at once.'

'And Clemmie? Where is Clemmie?'

'I'll tell you, Miss Timmis, but it's rather a long story.'

When I had finished, her little head had drooped on to her breast like a sleeping bird. I took her hand in mine and she turned to me.

'So the baby lived?' she said in a tiny voice.

'Yes, the baby lived. She became the great-grandmother of the man who Clemmie loves.'

Miss Timmis turned her head to stare out of the window. A long minute went by before she said in an anguished whisper, 'I did what I thought was right. I only had a moment to decide. I did what I thought he wanted.'

'It was you, wasn't it, Miss Timmis, in the aeroplane?'

She stared past me, her face a frozen mask.

'Why did you make her leave the baby?'

She responded by turning to look at me, her hand to her mouth as if she was frightened of the words that she must speak.

'It was what I thought he would have wanted. A baby like that . . .'

'He?'

'Mary's father. He trusted me to do what was right.'

'Why didn't she ever try to go back to see her daughter if she loved her so much?'

Miss Timmis's breathing was fast and shallow and she appeared much agitated. Her little hands kneaded the rug on her lap and she turned her head from side to side as if trying to escape from something. Will cleared his throat in alarm and sat forward on the edge of the bed. I could tell that he thought I should stop, that I had asked enough.

'I told her the baby was dead,' she whispered. 'I left it lying in the sun to die. It was half dead, you see, born prematurely and very weak. It was for the best. I thought it was for the best. She was very ill, you know. We told her the baby was buried at that place. That's why she wanted to be taken back there.'

'You left it in the sun to die? Oh, Miss Timmis!'

'It was all for love. All for love!' She had begun to

weep, and it was frightening to see her old face contorted by her anguish. Her tears clogged on her powdered cheeks, her breath came in little gasps and she held her hands to her head.

'But it didn't die, Miss Timmis,' I said urgently. 'Do you understand that? The baby didn't die. You didn't kill it. You might have thought you had, but I suppose the women must have found her and she survived.'

'It didn't die! It didn't die,' sobbed Miss Timmis. 'But it was such a poor scrap of a thing. I had no feelings for it, you see. No feelings. But it was a life, a human life. I did a terrible thing. A terrible thing. It was a mortal sin.'

I sat and watched helplessly. There was nothing I could say. Although I pitied her, it wasn't for me to forgive her.

'You did what you thought was right,' said Will gently. 'As far as sin goes, that surely makes a difference.'

We sat in silence for a moment while the truth settled around us. I realised now how very glad I was that Clemmie had insisted that we carry out Great-Aunt Mary's wishes. I was glad that what had been stolen from her in life was granted back to her in death.

'Miss Timmis,' I said gently. 'There was something

else, wasn't there? That envelope you gave us with the poem in it. There was something else that you removed, wasn't there?'

Miss Timmis gave a little moan and nodded. It was some moments before she could speak.

'Yes, my dear, there was. A letter from Mary which explained everything. I couldn't let you see it. I was too frightened that you would find out what I had done. I took the letter and left the poem, which I knew would mean nothing to you. That was just something that Mary knew by heart and loved. I think it must have reminded her of desert nights under the stars. The nights were so beautiful, I remember that.'

'Where is the letter?' I asked. 'Have you still got it?'

Miss Timmis began to fumble for her handbag and spectacles. 'Perhaps it's here somewhere,' she said, and I knew, suddenly, that she would never find it. She would have made sure of that. She had kept her secret for too many years. She would not have run the risk of being found out now. Her funny little furry face was troubled and her eyes swam with tears behind her glasses.

Poor Miss Timmis, I thought. Her devotion to her friend had cost her dear, but at least now she could rest in the knowledge that although she had done wrong, she was not a murderer. This story was as much about her life as anybody else's. What had begun with headstrong young Marie Barthelot falling in love, madly and unsuitably, in a far-off and unexpected place, had reached out, down the years, to touch us all.

From the corridor came the sound of the tea trolley and a little knock on the door. A cheerful woman put her head into the room.

'Cup of tea, dear?' she asked.

Miss Timmis shook herself and smoothed down the rug over her knees. She found a handkerchief in her sleeve and blew her nose.

'That would be very nice, Kathy,' she said. 'A cup of tea would be just the thing. Thank you so much.'

Already her face looked brighter, as if a cloud had lifted from the sun.

Later, Will and I walked to the top of the hill behind the farm, the hill that Great-Aunt Mary had so disliked. It was grey and foggy – a silent, secretive afternoon with a cold that bit into your bones. It was hard to remember the dazzling glare and hot sun of the desert.

'So you really believe she'll be all right, do you?' said Will, and I knew without asking that he meant Clemmie.

'I think so. Although it is supposed to be dangerous up in the north for tourists, she will be safe with Chamba. I'm sure of that. It's the perfect end of a fairy story for her. Remember how she always wanted to let down her hair like Rapunzel and be rescued? Well, she has been. By the Lion of Temesna.'

'And Miss Timmis? I can't believe that she has lived all these years with the belief that she killed that baby.'

'The truth will be a huge relief, won't it? I suppose it's never too late for redemption, and you could see how she had bucked up by the time we left.'

'And you, Em? How about you? You've had quite a time of it.' He took my cold hand and tucked it into the pocket of his coat.

'Me? I'm okay.' I meant it, too. The dread that I had felt on arriving back at Heathrow seemed to have evaporated. In two days' time I would be back at school, and I had begun to think about the children and realised that I had missed them and that I was looking forward to seeing them. Even Krissie Bignall. I needed to be doing something worthwhile again.

Although I could never replace Clemmie, whose absence would leave a great aching hole in my life, I had had two text messages from Hugh. Tomorrow night we had arranged that I would go round to his flat to help him treat his Dogon masks, which had turned out to be riddled with woodworm, and afterwards we would go out to supper. It wasn't exactly a fairy tale, but of such small beginnings great things may grow.

Towards the top of the hill the track was steep, a meandering sheep path cut through the short frosty grass and the dark clumps of gorse. We walked in silence, our breath coming in gasps which floated away in white trails. Up here the smooth, steep shoulders of the hill fell away to the valley below, and we could look down at the silent village, at the empty lane leading to the little grey church, at the neat rows of cottages and the bare trees, at the frozen allotments and the dark lines of the hedges, at the farm where I had grown up, with its sagging stone-tiled roof and empty yards, and the lane which wandered down the valley the half-mile to where Clemmie and the boys had lived since they were born.

Thin lines of smoke rose from one or two cottage chimneys; otherwise all was still and even the rooks in their black clots of nests in the high branches of the elms were quiet. Further away across the vale the mist thickened over the fields and the hedges and the dark knots of trees and distant farms so that they seemed to float on a white sea towards a white horizon. Will and I stood and looked for a long time at the dear, familiar scene and I knew that we were both thinking of Clemmie, and I hoped that maybe, in that far-off, unexpected place, she was happy and that she might be thinking of us.

SARAH CHALLIS

On Dancing Hill

'A fine novelist . . . a writer who can stand comparison with Rosamunde Pilcher or Joanna Trollope' *Blackmore Vale Magazine*

Kate and Josh Hutchins have been married for thirty years. For all that time they have lived on Dancing Hill Farm in Dorset. Here they brought up three children, expected to grow old, and imagined they would pass the farm on to one of their boys, like generations of family before them.

But things have not gone to plan. Neither of their sons is interested in the farm, their daughter is working in London, in love with a man who has no real liking for the countryside, and Dancing Hill itself is no longer the profitable place that it once was.

And Kate is restless. Longing for some time to herself, dreaming of what she might have achieved if she had not married so young. When her children give her a week's painting holiday in Provence she seizes it like a lifeline, hardly realising what a dangerous thing it is that she is doing.

'Sarah Challis is becoming a novelist to be reckoned with' *Dorset Life*

'Her evocation of the English countryside is elegiac . . . a pleasure to read' *Oxford Times*

0 7553 0039 4

headline
review

SARAH CHALLIS

Blackthorn Winter

In April, when blackthorn blossom clothes the hedgerows like a wedding veil, there sometimes comes a frost so severe that it seems as if the summer will never come. Country people call this a blackthorn winter.

For Claudia Barron, arriving in the Dorset village of Court Barton that April, blackthorn winter seems like a metaphor for everything that has happened to her. Hiding from her previous life, she adopts an assumed name and applies for a job in the local school. But villages don't much like mysteries and secrets and soon the inhabitants of Court Barton set out to find out what it is that Claudia Barron is hiding from and why.

Blackthorn Winter is Sarah Challis's third novel and once again she gives us her own particularly seductive cast of characters, old and young, woven into a story of drama and humour and love – set against the ravishing Dorset countryside which she knows so well.

'Sarah Challis is a fine novelist . . . someone who can hold the reader's interest from page one, creating convincing characters and realistic situations, throw in a few surprises, as fate so often does, and draw the various strands towards a compelling conclusion' *Blackmore Vale Magazine*

'Her evocation of the English countryside is elegiac . . . a pleasure to read' *Oxford Times*

'Wickedly well-observed . . . Sarah Challis is becoming a novelist to be reckoned with' *Dorset Life*

'[A] haunting story of heartbreak and friendship' *Peterborough Evening Telegraph*

0 7553 0948 0

headline
review

Turning for Home

Sarah Challis

A cantankerous, elegant old woman sits in her beautiful Somerset house while her family secretly plots to evict her. In the garden is her last loyal retainer, out at grass, her one remaining racehorse, prematurely retired, and in London the man she probably should have married – still her dearest friend.

Into this scene comes Maeve Delaney. Sole applicant for the job of companion to Lady Pamela, streetwise and outrageous, Maeve bursts into the old house like a firework. As open warfare settles into a wary truce between the two women, Maeve sets her heart on bringing the great racehorse, Irish Dancer, out of retirement, and everything changes.

'I really enjoyed *Turning for Home* . . . I thought it so perceptive . . . Lady Pamela a star . . . the horse-racing bit brilliant . . . and I particularly enjoyed the very touching romance' Rosamunde Pilcher

0 7472 6499 6

headline